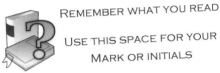

REMEMBER WHAT YOU READ

USE THIS SPACE FOR YOUR
MARK OR INITIALS

TiPS for LiVING

A NOVEL OF
SUSPENSE

RENÉE SHAFRANSKY

LAKE UNION
PUBLISHING

Published by Lake Union Publishing, Seattle

www.apub.com

ISBN-13: 9781542048118 (paperback)
ISBN-10: 1542048117 (paperback)
ISBN-13: 9781503949225 (hardcover)
ISBN-10: 1503949222 (hardcover)

Cover design by Kimberly Glyder

Printed in the United States of America

First Edition

For Nick

Think not, is my eleventh commandment; and sleep when you can, is my twelfth.

—Herman Melville, *Moby Dick*

From the *Pequod Courier*

Tips for Living

by Nora Glasser

Reasons to Leave the House

Residents of Pequod (Formerly Known as Middle Class): You've seen your property taxes climb astronomically this year, right? Thank the superwealthy city folk who have "discovered" our town. They're purchasing modest summer homes, renovating them into multi-million-dollar estates and driving property values sky-high. Developers offering deluxe waterside condos court more of the rich and fabulous. Meanwhile, you're transferring debt from one credit card to another so you can keep the roof over your head. So why not Airbnb your home for a profit to old-fashioned summer renters? They'll pay thousands for a decent city escape they can share with a dozen friends. You'll only have to replace your furniture and plumbing when they depart. "Good idea," you say, "but where will my family live in the interim?" How about those storage units out near the expressway? Lease one and put in an air bed. Set up a kitchen with a minifridge and microwave. Revive the chamber pot. Learn the time-tested skills of a homeless person. Think outside the box. Or live in one.

Chapter One

Helene Westing, the woman my ex-husband had an affair with and impregnated while we were married, joined my Pilates mat class a few weeks before Thanksgiving. Let me say that again. Helene Westing, the woman my ex-husband had an affair with and impregnated while we were married, joined my Pilates mat class a few weeks before Thanksgiving. I was there first, lying on my back. Just like with my husband.

Off-the-chart stress.

My Pilates teacher had been admiring my money socks—black with green dollar signs—when I heard the door open behind me. I bought the socks hoping to show money that it was welcome in my world, since money had made itself scarce after my divorce three years ago.

"Cool socks, Nora," Kelly said, going from standing on her mat in front of the class to sitting on it cross-legged in one smooth move—doubly impressive because Kelly's center of gravity had recently shifted. She was almost six months along and glowing with surging pregnancy hormones. Even her high, jet-black ponytail had developed a goddess-like sheen. It swung around gaily as she turned her head toward the door and chirped through the mike on her headset.

"Welcome! You must be the person who called yesterday. Helene, right?"

I tried to camouflage my gasp with a cough as Helene passed by close enough for me to smell her: L'Occitane Jasmin, a scent I used to wear. She stopped short and looked right at me for a second, then sniffed before smiling at Kelly and moving on.

"Sorry I'm late. I misjudged the drive time."

If Helene was fazed, I couldn't see it. She calmly laid out her mat and followed Kelly's instructions on how to engage her core. But her presence really shook me; I could barely focus on the class. Torturous memories of Hugh's betrayal came rushing back. The strand of blonde hair on my pillowcase. *Blonde?* The pair of maroon lace panties balled up under my bedroom dresser. *Maroon.* My stomach turning at the realization that this meant Hugh must be having an affair of such passion and abandon that he'd invited his golden-haired mistress into our bed and ravished her so thoroughly she'd forgotten to put on her underwear before she left.

I have to concede there were signs that Hugh had strayed before. There were certainly signs. I found a postcard of *Olympia*, the reclining nude by Manet, in our mailbox after Hugh returned from teaching a painting seminar in Philadelphia. On the back, no address or signature— just a phone number and two words: "Call me." Hugh claimed he had no idea who sent the card. He threw it away. Still, I paid close attention. No noticeable change in his behavior. No trips to Philly. Nothing suspicious at all. I convinced myself he hadn't crossed the line. But afterward I couldn't stop noticing the young women who hung on his words at parties and openings and gazed at him with moon eyes. Like I did when I was twenty-five and went to see his painting show in Chelsea.

Hugh Walker: New York Portraits. That was the show's title. Hugh was well on his way to art stardom then. I learned from his gallery bio that he was forty-three and from Virginia, and that he'd already shown his work at the Museum of Modern Art. The portraits were of his reflection in various store windows in the city's richest and poorest neighborhoods—from Tribeca to East Harlem. They were done in oil and awash in different glazes, which gave them a hazy, luminous effect. They were brilliant, I thought.

The moment Hugh entered the gallery, I recognized him from his paintings. He was tall and rakish, wearing khakis and a white Oxford shirt with the sleeves rolled up. He flashed me a charming, crooked grin before walking over to the reception desk to talk to the staff, and I found myself wishing I'd put on a sexier pair of jeans that morning. Between his clothes, wavy dark hair and brown eyes, I thought he looked like Jack Kerouac in the Kerouac Wore Khakis Gap ad.

After he finished at the reception desk, he headed straight for me. My pulse rate spiked. He introduced himself in a honeyed Southern accent and offered his hand. I felt the flutter in my chest as soon as our skin touched.

"Hello. I'm Hugh Walker. And you are?"

"Nora Glasser."

"May I ask what you think of the paintings, Nora Glasser?"

"I think they're beautiful and complex. Ethereal and political at the same time," I said. And then an irreverent urge took over. "But I have some not-so-great news."

"Oh?"

"They're out of focus."

Without missing a beat, Hugh's expression turned somber. He nodded and frowned. "Yes. I'm afraid I was experimenting with a new process. I put Vaseline in my eyes when I painted them."

"You're kidding, right?"

He winked and cracked another irresistible smile. "So were you."

I was practically melting from the heat we were generating.

Once we started sleeping together, Hugh began painting me. After *The Nora Series* showed in New York, his career skyrocketed. He called me his muse. "You're my dark, beautiful Jewess," he said. There was no one I'd rather spend time with. From then on, Hugh's was the first and last voice I heard almost every day for more than a decade. We were the passionate couple. We were the couple who loved to debrief in bed at night, feet entwined. "You first," he'd insist. "Tell me everything." If I occasionally expressed worry about the women who flirted with him? Hugh reassured me. He even invoked Paul Newman's famous quip on fidelity.

"Nora, why would I go out for a hamburger when I've got steak at home?"

We'd just come back from a vacation in Rome—sorely needed after my second fertility treatment failed—the week before the maroon panties and blonde hair detonated in our bedroom. I became so depressed afterward that I slept for the better part of four days. Finally, rising like Lazarus, I dragged myself into the kitchen so Hugh could tell me one more time that it was "a fling," that I was "the one." Apparently he met the woman, an art school grad student, while he was opening a gallery show in Austin.

"You were visiting your aunt when she called. She was in New York for the week and asked to drop over and see my new work," he said. "She brought wine. I had too much, Nora. Before I knew what was happening she . . . I'm sorry. Please, don't let this wreck what we have. Please. I don't care about her. I don't care about her at all."

I wanted to believe we would make it through. *Please don't let this wreck what we have.* I read books on how to heal from the trauma of sexual betrayal. "Don't expect miracles." "Rebuilding trust takes time." "Whatever you do, don't ask for details," they advised. During my long, emotional talks with Hugh, I tried to stay away from these land mines. "He succumbed from all the baby-making stress," I rationalized, and began to inch toward forgiveness. But less than six months later, as I was rummaging around his studio to find the zester that had gone missing (Hugh was forever borrowing kitchen utensils to achieve new and interesting textures with paint), I abandoned all hope.

Behind the antique Japanese screen that hid Hugh's paint-stained industrial sink, I saw the canvas leaning against the wall. It was an obvious takeoff on Annie Leibovitz's famed *Rolling Stone* cover—the one with naked John Lennon curled up in a fetal position around fully dressed Yoko. In this version, it was Hugh who was naked. And he was wrapped around a roundly pregnant Helene.

I stared at the painting, barely able to breathe, my body collapsing into its own fetal curl on the floor. *This is not fixable. From this we can never recover. He's stuck a knife in my womb and I am bleeding to death. This is dying.* Then I heard the studio door open and the floorboards creak behind me.

"Nora, I didn't mean for it to happen."

"But I wanted a baby. That was my baby. You broke us. And you broke my heart."

I made a silent vow that day in Hugh's studio: *I will come back to life no matter how long it takes, and I won't be a bitter, angry woman.*

Easier said. I started having violent fantasies of mowing Hugh and Helene down with a car. Then I was pulling a pistol out of my trench coat pocket like some 1940s gun moll and shooting them in their bed in flagrante delicto, which was more visceral and satisfying. I played that fantasy over and over again in my mind. It was so upsetting that I started seeing a therapist. Dr. Feld was the only one besides Hugh (and maybe Helene if he'd shared) who knew I'd actually drawn blood.

"Why don't you tell me exactly what happened?" Dr. Feld had asked, looking at me gravely during our first session, pen poised to write on his yellow legal pad.

"I attacked Hugh's work. Physically."

"When was this?"

"After I saw that painting in his studio. I couldn't get off the floor at first, I was so upset. Hugh kept saying we had to talk about this calmly. He kept calling the baby a 'mistake.' He said he didn't plan to get Helene pregnant, but it happened and she made the decision to keep it. He was waiting to tell me until after the baby was born. He thought I would be open to 'an arrangement' once I saw the child."

"What kind of arrangement?"

"He wanted me to go on living with him and become some sort of stepmother. 'Since you can't seem to get pregnant,' he said. We'd been trying. My ovaries weren't cooperating."

"You must've been very hurt."

"I was devastated. I accused him of sadism. He argued that I was being 'bourgeois and narrow-minded.' He said, 'Europeans make these arrangements all the time.' Correct me if I'm wrong, Dr. Feld, but isn't it usually the wife who bears the child? Not the mistress?"

"I'm afraid I'm not an expert on that."

"No, of course not."

"About the violence . . ."

"Yes. Well, I finally got off the floor. I saw Hugh starting to boil water for tea on his hot plate, as if we were a couple of Brits who could have a civilized conversation about how to handle this over a pot of Earl Grey. I looked at that painting of him with Helene again, and I actually saw red. It's real. That happens. The entire room went crimson. I picked up the nearest thing I could find to a weapon—the X-ACTO on his worktable—and I lunged. He grabbed my wrist before the blade touched the canvas. I accidentally nicked his hand."

Dr. Feld scribbled on his pad.

"How did he react?"

"'You're hysterical,' he said. I guess I was. But the thing is, I still have fantasies."

"Of what nature?"

I hesitated. Dr. Feld cocked his head.

"Of hurting both of them."

Dr. Feld wrote on his pad some more.

"What you said about being obligated to inform the authorities if I'm a danger to others or myself? You're not going to report me for having fantasies, are you?"

"No. But it would be good to explore some of that anger in here instead of acting it out."

"Can you say how many sessions you think we'll need? I'm worried about money. The meeting with my divorce lawyer was kind of a shock."

"How so?"

"Hugh and I lived together for over twelve years, but we'd only been married for one. It means the settlement won't be all that much. Between paying the lawyer, moving out of the loft, and covering living expenses until I find a job . . ." I sighed and shook my head, resigned. "Still, I don't want to spend years fighting for palimony."

"You'd rather move on."

"Right."

At $150 each visit, I couldn't afford to see Dr. Feld for very long, but at least I'd regained my equilibrium. I'm afraid that since Hugh and Helene moved to Pequod this May, I've begun to backslide. Some days I could swear there's a volcano in my chest. The energy I expend to keep it from erupting can exhaust me. I often feel depressed. But I make sure to renew my vow every day: *I absolutely will not let anger destroy my life.*

"The nerve of that woman," Grace huffed as we walked out of class down the corridor that led to the parking lot outside.

Grace Sliwa has been like a sister to me for twenty-three years, ever since we were freshman roommates at NYU. We even look like sisters. We both have long brown hair, oval faces, and prominent cheekbones passed down from ancestors who came from the same general part of the world: Grace is of Czech descent; my people hail from the Jewish ghettos of western Russia. We're both taller than average and long-waisted. "Modigliani model types," Hugh once observed. But my eyes are brown and Grace's are bright blue. She wears her hair straight and parted on the side. I favor a tousled, "sauvage" look with bangs. Grace doesn't need an excuse to put on a skirt or a dress. I'm happy in jeans 90 percent of the time.

Smart, talented, beautiful Grace also has a voice that purrs sex, which she uses to great effect on her interview show, *Talk of the Townies*, produced at WPQD here in Pequod and carried regionally on public radio.

"What she *should* have done the second she saw you in class, if she had a decent bone in her body, was *leave*," she hissed.

One of the qualities I admire most in Grace is her loyalty. She's as loyal as Lassie. After Hugh and I divorced, she wouldn't even deign to do a phone interview with him. Believe me, it would've been a coup for her, given who Hugh was. Grace was the only one of my friends who refused to talk to Hugh, fame or no fame, because of what he pulled with Helene.

"If I were you, I'd want to kill," she fumed.

Grace zipped up her fleece and took my arm as we emerged from the large, slate-colored concrete building into the chilly November morning. We steered toward our cars, parked side by side in the lot.

"So what are we going to do?" she asked.

"What do you mean?"

"We can't let that woman stay in class. There must be a way to get rid of her," she said, releasing me to open the back door of her Prius and toss her mat over a booster seat full of toys. Grace has two wonderful boys, two adorable munchkins—my godsons. After the first one was born, she and her family decamped to Pequod from Manhattan, intent on raising their kids outside the city. Her husband, Mac, grew up here.

"We need to have her banned," Grace said, turning back to the building. "Maybe we should go in there and tell Kelly and the rest of them what she's done . . ."

"No," I said firmly. "You know word will spread. I can't handle being the subject of gossip again. Remember when *New York Magazine* ran that paparazzi shot of Hugh and Helene, pregnant Helene, alongside my wedding photo? I was completely humiliated. I don't want to be a hot topic here."

"That SOB wedding photographer sold you out. What was the insult your aunt had for him?"

Sina Shluha vokzal'naja ve Siberia. Aunt Lada was so enamored of her Slavic roots, she'd studied Russian language and folk dancing in the midst of the Cold War. I knew most of her sayings but had to ask her to translate that one.

"Son of a whore who works a train station in Siberia." I sighed. "Grace, I just don't want people talking about me. I wanted to die last time, I was so ashamed."

"Don't get confused, Nor. The shame is on him."

Then why had I felt like ducking under the table whenever Hugh and Helene showed up at the cafés and restaurants I frequented while I still lived in the city? Why did I sneak out of friends' cocktail parties and gallery openings if they entered the room? I came to Pequod to start a new life. No, I wouldn't tell Kelly and the rest. I didn't want to advertise my past.

Grace was still simmering as she slid into her car's front seat. "Wasn't it lousy enough that they bought a house here? I mean, the entire point was for you to start over without those two in your face. Now she has to come to your Pilates class? She's a stalker!" she said, slamming the door.

I suspect buying a house in Pequod was Helene's idea. Hugh was nearing sixty with some health issues. He probably feared losing his twenty-seven-year-old wife if he didn't give her what she wanted. And she wanted a house near me. I imagined their conversation—it actually worried me that I imagined their conversations so often lately—went something like this:

"Helene, you know we can't get a house in Pequod. Nora lives there."

"But it doesn't seem fair. You said Pequod had the perfect light for painting," she'd plead in her Texas twang. "There's a beautiful, light-filled studio on the property. Are we going to give up our dream house on the chance that we might run into your ex-wife once or twice?"

True, Hugh claimed the light in Pequod was "as transparent as vodka," a result of air saturated with water molecules from the surrounding inlets and coves. We spent one idyllic August drinking it in—visiting with Grace and her crew, roughing it in a barn we rented so Hugh could work on larger paintings. We lit propane lamps in the evenings, took baths in a repurposed horse trough and loved every second of it. But the farmer sold his acreage to a condo developer the next spring, and we began renting a winterized cottage upstate to get away on weekends year-round.

Pequod is a summer place, really. Just under three hours east of New York City on Long Island's north shore. Our population swells tenfold from May through September, and then it's just us again. The Piqued. At last count 3,093 of us. A really small town. Hugh and Helene were Summer People, or more specifically, Summer Weekend People—a group whose sense of entitlement draws the ire of locals. The *Courier*'s "Letters to the Editor" featured a typical complaint in the Labor Day issue:

> Dear Editor,
> I was born and raised in Pequod, and I've been proud to call myself a resident of our town for almost fifty-one years. Recently, I've been angered by the attitude of some who share our community in the summer months. This past weekend I was standing in a long line

at the farm stand—typical during our high season—
waiting to pay for my corn. I was wearing my Pequod
Fire Department T-shirt, so there was no mistaking my
local status. When I finally reached the register, I heard
a man shout from the back of the line: "Hey, Townie!
Why don't you shop during the week, so we don't have
to stand here all fu**ing day?"

Being a public servant, I refrained from violence.
But like the bumper sticker says: SUMMER PEOPLE,
SUMMER NOT.

S. Ayers

Pequod FD

I'd spotted Hugh and Helene on weekends this summer. It seemed
as if every time I ran a Saturday errand, I had to cross the street to avoid
bumping into them. When the summer ended, I was relieved they'd
finally be gone. I never expected Helene Westing Walker (luckily, I
hadn't taken Hugh's name when we married—there was less chance
people in town would connect us now) to show up in my Pilates class
on a Monday morning in November.

The class meets three times a week in an unusual location: the
old bowling alley outside of town. Kelly and her husband brought the
failing alley back to life after finding it for sale on Bizquest. A tragic
event gave them the means: Kelly's parents died in their sleep from a
carbon monoxide leak in their boiler, and she came into an inheritance. Originally from Catskill, they changed the alley's name to "Van
Winkle Lanes" for the fabled Rip Van Winkle, who heard thunder in
the Catskill Mountains and discovered ghosts up there bowling nine-
pins. Kelly dubbed the alley's cocktail lounge The Thunder Bar. Her
husband bartends there.

"The Van Winkle name says bowling is awesome, bowling is time-
less. The name Pequod Lanes didn't say a thing about bowling," Kelly

explained for a story I did on the reopening. "Business is up seventeen percent since we changed the sign."

Until bowling hours begin, our Pilates group has the place to ourselves. Depending on moods and weather, between five and ten of us set our mats down in the shiny, oiled lanes. If you know your bowling, then you know the oil is what helps the bowling balls flow smoothly. What puts that sexy "slide and glide" on them. And if you don't know your bowling, I understand completely. I only have this information because my father, Nathan Glasser, did a lot of business in bowling alleys and bars when I was a kid, and he often brought me along.

I miss my dad. He died sixteen years ago, not long before I met Hugh. He was a complicated man with a big heart, and I was his "pearl of a girl." In some curious way, spending mornings in the bowling alley makes me feel connected to him again.

"Nor, snap out of it," Grace called out her car window.

I was still glued to the spot by the open trunk of my blue Toyota, having dropped my mat inside, anxiously watching the exit door of Van Winkle Lanes. I was thinking I should stay and say something when Helene came out, like, "How dare you! Go find your own damn class!" But really, I just wanted to cry.

"Why did Helene have to come here? Why?" I groaned.

"Are you going to be okay?"

"Maybe she won't come back," I said.

Grace frowned. "I heard her ask about Kelly's thirty-class card. I think she's buying it right now."

"Oh." I staggered for a second, grasping the trunk lid.

"Nora?"

"I'm a little thrown, that's all," I said, recovering. "I'll be absolutely fine."

"Just tell me you're not thinking of quitting."

"No way."

"Good. I can't come on Wednesday, but I'll try for Friday's class. This week is insane. Both kids have dental appointments and I'm interviewing the mayor about the new tax increases, so I have serious prep. Plus, I promised my mother-in-law I'd help her learn how to auction off her LPs on eBay. That could take *days*. Love you. Stay strong."

"Love you."

Grace drove her Prius out of the lot. I slammed the trunk and plunked down behind my steering wheel. I was dreading Wednesday morning's class already.

◆ ◆ ◆

The encounter with Helene left me agitated. I decided to drive directly to the *Courier* office rather than return home to change clothes. The oversize black sweater I'd worn to class would cover enough of my Pilates pants. I tried to think about the column I needed to write that morning, but I was too upset.

As soon as I reached the wharf, the sight of it began to calm me down. The cheery, green-and-white-striped snack stands dotting the long wooden pier. The wrought iron benches lining its edge like front row seats for the theater of the sea. Beyond them, light danced on the water under a bright fall sky. The air smelled of salt and burning leaves. I breathed in the scent, felt my tension release and turned left at the hand-painted PEQUOD EST. 1827 sign.

The name *Pequod* derives from the Pequot, the Algonquin tribe that thrived hunting whales off the coast here before the white settlers moved in. It's also the name of the whaling vessel in that epic tome *Moby Dick*, which I'd decided to reread during my "anger therapy." I'd tackled it in high school and remembered the story of one-legged Captain Ahab. He set out on the *Pequod* to kill the great white whale that cost him his limb, but he wound up going down with his ship. Given my fantasies about Hugh and Helene, I thought it might be wise to revisit a tale about the perils of seeking revenge.

I turned left again onto Pequod Avenue, the town's main thoroughfare, and drove between the rows of historic brick and clapboard buildings. The town's bones aren't all that different than they were in 1827. Stately sycamore trees line both sides of the street. The immense wooden doors of the library, painted a glossy cherry red, welcome readers into the landmark building. Pequod is a picture postcard. On the surface, a gem. But when I started work at the paper, the publisher and editor in chief, Ben Wickstein, warned me not to be fooled.

"It's a nasty little town," Ben cautioned. "Think Salem in the year of *The Crucible*. There are still wooden stocks behind the salt factory. And some people around here would like to see them get used. They'll call the health department if they see you bring a puppy into a coffee shop. They love their rules."

Grace encouraged me to try for a job at the *Courier* when I first mentioned wishing I could move to Pequod.

"I know the editor. I'll talk you up," Grace had offered. "He needs someone with your skills."

"You think? I've been out of the game for so long. And my last reference is Hugh."

Once we moved in together, Hugh had asked me to run his studio. "For a salary, of course." I was barely earning a living at a free downtown paper called *New York Spy*, covering everything from hip-hop clubs and pop-up galleries to rent strikes. I saw Hugh's offer as a win-win-win: a way to help him, earn decent money, and still have time to write. The studio job was demanding, but I managed to keep publishing. I even sold a feature to *The New York Times* on the Guerilla Girls, an anonymous group of feminists I admired. They donned ape masks and protested in front of museums on the dearth of women artists shown inside. They passed leaflets with slogans like **Do You Have to Be Naked to Get into the Met?**

But the fact was, I hadn't practiced the feminism they preached; I'd let my career take a back seat to Hugh's. Grace's proposal meant a chance to reclaim my identity as a writer.

"I'll tell Ben you worked with your husband. He'll appreciate that—his wife ran the paper with him," Grace said. "It's so sad. She was your age when she died of breast cancer last fall. He's raising Sam by himself now. He's a great kid. They're both just beginning to come back to life. Anyway, Ben won't cross-examine you. I'll let him know you had an agonizing divorce. No names. No details."

It worked. That was more than two years ago. I've been employed at the *Courier* ever since. I have a lot of respect for Ben; he has his priorities straight. He's proposed a ban on plastic bags for Pequod's stores and funding for affordable housing. He's made it his mission to stop overdevelopment and government corruption (which often go hand in hand).

As I pulled into a parking space almost directly in front of the *Courier* office's bay window, I could see Ben working, probably on his story about a new traffic camera that was generating a suspiciously high number of tickets.

He sat at his large oak desk, jammed between a file cabinet and a sagging bookcase, weighted with back issues, staring at his computer screen and pulling his left ear. Ben always pulled his ear when he was writing. He caught me watching him once. I could tell it made him really uncomfortable; he instantly found a reason to leave the room. He's a great editor, but on a personal level, he's about as open as a bear trap.

Ben stopped tugging abruptly and turned to say something to Lizzie, the junior member of our tiny staff. She left her desk and strode over in her lace-up army boots to study his screen with him. Lizzie has Orphan Annie hair, a pixieish freckled face and a petite frame that makes her look even younger than her twenty-three years. She tends to dress like a war correspondent to convince people she has gravitas. "The more you push for answers and don't back down, the more they'll take you seriously," I've advised, trying to be a mentor to her.

I exited the car and entered the three-story redbrick building, formerly a bindery in the mid-1800s.

"Morning," I said as I opened the office's old-fashioned, oak-and-glass front door.

Ben and Lizzie both looked up from his computer with solemn expressions.

"Uh-oh. Did the hard drive crash?"

"No," Ben said, swiveling his wooden swivel chair around to face me. As usual, he looked and sounded cranky, like he'd been yanked out of bed. The cowlicky salt-and-pepper hair, the deep shadows under his brown eyes and the stubble on his dimpled chin contributed to the effect.

"Then who died?"

"We just received another letter about your Tips column," he said.

I'd pitched Tips for Living as a creative way to give voice to the locals' gripes. Until I lived here full-time, I hadn't realized the impact Summer People had on the year-round community. "We need a new approach to talking about how tough things have become for the average Pequod resident," I'd told Ben.

I admit I came up with the idea after Hugh and Helene moved to Pequod. I could relate to the locals' aversion to having their hometown invaded by people who didn't treat them well. A snarky tone might let off some steam for all of us, I thought. So far, we'd run a half dozen Tips and received a fair amount of appreciative fan mail. But we'd also gotten a number of nasty letters.

"What does this one say?" I asked.

Ben turned back to his computer and read: "'Nora Glasser still thinks she's clever, doesn't she? Her Tips are an insult to people who are struggling to get by. There's real suffering out here. She should watch what she writes or she's going to regret it.' The letter is signed *Mad as Hell.*"

Ben folded his arms across his chest and raised both of his unruly eyebrows. "That's number two from *Mad as Hell.* I draw the line at threats. I'm not going to publish it," he said.

"And he's rethinking the column, too," Lizzie added.

Ben shot her an annoyed look, and Lizzie stared down at her boots, chastened.

Lizzie's father is Pequod's four-term mayor. All that campaigning for him has made her highly competitive. She compares word counts and story placement even if she's only writing the week's weather outlook. Ever since I started writing Tips, she'd been angling for her own column reviewing smartphone apps. But Ben won't sign off. He credits the paper's success with sticking to local angles.

"Is that true? Are you rethinking?" I asked, concerned. I loved writing Tips. It not only added something unique to the paper, but writing it finally brought me to life again after the divorce. At least in my work.

"Frankly, yes. I'm always rethinking," Ben said. "That's my job."

"You're blowing this out of proportion, Ben. It's two letters. People who write angry letters have already found an outlet for their hostile feelings." *Sobachny ne karyyty.* "Barking dogs seldom bite." That's what Aunt Lada would say. "Watch out for the quiet one that tucks its tail," she warned.

"It's the silent brooders you have to worry about," I told Ben.

"Don't be so sure," he cautioned. "I don't have to tell you how much resentment has risen with the cost of living here."

It's true. You can feel the tension in the air. Even the bar fights have escalated. Last July, an intoxicated plumber pulled a gun on a Summer Person over an unpaid fee for dealing with a backed-up toilet. The *Courier's* Police Blotter used to list a few DUIs and the occasional shoplifting incident. But we've reported a record four burglaries already this fall—all of vacant summer homes. Still, I believed what I said about not worrying about one irate letter writer.

"We've gotten lots of positive letters, too. And what about a free press? You didn't stop writing stories about the condo project because of the rock thrower."

After the *Courier* came out against a proposed high-end resort that threatened to pollute a tract of wetlands, a large rock crashed through the front window while Ben was working late. A note wrapped around the rock said, "Stay out of it." Grace even had Ben on her radio show to discuss the incident. Now he keeps a baseball bat by his desk.

Ben frowned at me, started drumming his pencil and then stopped abruptly. "Don't get me wrong; I like the column."

"So does my dad," Lizzie admitted.

"But one event is a data point. Several data points are a pattern. The column might not be striking the chord you think it is. If you receive any more letters like this," Ben said, pointing at his screen, "Tips is done."

"Got it."

I wasn't going to fight a hypothetical. I've learned to pick my battles with Ben.

"Is there any coffee left?" I asked, starting for the coffeepot on top of the file cabinet.

"We're out," Lizzie said, sheepishly. "Sorry. I know it's my turn, but I had to meet with my mom and the wedding caterer before work." She mimed shooting herself in the head. Lizzie was going to marry her longtime boyfriend next month—a sweet guy she's dated since high school. "I'll pick up a can at lunch."

I couldn't wait for lunch. I'd been waking up tired lately, as if I'd barely slept. Instead of my usual already excessive three cups to jump-start my brain in the morning, I seemed to need coffee all day long. I'd been putting off going in for a checkup. I knew I'd been mildly depressed, but was something else going on? As a child, I'd experienced this kind of fatigue from a vexing sleep problem, but I thought I'd outgrown it.

"I'll just run to Corwin's for coffee," I said. And a treat. I deserved a treat after Helene ruined Pilates class. I hadn't bought my favorite chocolate muffin in ages. "Anyone want anything? Muffins? Cheese Danish?"

"No, thanks. They're still charging summer prices over there," Lizzie said.

Ben let go of his ear and looked up. "How about one of Eden's donuts? Make mine jelly."

I left the office and headed across the street toward Eden's Coffee Shop, a bacon-scented haven in a town that's changed too fast for locals and not fast enough for Summer People, who want juice bars and gourmet takeout. I noticed a woman and two men emerge from a dark green Mercedes parked in front. They looked completely out of place. The woman wore a fur-trimmed black leather coat and heels. The men had on long, black cashmere overcoats with scarves at their throats. The shorter, silver-haired man locked the car and then ushered the others into the coffee shop while holding the door for them.

I paused as I recognized him. I hadn't seen him in a few years—he was probably close to seventy now, still spry, though his thick mane had thinned. He was wearing his trademark black turtleneck under the sleek black coat. He'd always looked and dressed like Sean Connery. Whether cooking one of his exotic dishes for Hugh and me in his loft or massaging egos at one of his gallery openings, he was impeccably outfitted at all times.

"Abbas?"

Hugh's longtime art dealer, Abbas Masout, of Chelsea by way of Lebanon, turned around and broke into a smile.

"My God, Nora!" he said, letting the door close behind his companions. "Dear girl, it's good to see you." He walked over and leaned in for a European "kiss kiss" exchange on both cheeks, then followed it with a hug, as he always did.

"Abbas, what are you doing here?"

"Taking some Paris collectors to Hugh's studio for the afternoon. They are desiring a little local flavor first."

A light in my brain clicked on. "That's right. It's Monday."

Art galleries were closed on Mondays in the city, making it a big day for studio visits. I used to arrange Hugh's schedule so Abbas could bring collectors and curators to view work on Mondays. That explained why Helene was in Pequod. She probably had my old job tending to Hugh's potential buyers.

"I heard you are also living in this charming place," Abbas said.

I got here first. "Yes."

He peered at me with concern. "You are managing?"

I remembered running into him in the checkout line at Barnes & Noble after the divorce. He'd asked the same question before insisting on buying the book I held, as a gift to me. Abbas was macho, but kind.

I blinked. "Of course."

"Excellent. You are looking wonderful, by the way."

"Thank you."

"I would invite you to join us," Abbas said, lifting his palms in helplessness, "but Hugh and his little girl are inside . . ."

I couldn't keep from glancing through the coffee shop's window. The Parisian collectors were just sitting down at a table, blocking my view of Hugh and his daughter. One of the newspapers had mentioned her by name. Callie.

"And Helene is coming," he said, apologetically.

"Right. Well, it would've been great to catch up, Abbas. But I'm late for work, anyway."

Just then Helene pulled up in a silver Lexus. She spotted me and raised a haughty eyebrow. I felt myself beginning to vibrate. My blood started to cook.

"Nice to see you, Abbas. Take care," I said.

"We must find a way to get together, dear girl."

"We will," I assured him, nodding and hurrying away. "We will."

No jelly donuts for me and Ben. We were going to have to pay for pricey muffins from the market.

On Wednesday morning, I headed for Pilates again, hoping Helene had purchased her class card exclusively for the Mondays she'd be hosting visiting art collectors. But her Lexus sat in the parking lot. In my spot. I considered turning around. Instead I parked and walked into the alley, fighting the urge to go home with every step—until I saw Helene. She was chatting up Kelly like the two of them were best friends, and she'd already set her mat down in lane seven. My lane.

I didn't make a scene. I didn't pick up a bowling ball and pitch it at her head. I took a deep breath and made another promise: no matter how hard it was for me to be around Helene, no matter how much discomfort I felt, I wasn't going anywhere. "You can feel your emotions without acting on them," Dr. Feld had said. "If you bottle up anger, eventually it explodes. It's called an *emotion* because it's meant to move. Just breathe and let it."

I was determined to let that inner river flow peacefully. To remain in the class and stay civil. I vowed to attend every Pilates class on the schedule, in fact. Helene already had my husband, my loft, and, arguably, the baby I hadn't been able to conceive. I wasn't about to let her take Pilates away. She wasn't going to mess with my core.

I drove home after class proud of the dignified way I'd handled myself. But as I stopped at the end of my driveway and pulled a cream-colored linen envelope out of the mailbox, my composure shattered. I recognized Hugh's handwriting instantly. Helene must have told him about joining the class on Monday. He'd always preferred letters rather than texts or e-mails for condolences or making amends. Had he

23

written to apologize for Helene's obnoxious presence? For their moving here? "I've made so many mistakes, Nora . . ."

Dear Nora,

I've been resisting writing because I know how angry you still are. But I can't wait any longer. I'm putting together a retrospective. A comprehensive one. I'd like to include an early sketchbook along with the paintings—to show how the work has evolved. The sketchbook I gave you on your twenty-eighth birthday is by far the best. Those first studies of you are some of my strongest. I hope you won't give me trouble on this. It's only a loan—and after all, it is my work. Can't you please try to let go of your rage at me, Nora? Hasn't enough time passed? Say the word and I can have my assistant call FedEx and arrange to pick up the sketchbook. I still think of you fondly.

Hugh

For a moment, I could barely breathe. What a fool I'd been to expect an apology. Hugh hadn't even acknowledged the distress his interloping had caused. He'd only written because he needed something. When would I learn? A little furnace in my belly fired up. Too damn bad! Hugh would have to do without his favorite sketchbook. I didn't even keep the book at home. I stored it at Aunt Lada's, along with other reminders of life with him. I wouldn't respond to the letter. Wait. Should I write him back and tell him what a selfish bastard he was? Or should I let him borrow the book to show how little I cared about him anymore? I couldn't decide which would be more satisfying.

Take your time deciding. You are not on his clock. And remember, you will not let this make you a bitter, angry woman.

The next evening, Kelly sent an e-mail canceling Friday's class. She explained that she couldn't arrange any other time for her sonogram appointment, and rescheduled us for Sunday morning.

Bleary-eyed after what felt like another poor night's sleep, at 7:30 a.m. on Sunday I dragged myself out of bed to get ready for class. I went into the living room, picked up the remote, and clicked on the local news before starting to make coffee. The screen was filled with uniformed police and squad cars with flashing lights. What was up? Lots of local and county cops involved. That looked like . . . What did she just say?

No. It can't be. Oh my God. Impossible. That's . . . Oh God.

I sat on the couch, eyes locked on the television. Questions swirled around in my head so rapidly I thought I might faint. *How? Who would do that? And why?*

In the midst of my confusion, I have to confess I felt a teeny, tiny bit of relief—relief that if the report was right, I wouldn't have to hate Helene and Hugh anymore.

Because Hugh Walker and Helene Westing Walker were dead. Someone else besides me had wanted them that way. Someone with a lot more nerve.

From the *Pequod Courier*

Tips for Living

by Nora Glasser

Where the Wild Things Are

We know how it works. Pequod's businesses raise
their prices in summer to carry them through the
slower months. Summer People expect it. They can
afford the markup. The rest of us hold our collective
breath until after Labor Day, when the town empties
out. No more. We're turning blue now that Summer
People flock here on weekends off-season, stealing
our parking spots and crowding our exercise classes.
Prices stay inflated, and we're paying a premium for
our muffins. We return from the market stunned
at how few groceries our money buys. We want to
help our local businesses profit, but we also need to
eat. So why not employ survival methods from long
ago? Methods used even before the wandering tribes
settled down to plant and harvest? Forget "farm to

table" and "artisanal." We're talking precivilization. Hand to mouth. Put on your boots and stalk that wild asparagus. You'd be amazed at what you'll find in that acre of woods the developers haven't cleared. Go down by the creek and pull up leeks, ramps and sorrel. Learn to love chickweed. How about acorn mash? It's nutty. Develop a taste for the "earthy," but remember: choose those fungi carefully, or you'll end up feeding the worms.

Chapter Two

I was numb. Everything had an aura of unreality. It was as if I were watching an episode of *Murder, She Wrote*. A small seaside community on a misty fall morning with stunned and sleepy citizens in robes and slickers gathered on the street in front of the victims' residence, the police working the crime scene and stretching yellow tape across the drive.

I began to click through other news channels mechanically. None of them had live coverage—the major media hadn't arrived in Pequod yet. I clicked back to the local station. With her windswept hair, orange rain poncho and exercise pants, their reporter was more the type you'd see covering the annual Bike for Breast Cancer race, not a murder. Or in this case, a double murder. While she addressed the camera, another woman in a hooded rain jacket waited nervously at her side.

"I repeat, police aren't telling us anything except that two Pequod residents, the internationally known artist Hugh Walker and his wife, Helene Westing Walker, were killed," the reporter said. "A neighbor confirmed that the housekeeper discovered the bodies around six thirty a.m. when she arrived for work. In fact, I have that neighbor right here. Sue Mickelson. Thank you for speaking with us, Ms. Mickelson. Can you tell us about what happened here this morning?"

Ms. Mickelson stepped forward and straightened her posture for the camera. She had an air of self-importance about her.

"Well, it was unbelievably awful," she said dramatically. "It was still dark and I was walking Jupiter, my Lab, when I saw a figure running down the Walkers' driveway into the street. She was screaming, *'Dios mio! Los están muertos! Los están muertos!'* I know Spanish. She was saying, 'My God. They are dead. They are dead.' I called 911 on my cell."

"You didn't hear anything else before that?"

"No. We live next door." She pointed off-camera beyond Hugh's driveway. "But you can see there's a huge stretch of woods between our place and theirs."

"How well did you know them?"

"Sometimes on weekends our daughter has playdates with their little girl, Callie. I saw their car yesterday afternoon and realized they'd come out, so I called to try and set something up for the kids. Thank God Callie was staying in the city with her aunt last night or she'd probably be dead, too. It's horrible. Just horrible."

"Yes, it is. Thank you, Ms. Mickelson."

The reporter did a recap and signed off so the regular news could begin. The facts were beginning to sink in. I felt panicky. Then another wave of disbelief washed over me. My mind wouldn't accept the killings, even as my body was trembling. Was I in shock? Was that the mind-body split I was experiencing? I wanted to talk to Grace. Talking to her would help ground me. Had she heard yet? I tried her landline. No answer. I tried her cell, and then Mac's. The same. Nobody picked up. Then I remembered that it was Sunday and sometimes the family went to an early church service with Mac's parents and out to breakfast afterward.

I couldn't just sit there. I should be doing something besides clicking the remote from channel to channel, shouldn't I? But what? I finally grabbed my trench coat, pulled on my Wellingtons over my pajama bottoms, and got into my car. I had no idea where I was going.

It was a damp, cold, foggy morning. I could see my breath. British moor kind of weather. I drove fast, speeding past the entrance to the nature preserve. Then I remembered the police often lay in wait behind the bayberry bushes nearby. I slowed down.

The roads were nearly empty. I just kept driving and trying to absorb what I'd seen on television. What they were saying still didn't seem possible. The man I met when I was twenty-five, the man I'd lived with and loved for more than twelve years had been murdered? Grief stabbed my heart. Then I remembered how Hugh betrayed me with Helene, and the jabbing stopped. The questions surfaced again: What kind of a monster had killed Hugh and the mother of his child? And why? I could practically hear Grace's voice in my head saying, "Karma, baby. You can always count on karma."

I reached into my pocket for my phone to try calling her again. But my phone wasn't there. I tried the other pocket and came up with a crumpled five-dollar bill. Damn. I must've forgotten it.

I switched on the radio to hear more details on the crime. Static. Dense woods on either side of the road interfered. It began to rain and I turned on my wipers.

"What the hell?"

They were making annoying clicking sounds, like a desperate smoker flicking a Bic low on fuel, and they moved intermittently, maybe one stroke for the usual three.

"In four hundred feet, turn left," my GPS ordered.

"Not now," I said under my breath.

My Toyota was a lemon. I bought it used, and within a month the GPS jammed—it wouldn't turn off. The electronic female voice gives me random instructions at random times. Fixing it would cost almost half of what I paid for the car, so I live with the malfunction. And now the wipers had decided to act up, too? I glowered as they made one of their irregular thumps.

"Turn left," GPS lady ordered again. "Turn left."

"Please shut up. If I turn left, we'll drown."

The woods had thinned out, and water appeared on my left. Dark gray water, stirred up and angry like the sky, which was now a moldy gray-green. The air began to smell briny, like sour pickles, as the road curved toward the bridge that connected the neighborhoods on this side of the harbor with downtown Pequod. Through my blurry windshield, I saw waves crashing into the harbor's stone breakwater. The dozen or so sailboats that remained in the water late in the season rose and fell violently with the surf. Sirens screamed somewhere in the distance. Could the police be chasing down the killer? I tried the radio again and found better reception on WPQD, catching the middle of a report on Hugh:

"Walker became internationally famous for his unusual self-portraits. His most recent major New York show, *Scenes from a Marriage*, received stellar reviews last year. Stay with us. We'll be speaking with Abbas Masout, Walker's longtime art dealer, right after this message from Pequod Savings Bank."

Abbas. Poor Abbas must be devastated. Hugh was one of the first artists he took on when he opened his gallery in New York. Originally, he made his reputation in Beirut selling modern art to visiting American and European collectors and movie stars during the city's golden age. Then, in 1975, the Paris of the Middle East became a war zone, and Abbas spent the next five years struggling to survive. He finally managed to flee to the States and use his art world connections to set up shop, initially in Soho, then in Chelsea. He'd become one of the most successful dealers of the last decade. Collectors loved him for his charm. Hugh loved him for that, too, plus being tenacious as a terrier on his behalf.

"This is WPQD back with our breaking story on the murders of Hugh and Helene Walker. We have Mr. Walker's art dealer, Abbas Masout, speaking to us from his loft in Lower Manhattan. Mr. Masout, what can you tell us about this tragedy?"

"I can tell you a great American artist who was my friend is dead, and my heart is crying. What evil creature did this? I don't understand. It makes no sense," he said. "How could this violence happen in such a peaceful place? And why to them?" His voice broke. "I can't speak anymore . . . I'm sorry."

"I understand. Thank you, Mr. Masout. Repeating, artist Hugh Walker, and his wife, Helene Westing Walker, were found dead in their home near Pequod, New York, this morning. An apparent double homicide. The police do not have a suspect in custody. Stay with us here at WPQD for the latest on the breaking story. And now for national news."

I pressed "Scan" on the tuner for another station. Nothing landed. I shut the radio off. On the other side of the bridge, I turned right, aiming for Eden's Coffee Shop half a mile ahead. My head was beginning to pound. Caffeine withdrawal. I hadn't thought to drink my coffee before leaving the house.

The sidewalks and most of the parking spaces were empty—Corwin's Market didn't open until 9:00 a.m. It was quiet. No double murderer in sight. No posse forming in front of the Laundromat, which is housed in a renovated nineteenth-century jailhouse. The plaque by the entrance says, "Three pirates captured by the whaling ship Cuttamonk were incarcerated here until they were hanged." It looked like a typical rainy, off-season Sunday morning in a quaint resort town.

Abbas was right. Despite the recent changes, Pequod was still an improbable setting for a double murder. A local homicide is the kind of story that gets framed and hung on the wall of the *Courier* office, along with coverage on bank robberies and hurricanes. We only have one homicide clipping up there—from 1972. The body of a teenage girl washed up on Crooked Beach. She wasn't even from Pequod. The tides brought her here. She'd been hit with a heavy object and dumped in the water, not drowned. Turned out her boyfriend caught her stepping out on him and smashed her head in with a skateboard. They called it "a crime of passion," which sounded to me like a justification.

The traffic signal in front of the pharmacy turned red and I stopped. I noticed Mr. Duck, with his dirty orange bill and mud-spattered feathers, sitting at the edge of the huge puddle on my right that forms during big rains in the alleyway between the pharmacy and liquor store.

Mr. Duck looked forlorn. And why wouldn't he? He'd lost the love of his life. Mr. and Mrs. Duck never left each other's side. You'd see the two of them mostly down on the wharf, except in a rainstorm. Then they'd waddle over to this puddle, ruffle each other's tail feathers and snuggle. Until another gray day, when one of the Piqued had complained, and a green van from animal control pulled up. They captured Mrs. Duck, but Mr. Duck escaped. He comes and sits here whenever the puddle appears, watching for her. I wrote a small item about him in the *Courier*. It elicited higher-than-usual reader response. One letter read: *My wife was taken by cancer. Some days I'm angry with her for leaving me. Other days I want to die and be with her. She was my best friend. I am Mr. Duck.*

I suspect Ben wrote that one and signed it with a phony name. People do crazy things when they hurt.

The signal turned green. Driving ahead, I saw that the lights were on in the *Courier* office. Ben would likely be there organizing coverage along with Lizzie and the rest of the staff, if they weren't already at the scene. Should I go there? They had probably tried to call me. Was I ready to talk with them? I'd need coffee first. I pulled into a space in front of Eden's.

I hesitated before stepping out of the car, realizing what I must look like. My pajama bottoms, men's dark navy plaid flannel with a drawstring waist, were conspicuous. I'd been wearing them for so many years, I'd forgotten until this moment that I'd appropriated them from Hugh. For a second my heart ached once more at the memory of him sleeping in them at my side, and then it went numb again.

I swung the visor down and quickly glanced in the mirror to check my hair. It resembled a bird's nest. I looked awful. There were puffy bags under my eyes. My normally flawless skin was splotchy. Oddly, there was a small cut on my cheek, like a cat scratch, near the top of my right cheekbone. Even odder, there were pieces of dead leaves in my bangs. I brushed them away. Something dry and stiff dropped out of my hair into my lap.

A twig.

I stopped breathing for an instant.

I flipped the visor back up. How did I get that scratch on my face, and where had the twig and leaves come from? I hadn't walked in the woods; I'd gone straight down the gravel driveway to the car when I left the house. I brushed my teeth the night before, and I hadn't seen any of those things as I looked in the bathroom mirror. I glanced down at my fingernails. They were a little ragged. I guess I could have run a rough nail across my face while I slept. But that didn't explain the twig and the leaves.

It couldn't be . . .

No. Nope. Keep your head, Nora. That's all over and done with. It stopped so long ago. Put it out of your mind.

The rain was starting to come down harder. I turned up the collar of my trench coat, bolted out of the car and ran for the coffee shop.

Stepping into the heart and soul of Pequod is like time traveling to the early 1960s, except for the flat-screen TV mounted on the wall. There were a few patrons scattered inside Eden's among the green-leather-upholstered booths and the chrome swivel stools at the soda fountain. I recognized the town's pharmacist. They were all looking up at the TV, transfixed by the news. The same local reporter I'd seen earlier was repeating information I already knew. What I hadn't noticed at first was Lizzie. She was standing on the far right by the register in her camouflage rain poncho and olive drab cargo pants. Her carroty hair was dripping wet.

"Nora!"

She spotted me at the door and hurried over carrying two coffees-to-go.

"I've been trying to call you. Have you heard about the Walkers?" I nodded.

"I'm so sorry. You must be completely freaked out."

"Lower your voice, please," I whispered, motioning for her to follow me to a small wooden table in an empty section on the side. "I don't want everyone in here to know about my connection to them."

"Right. Right. Of course," she whispered back.

I'd decided I had to tell Lizzie and Ben about my divorce the day she walked into the office and said a famous painter named Walker purchased the house at Pequod Point. The *Courier* publishes the largest real estate sales every month. Tracking them was part of Lizzie's job. I'd figured she would do her research on Hugh and find out soon enough.

She set her coffees on the well-worn tabletop. We both sat down.

"So how are you doing?" she asked.

"To tell you the truth, I'm not really sure. It's hard to accept that it's actually happened."

She nodded gravely. "That's normal. You're in shock."

It was almost reassuring to hear Lizzie confirm my self-diagnosis. It explained how crazy I felt.

"You're right. Shock would be a normal reaction, wouldn't it? What else have you heard? What does Ben know?"

"Ben is at the scene. I'm going over there now. He says they're not letting the press past the end of the driveway. He's working his contacts by phone."

"So, there's nothing beyond the preliminary report yet?" I asked, indicating the TV, which was airing the Sue Mickelson footage again.

"Well, one thing . . ."

"Tell me."

"But it's unconfirmed."

"What is it, Lizzie?"

35

She hesitated and bit her lip.

"Come on, spill."

"There's an unconfirmed report saying they were shot in the bedroom. In their bed."

"Oh shit." I felt the blood drain from my face.

"God. You've gone white as a sheet, Nora. I'm so sorry. I shouldn't have told you. Like I said, it's unconfirmed."

"No. No. It's okay. I'm glad you did. Who's the source?"

"I don't know. Ben got it from one of his people. Listen," she said, frowning. "You should take care of yourself and go back home. We have this covered. I'm on it. Ben is on it. No one expects you to deal with this. Ben certainly doesn't. He's worried about you."

"He is?" I was taken aback.

Lizzie nodded. "First thing he said, 'This is going to be tough for Nora.'"

"But I need to do *something*."

She noticed the time on her watch. "Damn. I have to get over there and snap some shots of the roadblock and cop cars. And we need quotes from neighbors." She picked up the coffees. "Nora, promise you'll go home?"

"Hmm?" I answered, dazed.

She looked at me sternly. "You. Home."

I waved her away. "Okay, okay. I will."

Lizzie left. I stared out the front window after her. Was it true? Had someone really acted out my fantasy and shot Hugh and Helene in their bed? How could I just sit on the margins listening to sound bites and watching looping TV images, waiting for other people to tell me what was going on? As my hands gripped the edge of the table, I felt the war inside me beginning, the wolf hair growing on my knuckles. I'd sworn I would never spy again. I promised myself.

"Coffee?"

"Huh?" I looked up at the waitress who'd appeared beside me.

"Sorry to make you wait. We just brewed a fresh pot."

"No, thanks." I stood up. "I just remembered I have to be somewhere."

As I walked out of Eden's onto the rainy street, I saw Mr. Duck waddling down the sidewalk toward me, quacking emphatically.

I got the distinct feeling that he was telling me to run.

Wipers thumping unevenly. Tires whooshing on wet pavement. Rain beating on the hood. I drove in a kind of trance. How many road trips had Hugh and I taken in all kinds of weather? Navigating a deluge in England or Ireland on the wrong side of the road. Crawling through fog along the northern Oregon coast. Winding through Zion National Park in the heat with a broken air conditioner. Plowing through snow-drifts on the way upstate to the weekend house. We were good traveling companions, Hugh and I. "Who'll be our trip master for the first fifty miles?" he would ask before we started out, sorting through the CDs we'd tossed into a travel bag. "Sinatra? David Byrne? Patsy Cline? You pick."

◆ ◆ ◆

Avoiding the roadblock was easy. I drove south on Old Route 20 wishing I'd bought that coffee. I had to keep the window open despite the rain to distract from the dull ache in my head. Passing Van Winkle Lanes and continuing beyond a stretch of undeveloped woodlands, I made sure no one was behind me before turning right at the two tall white pillars and cedar-shingled guardhouse that marked the entrance to the exclusive Dune Golf Club.

The Dune course closes the first day of November, so no one was there to stop me. No one had a list without my name on it that would prove I hadn't paid the $18,000 yearly fee. Dune members are primarily older, wealthy, conservative types. Most summer here and winter in Palm Beach. The public course is on the other side of town. Near the dump. Someday I'd do a story on the Dune Club's unwritten membership policies.

My mother would have loved a Dune membership. As much as her older sister embraced her Russian-Jewish ancestry, my mother denied hers, changing her maiden name from Sasha Levervitch to Sally Leer. "Sally Leer, my tush!" I heard Lada erupt during one of their fights. "You always wanted to fit in with the Waspy crowd. You pretend you have relatives who came over on the *Mayflower* instead of the cargo hold of a fishtunkina fishing boat."

The road continued to wind through the golf course's rolling, now-soggy brown lawns. I checked my rearview mirror. Still no one. I let out my breath and filled my lungs with salty sea air. The sea is never very far from any place in Pequod. A forest of pines and scrub oak at the edge of the course blocked the water from view at the club.

The sprawling clubhouse, another cedar-shingled affair, sat high on a hill at the top of the road's final curve. The grand-pillared, two-story building with the wraparound porch overlooked fairways, a lake, sand-pits and greens. Half-frozen red geraniums still bloomed in the window boxes, but the windows were shuttered. The club was deserted, just as I'd hoped. The parking lot behind the clubhouse butted up against the forest and I headed for it, nervously checking my mirror again.

Grace and I used to hike in this forest until we were put off by a gruesome accident—a hunter's arrow ripped into a hiker's leg. The Dune Club owners posted No Trespassing signs after that. I heard there were a few bold hunters who continued to show up when the club closed for the season, but I prayed they wouldn't be around.

Steering into the lot, I breathed more easily. Empty. No pickup trucks or maintenance workers' vans in sight. I parked at the edge nearest the woods, and when I turned off the engine, I could hear the howl of wind in the trees. Reaching over and opening the glove compartment, I rummaged through the detritus inside: sunglasses missing a lens, local maps, the car's manual and a miniature flashlight. Also, one small cellophane bag containing four chocolate-covered espresso beans likely purchased during another caffeine emergency. I popped them in my mouth.

I hadn't removed Aunt Lada's opera glasses since the last spying mission. Buried deep down in the well of the compartment, they had lenses capable of magnifying four times at a distance of three thousand feet—enough to see a performer's facial expressions from the top tier at Carnegie Hall. My great-grandfather Lev had left them to her. He was a "pacher" (Yiddish for clapper) at the City Opera in New York. Lev told Immigrant Services he was a cantor student back in the shtetl and a serious lover of music who knew all about opera. So, they got him a job at the opera house. Janitorial mostly, but one of his tasks was to use his knowledge during the performance to start applause at the right moments.

"He never left a diva in the lurch," Aunt Lada said.

Lada never let me down, either. She was always there to comfort. When my mother and father began fighting incessantly, I even ran off to stay with her in her East Village walk-up. She never married or had kids, and after both my parents were gone, with my father an only child and both sets of grandparents dead, Lada and I were all each other had left. The gold opera glasses were her most treasured possession, and she'd passed them on as a wedding present. I felt guilty as I pulled them out. Here I was, divorced and treating them like junk.

I stuck the glasses in my coat pocket, closed the window and stepped outside shivering. The rain had let up, but the cold, wet wind snuck up my sleeves. My face and fingers felt raw. I checked behind me again. No one there. I looked left. All clear. Then right. A sharp caw ripped the air at my back. I whipped around and saw a seagull open its claws. A clam plummeted to the asphalt. The big gray-and-white bird swooped down to the bits of cracked shell and pink slime and glared at me, daring me to approach its treasure.

"It's all yours," I said, trembling.

Pulling my collar high under my chin, I started across the water-logged grass for the woods and picked up the muddy hunting trail in a few yards. I slogged ahead, still trying to absorb the fact that Hugh was dead. I thought of the time he almost died and how intensely scary that was. He went into cardiac arrest during routine hernia surgery. I wasn't his wife yet, so the hospital called his next of kin. Hugh's brother flew up from Virginia to take charge. Tobias Walker was a born-again Christian and a real challenge for Hugh. "A fanatic," Hugh called him. He'd chafed at finding Tobias by his side when he woke up.

The rain was coming down hard again, slashing through the pines as I trudged along. The oaks that replaced them closer to the shore offered little protection. The storm had stripped off most of their leaves. Icy water ran down my hair, dripped beneath my coat collar and trickled down my neck. I picked up my pace, kicking through the dead leaves and skirting sinkholes of mud. Freezing, I shoved my hands in my pockets. Two fingers worried the leather strap of Lada's opera glasses.

I wasn't sure what was driving me. Was this a sign of trauma? Part of the shock reaction? I kept moving, squinting through the rain and walking faster, breathing hard. *I'm miserable, but at least I'm alive.* I could feel the sting of the icy rain, the cold air biting my lungs. I could see the trees and hear the wind and smell the sea. What could Hugh and Helene experience anymore? Nothing.

"Hugh and Helene. Hugh and Helene." What happened to "Hugh and Nora?" How did it all go so wrong? Had our brief marriage meant anything to him? We wed a few months after Hugh recovered from the surgery. But it wasn't simply so I'd be empowered in a health crisis to save him from the care of his zealot brother. We could've signed a health care proxy for that. We'd always talked about marriage in relation to having children, and after Hugh's brush with mortality, he turned to me in bed one morning, misty-eyed.

"Nora, let's do it. Let's get married and have a kid," he'd said.

I'd gladly accepted on both counts.

At last the scrub oaks thinned out and the view opened up. Down the slope at the end of the trail, thick, wheat-colored seagrass and reeds lined a ragged coastline. Beyond the grass, a channel of dark, windswept water churned. And because I knew exactly where to look amid all the vegetation, I spied the brown corner of the small wooden duck blind a few yards from the water's edge. Grace and I had spotted it on one of our hikes after a punishing nor'easter flattened the seagrass enough to expose the roofline.

I kept my head bent and tried to prevent the rain from pelting my eyes as I ran down the hill, tripping on roots and slipping on mud. I lost control and stumbled off the trail, careening through the high grass, finally stopping by shoving my hands out as I crashed into the back of the shelter. I caught my breath and checked myself; I wasn't hurt, just sore and winded. I pushed on the door. Sopping wet and shivering, I stepped inside the tiny wooden room and stood there, dripping puddles on the floor. *This is insane. Leave.* But I couldn't. I had to set eyes on the murder scene. As if it would prove to the disbelieving part of my brain that this had actually happened.

The dark interior of the blind smelled of wet cedar and sweet grass. Three walls had no windows. The fourth faced the water and was completely open except for the roof's extended overhang, which shrouded the inside in shadow. It rendered any hunter who sat there invisible to his prey. Friends or relatives of Mr. and Mrs. Duck might be coasting across the sky, feeling the warmth of the sun, enjoying a lift on a thermal when . . . Boom! Someone playing God would decide to end a life.

The blind had no furniture, no lighting. No heating device. Only a roughhewn wooden bench with an old army blanket folded on top. Removing Aunt Lada's glasses from my pocket, I stripped off my wet coat and wrapped the scratchy wool blanket around my shoulders. I sat down on the bench and tried to stop my teeth from chattering by clenching my jaw. Finally, I lifted the glasses to my eyes and peered across the inlet, missing the mark at first, getting lost in the choppy water before moving up into the trees. There it was on the opposite shore, perched on high ground in the wetlands of Pequod Point, glass walls and wooden beams soaring up through the pines. Hugh's house.

I'd never seen it in daylight before.

◆ ◆ ◆

I've never told anyone that I spied on Hugh and Helene. Not even Grace.

I spied on them the same day I found out they'd moved here, when Lizzie walked into the office with the town clerk's real estate list.

"Pequod Point sold for two point five million," Lizzie said, unwrapping a black-and-white Palestinian scarf from around her neck and setting down her backpack.

"The Miami developer who built the house last year as his summer escape couldn't pay off his construction loan. 'Mr. and Mrs. Hugh Walker' bought it from the bank. I bet you it's that famous artist Hugh Walker."

"What?" I gasped. "Can I see that list?" I couldn't fathom that Hugh would be cruel enough to add that much insult to injury by moving here.

"The property is great for a painter. There's a gigantic art studio—the developer's wife made pottery. I took those photos of her with her weird, misshapen urns. Remember? We ran them in Lifestyles? I call dibs on the feature story if I'm right," Lizzie said.

"I don't fucking believe this," I said, gawking at his name.

After I told her and Ben about my marriage and how it ended, Lizzie looked distressed and began fingering a tassel on her scarf.

"God, Nora, that's a terrible story. I mean, where was the birth control?" Her hand flew to her mouth. "Sorry."

"It's okay, Lizzie. Believe me, you're not the first person to ask about that."

She looked at me dolefully. "How long were you married?"

"We lived together for years. But we'd only been married thirteen months."

"Do you think getting married freaked him out? Is that why he messed around?"

I wanted to say, *Don't worry, your fiancé is not Hugh.* But I was embarrassed to be sharing any of this, especially in front of Ben, who was at his desk listening intently, rubbing his chin and frowning.

I shrugged. "I'd really appreciate it if both of you would keep this information to yourselves. Please, don't tell *anyone.*"

"I won't say a word," Lizzie said, crossing her heart.

Ben had an unusually emotional reaction. He apologized vehemently on behalf of his gender. "I'm sorry that happened to you, Nora. Men who behave like that make me ashamed of my sex." Given Ben's usual terse self, I was even more astonished he made it a point to say something nice again before the day's end: "You deserved a lot better, Nora. A whole lot better."

I could barely concentrate the rest of the afternoon. I was supposed to be working on my feature, "Canines for Heroes," about a pet adoption program designed to help Iraq War veterans recover from PTSD. Struggling to formulate questions for an interview with one of the vets, all I could come up with was a preliminary, "Have you ever owned a dog before?" Instead, I began playing the virtual slot machines on slotsofvegas.com, scoring $63,235. My highest total yet. I wished the games were real and legal, because my nest egg was gone. A small-town reporter's salary wasn't going to replenish it.

By six o'clock, everyone else in the *Courier* office had left for the day. It was a quiet time, good for taking another crack at the interview questions. Just as I reopened the work file, I heard the door to the street close. Seconds later, Al Rudinsky appeared. A sweet bear of a man with a buzz cut, Al was wearing his royal-blue Tidy Pools coveralls, and they were caked with mud. He stood in the office doorway wiping his dirty work boots on the mat. His meaty neck and broad forehead were streaked with grime and sweat.

"Am I too late? Did I miss the deadline? I brought cash." He gave me an anxious smile.

Al was married to Sinead, one of my Pilates classmates—Sinead O'Halloran-Rudinsky. Their Irish-Polish union produced four kids, and Al was always low on money. In fact, he was months behind on payments for his ads. Ben had reluctantly put him on notice. No more credit. This was the last day to buy space in the Summer Lawn and Garden insert, an important advertising platform for Al's Tidy Pools, Irrigation and Landscaping Service.

"The ad department is gone for the day," I said, indicating the closed door to the back office where our accounting and advertising staff work. "Everyone is. But I'll make sure Ben gets your money. He might be okay with extending the deadline since you brought in your payment today." I smiled at him. "In fact, I'll lobby for it."

Al crossed the floor in his bowlegged stride and handed me a manila envelope with his big, dirty hand. He looked down at the mud he'd tracked in, chagrined.

"Sorry, I tried to get it all off."

"It's all right, Al. No big deal. I'll sweep it up later."

He bent down and began to scoop up the clumps of wet earth with his bare hands.

"Can you tell Ben I'm sorry, I really meant to get here earlier? I had a rush job out at Pequod Point," he said, straightening up.

I drew back. My antennae went up. Could he mean Hugh and Helene's house?

"Oh? What job was that?"

He shoved the dirt into his coverall pocket and wiped his hands on his thighs. "Biggest property I handle. New owners moved in today, and they want everything done yesterday. Had to get the pool cleaned, replace the filter motor and dig out a busted sprinkler line. Four thirty came around, I told them I had to make an important delivery and I'd come back to finish," he said, indicating the envelope, "but the lady of the house *insisted* I stay or not come back at all."

I sat up in my chair and frowned, unable to hold my tongue. "That wasn't very nice."

Al nodded in agreement. "Summer People. But the husband is an interesting guy. An artist. I've done jobs for some artists out here in the summers before. They like the light." He spotted another clump of mud on the floor, snatched it up and pocketed it. "Saw him unwrapping paintings in his studio while I worked on the pool. He's painted lots of pictures of himself with his wife. One of them was pretty wild—with him naked, curled around her when she was pregnant." He shrugged. "Guess she inspires him."

"Sounds like it," I snapped.

Fortunately, Al didn't seem to notice.

"You know, I used to do some drawing. I drove in at night to take classes at the Brooklyn Museum. This is before Sinead and the kids. No time now," he said wistfully. "Well, I'd better get home. Thanks for putting in a word with Ben." He headed out, stopped at the door and turned back for a second. "Really sorry about the floor, Nora."

A kind of compulsion came over me. It grew worse by the hour. I had to see what Hugh's $2.5 million life with Helene was like. I waited until eleven o'clock. Then I drove to the Dune Golf Club and parked.

I wasn't frightened of running into anyone. The club closed after sunset. Even trespassing hunters didn't start stalking deer until October. I trekked under a full moon so bright there was no need for a flashlight.

The turnoff to the duck blind was easy to locate, marked on either side by large, gray rocks. I knew the spot would have at least a partial view of Pequod Point. The last time Grace and I hiked to the blind, we could see a house under construction across the water. I tramped down there, pushed open the door and sat on the wooden bench inside.

The house on the opposite shore was less than seventy-five yards ahead as the duck flies. Probably a five-minute slog through the seagrass along the inlet's shaggy coastline, or on higher ground, a two-minute run. The view was even better than I expected—an almost-clear sight line over the top of the grass. I could only make out the parts that were lit, but with Aunt Lada's glasses, they were visible in detail. On two sides, towering walls made of glass revealed an open-plan kitchen, dining and living room area with a mammoth stone fireplace. A de Kooning hung over the mantel, a Rauschenberg on the adjacent wall. Even with moving boxes all over the room, it was easy to see this was a spectacular home.

It was cool that May night. Hugh reclined on the couch in jeans and a sweatshirt. Helene came out of the kitchen carrying two glasses of wine. She wore shorts and what I recognized as one of Hugh's flannel plaid shirts. She sat down and snuggled against him as they sipped their wine in front of the fire. Watching him wrap his leg around hers, I felt a tug in my chest. I knew the warmth and firmness of his thigh. For the first time in years, I let myself miss Hugh's touch. He rolled over and kissed her, and I remembered his salty taste. The light flick of his tongue. The way he liked to blow softly on the back of my neck. My heart ached so badly, I thought I might be having a heart attack. He fondled Helene's breast, and I couldn't look away. Was I that masochistic? Would I actually stay and watch them make love?

Their daughter saved me from myself. Callie staggered into the living room in her pink pajamas, rubbing her eyes, apparently unable to sleep. Built long and lean like her father, she had Hugh's dark curls. I couldn't distinguish her features under her mass of hair, but I was sure she must be beautiful because both her parents were. Helene pulled her close. I watched her stroke Callie's head and comfort her, and as I did, I wept. I dropped Aunt Lada's glasses and doubled over, hugging myself, wailing, rolling on the blind's dirty floor like I was possessed.

"How could you give her my child?" I gasped.

I cried so much I was sure there was no feeling left.

At last I'm done, I thought. *I'm cured.*

From the *New York Journal*

Picks of the Week: Hugh Walker's

Scenes from a Marriage

By Davis Kimmerle

Hugh Walker's show at the Abbas Masout Gallery is nothing short of a revelation. Walker has taken artistic risks before, for better and worse. His early self-portraits, works like *Self-Portrait with Monkeys*, an homage to Frida Kahlo, were bold but essentially derivative. His *New York Portraits* delivered both originality and a distinctive style. With *The Nora Series*—self-portraits that included his ex-wife, Nora Glasser—we saw a major American artist heading into his prime. But in *Scenes from a Marriage*, his first show since last year's very public divorce, Walker has succeeded in securing his place in the pantheon as a mature artist capable of depth and pathos.

The front room of the exhibition offers the prosaic *Self-Portrait with Nora Making Coffee*, *Self-Portrait with*

Nora Bathing and other tranquil, domestic scenes. From there, Walker delves into the darker aspects of his personal life. *Self-Portrait with Nora in Cell* is a frightening, claustrophobic image of his former muse beside the artist in a shadowy, tunnel-like space. In another powerful, untitled work, Nora is depicted, disturbingly, as part mythical beast looming threateningly over the sleeping artist in their marital bed.

The back room of the gallery introduces Walker's new source of inspiration by way of homage to Ono and Lennon. The jubilant *Self-Portrait with Pregnant Helene* (interestingly, not for sale) has an entire wall to itself. Hanging opposite is the show's pièce de résistance: the artist sketching Nora, who lies curled on the floor of his studio, having discovered the fact of his mistress's pregnancy. Walker titled it *Self-Portrait with Nora, Knowing.*

Walker manages to capture the deep psychological pain and turmoil that comes when a marriage unravels, as well as the hope new love can inspire, all while pushing the aesthetic boundaries of the self-portrait form. This is a masterful show. Don't miss it.

Chapter Three

Two dark blue Crown Victorias with county police seals were parked in front of the garage. Alongside them, a white county coroner's "Crime Scene Section" van. Aunt Lada's opera glasses provided a fragmented view of the entire spread in a series of close-ups that I could piece together for the bigger picture. Panning from left to right, I came across one of Pequod's police officers standing guard in the driveway. He looked like Lt. Crawley but it was hard to tell if it was him for sure. He had the hood on his yellow slicker drawn up.

Crawley knew me from my weekly drop-ins to the station. Editing the police reports for the *Courier*'s Police Blotter was part of my job. When I picked them up at the precinct, I'd usually find him reading the sports pages and resenting the interruption. Besides Crawley, I counted eight county officers in gray Stetsons and black rain gear patrolling the woods that shielded Hugh's estate from the road. Without a doubt, this was a murder scene.

Rain pelted the roof of the blind as I continued to scan, hands shaking from the cold and jiggling the opera glasses so that everything blurred. I should leave immediately. Since that May night, I promised myself I'd never play Peeping Tom again. What more could I actually learn out here? I should hike out and drive home right now, or head for a bar. Instead I wrapped the army blanket around my shoulders more tightly and tried to steady my hands as I examined the scene.

Not even this ugly weather could diminish the grandeur of the house and property. The operatic great room's glass walls shot up to the treetops, offering dramatic, one-hundred-eighty-degree views of the secluded woods and cove. The other walls were constructed of large stones and trimmed with honey-colored timber that blended in naturally with the landscape. At the far wall, I could see a hallway that led to the rest of the house. The place was so large, there must be rooms and rooms and rooms back there. A separate three-car garage was situated to the left. A slice of another glass-and-wood building was visible on the right behind the main structure, past the pool. Hugh's studio, I surmised. It was built to take advantage of the views as well.

A tall, bald man in a brown tweed sports coat and a tie gestured animatedly in the center of the great room while talking on his cell. He must be the lead county homicide detective. Around him, figures wearing hooded white jumpsuits and blue plastic gloves crawled on the floor marking, measuring and putting random items in Ziploc bags. I knew this to be forensics procedure, but it looked like performance art.

As I panned back to the fireplace, a white light suddenly exploded in my eyes. I dropped the glasses and blinked at the orange balloons floating on my retinas. They faded quickly, but bursts of light continued to strobe across the choppy waters. Camera flashes. The police were taking pictures of the crime scene.

I picked up the glasses and peered through them again just in time to catch the bright red of an ambulance rolling up the drive. Who needed an ambulance? The news hadn't mentioned any other victims who'd survived. And if there *were* survivors, why were the EMTs arriving so late? It took a moment before I grasped that the ambulance must have come at the county coroner's request. To cart Hugh and Helene away for autopsies. I shuddered at the thought.

With a little maneuvering, the vehicle turned and backed up to the house, revealing a Pequod Volunteer Ambulance insignia on the side. The driver's door opened and an unmistakable head of thick, snowy hair appeared. Grace's husband, Mac, had gone gray at twenty-five. "He thinks of emergency calls as a vacation," Grace had said when Mac first signed on for the ambulance team. After leaving his job on Wall Street to move to Pequod, he began day-trading from home. Mac has attention deficit disorder, and like many people with the affliction, he gets calm and laser focused in high-stress situations. That's why he's drawn to trading and EMT work.

Mac climbed out of the ambulance and drew his hood up against the rain. Another man came around from the passenger side to join him. Al Rudinsky. I knew Al volunteered with the ambulance corps, but I don't think I'd ever seen him out of his bright blue Tidy Pool coveralls. Like Mac, he wore jeans and a red crew windbreaker.

A third man in the same outfit clambered out of the double doors in the back. I was surprised to see Kelly's husband, Stokes. When had Stokes joined the ambulance corps? I wouldn't have expected him to give up his bowling time.

"He's dreamed of running an alley ever since his first bowling party at ten," Kelly told me the morning I interviewed the couple for my piece on Van Winkle Lanes' reopening. "He's a maniac about bowling," she said of her athletic but baby-faced husband, who barely said a word. "He practices every day. At least three hours. Even when he isn't competing." I remember thinking that could explain his freakishly overdeveloped right arm.

Now Stokes was using his considerable upper-body strength to unload gurneys. The front door of the house opened and the tweedy detective appeared, giving the men a thumbs-up. Mac pushed the first gurney in alone while Stokes and Al waited, hunched over the second. When Mac was fully inside, the other two shoved their gurney across the threshold. But Stokes let go. He allowed Al to continue wheeling the equipment into the house while he stood in the rain like a statue. Why had Stokes stopped? Was he afraid of what he would see inside?

I tried to keep the violent images at bay by picturing Hugh at work in his old studio. I knew that scene so well, I could create it easily in my mind. Hugh wearing jeans and a faded blue plaid shirt with the sleeves rolled up. Three buttons open at the top, soft brown chest hair peeking out. Paint stains on his calloused hands. The boyish nape of his neck as he looked down at his palette to mix more paint. I could almost smell the turpentine. I suddenly missed being in the studio with him, posing for his paintings and sketches while he played Bach CDs on his ancient, paint-splattered boom box. I missed being his muse. I missed his making tea for us when we took breaks. He'd show me the new work, excited. *When had I made him claustrophobic? He never told me he felt like that. I had to learn it from a critic's review of a painting I never saw.*

Stokes finally moved. He reached inside his windbreaker pocket, pulled out a pack of American Spirits and went to stand under an eave at the side of the house. Stokes smoked? That was odd. With Kelly such a health-conscious type, not to mention pregnant, she couldn't approve. Maybe she didn't know? I watched him light the cigarette, toss the match and take a long draw, as if it were the deepest breath he'd taken in years. As he exhaled, something caught his attention and his head jerked to the left. I followed his sight line.

Two jumpsuited men had come out of the house carrying what was obviously a large painting wrapped in clear, heavy plastic. Was it the de Kooning or the Rauschenberg? Or could it be one of Hugh's paintings? And why were the police removing it?

The men walked it slowly and carefully down the path past Stokes. When they reached the crime scene van, the man holding the bottom of the painting used one hand to slide the van's side door open. They both tilted the canvas and began brushing rainwater off the plastic before loading it in. The covering fell away and I recoiled instantly. Before they could put it back on, I saw Hugh's *Self Portrait with Pregnant Helene* with two large, vicious gashes sliced into the canvas: one in the vicinity of Hugh's heart and the other across Helene's belly.

A shiver ran through me as I lowered the glasses, like dark tar seeping through my veins. Even at this distance, I could sense the rage in the gesture, the ferocious need to destroy. It was a horrible feeling. And how crazy was it that whoever committed the crime had the identical impulse I'd had?

Only they'd succeeded.

Shaken, I lifted the glasses to my eyes and searched for Stokes, but he wasn't under the eave anymore. Instead I found Mac and Al bowed against the driving rain, pushing a stretcher loaded down with a bulky gray body bag on the path toward the ambulance. Was Hugh's body in there? I couldn't bear to think of him suffocating in that airless bag. I whispered a plea: "You're smothering him. Unzip it."

Unable to watch anymore, I closed my eyes and took myself back again. To the roof of our loft building this time. Late at night. The streets below empty except for a grinding garbage truck and an occasional shift-changing cab. The skyscrapers of Lower Manhattan sparkling around us like Oz. An older, white brick office building sitting directly across the street has its lights out and its blinds drawn. The office cleaners have finished vacuuming, mopping and taking out trash. Hugh has a 16-mm projector on a stand. He's threading a reel of film, turning on the bulb. He picks the machine up and aims it at the building.

Fred Astaire and Ginger Rogers appear. They're at least thirty feet tall. Ginger, dazzling in a backless satin-and-ostrich-feather gown; Fred in white tie and tails. He's singing, silky-voiced, as he floats her across a dance floor. Their cheeks touch. He's in heaven, he croons.

The garbage men stare up from the back of the truck. They are mystified. We laugh in delight. We sing along. Hugh puts the projector down and grabs me for a dip and spin as the orchestra plays on.

I smell his musky scent. He is solid and strong. Playful. Alive.

Snap.

I opened my eyes. What was that?

Snap.

A breaking branch?

Crunch. Crunch.

Rustling leaves?

Someone was behind the blind. A hunter? The police? How bad would it look if they found me spying at the murder scene? Another *snap*—this one closer. What if it was the killer? What if a gun-toting, knife-wielding maniac was still out there?

Heart pounding, I threw on my trench coat, shoved the glasses into the pocket and climbed through the front of the blind. Crouching low, I made my way deep into the tall grasses by the shore, the muddy ground sucking at my Wellingtons, the long, wet blades lashing my face and soaking my pajamas, my hair. But the grass was good cover, thick and high. A wall of wheat-colored straw. Breathless, I stopped to wait for whomever was out there to leave. If it was a police officer, what story would I tell? Would he believe me if I said I was trying to cover the murders for the *Courier*? From here?

What if he discovered I was Hugh's ex?

I tried to listen beyond my chattering teeth. Maybe it was only rain I'd heard before? Or a deer foraging near the blind?

I longed to stand—my knees and thighs ached from squatting. I parted a section of grass and scanned. No one there. It seemed safe to make a move back to the trail. I started to rise. Suddenly I sensed the reeds shake behind me. My muscles tensed. Something rustled very close by. I stopped breathing and heard a voice inside me say, *Run!*

Taking off like a rabbit, I thrashed through the seagrass and reeds, adrenaline pumping. I steered inland, kept running and finally emerged from the grass, panting and sweating, into a small clearing only partially obscured by some bayberry bushes. It was about thirty yards from the house.

"Hey!" a male voice whispered hoarsely.

I whirled to my right. Standing a few yards ahead, soaked to the bone just like I was, was Stokes.

Chapter Four

"What the hell?" Stokes rasped. "You can't be here."

Stunned to encounter Stokes, I'd almost forgotten about the police. I dropped to a crouch and crept back behind the bayberry bushes. I waved at him to follow.

"C'mere. Over here."

Stokes looked at me dubiously. "Are you nuts?"

He might well think so. I'm sure I looked like I'd escaped an asylum. And we hardly knew each other. I'd done that interview with him and Kelly, chatted casually at the Thunder Bar and exchanged "hellos" if he showed up at the alley during our Pilates class. That was it.

"Please," I whispered.

Stokes frowned and joined me in the bushes. Once we were safely out of view, he admonished me some more.

"This is a crime scene. No reporters. You'll get yourself in big trouble nosing around."

So he thought I was here to get a scoop for the paper. Good.

"It's okay. No one saw me."

I'd been lucky. The patrol must've been checking around the other side.

"How did you get past the roadblock?"

I waved vaguely behind me. "I came on the hunting trail from the Dune Club."

He maneuvered around me, pushed aside some shrub branches and squinted in the direction of the camouflaged blind.

"There's a hunting trail back here?" He turned back to me. "You've got half the trail in your hair."

I reached up and brushed out debris. More leaves and twigs. I paused . . . the same sort of fragments I'd found this morning. I went on the offensive.

"What are *you* doing here, Stokes?"

"What do you mean? I'm on the ambulance team."

"Then why aren't you doing your job? Why are you sneaking around in the bushes out here?"

His boyish face suddenly looked tired and old. He ran his fingers through his dripping-wet black hair and lowered his eyes. For the first time, I noticed what incredibly long lashes Stokes had.

"I wasn't sneaking. It's only my second time out with these guys. My stomach didn't feel so good. I thought I was going to hurl, and I didn't want to do it in front of the crew and the cops and everyone."

He pulled out his cigarette pack and quickly stuffed it back in his pocket again, probably thinking the better of sending the police smoke signals. He grimaced and looked up, shaking his head.

"When they called me this morning, I had no idea where we were going. Then Mac told me *who*." He looked like he was about to cry. "And *what*." Taking a deep breath, he let out a groan before speaking again. "It's so fucked."

My stomach dropped to my groin. I was feeling queasy myself. I wavered for a second.

"What did Mac say?" I asked, my voice cracking. "Tell me what he said."

"Hey, take it easy. What's going on?"

Stokes, along with everyone else, was going to find out soon enough.

"He was my ex-husband."

"Who?"

"Hugh Walker."

"No." He took a step back. "You and Walker were married?"

"We divorced three years ago. He got Helene pregnant while we were together."

His eyes widened. "Fuck, no. Jesus. She . . . no. Mother of God." He stared at me with his mouth open for a few seconds before he blinked and closed it. "She got herself knocked up by him while he was married to you?"

I nodded. He seemed to lose focus and mumble something I couldn't understand.

"Excuse me?" I asked.

"Nothing. That is seriously fucked up."

"Tell me about it."

He mumbled again.

"What did you say?"

"I'm . . . I'm sorry for your loss. I guess."

"So what exactly happened to them?" I prodded.

He looked at me blankly for a moment. Then he seemed to come back to himself. His tone turned official, and he puffed out his chest.

"You should go home, Nora. I can't tell you anything. I'd get kicked off the crew if anyone found out I leaked information. We're not allowed to discuss the jobs we do for the coroner. Mac said so."

"I'm a reporter. I never reveal my sources. Come on," I begged.

Stokes just looked at me with a stony expression.

"Didn't Mac give you any specifics? Were they shot in their bed?" I blurted. I was obsessed with knowing how Hugh and Helene were killed. Could he verify the unconfirmed report?

"Whoa." Stokes frowned. "You're his ex, and you're skulking around back here, sniffing out the gory details on his murder? I don't care if you *are* a reporter. That's just wrong."

"But I—"

"You'd better get going." He pointed in the direction of the blind. "Now."

I felt ashamed. Stokes was right. I was acting like a creep, asking these questions. A ghoul. I didn't belong there. But I'd become irrational. The slashed painting had finally put me over the edge. I'd started adding it all up. My fantasy of shooting Helene and Hugh in bed. The scratch. The leaves and twig in my hair. I was tormenting myself with an absurd idea. *"Ne eshee byidi beda sama tibya nadyet.* Don't trouble trouble till trouble troubles you," Aunt Lada would say. She'd be right.

I glanced up at the sky. The clouds above us had swelled up and darkened again. Whatever Stokes knew about the crime scene, he wasn't going to tell, anyway. Rather than offering any closure, coming to Pequod Point had messed with my head. I had to get out of here. If I hurried, I might be able to beat the next downpour. And if I didn't change these freezing, wet clothes, I'd catch pneumonia on top of losing my sanity.

"All right, I'm leaving. But please don't tell anyone I was here."

He raised his huge right hand and pledged. "Scout's honor."

I stayed low and set my nose for the blind, loping back through the seagrass. Before I'd gone very far, Stokes called out to me in a loud whisper.

"Nora, wait."

I turned around. He looked young again, huddled in the bushes, a wet, Elvis-like curl spiraling down his forehead. Young and innocent and scared. Like a little boy who'd gotten lost playing hide-and-seek.

"You think maybe I could get a ride with you to the alley? Mac and Al don't really need me. It's almost nine forty-five. I usually open the lanes by ten."

Strange. Was he just going to walk off the job? Leave them wondering where he went? I nodded and waited for him to catch up. But the rain didn't wait. It came down in sheets as we ran.

Breathless, we reached the car and jumped inside. I opened my coat and began wringing out my baggy pajama bottoms. Luckily, the police didn't see a woman in soaking wet pajamas sneaking around the scene of her ex-husband's murder. What was I thinking? The dark pajama water pooled under the gas pedal. The ride back would be tricky, not just for a car with funky wipers, but also for anyone traveling outside of an ark. I turned the key, cranked the heat and pulled out of the Dune Club lot. It was like driving through a car wash.

Stokes didn't seem to notice the monsoon. He was making a call on his cell.

"Mac? No, I'm sorry. I wasn't feeling well. I didn't want to walk into the middle of . . . of . . . a crime scene and be sick. I hitched a ride from one of the neighbors who was on his way to church. I would've called sooner, but I just got cell service."

A convincing liar, Stokes was, innocent face and all.

"Sure thing," he said.

He hung up and stared out his window. His jaw was clenched. He'd turned distant and morose. We rode without speaking as the rain pounded the hood. I kept thinking about the gray body bags. The mauled painting. The sickening violence. The dreadful suspicion I'd tried to suppress kept surfacing. I needed to focus on the slippery, winding road, or I'd spin out. The wipers were functioning slightly better at the moment, only missing one beat out of four. Still, the driving was treacherous. Suddenly there was a lightning flash, and a blinding torrent of water cascaded down the glass. I flinched at a thunderclap.

"Shit," I said, hunching over the steering wheel and trying in vain to see the road ahead clearly.

"Make a U-turn," Lady GPS ordered. "Make a U-turn."

That snapped Stokes out of his fog. He scowled.

"What's up with your car?"

"It has Tourette's."

"What?"

"Nothing." I groaned. "Who ever heard of a lightning storm in late November?"

"You know, they had a tornado in Catskill last month. The oil companies want us to think it's a 'natural cycle.' Bullshit. The earth is a living thing, like an animal or a person. When it's threatened, or attacked, it fights back." He folded his powerful arms across his chest and glared straight ahead. "To the death, if it has to."

Anger was swirling in the air around him, as if a tornado were right there in the car with us. What was he so ticked off about?

I struggled to concentrate on driving. We sat in silence again except for the drumming rain and the intermittent click and squeak of the blades. I was exhausted, emotionally drained. I just wanted to drop Mr. Moody off, go soak my frozen bones in a tub and clear my mind of disturbing thoughts. Then, as we passed the Tea Cozy, the rain miraculously let up. Within seconds, it stopped completely. I leaned back into the seat and shut off the wipers. Stokes turned to face me.

"Have you ever seen a dead body?"

"What?" I glanced over at him. His long, girlish lashes framed intense, dark eyes that glared into mine.

"Have you ever seen a dead body?"

Spooked, I looked back at the road. "No. Fortunately, I have not."

"I have. I found my in-laws in their bed. Curled up next to each other like honeymooners. They looked so healthy, I didn't realize they were dead at first. Their cheeks were all flushed pink like they'd just come back from a run. That's what the CO_2 does."

He cracked a few knuckles. I winced.

"I ran around opening windows and doors, but they'd died hours before. That's what the coroner said."

"It must've been awful for you."

"Yeah, it was bad. But I didn't like them much." Another knuckle sounded. "You know what was totally weird? Finding them together like that—snuggled up. They hated each other."

I peeked over at him again. He was clenching and unclenching his fists.

"They made everyone around them miserable, too. My father-in-law was a cheap son of a bitch. Sitting on a pile of money he'd made selling some of his farmland to a fracking outfit. I think death by gas was . . . what do you call it? Poetic justice. He never gave any money to Kelly and me. Never helped us out. The bastard even made us pay our share whenever we ate dinner there. He'd show us the grocery bill. And Kelly's mother had battery acid for blood. Nothing good to say about him, or us, or anyone. But there they were, spooning."

I was amazed Kelly had turned out as well as she had, given Stokes's report on the people who raised her. But even if the murder scene had triggered his memory of finding his in-laws' corpses, why air all this family laundry with me?

"I guess you never know what goes on between couples in bed," I said.

Relieved to see the bowling alley coming up on my right, I flicked my turn signal on.

"Here we are."

I steered into the parking lot and stopped next to the hulking, unlit VAN WINKLE LANES sign. Stokes unbuckled his seat belt and hesitated. He turned and studied me for a few seconds.

"What?" I asked, uncomfortable.

"Mind if I ask you a personal question?"

I worried he was going to ask details about the Hugh and Helene affair in some inappropriate fashion.

"Um, how would I know until you ask it?"

"Did you still love him?"

"Ah," I sighed.

I wasn't expecting that one. But I'd asked myself the same question after Hugh moved to Pequod. How could I not still love him a little? We shared so much history—I'd spent almost a third of my life with him. There were so many bittersweet memories. And yet, whenever I thought about the way we ended, I felt a cold, black stone in my heart.

"I'm not sure."

"Because if it were me, I think I'd be grateful someone offed him," he hissed. "Her, too." He was practically spitting the words. "I'd want anyone who screwed me over like that to be fucking dead."

"Good to know," I said, startled by his vehemence.

Stokes stepped out of the car.

"Thanks for the ride."

He slammed the door so hard that I jumped. I felt like I could finally breathe again as I watched him stride off and disappear into the alley.

I was about to drive off when a giant yawn overtook me. I sat there, bleary-eyed and groggy, as the Van Winkle sign woke up. Blood red letters flickered against the pale gray sky. I stared at them and thought back to those worrying days of my childhood when I'd first known this level of exhaustion. Troubled, frightening days that began as I understood the darker side of my father's world—a place of angry, violent men.

How many times had I held my father's hand as we strolled past neon bowling alley signs in the early morning hours? He'd be nattily dressed in a suit and tie, Clark Gable-handsome with slick black hair. So many Saturday mornings, while my mother primped at a beauty salon or took tennis lessons at her club, I would go with Nathan Glasser to visit a bowling alley in our suburban township or a neighboring one. Bellport Lanes. Bayshore Lanes. Pro-Bowl at Hempstead. Nathan with his black book of numbers. His 1984 Mercury Grand Marquis wagon full of cigarette cartons and racing forms.

All the alleys seemed the same to me: cavernous concrete buildings, dark inside except for a dimly lit concession stand or small bar. Quiet except for the hum and buzz of soda machines, refrigerators and a whirring floor buffer if the night janitor was still there. On occasion,

Nathan would get a lane switched on and hand me a sparkly blue or pink child-size bowling ball, so I could roll it at the pins while he and the owner spoke in hushed tones.

"I have dozens of men working for me all over New York," he liked to brag. He told everyone he was president of Nat-o-Matic, a statewide vending machine distributor. In truth, he worked for the Mob, stocking their alley and bar machines with contraband cigarettes. He also booked sports bets for them on his route and skimmed some of the profit off the top for himself. It was a cash business. He didn't think his bosses would find out. If they did, he'd pay them back with interest from his winnings at the racetrack. The problem was, his horses lost. He hid this from my mother and me. By the time his lies came to light, they'd ruined us all.

Both my parents had secret lives back then. Sally the Country Club Wasp née Sasha, the Russian Jew from East New York. Nathan, the bookie, gambler and money launderer.

So did I. Another life I lived only at night. A potentially dangerous one.

Chapter Five

Dark. I'm standing in the dark in my pajamas. My whole body tingling like a sleeping foot. Confused. Scared. *Dad? Mom?* Where am I? Start to rub my arms and legs to stop the tingling, but there's something in my right hand. A metal stick. Thin and long. Squeezing it tight. What is going on? Eyes adjusting. I recognize this place. The downstairs hallway by the front door. But this makes no sense. How did I get here? No one carried me. I must have walked out of my bedroom, across the hall, all the way down the stairs and down another hall. I don't remember any of it.

You woke and had to go to the bathroom. You were sleepy; you got confused in the dark.

But the bathroom was only a dozen steps from my bed. No. I hadn't been sleepy. Or confused about where the bathroom was. I must've actually *been* asleep. Sleepwalking. And the stick in my hand? A golf club. My mother's golf bag was leaning against the hall closet. I was standing at the front door clutching a golf club. But why?

I was almost twelve the day my symptoms started. My mother had already left for her beauty salon appointment that Saturday morning when my father tapped on my bedroom door.

"No bowling alleys today, kiddo. We're going to the movies. They've rereleased *The Pink Panther Strikes Again*. You'll love this one."

We were movie nuts, my father and I. His "work hours" were flexible, so he would treat me to matinees after school or on weekends—whenever the mood hit him. We'd seen *Top Gun* the week before, and I fell in love with Tom Cruise. We also shared a love of big band music. He introduced me to Benny Goodman and taught me to swing dance by the time I was seven. My father was fun and spontaneous. Unlike my mother, who was beautiful but rarely relaxed enough to smile.

Halfway to the movie theater, I noticed my father was driving fast and glancing in his rearview mirror every few seconds.

"What are you looking for, Dad?"

"Nothing, kiddo."

When we reached the theater, he pulled into the back lot and surveyed our surroundings nervously before parking the car.

"Really, what are you looking for?"

"Let's hurry so we score some popcorn before the trailers start," he said, ignoring my question.

We went into the lobby and joined the concession line. The men walked in seconds later. There were two of them in sharp-looking overcoats, sunglasses and shiny shoes. The tall one unhooked the velvet rope. Nobody behind us said a word when they cut the line, I think because of the bullying energy they gave off. I grabbed my dad's hand, intimidated.

"Hello, Nathan," said the short one with the newspaper rolled up under his arm. He had a small, pointy head with a lot of dark, fine facial hair. Like a rat. How did my father even know this man?

"Hello, Brizzi."

"Have we done something to offend?"

"No, not a thing. We're all good here."

Brizzi leaned down until his face was inches from mine. He stank of cigarettes, and his teeth had brown stains. There were tiny pimples on the pale skin around his wispy moustache. My father tightened his sweaty grip on my hand. I squeezed back, afraid.

"You think your father is telling the truth?" he hissed.

"Please. Leave her out of it," my father whispered, sounding desperate, which only increased my alarm.

"He says he's not upset with us. So why do you think he's been avoiding us? Not answering our phone calls? Not showing up for our appointments? Not very polite, is he? Could it be he's forgotten his debts?"

Now I was petrified.

"She's only a kid. Please."

Brizzi straightened up and touched his sunglasses. He sucked in air between his teeth, took the rolled-up newspaper and tapped my father's chest.

"Because you asked nicely, we'll just have a brief mano a mano out there," he said, aiming his paper across the lobby toward a metal door marked EMERGENCY EXIT.

The taller man, who had a shiny, hairless head and was built like a giant thumb, unhooked the black velvet rope from the stand again and gestured for my father to walk through the opening.

"Wait here, Nora." My father released my hand. I tried to take it again, but he waved me back. His voice was sterner than usual, his face tight. "We're just going to talk for a minute."

The men flanked him as the three walked across the royal-blue carpet. I looked on helplessly, my heart thundering in my chest. Before they reached the exit, my father glanced back at me. He had that look in his eyes, like the soldier in the *Tarzan* film who slipped into a pool of quicksand. When the sand reached his chin, he stopped yelling and struggling, but his eyes still screamed—the way my father's were screaming right then.

I felt like I was going to explode and collapse all at once. I wanted to save him, but my feet were lead. My skin felt hot, and then someone turned the lights out. The next thing I knew, I was floating on my back in an ocean of blue carpet looking up at concerned but unfamiliar faces. Until my father pushed through them. He knelt down and cradled my head, searching my eyes with a pained expression.

"Kiddo, kiddo, kiddo," he said.

◆ ◆ ◆

I'd been afraid to wake my parents the night of that first sleepwalking incident. They'd ask a lot of questions. It could lead to telling them how anxious I was about those horrible men. My father was in enough trouble already. He'd begged me not to say anything to my mother about what happened at the movie theater. How could I speak of it without betraying him? I went back to bed, but I lay there with eyes pinned open. The next day, I was sapped.

The following night, I woke up standing in the kitchen. The house was dark except for bright moonlight coming through the white eyelet curtains on the windows. So quiet I could hear the crickets outside and the faint hum of the clock on the wall oven. The clock said 1:12 a.m. There was an open kitchen drawer. On the counter above it, something slender and silver glinted in the moonlight. My mother's favorite Wüsthof carving knife. Her largest and sharpest carver of flesh. Someone had taken it out of its velvet-lined case in the kitchen drawer. Did I do that, too? My twitching gut said yes. I put the knife back and tiptoed up to bed.

I stayed awake and worried again. If I told my mom, she would be so angry with my father, she'd divorce him. Maybe I should talk to Aunt Lada? I would be staying at her apartment in the city that weekend—one of the rare occasions my mother let her babysit. She thought Aunt Lada was a questionable influence. "That Ukrainian boyfriend of hers? Does he even work? And they both smoke those disgusting cigarettes." Balkan Sobranies. "God bless the stink of

Minsk," Lada would say whenever she lit one up. Lada has never been to Minsk. She's only seen pictures my Minskian grandfather took.

But I didn't speak of it to Lada when I arrived—you can't just launch into something like that. *I'll try at dinner,* I thought. *No. I'll say something after we watch our television shows.* The big perk at Lada's was staying up late with her, watching television shows.

Sybil. Of all the movies that could have aired that night, an old TV movie called *Sybil* was on. The story of a woman with multiple personalities. A woman who had other people living inside her who did things she never would.

"You'll get nightmares. She's *bezumny,*" Aunt Lada explained as she turned the television off before the second commercial—after Sybil had punched her hand through a glass window during one of her episodes.

"What is *bezumny,* Aunt Lada?"

"A nut. A cuckoo lady. She has mice running around in her head."

I took the movie as a sign. I was like Sybil. That cinched it. I couldn't tell anyone. I was convinced I'd be locked away if they found out how crazy I was.

My mother took me to the doctor a week later to figure out what was causing the worrying symptoms I'd developed. But I didn't give either of them the whole story. I guess I was too frightened . . . and confused. I was young.

I sat on the edge of the exam table in my jeans and T-shirt, hugging myself. The white paper crinkled under me as I nervously kicked my sneakers at the base.

"Stop fidgeting and sit up straight," my mother said. She pointed to my feet. "How did your sneakers get so scuffed?"

"Where?"

"That black mark on the side. Right there."

She frowned from her post in the white plastic chair next to the door.

"Can't you keep anything nice for five minutes?" she scolded.

That was another reason I wasn't entirely truthful. My mother had a lot invested in perfection. She wasn't the easiest person to confide in when something was wrong. She had a way of making the problem your fault. I started kicking the exam table unconsciously again.

"Nora!"

She eyed me angrily. But the neurologist didn't seem to mind my nerves. Nerves were his business. He stood at a counter studying the papers attached to my chart, obviously pleased with the results.

"I'm happy to say there's no sign of a head injury. And Nora's wiring looks completely normal. EEG, EKG. Her brain. Her heart. Blood work. All normal. Reflexes. Everything."

"That's a relief," my mother said. "I was worried it might be a concussion."

The doctor turned to her. She crossed her shapely legs and smoothed the skirt of her turquoise mohair suit full of little poodle-like nubs.

"And her symptoms began a week ago, you say? She fainted twice in one day?"

My mother nodded and tugged at her pearls.

"I wasn't there the first time. She was at the movies with her father. She fainted again when they came home. At first, she seemed normal otherwise. But then I noticed she was more and more tired every day. Exhausted."

"Any headaches?"

"No. Just tired."

He looked at the chart again and shook his head. "Her blood work is normal." He looked at me. "Talk to me about the blackouts, Nora. What did you feel?"

"I got dizzy. Then I fell."

"Did you eat or drink anything before they happened?"

70

"No."

"Were you hungry or thirsty?"

"No."

"Did the movie scare you?"

"We hadn't seen the movie yet."

"Anything unusual you can tell me about?"

I glanced at my mother and heard my father's voice. *She'll leave me, Nora. She'll go. You don't want the family to break up, do you? I promise you I'll fix this.*

"Think for a minute," the doctor urged. "Anything at all?"

"No, I don't remember anything special," I told Dr. Nerves.

He kept watching me as he spoke to my mother. By then I think he'd figured out I was holding back information.

"How is Nora sleeping?"

How did he know about that? *Get out of my head.*

"Fine. No problems there," she said.

"No problems," I echoed.

Fainting twice was one thing, but these other . . . what to call them? Zombie spells?

"I'll need you to step outside for a minute, Mrs. Glasser," the nerve doctor said.

"Oh?" My mother looked surprised and a little put out, but she stood up and smoothed her skirt again. She fiddled with the delicate pins in her strawberry-blonde, perfect French twist.

"I'll be out there, Nora. Right outside in the hall."

She left and closed the door. The doctor stood next to the exam table, but behind me so I couldn't see him. What was he up to? I wouldn't tell him my secret, even with my mother out of earshot. I didn't want to wind up being committed to a mental institution.

"Raise your right hand," he said.

I put up my hand. "Is this another reflex test?"

"Quiet, please. Do as I say. Raise your *right* hand."

I checked my hand. Yes, my right hand was in the air.

"Didn't you hear me?" he asked, impatiently. "The *right* hand."

My face flushed. I felt confused. I stretched my fingers. *I pledge allegiance to the flag* . . . Right crosses to heart on left. This was definitely my right hand. I lifted it higher.

"Are you telling me you don't know your right from your left?"

Why are you being so mean? I'm trying.

"Dammit. Just do it, Nora. I'm waiting."

My eyelids fluttered. The fluorescent lights dimmed. Heat blossomed in my chest and spread to my limbs. I leaned forward, almost falling off the table. The doctor's arms caught me.

"It's okay, Nora. It's all right. I apologize. I had to see if I could induce a fainting spell."

He put two fingers to the side of my neck and stroked my forehead with his other hand. How soothing his touch felt. A balm for my distraught state.

"You're fine now. Just lie down here."

He eased me back onto the table and then walked over to the door. Cracking it open, he beckoned. "Come in, Mrs. Glasser."

"What happened?" my mother asked, alarmed to find me lying there limp.

"Nora just had another fainting incident. A 'neurocardiogenic syncope.' Her vagus nerve went into spasm and cut off the blood flow to her brain. The situation rights itself after the person falls and blood pressure equalizes. How do you feel now, Nora?"

"I feel good," I said. And I actually did.

"That's likely what happened in the movie theater and at home afterward. The biggest danger lies in getting hurt from the fall itself. This is the typical age for the start of the problem. Sometimes it's paired with other symptoms like sleep disturbances, which may indicate a more serious psychological disorder."

Sybil?

"But Nora seems to have only the one," he said, patting my arm.

"Tell me this is curable," my mother implored.

"It is, in the sense that children usually grow out of this by the end of puberty."

Was he saying this could continue for years? I felt myself growing dizzy again. I closed my eyes and lay unmoving on the table. That seemed to help.

My mother twisted her pearls. "What causes it?"

"In Nora's case, stress. You've got a highly sensitive child here."

So I wasn't crazy; I was sensitive. Wasn't sensitivity a good thing? I'd had a stress reaction to those scary men. My dad promised he'd pay them so they wouldn't bother us. After he paid, I could go back to being sensitive and normal again.

"Are there any drugs she can take?"

"I'm afraid not. The best thing is to try and reduce her tension. Nora needs to become aware of her emotions before they get the better of her. Help her identify anxiety, fear, anger, et cetera. Some kids don't know what they're feeling until they're completely overwhelmed."

My fainting stopped as I learned to pay better attention to my feelings. But I had more sleepwalking episodes after my father came clean about his real job to my mother and their terrible fights began. I didn't confess then, either. I was afraid it would make everything worse. The sleepwalking ramped up again when we sold our house to pay his mob debts, and as my parents went through their divorce. Then it disappeared for six years. Until I was a college sophomore.

Axel Bartlett, my boyfriend since freshman year, had just broken up with me. He said he thought we'd reached a point where we should stop dating and "just be friends." I was stunned and hurt. "You've met someone else," I wept. He vigorously denied it. But I saw him that evening in the student lounge with his arm around a girl I recognized from our Crime Reporting class.

Grace and I were roommates by then. She woke up at three a.m. the following morning and discovered me sitting on the floor of our dorm room in my nightgown with scissors in my hand. Between the blades was the hoodie Axel had taken off and insisted I wear one night when we were both freezing in Washington Square Park. "Keep it. It looks sexy on you," he'd said.

"Nora? What the hell are you doing?" Grace told me she asked, having no idea I was asleep. I woke up then, confused and disoriented. I stared at the giant heart cut out of the front left side of the sweatshirt I held, bewildered.

"Holy shit," Grace said. "You must be really, really angry at him."

Finally realizing what I had done, I was appalled. I told Grace about my sleepwalking history then, distraught that the problem had returned after so long a hiatus, and that I'd acted with such aggression. Grace was incredulous. "Seriously? You were sleeping? You looked wide-awake! That's scary. That's supremely scary, Nora."

"Nora Scissorhands," was how she referred to the episode.

It was the last one. Nothing remotely like that has happened since. The doctor was right. End of puberty, end of problem. It's been twenty-one years. If I ever wake up in the middle of the night, I'm at home in my bed like any normal person.

From the *Pequod Courier*

Letters to the Editor

They're back! Nora Glasser was right. The Summer People are turning into Fall People. Did anyone else notice how many of them were treating us to their usual rudeness on Halloween weekend? A BMW cut me off for a parking space on Halloween morning. I saw a Mercedes run the red light on Pequod Avenue. (Why aren't the police ever around when that happens?) They bought out all the candy corn at Corwin's Market. Next thing you know, we'll be overrun on Thanksgiving and they'll raid the pumpkin pie. Will they steal Christmas like the Grinch? Why don't the Summer People stay where they belong until after Memorial Day? How will we deal with them all year round?

Dawn Murphy

Pequod, NY

Chapter Six

Mad. Sad. Bad. Glad. Those were the "check-in" words Dr. Nerves recommended to help me identify if I was feeling anger, grief, shame, or happiness. I had nothing to lose by trying the technique again. As I headed toward home, I determined that I was Glad. Glad that a sunny, crisp fall morning had arrived unexpectedly after the storm. A heroic day. Blue water sparkled in the harbor. Light played on the sailboat hulls. Some of Pequod's citizens walked their dogs on the wharf. The world turns. It really does. But I was also Sad. Hugh had died too young and in such an awful way. Who took his life? Who slaughtered both of them?

Squinting, I flipped down the visor to block the sun as I drove back over the bridge. I caught my reflection in the mirror again. That scratch had grown redder. That mysterious scratch. *You never had any physical marks from sleepwalking before.* There it was. I'd finally let myself hear the whisper in my psyche. Had I begun sleepwalking again? After twenty-one years without any incidents?

I tuned out the worrying voice, even as the scratch's unexplained source gnawed at me. So did my hunger. The clock on the dashboard read 10:11 a.m. I hadn't eaten since Mao's Chinese take-out shrimp and broccoli the night before. Despite everything, I had an appetite. As I turned off Crooked Beach Road onto the dirt lane that led to my driveway, I looked forward to fried eggs, a hot bath and clean clothes.

I live in the Coop, as it's known. A white clapboard chicken coop. The long, low, shoe box–like structure sits at the back edge of a former strawberry farm next to a swath of county-owned woods. The landlords are Summer Weekenders, a gay couple whose renovated 1880s farmhouse is on the other side of the property and who had returned to their city residence in early September.

They did a lovely job on the farmhouse, forgoing the typical million-dollar expansion and staying within the existing footprint. They installed solar panels, a copper roof and oversize casement windows, but those cost more than they'd budgeted, and they couldn't fix up the Coop as they'd planned. No solar for me. I have space heaters and a Danish woodstove, along with lots of old, leaky, wood-frame, six-over-six windows that fill the Coop with clear "vodka" light. The rent is reasonable, the place is charming and has real potential, but it's freezing in winter.

When I spotted the red Prius parked in my driveway, I almost turned the car around. Grace had used her key to let herself in. As much as I'd wanted to see her earlier, I wasn't up for her company. I was worn out and wary of questions. Grace is an expert interviewer; I could feel the heat of her grilling already. She'd want to know where I'd been. I was reluctant to admit, even to my best friend, that I'd been spying at the scene of Hugh and Helene's murder. And that I worried I'd been sleepwalking. And worse . . . No, that was absurd, and I refused to even think about it.

I parked and walked wearily to the front door. As I reached for the knob, the door flew open. Grace stood there talking into her phone.

"She just got here, Ben. I'll call you later." She hung up and threw her arms around me. "Nora. I was so worried. You heard about Hugh and Helene?"

"Yes, I did. It's horrible."

She released me and stepped back, scowling down at the consequence of our hug: streaks of mud from my trench coat decorated her NPR T-shirt.

"Are you okay? Where were you?"

I hesitated. Was a lie of omission still a lie?

"I went for a drive."

I scooted around her into the living room, noticing how it had been tidied up. I'd let my housekeeping slide with my depression. There were no clothing and magazines strewn on the wicker couch or kilim-covered floor. The take-out food cartons had been cleared from the pine dining table. The aroma of fresh coffee wafted through the rooms.

Grace followed me inside and shut the door. All this domestic handiwork was hers. In college, she managed to make staying in and doing laundry on a Saturday night seem like a party. Of course, smoking pot always helped.

"You went for a drive? Really?" She evaluated me skeptically. "That explains why you look like you've crawled through a sewer."

I averted my gaze.

"And how you got that nasty scratch under your eye."

I heard my cell phone—my only phone—ring in the kitchen. Saved by the bell.

"You've had about ten calls since I got here," Grace said, trailing me as I went to fetch it. "One was from Lada, but I didn't answer because I couldn't tell her where you were. I'm sure she's upset."

The phone sat on the butcher-block kitchen counter next to a pile of mail. Its face read "Unknown Caller." I silenced the ringer.

"You should call her," Grace said.

My back was to Grace, blocking her view of Hugh's letter. It still sat on top of the mail stack. I'd reread it a dozen times but couldn't make a decision about how to respond. Grace obviously hadn't noticed the return address or she would have said something. This was not the moment to show her a maddening letter from Hugh. There was no point in letting her know he'd hurt me again, or in stirring up anger at him. I picked the envelope up discreetly and stuffed it in the pocket of my trench coat.

"Nora?"

"What?"

I pivoted and walked back to the living room with Grace still on my tail.

"You should let her know you're okay."

"Who?"

"Lada! *If*, in fact, you *are* okay. Have you heard one word I said?"

I flopped onto the couch and began the struggle to take off my Wellingtons, twisting and yanking first one, then the other to no avail.

"Talk to me, Nor."

"Fuck!" I yelled as a boot finally gave way and I pitched it across the room. The toe grazed the framed photograph of my father that sat on my desk and toppled it, filling me with regret. Grace came and stood over me, her brow furrowed.

"Give me that," she said, pointing to my remaining booted leg.

I lifted my leg and she calmly eased the boot off.

"I want to know everything," she said.

Grace makes the most delicious fried eggs. Mine always cook up rubbery, but she gets perfect, crispy whites and syrupy yolks. Eating them in my oversize, claw-legged bathtub between sips of strong coffee makes them taste even better. The tub sits next to a window that looks out over a small garden and across an open field ending in dense cedar woods—a welcome change from the bleak views in my post-divorce city apartment.

Pink roses bloomed just under the window the first spring I spent here. But the deer munched the petals like candy and left only thorny stumps. I've been meaning to clear out the dead rosebushes and plant daffodil bulbs before the frost hits. The man from the garden center said the deer have zero interest in daffodils. But I haven't gotten around to taking the bulbs out of the shed yet. Sometimes I think I'm like those bulbs. Dormant. Sitting around in dull, protective wrapping.

Instead of working in my garden, I spend a lot of time soaking in this tub. I watch squirrels, chipmunks, blue jays and cardinals. I daydream about the usual topics: money, worldly recognition. Love. I imagine having enough money to buy a house of my own, writing a great piece of journalism and winning a Pulitzer, meeting a man. This would be a romantic place to make love if I ever met the right one. I tried dating last spring. A photographer Grace knew from the city who was doing a book on Pequod's historic houses. A smart, funny guy. After three dates, I invented a reason to withdraw. I told him a long-distance relationship wouldn't work.

Aside from the excellent tub, my pale blue bathroom has wall sconces, a side table and a Shabby Chic armchair in the corner—my version of a Jane Austen sitting room. Hugh would not have tolerated this decor. I've discovered that one of the benefits of living alone is you can have as much chintz as you like.

After serving me, Grace returned to the bathroom with a cup of coffee for herself and curled up in the rose-patterned armchair.

"So, out with it. How did you get so filthy? Where did you go?"

Despite her questions, I had to admit hanging out like this with Grace was comforting. We'd spent about a zillion hours talking to each other in our dorm bathroom back in the day.

"I drove to the beach and took a long walk. I was trying to wrap my head around what happened." I set the empty plate on the floor, leaned back against the porcelain wall of the tub and sank further into the water. I hated lying to Grace.

"And the mud?"

I swallowed hard and said the only thing I could think of.

"When the storm hit, I ran for the car. I tripped and fell into a puddle near where I parked."

Somehow lying to Grace while I was naked made me feel more sinful—like Eve in the Garden after the apple. She came over, picked the plate up and looked me right in the eye.

"You must have been so upset," she said, softening. "You were in shock."

Shock. Yes. Lizzie and Grace had both come to the same, logical conclusion. That would explain my irrational thinking.

"I wasn't in my right mind," I said.

Grace went back to her chair and put the plate on the side table.

"I just wish you'd called me before you went off like that."

"I did. I couldn't reach you," I said, relieved to be honest for a moment. "So you spoke to Ben? Does he know anything besides what they said on the news?"

"He's tried his contacts at the county police but hasn't heard back yet. He's thinking it was a home invasion or a robbery gone bad. It's just so insane."

A home invasion. A robbery gone bad. I sank lower into the water and closed my eyes. Hugh's and Helene's faces appeared. Flesh reduced to gory masses of red-and-purple mush. The work of a shotgun blast. I gagged and sat up.

"Like the Clutters."

"Who?"

"The Clutters. The family those robbers shot in Truman Capote's book *In Cold Blood*." I covered my eyes. For the first time since I'd heard about the murders, tears poured out.

Grace rose again, came over and knelt next to the tub.

"Breathe, honey. That's right. Just breathe," she said, rubbing my back.

"This whole thing is so unspeakably awful."

"Yes, it is."

"I just feel . . . fuck. I don't know what I feel."

"It's traumatic for you." She stroked my hair. "And with all the times you must've wished them dead, maybe you feel, I don't know. Guilty."

She'd hit a nerve. I straightened up and glared at Grace. "I do *not* feel guilty," I said defensively.

"Okay. Sorry. Simmer down. I just said that because . . . I don't know why I said it."

She knew me so well. Was she picking up on the fear I was trying to squelch?

Grace got to her feet, dried her hands on a towel and studied me closely.

"I'm worried about you, Nor. Even before all this. You've been looking exhausted." She took a step back, hesitating before asking. "You're not having any more of those sleepwalking episodes, are you?"

I stiffened. "Why would you think that? You know I grew out of those, like, forever ago." I was trying to reassure myself as much as convince her.

Grace sat on the rim of the tub now, a vexed look on her face. "But you're so tired. You haven't been yourself. I guess it's because you're depressed. You've been depressed ever since Helene and Hugh moved to Pequod."

She was right about the timing. The doorbell buzzed.

"You expecting someone?" she asked.

"No."

"It could be a reporter."

"Fuck."

"I'll get rid of whoever it is. And then we'll pick the rest of that crud out of your hair. You must've fallen into a very dirty puddle."

The buzzer rang again. Grace left the bathroom, and I ran my hands through my filthy locks. Bits of dead leaves and another tiny twig, similar to the debris I pulled out earlier, fell into the water. I sank down and watched the flotsam and jetsam float on the surface, feeling an overwhelming desire to go to sleep. I splashed water on my face.

A male voice began murmuring outside along with Grace's. And then it struck me: reporters generally don't ring doorbells. They call for a comment. Or lie in wait at the property line until their target comes out. Maybe it was Mac? Could he have returned from the morgue already?

While I was contemplating this, my eyes caught a movement out the window at the edge of the forest. A form lurking among the tree trunks and ferns. I wasn't tired anymore. I was on alert, my muscles tense. I sank deeper into the tub to hide my nakedness and tracked the dark shape outside, fixing on it for a second and then losing it again. Someone was definitely out there. I started to reach for a towel to cover myself but stopped when I saw a fluffy bit of white flitting between the cedars. I let out my breath and relaxed into the tub. That would be a doe—a worn-out doe running from another horny stag, her white tail lifting in alarm. We were at the end of rutting season.

She came forward to the edge of the woods, stepping slowly on her slim legs. Tall and elegant with a thick, grayish-brown fall coat, she held her head high. Her black nostrils twitched. Her brown eyes were wide and watchful.

She knew how vulnerable she was. Had her trust meter hit the red zone? She seemed to be trying to decide if it was safe to go for that patch of green still growing out there in the sun. Or that group of acorns under the oak. Could she nibble the last bit of sweetness before winter kicked in and the bitter, hungry days began? Perhaps she was pregnant already. Did she need extra food for the babies she carried?

I thought of Helene's pregnant belly in the painting.

Ripped open.

Hugh's heart.

Cut out.

That didn't read like a home invasion or robbery gone bad. That felt personal. The vengeful act of someone with a grudge. *Like me?*

"Nora."

Something outside startled the doe. She turned tail and ran back into the forest as Grace slipped inside the bathroom and shut the door, looking uneasy.

"The police are here," she said.

Chapter Seven

"You're creating another Richard Jewell situation," I heard Grace complain as I stepped out of the bathroom wrapped in my robe. She was referring to the security guard wrongfully accused of planting a bomb in a trash can at Atlanta's '96 Olympics.

"You're going to start a witch hunt," she said as I tentatively entered the living room. "You'll set off a media frenzy."

The bald cop in the tweed sports jacket who had been running the crime scene was facing her. He had his hands folded across his corduroy-covered privates. Through the window behind him, I saw a county police officer sitting in a squad car in my driveway. Grace had been expressing worry that the press would discover them here and assume that I was a suspect.

"Ah, hello, Ms. Glasser," the cop said over her shoulder.

"Hello."

Grace turned around and mouthed, "Are you all right?"

I nodded.

"Detective Larry Roche. County Homicide." He flashed his badge. "I was just about to tell your friend Grace here that none of the reporters saw me leave. I instructed our media liaison at the scene to issue an official statement just before I took off. They were too focused on getting their quotes to track me. I promise you, the press did not follow me here."

Just then his cell phone began to play the theme from *The Godfather*. "Excuse me," he said.

He answered the phone with a brusque "Roche" and ran his free hand across his smooth, shiny head. "Tell him *I'm* authorizing overtime. I want the blood work. Stat." He frowned at whomever was on the other end. "Well, get the dive unit on it. And while you're at it, find out who's leaking information out there." He hung up and addressed me again.

"Sorry, Ms. Glasser. I wondered if we could ask you a few questions. On a totally volunteer basis, of course. Any leads you give us will be a big help. We're groping in the dark here."

So they didn't have a suspect. They wanted my assistance, my knowledge of Hugh's friends and associates.

"Sure."

"Would you mind coming down to the county precinct in Massamat for the interview?"

I blanched. Grace launched into full-on protective mode, hands on her hips.

"I don't understand," she said. "Why do you need to take her to Massamat? Why can't you ask your questions here?"

An interview was an interview to Grace. Unlike me, she was not a TV crime-drama buff. No binge-watching Helen Mirren play Detective Chief Inspector Tennison in *Prime Suspect*. No indulging in cheesy *Law and Order* marathons. Those shows help me believe there's order and justice in the world, if only for an hour or so. If Grace had watched as many crime shows as I had, she would know the police liked to conduct interviews on their own turf in order to intimidate and confuse suspects. They're hoping their guests will incriminate themselves or confess before they "lawyer up." Roche's request could mean I was under suspicion. My insides were quaking while I tried to look calm.

"A formal environment usually helps jog people's memories," Roche said reassuringly. "There might be a seemingly innocuous event in Ms.

Glasser's relationship with Mr. Walker that could help point us in the right direction."

"But there was no relationship anymore," Grace argued.

"It's all right, Grace," I said. "I want to help."

Maybe I was misreading this and the police really wanted my assistance. It was entirely possible I did have a piece of information that would lead them to another suspect. Besides, what was the alternative? Calling a lawyer or refusing to cooperate would make it seem like I had something to hide. Except for visiting the murder scene this morning, I didn't. Or did I?

"Thank you," Roche said, making prayer hands in my direction.

He was so dapper and polite, he might have been a date picking me up for a Sunday brunch.

Grace turned to me, worried. "Nora, I don't know about this."

"It's all right," I repeated. "Just let me put on some clothes."

Grace—trying to promote goodwill, I guess, or deal with the awkwardness—offered Roche one of her excellent lattes while he waited. He declined.

Nervous, I retreated to my bedroom and began to dress, pulling my sweater on backward at first. As I grabbed my watch on the night table, I glimpsed *The Role of the Muse in Contemporary Art* by April Krim sitting at the top of my reading pile. The morning I received Hugh's letter, I'd ordered it on Amazon. I'd remembered reading a review of the book, and I intended to learn how other muses dealt with betrayal by the men who immortalized them. I had devoured it as soon as it arrived.

I didn't want to end up like Dora Maar. Known as Picasso's "weeping woman," the sad, French-Croatian beauty with pencil-thin eyebrows and sensual lips was Picasso's lover and inspiration for many years until he replaced her. She never had an intimate relationship with a man again. She gave herself to Catholicism. "After Picasso, God," she said.

They found Picasso's artwork in her apartment after her death—gifts he had given her that she could have sold for a fortune but kept for sentiment. His portraits of her fetched "ooh la la" prices: Sotheby's auctioned off *Dora Maar au Chat* for more than $95 million a decade ago. Proving, to me at least, that musing was a woefully undervalued profession.

The bedroom door opened a crack and Grace poked her head in.

"Nora?"

"Coming."

I returned to the living room. Roche was checking out the titles on my bookshelf. He stopped and faced me.

"Are you ready?"

I walked to my desk. "I just have to find my keys."

"You left them by the sink, honey," Grace said, disappearing into the kitchen.

As I lifted my trench coat off the back of my desk chair, Roche strolled over. He insisted on playing the gentleman and helping me on with it. "We really appreciate your agreeing to take a trip downtown with us, Ms. Glasser."

I hoped he didn't notice my trembling hands. I had nothing to fear, I told myself. Unlike my father, who dodged the police half his life. My father, who avoided jail but wound up living in someone's basement after the divorce—he'd given what money was left to my mother and me. "I know people say lousy things about me, Nora. But remember, all I wanted was for you and your mother to have the best. Everything I did, I did for love."

My father, who bent down and held my face in his hands the day he moved out and said, "Here's a tip, kiddo. A tip for living. This world is rough, and it's going to keep throwing things at you. Don't let them break your heart."

I tried to steady my fingers enough to button my coat.

"I want you to find whoever did this, Detective."

I meant it.

Grace handed me the keys as Roche opened the front door, gesturing for me to walk through ahead of him. But I lifted my father's photo first. With the sleeve of my trench coat, I cleaned Nathan Glasser's sad eyes of the specks of mud that hit them when I hurled my boot before. Then I set him down and went outside.

"Don't worry, Nor. I'll be right behind you," Grace called out. "You don't have to say anything to anyone, you hear?"

◆ ◆ ◆

As I walked toward my Toyota, Detective Roche called my name and pointed to the waiting squad car with a county police officer behind the wheel.

"Can't I take my own car?" I croaked.

"It would be more convenient if you came with us. We'll arrange to get you home later; don't worry." He strode over and opened the rear door to the spot usually reserved for suspects.

"Careful of your head," he said, patting my scalp with his hairy hand as I ducked in.

Whenever I saw the police make this gesture on crime shows, I imagined a warm palm placed protectively on the crown could feel soothing momentarily, especially for an innocent scared out of her wits, and maybe even for a serial killer like Ted Bundy. But in reality, it felt manipulative. Psyops for cops. "We are your friends. We want what's best for you. We care." A devious message from folks who hoped to lock you away for life or fry you in an electric chair. A hedge against a lawsuit if you hurt yourself.

"Fasten your seat belt. We wouldn't want you banged up if we make a sudden stop. Or hit a pothole," Roche cautioned. "We've already seen some big ones this year."

"You might consider reporting them to the highway department," I said.

I could hear my father's voice whispering in my ear. *Don't get cheeky, kiddo. This is serious business here.*

I buckled up, noting the car's sickly sweet chemical smell, like the inside of a Port-O-San, and the stiff, uncomfortable back seat made of molded gray plastic. *Probably easier to clean if anyone vomited, pissed, or bled,* I thought, repulsed. What was that curious silver ring bolted to the middle of the floor?

"What's this metal ring for?" I asked through the security screen as Roche climbed in the passenger seat up front. The blue-black edge of a tattoo snaking along his collar line finally exposed the ruse of his country-squire look. He glanced over his shoulder.

"Securing a prisoner's leg irons," he said.

The remains of whatever bravado I'd conjured disappeared as we sped out of my driveway, the police radio crackling with addresses and codes. My heart began hammering. My hands resumed their shaking. My stomach churned. The scratch on my cheek even throbbed for a second. How had it gotten there? Then . . .

Kathump!

My head hit the car roof.

"Damn pothole! You okay back there?" Roche asked.

No, I wasn't okay. I felt scared and alone. I wanted to call Aunt Lada and be soothed by her voice. But I was afraid she would hear how frightened I was, and it would worry her sick.

"I'm good," I said, and repeated it more for myself than for him. "I'm good."

From the *Pequod Courier*

Letters to the Editor

Dear Editor,

Thanks to "Tips for Living" for bringing some levity to the struggles faced by average residents. You can tell Ms. Glasser is "one of us." She probably drives a car that's more than two years old. At least I doubt she owns a 7,500-square-foot summer home along with a Manhattan penthouse. Make no mistake about it: there's a class war raging in Pequod, and I know who is winning. The greedy real estate developers who are profiting by polluting our wetlands and scarring our beautiful landscapes. The superrich Summer People who build giant vacation homes and then charter helicopters in their rush to get here and "relax," inflicting deafening noise on the rest of us. Why is nothing ever enough for any of them?

Tim McNulty

Pequod, NY

Chapter Eight

Compared to Pequod, Massamat is a big city. Population over thirty-two thousand, according to the last census. But the downtown area was depressed. We were driving through a ghost town. At least on weekdays, you'd see some shoppers. Or young and old men in front of the empty display windows of vacant stores on State Street. They sit on graffiti-marked benches or overturned milk crates, smoking and shooting the bull while waiting for contractors to drive by and hire them as day laborers. Today everyone was at the discount mall.

The financial crisis or prolonged recession or end of the great capitalist experiment, depending on your point of view, has made downtown jobs scarce while creating other employment opportunities. Some of Massamat's formerly college-bound youth have been joining gangs and dealing drugs. The quarterback for the Massamat High School Mastiffs became involved with a gang and was arrested for selling Vicodin and meth. Last year saw three homicides—two of them gang-on-gang kills. The third was a gas station attendant shot during a robbery. The police suspected gang involvement there, too. Just 10.8 miles from Pequod, there's a growing culture of violence.

What if some of Massamat's angry desperados rode over and shot Hugh and Helene in the course of robbing them? Or it could have been a gang initiation rite. Killing someone to become a member of the club. Maybe they'd slashed Hugh's "artsy" self-portrait in a final gesture of contempt? It was possible, yes. Especially if Hugh had shown up on their radar because he was buying drugs. I'd known him to indulge in the past. Besides spreading through America's suburbs like the plague in the last few years, heroin had become hip in the art world again, reprising the '70s, when artists snorted in the toilet stalls at Max's Kansas City and the Mudd Club. At least that's what *New York Magazine* said. Maybe Hugh and Helene were using and abusing?

I let my head fall back against the car's hard seat.

There were surely people besides myself with motives to murder Hugh and Helene. Killers with guns. In my muddled thinking, I'd failed to consider that if the unconfirmed report was accurate and Hugh and Helene were shot . . . well, I didn't own a firearm. I wasn't 100 percent certain how the police viewed me, but my own lurking, illogical doubts eased.

We drove by city hall and pulled up to the new police station conveniently located next to the county court complex. Unlike the rest of Massamat's traditional brick government buildings, the station was conspicuously modern—all black steel and dark, tinted glass. Some failure of the imagination had led to the placement of a large bronze badge "sculpture" in the middle of the concrete front walk. A good portion of the county's boom-year tax dollars went here when property values rose: not to job retraining or after-school programs, but to law enforcement and monuments. The police budget was a hot issue in Pequod, too.

Detective Roche came around to the back of the car, opened the door, and guarded my skull again. "Careful there, Ms. Glasser."

Flanked by Roche and our golem-size chauffeur, whose nametag read "Sgt. Klish," I climbed the marble stairs of the massive precinct as if I already dragged a ball and chain. You are small and helpless and dwarfed by our power, the building said. The lump in my throat felt as big as a walnut. I entered the immense lobby with its floor made of black polished stone and a vaulted ceiling overhead, three stories tall.

Metal detectors and conveyor belts blocked access to a glassed-in front desk. Likely bulletproof. The setup resembled a security gate at an airport, except there were no lines. I was the only passenger on this trip. For a second, I wondered if Massamat's criminals took Sundays off. But the constant squawk of Klish's hand radio told me the town's gangsters were still busy on the Day of Rest.

"I'll take the phone," Klish said gruffly. "Outer garments, purse, and shoes go on the belt. Empty your pockets of keys, lipstick. Anything metal. Deposit them in the plastic cup."

I removed my coat. "The scarf, too?"

He flashed me an icy smile. "I said outer garments."

Give a former C student some authority and Klish is what you get. I did as he instructed and passed through the metal detector. An Asian officer with a big gray plastic wand met me on the other side of the arch. Pretending he was about to cast a protective spell made me feel less anxious for about a second. He waved the wand over my jeans and black cardigan, and it dawned on me that for weeks I'd been wearing nothing but black: black jeans, black Pilates pants, black T-shirts and black sweaters. Yet another symptom of my dark emotional state.

When the officer finished, he directed me to Sgt. Klish again, who lorded over my belongings at the end of the conveyor belt. I refilled my purse, gathered up my coat and scarf and bent over to put on my black boots, vaguely aware of something fluttering to the floor as Detective Roche's voice warned from behind.

"Don't forget this."

Straightening up, I turned around. Roche held out the cream-colored envelope I'd taken from my kitchen. I nearly snatched Hugh's letter from his hand, but caught myself.

"Thanks," I said, casually taking the letter and returning it to my coat pocket.

"The other shoe, Ms. Glasser."

"Huh?"

"If you'll put on your other shoe, we'll get going. We've got room six. Best in the house," he said. As if we were checking in to a five-star hotel.

I slipped the boot on and followed Roche through a reception area—a less intimidating space decorated with local travel posters ("Moon over Massamat Harvest Festival"), potted plants and orange plastic chairs. The chairs were empty except for a Hispanic woman with a cooing infant on her lap. We walked down a long corridor next. No softness or warmth anywhere. Fluorescent lights, beige linoleum floors and bare white walls. Room six was also white. No windows. Just a gray metal table, three gray metal chairs and a gray metal door. A black electronic device sat on the table, likely a tape recorder. The mirrored wall behind the two chairs had a dark tint. One-way glass. My mouth was dry as sandpaper.

"Have a seat here." Roche indicated the single chair with its back to the door. "Are you thirsty? Can I get you any coffee? Soda? Water?"

My new best friend.

"Coffee would be great, thanks. Black is fine."

Roche picked up an intercom handset on the wall and asked someone to bring coffee to room six. Then he sat down opposite me. It was so quiet I could hear the nervous gurgling in my stomach. I noticed my hands were tightened into fists and opened them.

"All right then. Let's get started."

He flipped the switch on the electronic device and a little red light came on. He leaned forward and then instantly back, probably catching a whiff of my stress breath. After clearing his throat, he said, "Interview with Nora Glasser by Detective Lawrence Roche. November sixteenth. Massamat station. 1:47 p.m."

Then Roche paused and reached inside his jacket. He pulled out a folded copy of the *Courier* and laid it down on the desk with my recent Tips column faceup. I thought of my caustic remarks about Summer

People, and gulped. My complaints about how they clogged exercise classes. Did he know Helene was in my Pilates class?

Roche focused his dark, sly eyes on me.

"Are you Nora Glasser of number three Crooked Farm Lane, Pequod?"

"Yes."

"And you've been employed as a writer at the *Pequod Courier* for the last two and a half years, approximately?"

"Yes."

"Hugh Walker is your ex-husband, Ms. Glasser. Is that correct?"

I nodded.

"I need a verbal, please."

"Yes."

"When was the last time you had any contact with him?"

Was Hugh's letter technically contact? It wouldn't make me look good.

Can't you please try and let go of your rage at me? Hasn't enough time passed?

Unless the mailman read and memorized return addresses, there was no way the police could know the letter existed. I'd take that chance.

"Just about three years ago."

"You haven't seen him since?"

"Well, I *saw* him. A number of times."

"Exactly where and when most recently, if you can remember?"

"Outside the Pequod hardware store. This past Labor Day."

"What were you doing there?"

"I was going in to buy some DampRid. He was coming out. He had two armfuls of tiki torches from the end-of-season sale."

"And you didn't talk to each other?"

It was the one time I couldn't avoid Hugh. There might have been a witness. I had to tell the truth.

"Actually, I misspoke. We did have contact."

"Oh?"

"He said hello. He told me I looked great."

"That's all?"

"He asked me if I was seeing anyone."

"And did you respond?"

I hesitated and wiped some moisture off my upper lip.

"Ms. Glasser, did you speak to Hugh Walker?"

"Yes. I told him to light up a tiki torch and shove it you know where."

Roche smiled slightly. "No, I don't," he said.

My face reddened. "His ass," I said, softly.

"For the recorder, please."

"His ass." Damn.

"So, you were not on friendly terms."

"We really weren't on any terms at all."

Roche eyed me steadily. He put his palms on the table and spread his fingers. "Ms. Glasser. Do you know of anyone who might want to harm your ex-husband or his wife?"

I relaxed a little, grateful we seemed to be moving on. "I have one idea," I said.

Roche slid his chair in closer and clasped his hands on the table. "Go ahead."

"A drug dealer. A dealer who felt ripped off or dissed by them."

"Are you saying the Walkers were drug addicts?"

Was he trying to put words in my mouth? "Maybe not addicts. But I bet they got stoned a lot."

"Do you know that for a fact?"

"No." I'd said "idea," not fact. Was he setting some trap? I felt light-headed. I tried to control my breathing. Mad. Sad. Bad. Glad. *Bad.*

"Then what makes you think they did?"

"It's an artist thing. Hugh used to partake sometimes when we were together. Drug habits tend to get worse over time when there's a lot of money. Hugh certainly had plenty." Oh shit. That sounded bitter. I was not a bitter, angry woman. Or was I? I guess I *did* feel cheated by Hugh, but Roche didn't need to know that.

"I see," he said, sitting back again and crossing his arms. "That's interesting information, Ms. Glasser. We'll look into it."

"I really think you should."

"Did he have enemies? Was anyone very angry about his treatment of them?"

I was sure he meant me. I tried to think back, determined to come up with alternatives.

"Well . . . I remember he thought his accountant did a lousy job on his taxes and fired him. But that seems pretty far-fetched." Who else? Who else? "How about the housekeeper? The one who found them. Maybe they didn't treat the help very well?"

Roche nodded, paused for a few seconds, then uncrossed his arms and pulled on his chin. "I understand Hugh and Helene Walker bought their house at Pequod Point last spring. I can imagine you must've had some feelings about them moving here?"

I shifted in my chair and Roche registered it.

"It's a free country," I said. Now I sounded defensive. This was not going well at all. I noticed my palms were glistening with sweat. "I only meant . . ."

Roche interrupted. "And where were you between the hours of midnight and three a.m. this morning?"

"Where was I?" I began blinking nervously. I was definitely on his radar.

He nodded.

"At home. Sleeping."

"Are there any witnesses? Anyone who could corroborate that?"

"I was sleeping alone, if that's what you mean."

"How did you get that scratch on your face?"

I felt the blood drain from my cheeks as I touched the cut under my eye.

"This?"

I was floundering for an answer when the door behind me opened unexpectedly, causing Roche to look over my shoulder and scowl. "What is it?"

"He claims he's her lawyer."

I was confused. "Who is?"

I turned and saw Sergeant Klish with my coffee in his hand. Douglas Gubbins, the lawyer with offices upstairs from the *Courier*, stood off to the side behind him. Gubbins was suited, tied, and carrying a leather attaché case. A beanpole of a man in his sixties with a neat helmet of graying brown hair, clear-rimmed glasses, and pasty skin—Aunt Lada would call him a "nebbish"—he stepped forward.

"Ms. Glasser, I came as quickly as I could."

He extended his hand palm up, as if he were asking me to dance at a ball. Roche groaned. I was flabbergasted. What was Gubbins doing here? I barely knew him—our interactions had been limited to polite "hellos" in the hallway of the *Courier* building or in Eden's Coffee Shop, where I'd often see him having breakfast or lunch. But that little voice inside told me not to ask questions, just to waltz out of there with him. I pushed back my chair, stood up and put my hand in his. I could swear Gubbins bowed before he led me to the door.

"Ms. Glasser has cooperated in good faith thus far, Detective. And I am advising her, as is her right, not to answer any further queries just now. Thank you for your time."

With that, I heard Detective Roche curse as Gubbins whisked me out of the interrogation room. As the door closed behind us, I sagged against Gubbins's shoulder for a moment. I was so relieved.

"Thank you so much. Who sent you?"

He took my arm.

"Let's walk and talk," he said, and steered us down the hall toward the reception area. "Ben Wickstein phoned me on your behalf. I hope you're not peeved about my fibbing in there."

"Ben called you?"

"You needed a lawyer, pronto. They don't have enough to charge you, but you are definitely a person of interest in a capital offense."

"You mean a person of interest, officially?" My voice broke. "They didn't tell me that. Jesus."

"I could represent you, if you wish, until you have time to research and secure other counsel," he said.

"Wait." I stopped short and spun around toward him. My adrenaline was up. "There's no evidence. If this is just because I'm Hugh's ex, well, that's prejudicial. That's . . . divorcist."

"Perhaps. But it is what it is. And we don't know how far or fast this will progress. As a young lawyer, I did have experience in the county DA's office before I went into private practice, and I can tell you these matters are unpredictable. A lawyer is necessary."

"This can't be happening," I croaked.

Gubbins's serious demeanor said it was.

"Let's hope they find other suspects," he said.

"How about finding the killer?"

Gubbins nodded so vigorously his glasses slipped down his nose.

"The killer. Of course, yes."

He urged me forward again, and as we neared the reception area, I spotted Grace speaking on her phone in a corner by a potted palm. She hadn't seen me yet. But Ben, who'd been sitting next to the Hispanic woman and tickling her baby's toes, had. The relief on his face was evident. He instantly patted the infant's thigh, stood up and rushed over to meet us. I flushed, both embarrassed and grateful to see him.

"Nora! Are you okay? I jumped on this as soon as Grace called me."

I lowered my voice. "Am I really a person of interest? Officially?"

"Yes. But the police are on a fishing expedition. They're trying to bait you, and they're about to get straightened out." He put his hand on Gubbins's shoulder. "Doug, can we speak for a sec?"

"Of course."

Grace saw me and hurried over as the two men stepped away.

"Nor! Thank God you're out of there. How awful was it?"

I glanced over at Ben and Gubbins huddling together and whispering in a way that seemed urgent.

"I'll tell you at the nearest bar. Do you know a place around here?"

She sighed and looked distraught. "I wish I could go out with you. I can't."

"What's wrong?"

"Mac just called to say Otis had a tummy upset. He's asking for me. I really should go back soon."

Of course she should. Grace had been at this with me for hours. Now Otis needed his mommy. I felt rotten about keeping her from him even one minute longer.

"I'm sorry, Gracie. I've taken up your whole day with this mess. Can you just drop me home on your way? I've got some vodka in the fridge. I'll be fine as soon as I knock myself out."

"Don't be silly. You're coming to stay with us. The boys would love it. Grams is making dinner tonight."

"No. Otis isn't feeling well. You need to focus on him. And I don't think your in-laws would appreciate you bringing home a . . ." Choking up, I pressed my hand over my mouth to stifle a whimper. Grace reached for my other hand and squeezed it until I was able to speak again. "I don't think she'd like you bringing home a murder suspect."

"A person of interest," Ben interrupted as he joined us. "First rule of reporting, Glasser. Have your facts straight. Don't get me started on how many so-called journalists screw that up."

Ben offered to give me a ride back to the Coop. I insisted that Grace go home and pay attention to her family, and she didn't argue with me, for once. While Ben went off to the parking lot, I lingered on the station steps taking advice from my new legal representative. All the while Gubbins was speaking, I worried about how I was going to pay his hourly rate on top of all my other expenses.

"There are some rules, Ms. Glasser. Number one: don't leave the county. Not because the law forbids it, but because the police will likely put you under twenty-four-hour surveillance, seven days a week, if you do."

"How will they know I've left?"

"Believe me, they will. They've probably already flagged your charge cards and started tracking your car's GPS."

"That can't be legal."

He shrugged. "Once they start following you full-time, they'll tend to see all your actions as suspicious. It's the observer effect. Watching changes things. Number two: don't speak to the press."

"But Ben is the press."

"Ben is an exception—he's already involved and sworn to stay off the record. In fact, don't talk to anyone you can't completely trust, including and especially friends and relatives. You have no idea what trouble can come of that. I had a client charged with insurance fraud whose sister testified against her in order to take over the family business. And my client's husband, as well. What about your friend Grace and her family? Do you trust them?"

I was choking up again, upset. I cleared my throat and nodded. "They won't gossip. And as far as relatives, there's only my aunt. You don't have to be concerned about her."

I couldn't put off calling Aunt Lada any longer. Not hearing from me at all would freak her out more than hearing from me in a state of distress.

Gubbins frowned. "Discretion is all." He took his car keys out of his camel hair overcoat. "Come to my office tomorrow afternoon. By then I'll have the paperwork for you to sign and a strategy to discuss."

"Is that what you and Ben were talking about inside? A strategy?"

"Oh no, no, no." He smiled nervously. "That was about something else altogether."

I didn't believe him. And I didn't think it was a good thing not to be able to trust your own lawyer. But Ben trusted him, and he was no fool.

"Please try not to worry too much," Gubbins said.

He shook my hand and then scurried down the steps. Belly roiling, I sat down on the low cement wall at the edge of the landing. Knotted muscles had a painful grip on my neck. How could I help but worry? Recognizing that Aunt Lada would be growing more anxious by the minute, I took out my phone and called her apartment at The Cedars.

The Cedars is the assisted-living complex I found for her sixteen miles from Pequod. She'd worked as a photo librarian for the Associated Press well past retirement, but her crippling arthritis eventually made navigating the city impossible. The Cedars is much nicer than those claustrophobic urban senior residences. Lada seems happy there, and the proximity means I can visit her every week. The only downside is that I need to make up the difference between what they charge, what Medicare pays for and what Lada can afford. But I feel good about setting her up in a safe environment. She moved just in time. She's begun to drift.

Lada's line trilled and trilled, eventually rolling over to the front desk. I left a message with Yvonne, the receptionist, asking her to tell my aunt that I was fine and I would visit as soon as I could. The loud rumble of a motorcycle had me shouting the last few words before I hung up.

A dark-green-and-chrome bike—a vintage model—thundered along the perimeter of the parking lot and stopped at the base of the steps. Amazingly, Ben straddled it. I walked down to meet him, incredulous.

"Since when is this your ride?" I asked over the engine idle.

Ben pushed the visor of his helmet up.

"My car is in the shop." He patted the Triumph logo on the gas tank. "This was Sam's graduation present. A '92 reissue of Steve McQueen's bike. She needed some work, so Sam left her home for first semester. She's perfect now."

He pulled a second helmet from the bike's saddlebag and offered it. "Hop on."

I hesitated.

"It's okay. I know what I'm doing. I had a Harley in college."

"It's not that. I'm just . . . I'm not ready to go home yet."

He looked at me for a long moment, seeming to search my face for I don't know what.

"Understood," he finally said. "How about we find a bar in Massamat, or go back to Pequod and stop at—"

"The Tea Cozy," we said in unison. I smiled. I felt lighter already.

I strapped on the helmet and climbed on behind Ben. As I leaned into his broad back, I was surprised by its firmness. I wrapped my arms around his center. No beer gut. He was in pretty good shape at forty-seven. But it felt strange to be embracing a man after so long, and even stranger that the man was my boss. I was used to taking assignments and editorial notes from Ben, not motorcycle rides. He put his hand over mine briefly and squeezed. I was both surprised and comforted.

"Hang on tight," he said.

With a flick of his foot, the kickstand went up, the bike lowered and we took off with a jerk and a roar. Ben steered us out of the lot heading east toward Pequod, but not along any route I'd driven before. We zigged and zagged through sketchy residential streets, passing boxy houses, unmowed lawns and broken, weedy sidewalks until we met up with a narrow country road that hugged the shore.

Ben drove faster on the winding road. I leaned in with the dip and swerve of the bike as we rounded the curves, taking pleasure in the movement and in the vibration alternately hastening and slowing between my legs. I breathed in the salty sea air. The late afternoon sunlight flickered through the bare trees, lulling me into a pleasant trance. Ben's body blocked the wind, and the heat of him warmed my chest. Only my bare hands were cold; I hadn't thought to wear gloves.

As if reading my mind, Ben took my right hand from his waist and placed it inside the pocket of his parka. It felt intimate—a gesture a boyfriend might make, and I tentatively followed his lead, slipping my left hand into the other pocket. It met with something metal. About four inches long, an inch or two thick, smooth on the sides, and ridged in between. A folded knife. A big one.

I pulled my hand out, alarmed, and felt Ben's body stiffen. What was he doing walking around with a knife like that? *Chill. You are a paranoid mess right now.* I slid my hand back in.

Eventually we made a turn onto the straightaway that cut across a bay just outside of Pequod, a strip of flat, sandy land with nothing but seagrasses and water on both sides. The landscape looked so magical in the waning crimson-and-orange light that if I had even half of Hugh's talent, I would paint it.

All that talent gone, I lamented, starting to slip into melancholy. Hugh would never paint again. But I recovered quickly, sat up tall and tightened my thighs around the saddle. Removing both hands from Ben's pockets, I stretched my arms out to the sides, attempting to take in the striking beauty all around. I was perfectly balanced, thanks to Pilates. My core supple and strong. Ben opened the throttle, and we flew down the road with the wind at our backs. For a few short, ecstatic moments I forgot all my troubles. Then a dark thought swept in.

I might not ever feel this free again.

"Two-for-one hour" was just gearing up at the Tea Cozy. The cranberry-colored clapboard roadhouse used to be a tea parlor, though the Cozy has always served stronger brews than tea in its cups. Protected by a police department paid off by the gangster Dutch Schultz, it was the most popular of the "Rum Row" establishments that opened up near the coast during Prohibition. Mostly because Captain William McCoy, a rumrunner known for his high-quality giggle water, stocked its shelves. The Piqued like to encourage the myth that the phrase "the real McCoy" referred to the enterprising captain's goods.

The Cozy lived up to its adjective. The main room had a stone fireplace, wood-beamed ceilings above wide-board pine floors and booths with small, shaded lamps on the tables. Yet from the moment I entered, despite the glowing hearth and warm decor, I felt a shiver so deep in my bones I had to keep my coat on.

Kevin Coates, the African American owner and a former state wrestling champ, signaled us from the far end of the busy bar as we walked into the room. Kevin is a leading member of Pequod's small African American community. His roots go back to the years when escaped slaves came north and took tough and dangerous jobs on whaling ships alongside Native Americans and white men. Kevin is descended from one of those slaves who eventually became a whaling captain. The Coates family has seen a lot of social and economic upheaval in Pequod over almost two centuries. He wanted to talk about the murders.

"You hear anything off the record? Was it a botched robbery? A home invasion? Did someone have a big, fat grudge?"

Ben and I shook our heads. In an unspoken agreement, we feigned ignorance of anything that hadn't already been reported. We certainly didn't tell Kevin I'd been taken in for questioning.

"The police are being tight-lipped so far, Kev," Ben said.

Kevin continued to speculate as Ben put in our order for two vodka tonics.

"If there's a serial killer on the loose, we should form neighborhood watch committees like they did for that Zodiac Killer."

A boozy woman sitting a couple of stools down the bar chimed in. "I'm going to the shelter tomorrow and adopting a pit bull."

After a few more similarly anxious comments, we escaped to a booth in the back.

"People are really scared," I said.

Ben's expression darkened. "Yes, they are. These murders are going to create a lot of anxiety even after the killer is caught. We're a small town. The sense of basic personal safety is gone." He squinted and pointed under my eye. "I've been meaning to ask, what happened to your face?"

I touched the tender wound. "Nothing. Just scratched it with my nail."

If I only knew for sure that was the case, I'd feel a lot less stressed.

"It looks angry. You should take care of it."

"I will."

We sat in awkward silence for a moment. I was grateful when Sinead O'Halloran-Rudinsky appeared with our drinks. A big-boned, muscular Irish lass in a black waitress uniform, Sinead wore her straight brown hair in a bowl cut. Unfortunately, it made her look a bit like a prison matron. She had come here from Dublin as an au pair and fallen in love with Tidy Pool Al the day he repaired her employer's hot tub. With their twins in college and the two younger kids heading there soon, she works weekdays at the Pequod Savings Bank and weekend shifts here to earn extra cash. Somehow, she still makes it to our Pilates class.

"Hi, Sinead," Ben and I said simultaneously.

"Evening, Ben, Nora," she said, setting out the drinks. "A sick thing, these killings, isn't it? You'd never dream this could happen in Pequod." She reached out and touched my shoulder. "Nora, I know this must be hell for you. Even after that shite thing your ex did. And then Helene signing up for Pilates? That woman was shameless. I wanted to say something, but I took my cue from you. You were such a lady about it."

I felt my face flush.

"So you knew who Helene was when she joined the class? You knew about her and my divorce?"

Sinead nodded. "I did. Lizzie Latham told me after the Walkers moved here."

I turned to Ben, livid. "Did you hear that?"

"Easy, Nora . . ." Ben warned.

I drew in a slow, steady breath. "That's just great."

"What did I say?" Sinead asked, her face coloring.

My voice rose. "Un-fucking-believable."

Heads turned at other tables.

"For jaysus sake," Sinead whispered as she picked up her tray and skulked away to the bar.

"Nora, if I were you, I'd keep my cool right now," Ben said.

"But I specifically asked you and Lizzie not to talk about that to anyone."

Ben watched me quietly while I steamed.

"I'm sorry she broke your confidence," he finally said. "You should know that from now on, there's going to be a lot of talk. People felt free to poke around my world when my wife died, but it was nothing like what's about to happen to you. I wish it weren't the case, but there'll be press."

"I've been a public spectacle before. I hate it."

"Fame and murder take it to a whole other level. You're going to have to toughen up. They're going to be prying, coming at you with questions like crowbars."

Ben was right. I knew the public's appetite was insatiable when it came to what veteran journalist Pete Hamill called "murders at good addresses." They couldn't get enough of Claus von Bulow and O. J. Simpson. That investment banker, Ted Ammon, who was found naked and beaten to death in bed at his East Hampton mansion? People fed off that story for months. I felt betrayed by Lizzie, but I needed to settle down and stop taking things personally.

"Point taken," I said. "Now I've got a question for you, Ben."

Ben took a sip of his drink. "Shoot."

"What were you and Douglas Gubbins talking about at the police station? I have a feeling it was about me."

He nodded solemnly and pushed my vodka closer. "Don't you want your drink?"

"You're saying I need one to hear this?"

"Recommended."

I took a long, slow pull on the vodka tonic while Ben checked around us for eavesdroppers. When he was satisfied we had privacy, he leaned in.

"Remember my Deep Throat in the DA's office?"

"The one who tipped you off to the embezzlement charges against the county highway superintendent?"

"Same guy. He told me what they have on the Point murders."

"The Point murders? That's what they're calling them?"

"He spoke off the record. Nothing they're releasing to the press." He tapped my glass. "Have some more vodka. I'm driving."

I gulped more of the drink, but too fast. The bubbles backed up into my nose. I picked up my paper cocktail napkin with the teacup emblem and sneezed into it.

"Bless you."

"Thank you."

Ben took a deep breath before speaking.

"There was no forced entry. Hugh or Helene, or both, likely knew their killer. The police haven't found the murder weapon yet, but they were each shot at point-blank range with a .22," he hesitated, "in bed." He paused again. "And they were shot in the face."

I gasped and squeezed my eyes shut. I felt both relieved for myself and nauseated. This confirmed the shooting. A gun was involved, and I didn't have one. But I couldn't lose the image of Hugh's head resting on a fluffy white pillow, dark red syrup oozing out of the charred, fleshy crater where his nose used to be.

"Don't look at it, Nora."

How was he so tuned in to what I was thinking?

"Draw a curtain in your mind," he instructed.

I tried to do what Ben said. A plush, blue velvet curtain like the one they have on the stage at Pequod High School appeared and blocked the horrific image. The sick feeling passed. I opened my eyes and they met Ben's. I could feel how present he was. So with me. So *there*. More than a boss, a friend.

"That's not all."

I shifted in my seat, bracing myself.

"Finish your vodka first," he said.

I drained the rest of my drink.

"There was a painting on the wall in their bedroom. Of Helene Walker with Hugh wrapped around her when she was pregnant. You know it?"

I nodded, cringing internally as I pictured the mutilated painting. "Unfortunately, yes."

"The canvas had been slashed up with one of their kitchen knives."

I feigned surprise. "Oh my God."

"As if killing them once wasn't enough." He hesitated. "And the bodies were posed."

I gulped. "Posed?"

"Posed naked. In the bed. To mimic the painting."

I could feel the skin on my forearms prickle and the hairs at the back of my neck stand up. I closed my eyes again and saw the scene as if I were the killer: my gloved hands pushing and pulling Hugh's limp torso and limbs into a fetal position; adjusting his faceless head;

arranging Helene's hair on a snowy-white sheet like a stylist composing a macabre magazine spread. Pollock-like blood spatters on the wall behind her. How could I see it so clearly if I hadn't been there? I let out a whimper.

"Use the curtain, Nora. Don't dwell."

I drew the curtain quickly and masked the bodies. When my lids fluttered open, I saw how worried Ben looked.

He gave me a strained smile. "You all here?"

"Uh-huh. How did you know about the curtain thing?"

"I used to keep seeing Judy in my mind. In that hospital bed. Skinny, bald and full of tubes. I had to figure out something to keep from torturing myself."

"Do you still see her?"

"Only in happier places." He checked the room again to make sure no one had started paying attention to us. "Someone is trying to set you up, Nora."

I frowned. "That doesn't make any sense."

"Yes, it does. You're perfect."

"How could the police believe I'd commit a double murder, leave all those clues to incriminate myself and stick around? They'd have to think I was an idiot."

"Or very smart. Trying to make yourself the obvious suspect so they'd view you as *too* obvious. The person trying to frame you is hoping the police will think you're attempting to con them. The killer would have to be someone familiar with your history." He glanced at Sinead. "We don't know who else Lizzie and Sinead shared your story with in the past few months. Not to mention the ones who read the press on you in the past. By now there's a long list, I would guess."

Maybe Ben was onto something.

"You really believe that I'm being framed?"

"I'm sorry, but it looks that way."

"What do you think I should do?"

"If the DA does bring charges, I know an excellent criminal attorney in New York. For now, you're better off sticking with Gubbins. He's got connections. The DA knows him. Hiring a city lawyer will only make you seem guilty."

"Excuse me for a second."

"Sure."

I slid out of the booth and made a beeline to the ladies' room, lurching through the door and rushing into a stall. I locked the door, sat on the toilet and inhaled deep breaths with my head between my knees. When I finally settled down, I reviewed Ben's information: the victims had been brutally murdered and then posed to mirror the painting, which had been savagely slashed. Both acts reinforced the idea of revenge. Add the fact that Hugh and Helene knew their killer and it would all seem to lead to me, the "hell hath no fury" suspect. Maybe someone *was* setting me up.

Better than having killed them yourself. But which was it?

I frantically ran through more possibilities. If Hugh was up to his old tricks despite those happy-couple pictures with Helene in the press, the murderer could well be another woman he'd slept with—some insanely jealous "psycho fuck." She could've slashed the painting and posed their bodies. And what about the idea of their drug dealer having gone all *Scarface* on them? That was still a reasonable guess. I wasn't necessarily the only person with a motive to whom they might have opened the door.

I looked down and noticed something had fallen out of my pocket onto the floor. Hugh's letter again. I'd instinctively understood Roche would view it as incriminating.

As I picked the letter up, the restroom door squeaked open. I shoved the paper deeper into my pocket. Heels clicked across the tile floor into another stall. I stood and walked out to the sink to splash water on my face. What I saw in the mirror made me even more distraught. No wonder Ben asked about the scratch. It had become elevated and angry.

There was a small dot of pus in the center—a sign of infection. It looked like a tiny erupting volcano. I winced as I dabbed it with a wet paper towel and cursed my uneven fingernail.

And what if your fingernail wasn't the culprit? That scratch, the twigs and the leaves could have come from thrashing through the woods at night. Fleeing Pequod Point in your sleep the night of the murders. You can't dismiss the idea completely.

I threw the towel into the trash and silently lectured myself in the mirror.

Nora. Just cut those damn nails before you scratch your face again.

Still feeling fragile, I left the ladies' room and made my way back to the booth just as Hugh's neighbor, Sue Mickelson, appeared on the TV screen over the bar. She wasn't in her sweats anymore. She sat, dressed alluringly in black riding pants and a red silk shirt, on a massive white couch in what I guessed was her living room. I heard her say, "They were such an attractive couple, and they seemed so in love," as I slipped into the booth across from Ben. He was staring at his BlackBerry, looking grim.

"What's wrong?" I asked.

"I just checked the *Courier's* e-mail."

He passed me his phone, and I read:

Dear Tips for Living,

Why didn't you print my letter? Are you afraid your readers would agree your column is garbage? Where do you get off making fun of our problems? You act like you're better than the rest of us. I'm warning you again. You need to stop. You're going to be sorry if you keep this up.

Mad as Hell

"Two letters in one week. A real fan," I said evenly, though I was dismayed that *Mad as Hell* was continuing the campaign.

"That's three letters total from this 'fan.' It's an obsession now. I don't like the tone. The column is off."

"But that means the intimidation worked," I countered.

"It's off."

"Permanently off?"

"We'll see."

I was upset. "You're really going to kill the column because of one disgruntled reader."

"Like I said, the town is tense. We're not going to add an edgy column to the mix. Especially when it inspires hostility toward you during an investigation of your ex's murder. Do a follow-up on the 'Canines for Heroes' story. It's been almost six months," he said, standing up. "I'm taking you home. You look exhausted. No arguments."

Funny, Ben seemed very much like a boss again.

I hunkered down on the motorcycle, held on tight to Ben, and felt the wind's bite through my trench coat as we rode into the dark evening. Not even six o'clock and the sun long gone. The trip home from the Tea Cozy took only minutes, but if we'd driven any longer, my legs would've frozen in straddle position. We turned down Crooked Beach Lane. The bike bounced and rattled on the unpaved road. The moon hadn't risen above the trees yet, and the Triumph's single headlamp cast the only light as we pulled up in front of the Coop. I climbed off stiffly, handing the helmet back to Ben. He dropped it into the saddlebag.

"Listen, about Tips," I said. "I know you're trying to do what you think is best. For me, for the town. All I ask is you keep an open mind."

He nodded. I sensed something else weighed heavily on Ben's mind, but he was quiet. I couldn't see his expression through the shadowed visor on his helmet.

"Well, thanks for everything," I said. "I mean thanks for calling Gubbins, for the ride, the drink. The intel."

No "you're welcome" was forthcoming. There was only the sound of the idling bike engine while Ben sat there looking like Darth Vader. What was going on with him?

"Okay, then, good night," I said.

I started for the door and Ben's hand shot out unexpectedly. He caught my arm, spinning me back. What was he doing? He flipped his visor up and fixed me with his eyes. The air between us began to vibrate. My pulse soared as he pulled me closer. His warm body was trembling. I could smell his spicy scent. He lifted my chin and kissed me full on the mouth. A deep, passionate kiss that left me breathless. I liked how it felt.

"Get some sleep," he said, and quickly popped the visor back down.

He kicked the bike stand up, rolled out of the driveway, and roared off into the night before I could gather my wits. I wasn't cold anymore. I stood in the driveway, flushed, my heart racing, trying to take in what had just happened. He was my boss. He was my friend. He was my boss. He was a man. He was my boss. He tasted good.

What had that kiss meant? How long had Ben been attracted to me? Did I miss the signs? Or had he given in to a spontaneous urge? Why the approach now, after the police labeled me a person of interest in my ex-husband's murder investigation? My head was trying to tell me that what just happened was wrong even as my body said it was right.

I heard the faint crunch of gravel behind me and I spun around, frightened. Nothing but darkness. The sound was there and then it wasn't. I listened closely. Nothing. Then crunching again. I whipped out my keys and hurried to unlock my door. Safely inside, I switched on the outside light and peered through the window. Something moved at the end of the drive in the shadows by the trash can. Then it was gone. Probably a raccoon trying to dine on the garbage.

I checked the door's lock, peeled off my coat and wrenched off my boots. Still abuzz with adrenaline, I marched to the kitchen, removed a bottle of vodka from the freezer, poured a shot and drank it down. Tracing my moistened lips with my finger, I closed my eyes and relived Ben's kiss. I forgot my heart could flutter at the thought of a man. Ben's eyes. Soft beagle eyes. How had I not noticed Ben's eyes before?

Hold on. Eyes or not, this was complicated. Had Ben really gotten over his wife? How much emotional baggage was he carrying?

Mad. Sad. Glad. Bad. *Jumbled.* That's what I was feeling. Part of me wanted to snuggle up under the covers and fantasize about Ben. But the other part was resisting. I made my way to the bedroom, hoping I'd finally manage to sleep deeply.

Maybe I'd dream about him.

Chapter Nine

I woke naked and cold, tangled in sheets with the cell phone vibrating next to my head. The lights in the bedroom were blazing. I thought I'd turned them off? I grabbed the phone as the buzzing stopped. Unknown Caller again. Should I try Grace? Not now. I needed to check the news on the murders.

I wrapped myself in my blanket and went to the bedroom window first, parting the curtains to check the garbage can. It stood upright. No trash in sight. If a raccoon had been foraging out there, it hadn't done any damage. I thought of Ben for a moment as I trundled out of the bedroom, still amazed and confused by what had happened.

I paused when I saw that the lights in the hallway were on. And in the bathroom, too. I didn't remember leaving them on, either. Had fatigue made me forgetful or . . . I pulled the blanket around my body more tightly.

Stop.

There was good news in the medicine cabinet mirror. The antibiotic cream that I *did* remember putting on before I went to bed had worked. The scratch was healing. I dropped the blanket, snatched my robe off the hook and headed for the living room to switch on CNN.

They were already in the midst of airing *Point Murders: Special Report*. A graphic labeled the petite Latina woman onscreen as the

Walkers' housekeeper. She was exiting her home and explaining tear-fully in Spanish what her teenage son translated as: "The district attor-ney told her not to talk to anyone." Could the housekeeper have killed Hugh and Helene? She was such a tiny, frightened-looking woman. She seemed genuinely upset. It was hard to picture her putting bullets in people's heads and posing dead bodies.

But you've already pictured yourself doing it, haven't you?

The glass exterior of the Masout Gallery in Chelsea appeared next. A voice-over identified it as the gallery that represented Hugh Walker. The program cut to a dapper but grief-stricken Abbas standing outside his loft building on West Twenty-Second Street, flanked by some of the artists he represented.

"I am so very sad to lose my good friend. I am sad for the families and sad for the art world," he said. "Hugh was a great talent. One of the finest artists of the twenty-first century."

What a loss for Abbas. He'd supported Hugh all through the lean, early years. Even helped him with rent. "Abbas basically adopted me," Hugh had said.

As the report shifted into a teaser for a documentary on southern India, I began fixating on the lights again. Why had all the lights been on this morning? Instinctively, I rushed into the kitchen. Why hadn't I thought of this yesterday? I checked my knife rack and calmed down. I was reassured to see all the knives in place.

Coffee next. There was still half a pot from yesterday. Screw it. I poured a mug full and zapped it in the microwave.

"This is Wolf Blitzer for CNN's special report: *The Point Murders.* Coming up next, we'll have Tobias Walker, the brother of murdered Hugh Walker, with us here in the studio."

Tobias. The last time I'd seen Hugh's brother was at my wedding.

I grabbed the coffee and rushed back to the living room, only to have to wait through a commercial. As I chugged the bitter brew, I thought back to the way Tobias behaved at the hospital during Hugh's heart event. He'd put a picture of Jesus under Hugh's pillow and sat there reading articles from *Christianity Today* and *The New Baptist Newsletter* to his half-conscious brother—his captive audience. Then he organized other ICU families for daily prayer circles in the waiting room, giving out prayer cards to the doctors and nurses. Hugh had been mortified.

Wolf was back.

"Thank you for joining us, Mr. Walker. I'm sorry for your loss," he said.

"Thank you, Wolf."

Sad, red-eyed Tobias sat across from the CNN host. Tobias's familiar face sent another tremor of grief through me. There had always been a strong family resemblance between the brothers. Tobias was the taller, skinnier, less sensual version. With Hugh dead, it pained me to observe their similarities.

"I understand you had just come from Virginia to New York City on Friday for a 'Save the Family' Conference," Wolf said. "And on Sunday morning you received the shocking call that your brother and sister-in-law had been killed."

Tobias swallowed hard. "That's right. Ironic, isn't it?"

"Do you have any idea who committed this horrific crime? Or why?"

"None. It's beyond tragic. Hugh and Helene both had so much to live for. Hugh had his art and a wonderful wife. They had a child they loved. My niece, Callie."

"It was incredibly fortunate that she happened to be staying with her aunt in the city for the weekend," Wolf said.

Tobias nodded. "I'd spoken with Hugh on Saturday morning just as he was dropping her off downtown with Helene's sister before heading out to Pequod. We lamented that our schedules didn't permit our getting together this trip. If I hadn't been so busy with the conference, I would've seen Hugh before . . ."

Tobias looked down. He paused and then cleared his throat. "Anyway. I thank the Lord for the fact that Callie wasn't in that house with them. It was a miracle."

"One bit of light for you in this dark time," Wolf noted gravely.

"Yes. She's a lovely child."

"I'm sure I speak for many people when I say our hearts are with you."

"Thank you, Wolf."

Wolf returned the thanks and the show gave over to a boxing match promo.

Tobias had been in New York City over the weekend? Hugh would never have "lamented" not meeting with him. Hugh avoided his brother. He barely saw him after their parents died. We'd even been ambivalent about inviting him to our wedding.

I remembered how Hugh prepared me to meet Tobias for the first time.

"Tobias makes his living teaching biology laced with creationism at an evangelical school," Hugh scoffed. "He married a local kindergarten teacher. They have one boy, Gideon, I assume named after the Bible.

"Don't be surprised when he talks about Christ like he's a member of the family. Or his superhero best friend," Hugh warned. "We were baptized Lutheran, but only Toby took it seriously. Really seriously. Until he left for college, we shared a bedroom, and he'd harangue me at night by reading the Bible aloud. Or quoting religious scholars. I can still hear him reciting Martin Luther's anti-Semitic screeds. 'We must drive the Jews out like mad dogs, so that we do not become partakers of their abominable blasphemy.' 'Their breath stinks with lust for the Gentiles' gold and silver . . .' That's the kind of religion Tobias is into."

I could never look at Tobias without thinking about those words and resenting him.

Wolf Blitzer returned and introduced footage of Callie, who was holding the hand of a frazzled, auburn-haired woman wearing a leather motorcycle jacket. He identified the woman as Helene's sister. Callie's aunt. The pair was exiting a grungy loft building in Chinatown, fleeing the paparazzi and rushing into a cab. Little orphaned Callie. I could finally see her face and was thankful she didn't look anything like Hugh except for the dark, curly hair. She was so frightened and pale. What would happen to her? Who was responsible for causing all her misery? Whoever it was should be locked up forever.

Was it me?

I loosened my robe. Suddenly the room had turned warm and airless.

The special report ended and I surfed more news channels. None of them reported progress on the case. My cell buzzed again from the bedroom. I dashed back to answer it, disappointed that the ID said Lizzie. I hesitated. I wasn't eager to talk to her after Sinead's revelation that she'd been gossiping about my divorce, but it might be something important about work. I picked up.

"Hello, Lizzie."

"Where are you?"

"Home."

"I've been calling and calling. You looked so upset at Eden's yesterday. I was starting to worry when you didn't answer."

"No need."

"Well, it's a zoo here. People are dropping in to ask questions every few minutes. Basically, they just want to talk because they're flipping out. There were satellite vans along Pequod Avenue with reporters filming people's reactions. It looks like they've left. But the phones don't stop. It's so nuts in here, no one can concentrate. Ben went home to make calls and see if he could wring out any more information from the DA before he writes the front-page story. He gave me seven hundred fifty words on Walker's career, but I can barely get any work done—"

I interrupted. "Is that why you called, Lizzie?"

"Oh. Well, no. Ben just phoned and said to tell you not to come in. You know, to take some time to process all this. I'll cover you."

I felt a twinge in my chest. Why hadn't Ben phoned to tell me this himself?

"Thanks for letting me know," I said, and then it just popped out. "And thanks for gossiping about my marital history."

"Me?"

"That's what Sinead said. Why would you do that, Lizzie?"

Lizzie went silent for a few seconds. Then she groaned.

"I guess I did say something."

"But I specifically asked you not to."

"I'm so sorry, Nora. It was the day you told your divorce story. That night Danny and I had a stupid fight over the invitations to our wedding reception. He stormed out, and I kept thinking about you and your ex. How you'd been together for so long before you made it official. Just like us. How it could end so miserably. Just like that. I was upset and went to the Tea Cozy and got a little loose. Sinead wouldn't let me drive. She took me home. We were talking and it slipped out." She paused. "I'm really sorry. Really."

I heard a car slowing down outside.

"So, you weren't just gossiping about me then," I said, walking to the window.

"No! I wouldn't. I feel awful."

"That feels better." I sighed. "Let's just forget it. I hope you and Danny are back on track."

"We're great."

"That's good. This should be a happy time for you both." I pulled aside one of the curtains. "Oh no."

"What?"

"The press."

One, no . . . two white TV vans already sat at the edge of the driveway, and two more cars were pulling up.

"Shit. There's a small army out there."

Altogether, nearly a dozen people spilled out of the various vehicles. They were from the city, judging by their mostly black clothes. Some had long-lens cameras hanging from their necks. Two men lugged video packs. One labeled CNN, one FOX.

"What are you going to do?" Lizzie asked.

"I don't know."

I felt cornered. I stepped back from the window and let go of the curtains, frustrated that Hugh had succeeded in turning my life into tabloid trash again from beyond the grave. But did I deserve it this time?

"Why don't you give me the exclusive?" Lizzie asked.

"Exclusive what?"

"Interview with you. I'll come over and tell them they're too late—we have a contract. You aren't allowed to answer any questions except mine."

"I'm not giving interviews, Lizzie. I want less publicity, not more." I peeked out the window again, dismayed.

"Unless you talk to them, they'll probably be there until the police announce they've caught the killer."

I winced. Lizzie could be tactless. "Great. I'll be ordering in food then."

"FYI. I do know *one* thing about whoever did it," Lizzie said. "It was someone they knew."

Only the police and the DA's office had that information. And Ben.

"Ben told you that?"

"He didn't have to. It's obvious. There's no mention of a robbery in the police statement. Random 'break in and kill the rich in their mansions' murders don't go with the zeitgeist—too Charles Manson. We're in the era of public executions: Sandy Hook Elementary, the Aurora movie theater. That church in Charleston. It has to be someone they knew and let into the house. They had no idea they just invited their killer in."

I had an unpleasant thought. I tried to ignore it.

"Nora? Did you hear me? Don't you think I'm right?"

Was Lizzie trying to imply something here, or was I paranoid again?

"They knew whoever killed them," she repeated.

I couldn't contain myself.

"I think you should just say it, Lizzie."

"Say what?"

"You think I'm the prime suspect."

"What? No! That's crazy."

"Is it so crazy to think anyone who knows my history with Hugh and Helene is going to entertain that idea? And judging by the amount of media here, the entire country could come to the same conclusion by the evening news. I'll be tried and convicted in the court of public opinion."

"Well, if I'm going to be completely honest, it did cross my mind . . ."

"I was right," I said, unable to hide the hurt in my voice. "And that's why you're so eager for an interview."

"No! I didn't mean that you killed them, only that people might suspect you."

"Oh."

"I'm sorry if you have to deal with that. It's really unfair."

I had to find my balance. Lizzie was only trying to help. "Lizzie, I'm not thinking rationally. I'm exhausted. I'm really sorry I misjudged your intentions. Please forgive me."

"It's okay," she said, sounding relieved. "You're not mad anymore, right?"

"No, I'm not mad." I heard another call beep. "But I have to get off now."

"You're sure a sympathetic interview wouldn't help?"

"No interviews. Goodbye." I clicked off and saw that the other caller was "Unknown." I rejected it.

I sneaked another look outside. The reporters were slouching in their open cars and vans, talking on cell phones and working on MacBooks. A few of them were eating Eden's powdered jelly donuts and brushing the white sugar dust off their black outfits. They were in no rush to go anywhere. I wanted to scream.

Instead I sat down on the edge of the bed and thought it over. Lizzie's proposal actually had some merit. It might be smart to engage with the press, but in a manner I could control. Not an interview—a statement. A compassionate one. If anyone tried to paint me as Hugh's murderous ex, I could draw a different picture. It might just be enough to get rid of these reporters, and also help clear any cloud of suspicion hanging over me. Despite Gubbins's warning, I decided to face the press.

My jeans lay in a clump at the foot of the bed. I pulled them on, slipped into my UGGs and returned to the living room. Remembering how washed-out I'd appeared in the bathroom mirror, I fished a makeup pouch out of my shoulder bag and hurriedly dabbed cover-up on the scratch. Then I ran "Cherry Lush" red lipstick over my cracked lips and rubbed some on my cheeks so I wouldn't look like death. Hair fluffed. Trench coat on. I was ready. *I can do this,* I thought.

"There she is!"

They scrambled like roaches as soon as I opened the door. Within seconds, they'd regrouped at the bottom of the driveway with their gear. A barrage of cameras whirred and clicked. There were frantic shouts.

"Ms. Glasser! Over here!"

"What's your reaction to the murders of your ex and his wife?"

"Why did the police bring you in to the Massamat precinct?"

At the last question, I shuffled back a step, startled. Someone leaked my visit to the station. *Damn.* That would only foster more suspicion. *Fuck*. The recording light on one of the video cameras flashed red. *Think. Get it together fast.* I concentrated on making my expression unreadable and my posture perfect and then strode slowly, purposefully ahead, heart pounding. Aiming my gaze at the camera lens, I felt like Norma Desmond going for her close-up. I stopped and took a breath.

"I want to express how shocked and saddened I am. The Walkers' murders are devastating. My heart goes out to Hugh's family. And his wife's family. It's especially tragic for their little girl. I can't imagine who would want to do such a monstrous thing. The police were hoping that I might have some additional information that would help them solve the case. They're leaving no stone unturned and doing everything in their power to find the killer as quickly as possible. And I'm praying they will."

Boilerplate, but appropriate. And actually sincere.

The reporters instantly began shouting more questions, ratcheting up my heart rate again. I had tunnel vision—all I could see was my front door. Shaking my head, I tried to smile and politely refuse them as I determinedly walked toward it and escaped back inside. I stole another look through the curtains. The reporters remained at the foot of the driveway, most of them talking on their phones. But one black-clad cameraman was still aiming at the front of the Coop. I jerked my head away from the window. In a few minutes, I checked again, even more discreetly. Everyone was packing gear and dispersing except him.

I tried to ignore the fact that he was out there and went to my desk to check e-mail and Facebook. There were condolences from old friends, but still no Ben. My phone buzzed with more unknown callers. Likely tabloid reporters who'd found my cell number through illegal methods. They left voice mails. I didn't listen to any of them. Staccato phrases popped in and out of my mind: "The killer was someone they knew and let in." "Did you have a reaction to them moving here?" Yes, Lizzie was right. The suspicions were unfair. And awful. And scary as hell.

I called Grace to see how Otis was feeling and give her an update. She didn't answer. I sneaked a look out the window again. The lone cameraman waited.

The apparatus on his shoulder seemed more and more like a gun.

Chapter Ten

I must've dozed off. The sleep had helped. I woke just past noon with a clearer head, feeling stronger and resolving not to be a prisoner in my own house any longer. Let the paparazzo have his shot. We both needed to get on with our lives. I counted to three, strode to the front door, took a deep breath and opened it. But the only things in the driveway were my Toyota and the trash can. The cameraman had left.

Relieved, I closed the door and checked my cell phone. A concerned voice mail from Grace asked how I was doing. There was bawling in the background. She reported that Otis had recovered, and she was at the dentist with both the kids. Grace had her hands full, but like the true friend she was, she urged me to call or come over if I needed her.

Lizzie had also phoned. She probably wanted to try selling her interview idea again. She'd obviously taken my advice on persistence; I'd give her that. Before figuring out what to do next, I turned on the TV news for an update.

FOX had already begun airing the segment. I should have known they'd start with the sordid bits. Our wedding photographer was making money off us again. There I was, leaning on Hugh, wearing a happy bride smile and a white satin wedding gown, clutching a bouquet of daisies. The voice-over began:

"Nora Glasser and Hugh Walker were practically newlyweds when the artist's affair with Helene Westing resulted in pregnancy . . ."

Offended, I pressed "Mute" on the remote. More pictures of our wedding intercut with Hugh and Helene's "budding" romance, before they finally showed me stepping out of the Coop. I clicked on the sound. The last reporter's inquiry was the only one they'd included: "Why did the police bring you down to the Massamat precinct?"

"Please, no, no, no," I pleaded with the screen as I watched the caption crawl by underneath: "Walker's former wife taken in for police questioning." I switched to CNN. "Police question Walker's ex-wife" rolled by under my close-up. Even more condemning, I was smiling and wearing way too much makeup—the slash of beige below one eye resembled war paint. Ditto for the bright red blotches of lipstick smeared on my cheeks. There was even lipstick on my teeth. I didn't appear sad at all. I came across as fairly insane. The final image was the cameraman's shot of me peeking out the window like a fugitive surrounded and weighing surrender. It all added up to one guilty-looking woman. My knees almost went out from under me. This had totally backfired.

First thought: call Aunt Lada immediately. She might be watching this and panicking. The stress would aggravate her dementia. She picked up almost instantly, as if she'd been holding the phone, waiting.

"Hello?"

"Aunt La—"

"Nora! Are you all right? Did the police take you in? Are you a suspect?"

"I'm fine. The press got it wrong. I went in voluntarily—to help them."

"Beshot lapshe na ooshe," she said. *Don't hang noodles on my ears.* "Don't deceive me," to a Russian.

"I'm not hanging any noodles, Aunt Lada. Did you get my message yesterday? I didn't want you to worry."

"Yes, yes. But I just saw you on TV. The headlines they put! And you don't look so good. Are you sick? There's a stomach thing going around."

"I'm just tired. Really. It's okay."

"I've been watching the reports, Nora. It's terrible. So terrible. I keep thinking about it. Hugh and that woman were miserable people, but they deserved each other—not this. And that poor little girl is scarred for life."

She was right, I thought sadly.

"Don't watch any more coverage, Aunt Lada. Please. It will just make your blood pressure go up. I'll visit you tomorrow. I promise." I was reluctant to drive to The Cedars before then. Lada could read my moods even with her compromised brain. She'd realize how freaked out I was. Best to wait until I calmed down. She sensed my reluctance to talk and chose not to press.

"Okay. But make sure you sleep, you hear me? Take good care of yourself," she said.

The instant I hung up, the doorbell rang. I stole a look out the window and caught a glimpse of a camouflage jacket and Lizzie's ginger curls. She rang again. I opened the door, exasperated. Lizzie stood there, her freckled nose scrunched up in a scowl.

"Why don't you answer your phone?" she pouted.

"I meant what I said, Lizzie. Please. Give it a rest."

"I'm trying to make amends here. You're worried about being labeled as an O. J. if they don't figure out who the killer is, right? Well, I might have an idea who did it."

"What? Who?"

"Are you going to invite me in?"

I motioned her inside and shut the door.

"At least the press took off," she said.

"For now."

Lizzie sat down on the couch, clasped her hands in her lap and looked up at me, excited.

"What's your idea?" I asked.

"You agree it's my story if what I tell you checks out?"

"For God's sake, Lizzie, yes."

"Well, I remembered something Sinead told me driving home from the Tea Cozy that night. She said she'd heard of the Walkers before but didn't realize you had a connection to them. She heard about them from the guy who built Pequod Point."

"The Miami developer. The man who lost it?"

Lizzie nodded.

"Mr. Miami came into the bank to meet with Sinead's boss. She heard the whole conversation. Seems he'd raised the cash to buy his house back, but too late. The bank accepted the Walkers' offer the day before. The guy was extremely agitated about it."

"It's quite a stretch from there to murder, Lizzie."

"No, wait. He told Sinead's boss he'd tracked the Walkers down and made an offer with a healthy profit. He explained to them that he'd built the house for his wife, that she loved her pottery studio, etc., etc. He pleaded with them. The Walkers said no. The next day, they had their lawyer call and tell him to lay off. Or face a restraining order."

"Well, *that* was harsh," I said, taking a seat in the wicker armchair across from Lizzie. This was getting more interesting.

"So, he comes into the bank and tells his story to Sinead's boss. Asks if there's anything the bank can do to help him get his house back. He'll pay. The boss says sorry, there are rules. Mr. Miami calls the Walkers a few choice names, blames them for his wife lapsing into a serious depression and then splits."

"Okay . . ."

She pulled a paper from her jacket pocket and handed it to me. "I went back to our Lifestyles piece on the wife. These are the names, right here."

"Diane and Jeffrey Volani spend the rest of the year in Miami Beach, Florida," I read.

"I found their number through the reverse directory. I had a hunch. I thought I'd call, and if Mr. Volani answered, I'd say something like, 'Lizzie Latham of the *Pequod Courier* here. My sources tell me you were seen turning into the driveway of the house you built on Pequod Point this weekend. You may have been the last person to see the Walkers alive. Any comment?'"

"Smart. Take him off guard. See what kind of response you'd get."

"Right. And if the wife answered instead, I'd pretend interest in one of her lovely urns for my wedding centerpiece. Chat her up. Try to learn if her husband had an alibi over the weekend. But I didn't talk to either of them." She sat back, looking pleased with herself.

"So, what happened?"

She mimed talking into her phone. "'Hello, may I speak with Jeffrey Volani?' I ask. An old man's voice answers, 'I'm sorry. Jeffrey is out of town.' Bingo. Out of town in Pequod, maybe? 'Oh. Then may I speak with Diane?' But there's this really *loong* silence from the old man.

"'Who is this, please?' he finally asks, but his voice sounds all funny. Something tells me not to say I'm a reporter. 'It's Lizzie Latham. From their old neighborhood in Pequod.' Not a total lie, right? He chokes up. Turns out the old man is Jeffrey's father, and he tells me that on Labor Day weekend, Diane Volani killed herself."

"Whoa." I let out a long breath.

"Volani's dad was eager to talk to someone who knew them when. It felt kind of icky to mislead him, but check this out: he told me that he moved in with his son because he's '*very* worried about his mental condition. The toll this has taken.'"

"I see where you're going with this." I stood and began to pace. "If Volani Jr. already blamed Hugh and Helene for his wife's depression, he's got motive. And if he'd been brooding for months, he could have snapped when she killed herself. He could have completely cracked . . ." At last, a viable suspect. Someone enraged at both Hugh and Helene. Someone unhinged. I stopped pacing. "Great job, Lizzie."

She glowed. "Yeah? It means a lot that you think so."

Sometimes, under all Lizzie's competitiveness, I forgot that she wanted my approval.

"I called upstairs to see if Gubbins could add anything, but he'd left for lunch," she said, getting up. "Listen, I need to go back to the office. I'll take the information to the police after I talk to Gubbins. If this Volani guy turns out to be the killer, I'll be ready to run with the story before anyone else."

"I don't understand. What does Gubbins have to do with it?"

"He handled the Pequod Point purchase for the Walkers."

◆ ◆ ◆

The chances of finding Gubbins lunching at Eden's were good. And if I guessed wrong, I'd try the pizza place on Bridge Street or pop over to his office and wait for him there. No media vans were visible on Pequod Avenue, so I was fairly confident the press wouldn't accost me. I parked and strode into the coffee shop, impatient to confront my lawyer. How could he withhold such an important piece of information? How could I trust him?

Gubbins sat in the last green-leather booth at the back of the room, wearing his shiny brown suit, eating a piece of pie. He didn't notice me come in. His attention was split between the pie and the TV on the wall. FOX News was reporting on another round of deadly flooding in Haiti. I paused for a second and took in the heartrending images of homeless, grief-stricken survivors covered in mud, of inconsolable children crying for missing parents. That put things in perspective. I said a silent prayer for them and continued across the red linoleum floor, plunking down across from Gubbins, giving him a start. I kept my voice low.

"Why didn't you tell me that you were Hugh and Helene's lawyer?"

Gubbins pushed away his slice of key lime pie and wiped his mouth with a napkin.

"It wasn't relevant."

"Of course it was relevant. And what about legal? Or ethical?"

133

"I did not solicit you, Ms. Glasser. Ben Wickstein solicited me on your behalf."

"I know, but—"

"I was the Walkers' attorney for a single real estate transaction. They're dead now. As such, they're no longer my clients. But since they once were, confidentiality seemed appropriate."

"Okay, but—"

"I really do take offense at your implication."

"I'm sorry."

"If you prefer not to accept my representation, that's fine."

"I didn't say that—"

"So, for the record, you still wish to be my client?"

"Well . . . yes."

"And you agree to listen to my advice?"

I nodded. At that moment, I could imagine Gubbins in a courtroom pretty easily.

"I saw that you spoke to the press," he said, gesturing at the TV screen. "I hope you've gotten that out of your system. It's dangerous territory. I'm not sure you've created the desired effect."

I bit my lip. "You mean I made it worse."

"Indeed."

"But I felt I had to say something. I'm nervous about the way people are viewing me in all this."

"Once again, I advise you against it. The media is tricky. It's easy to give the wrong impression."

He'd been right about that. What was the matter with me? If I was going to trust anyone, it should be him. I had to bring him up to speed on Volani. As he signaled for his check, I bent my head toward him and whispered, "You knew the previous owner of Pequod Point, right? The man who tried to buy his house back? Jeffrey Volani?"

"I've spoken with him, yes."

"The police need to focus on Volani."

Gubbins gave me a questioning look.

"He was angry with Hugh and Helene. He blamed them for his wife becoming depressed because she couldn't have her house back. Well, the wife committed suicide a couple of months ago. It destroyed him. And I learned he wasn't in Miami the night of the murders. He was 'out of town.' He could've come here to take his revenge . . . maybe."

Even as I proposed Volani as the killer, I had reservations. The scenario suddenly seemed too far-fetched. Why would Volani slash the painting? Pose the two in bed? If he were trying to frame me, he'd need to have known my history with Hugh and Helene, and that I lived in Pequod. It was doubtful he even knew I existed. Or had he done research on Hugh and discovered our connection? Or had I just latched on to Volani because I was desperate to find a suspect? My mind was on fire with arguments and counterarguments.

Gubbins sighed. "Who told you all that?"

"I have my sources."

"Well, it's impossible. He couldn't have killed them."

"Why not?"

"Because he faxed me last night from Dubai. He's developing a hotel there. He saw the news about the murders and wanted to know if I had the name of Hugh Walker's estate attorney, so he could try to buy Pequod Point again. True, Mr. Volani is obsessed with that house, but he was in Dubai on Saturday night. He can't be in two places at once."

I slumped down in the booth, deflated. An older waitress delivered the check and began to clear the table. Gubbins took out his wallet, removed a hundred-dollar bill and set it down to pay.

"Thanks, dear," he said. "I hope it's not too much trouble to break that hundred. I don't have anything smaller."

"No problem, Mr. G."

As she reached for the money, she caught sight of my face and did a double take. She deliberately avoided my eyes and slipped away to bring Gubbins his change.

"Did you see that?" I asked.

"What?"

I groaned. "The way she looked at me. I *did* make it worse. It's like everything is conspiring to make me look guilty. Even my own efforts."

"Try to keep calm, Ms. Glasser."

"But I'm worried. Do you know the way Hugh and Helene were murdered? Do you understand what's happening here?"

"I do." Gubbins nodded, his expression grave. "The killer set the scene to frame you."

I leaned back and felt some of my tension drain. Gubbins believed what Ben believed.

"So that's your take, too?"

"We're dealing with mental illness, Ms. Glasser. A very sick, but very clever person did this. Someone diabolical."

I shuddered. "Yes."

"*But*, since the police haven't come to your house looking for evidence, I believe they subscribe to the theory that whoever murdered the Walkers is trying to implicate you. The lack of a warranted search of your premises is a very good sign that the police are not buying you as the killer. You're a person of interest because of your relationship to the victims. I truly doubt you're the focus of the investigation."

I straightened up. "That's excellent," I said, slapping the table. I had to refrain from breaking into a happy dance.

Gubbins scowled. "Now, listen to me. Keep a low profile. Stay away from the press until the police find the murderer, which they will. This is a small town. Someone will have noticed something that will lead them in the right direction."

Gubbins's optimism gave me back my appetite. I told him I'd meet him at his office in a few minutes to sign the papers that said I was officially hiring him. When he left, I ordered a large container of Eden's legendary clam chowder at the register. While I waited for my soup, my own voice began speaking from the TV set. I glanced over my shoulder.

On the screen, a deranged-looking version of myself was making a statement. I wanted to fall through the floor. What a stupid mistake I'd made taking on the press. The other patrons in the coffee shop were turning their heads from me to the TV and back again, stunned. I lowered my eyes and focused on a bowl of mints by the register until the waitress handed over the container of soup. She took my cash in silence.

"Keep the change," I mumbled and quickly headed for the door.

As I reached the street, a woman I recognized as the wife of Kevin, the Tea Cozy's owner, walked by with her little boy. She pretended she hadn't seen me and looked away nervously.

Pequod's Pariah. That's what I'd become. That's what I'd remain until the police caught the killer. I cringed. I hadn't been convicted, but I was already in solitary. How long would it take for the police to do their job? Judging by my interview with Roche, they didn't have any suspects. If one of Pequod's residents had "noticed something," I wished they would hurry up and report it.

I crossed the street to the *Courier* building, planning to stop in and see Lizzie before going upstairs to sign Gubbins's legal papers. She needed to know that Jeffrey Volani had an alibi. I purposely slowed down to see if I could spot Ben through the front window. He wasn't at his desk. No jacket on his chair. No motorcycle out front, although he might have parked in the small lot around back. I felt like a schoolgirl with a crush.

I stepped into the office. Lizzie was at her desk in the corner just getting off the phone. Still no sign of Ben. It was probably for the best. Our first post-kiss encounter was going to be awkward. I'd rather not have Lizzie witness it.

"I just spoke to Gubbins," Lizzie said, shaking her head, disappointed. "Looks like Volani was on the other side of the world. Too bad. I thought I had him."

"It was first-rate investigative work, Lizzie."

"Thanks." She studied me and frowned. "Remember what Ben said. You sure it's a good idea for you to come back to work today?"

It occurred to me why Ben would prefer I stay home. He could dodge the discomfort for a while longer.

"I'm not here to work. I have an appointment upstairs."

"Oh." She gave me a knowing look. "Going with local counsel. Good idea. Really good."

Gubbins was in a conference, so he'd left the papers with his receptionist. I filled them out and then headed back downstairs. My phone rang as I reached the landing.

The caller ID read "Grace." I picked up.

"Why can't that Detective Roche control his people? Someone deliberately leaked your visit to the police station. They had to know the media would jump on it and label you a suspect. I'd like to strangle whoever it was. You were brave to go out and talk to the press, Nora."

"How do you think I came off?" Like a guilty, mentally disturbed ex-wife?

"You seemed . . . sincere. To me, at least."

"You're not a very good liar. How's Otis?"

"Better. Come for dinner."

I was feeling too low. Like I might contaminate the kids with despair. "Thanks. Another time."

"C'mon, Nora. Don't isolate, honey."

"I'm not. I'm just. I'm just . . . not in the mood."

"Okay. I won't push you today. But we're here for you. Remember."

"I know. You're the best."

I signed off. As I passed the *Courier*'s office door, I saw Lizzie's dad through the glass panel. Mayor Latham was sitting across from Lizzie at her desk, talking animatedly.

About the murders, I was sure. That was all anyone was talking about. Shoot me now.

Back at the Coop, I devoured the chowder and checked e-mail again. Still nothing from Ben. I berated myself for being naïve. What I'd begun to think of as Our First Kiss was probably the result of too much vodka. While I stretched out on the couch with my laptop, trying to determine whether I was disappointed or relieved, an e-mail with the subject line *Funeral* arrived. I was stunned to see who the sender was: twalker@ fundfortheamericanfamily.org. I clicked on it.

> Dear Nora,
>
> I caught your statement on the news and though we have never been close, your grief touched me deeply, along with your willingness to help the police. Christ, in his infinite compassion, forgives Hugh and Helene. I'm glad to hear you have forgiven them, too.
>
> I've arranged for the funeral to be held at 10:00 a.m. this Friday here at the Charlotte's Cove Chapel. There will be a larger memorial in NYC at a later point. This is exclusively for family and a very few local friends. I'm sending this in hopes you'll attend. You were such an important part of Hugh's life.
>
> Go with God,
>
> Tobias

At least Tobias didn't suspect me of killing his brother; he'd interpreted my unhinged appearance as angst. He was showing empathy, reaching out. But this was such a turnaround from the arrogant Tobias I remembered. So was his emotional response on CNN. Could Hugh's death have changed him, at least for now? Still, I wasn't sure it was appropriate to attend. I doubted he'd cleared the invitation with Helene's family. They probably wouldn't appreciate seeing Hugh's ex at his funeral.

I felt beaten up emotionally and physically. A movie might be comforting, I thought. I'd checked a DVD out of the library a few days earlier but hadn't viewed it yet: *Double Indemnity*, a classic film noir starring Fred MacMurray and Barbara Stanwyck. Watching it turned out to be a bad idea. The two of them were so evil, so icily calculating in their attempt to commit the perfect murder, that they only increased my stress. I shut the film off halfway through and, despite the early hour, headed to bed. I was so tired in my bones, I thought I might sleep for a year.

Click. *Turn off the lights in the living room.* Was "The Point Killer" as clever as the killers in the film? Click. *Turn off the lights in the hall.* Would the plot to frame me succeed, or was there a flaw in the plan? Click. *Turn off the lights in the bedroom. If you find the lights on in the morning . . . you'll know. You'll know if a frame-up is wishful thinking. Or if you've started sleepwalking again.*

Pitch this after Ben cools down?

Tips for Living

Piqued? Do Your Civic Duty

Ever wonder if instead of protecting you, the local police are out to get you? I'm talking about those speed traps, peppered all around Pequod. Nice way to fill the town's coffers, eh? Where are the police when a Summer Person in an Escalade speeds through a crosswalk and nearly flattens a pedestrian? They're lying in wait at one of those back-road snares hoping to ambush one of us. Why not take your morning coffee, cruise by a few of the setups until you discover where the cops are hiding? Then park a half mile ahead and flash your lights to give drivers a heads-up. No problem if you're caught. Just say, "Officer, I've got an electrical short and I'm testing my headlights." Vive la Resistance!

WHAT are you thinking? Are you insane?

Chapter Eleven

I closed my black-and-white composition notebook, put down my pen, and finished my coffee. I'd woken up in the morning, reassured. All the lights were still off. Nothing out of place. No new marks on my skin. And for the first time in ages, I felt rested. I'd slept deeply and well. It was good to be back in the world feeling human again.

After dressing, I walked out of the Coop under a sunny sky of saturated blue—the rich hue of an old Technicolor film. A blanket of white spread over the front yard. Glimmering, gossamer white. I stopped short, exhaling cloud puffs. That lacy covering on the lawn was frost. It meant there was no chance to plant daffodils anymore—the earth was too hard and unwelcoming. The bag of bulbs would have to stay in the garden shed until next year. My mood took a dip.

As I backed the Toyota out of the drive, "Unknown Caller" rang. Another reporter, I was sure. It rang again moments later. My landlord. What did he want? Had he seen my statement on TV? Did he suspect me, too? Would he make up an excuse about why he couldn't rent the Coop any longer? I let the call go. Another ring as I reached the paved road. Grace again. I picked up.

"Listen, you really need a break from all this stress. The kids and I are going to Charlotte's Cove Farm this afternoon to walk the corn maze and watch them make cider. It's their reward for not biting the dentist's fingers. We miss you. Come with us."

I wished I could. It would be a soothing distraction.

"I'd love to, Gracie, but I'm going to see Aunt Lada today."

"Oh, I'm glad, Nor. That will be really good for both of you. Then let's plan on Pilates tomorrow."

"I don't know . . . the thought of facing everyone in class . . ."

"I get how you might be nervous about going. But you can't give up exercising and turn into a slug. Besides, exercise helps fight depression."

"Um. Let me think about it."

"The women there know you. They'll be supportive."

"I hope you're right." Grace usually was.

"So you'll come?"

"Okay. But let's meet out front. I want to catch up before we go inside."

"Seven thirty in the lot?"

"I'll bring the coffee."

I spotted Lt. Crawley on the opposite shoulder.

"Gotta go. Phone bust."

I dropped the phone into my lap and put on my poker face as I drove past him, even though I was certain he'd seen the cell at my ear. Crawley lived for the cell phone traffic stop, the easiest bust aside from speed traps. But when I checked the rearview mirror, his car hadn't moved. What a mensch, I thought. He's giving me a break. He knows the trauma I've been through. But by the time I reached the bridge, I decided Crawley was a spy. The police never monitored speeders that close to my house—not enough traffic. Crawley must be keeping tabs on my comings and goings for Detective Roche. If I was right, then Gubbins was wrong about me being off the hook.

Flustered, I crossed the bridge and drove through town without stopping for breakfast at Eden's. I'd rather avoid the stares, and I felt anxious about running into Ben. He often grabbed breakfast there. Another distressing thought popped into my head: if Ben hadn't called because he woke up mortified about the kiss, would he fire me to avoid dealing with me at work? No, he would never do that. We'd both have to find a way to cope with the discomfort and embarrassment.

Thirty minutes later, I was driving up the tree-lined drive of The Cedars, a collection of sprawling stone buildings set atop a wooded hill. The largest had a castle-like arched entrance (albeit with wheelchair ramp and automated doors), balustrades and multiple chimneys. Think Manderley in Hitchcock's *Rebecca*. The developers purchased the thirty-two-acre compound in 1973 during the first US oil crisis, probably for a song. It was a Buddhist monastery in a previous incarnation, and before that a Jesuit one. But the heating bills daunted even austere monks who dialed their thermostats down and exalted their shivering.

Going from the visitors lot to the main building required an uphill hike along a cedar-chip path that cut through a large stand of cedar trees. The preppy young sales rep had pushed the cedar thing heavily when I'd attended the open house.

"The Cedars was named for the magnificent cedar tree—worshipped in ancient Sumeria," she said. "We've planted one hundred fifty cedars around the main building. We want the trees to be an inspiration for our residents. It's often called The Tree of Life and can live to be one thousand years old."

"I don't expect my aunt will be interested in living nearly that long," I'd said.

She ignored me and went on with her sales pitch.

"We've added three other buildings in the same architectural style for a total of one hundred twenty beautiful apartments, all with the option of supervised home care. Residents and their loved ones can feel secure knowing there's an on-site clinic, rehab center and hospice."

At $75,000 a year. Plus extra for the clinic, rehab and hospice. At least Lada had quit smoking the Balkan Sobranies, which would improve her chances of staying healthy. The challenge was how to afford to keep helping her pay for her longevity.

I entered the lobby, a grand oak-paneled room with a sweeping wooden staircase and two giant, intricately carved fireplaces you could walk into if you got the urge to self-immolate.

Yvonne, the sunny, buxom Jamaican receptionist fond of hair accessories, waved from the front desk. Shiny orange and yellow beads bounced at the ends of her dreadlocks as she moved her head. A carved wooden turkey wearing a pilgrim's hat stood on the counter next to her. No Fowl Language read the sign that hung around its intact neck. I wondered if Yvonne had caught me on the news and how she'd react.

"Ah, Nora, dare ya are."

"Hi, Yvonne. How've you been?"

"The lord shinin' his love on me. Giving me extra shifts. Yourself?"

Yvonne seemed unaware of my drama. She was probably much too busy to watch television with all the hours she worked.

"Good. I'm good. How is my aunt?"

"She's been missing ya. Acting a bit spacey. Mostly she go to a happy place, but sometime she go paranoid. She call security yesterday evening. Say someone stole her can opener. Turns out she put it in her refrigerator."

It was always a blame game with Lada lately. Always a mysterious "someone" responsible for petty crimes against her. But there'd been nothing really alarming yet.

"Here you go, child. Sign on the line," Yvonne said, pushing the registration book toward me before she buzzed Lada's apartment.

I be no child, I thought, tracking the brown spot on my hand as I wrote my name. Was that a freckle or a liver spot? Whenever I came to The Cedars, my fears of aging bubbled up.

"Nobody home. Try de Panic Room," Yvonne said, hanging up the in-house phone.

That was what residents had dubbed their lounge area, the place they went when they couldn't bear spending any more time alone in their apartments but didn't have the energy to entertain.

"If I invite people over, I've got to serve coffee and a nosh, at least. Then I have to clean up after them," Lada told me. "Old age takes it out of you, Nora. *Syakomu ovoshchu svoyo vremya.* Every vegetable has its time. Mine is over. I'm rotting in the bin."

My heart broke when I heard her talk like that. I wished I had something to say to make her feel better—some sage advice, some really useful tips for living. But *Mad as Hell* was right. I was glib. If Ben had published the letter and I had the guts to be totally honest, I would have written this response:

> Dear Mad as Hell,
>
> Here's why I write the column in the way that I do:
> I'm covering up for the fact that I have no idea how
> to deal with the reality of people's pain and fragil-
> ity. I don't have a fucking clue how to help with my
> own, let alone theirs.
>
> Nora Glasser, alias Total Fraud.

I thanked Yvonne and took the elevator to the second floor, where I walked down a corridor whose walls featured decorative paper cutouts of smiling Native Americans in headdresses, pilgrims and cornucopias. The Cedars wasn't exactly politically correct. My spirits lifted as they always did as soon as I entered the Panic Room. It reminded me of New York's Algonquin Hotel—the dark wooden paneling, clusters of high-backed Edwardian chairs, antique tea tables and velvet couches. Back when I lived in the city, I used to hang out in the lobby of the famous old hotel for inspiration. I'd imagine Dorothy Parker and her *New Yorker* friends trading witty stories at their Round Table luncheons there.

The Panic Room was full of character, but it was also redolent with the stink of mothballs—all those wool sweaters and shawls that residents had pulled out of storage with the arrival of the cold weather. Surprisingly, the cedar-obsessed owners hadn't installed cedar closets when they renovated. My nose started running from the sickly sweet odor of naphthalene.

Aunt Lada and another white-haired woman were playing cards near the window. Even from across the room, I could see that Lada had a "tell." She looked so much like my mother in that moment that I had to stop and catch my breath. It wasn't just that Lada and Sally Levervitch had prominent Russian foreheads, feline eyes and similar wavy hair (though my mother dyed hers strawberry blonde to hide her ethnicity, while Lada had lived to see her brown hair go completely gray), it was the astonishing height to which Lada's left eyebrow could arch when she disapproved of something. My mother had the same ability. Lada's eyebrow was aimed at her cards, and it said, "I don't like the hand I've been dealt."

"Nora!" Lada exclaimed, lighting up when she saw me. "I told you she'd come," she said to her card-holding friend.

I didn't recognize Lada's companion—a handsome Asian woman with unusual ethnic bracelets and earrings that complemented long silver hair she wore twisted into a bun. She must be a new resident, I surmised.

"Nora, this is Ann Kogarashi. She took a one-bedroom on the third floor. She's an anthropologist."

Ann looked me over and smiled.

"Anthropologist, long retired. Lovely to meet you. Your aunt raves about you," she said. There was no hint of her having seen me on the news, either. Was she just being discreet out of respect for my aunt?

A whirring sound came from behind as Mort pulled up. Mort, who was eighty-nine, had a tube running from his nose to an oxygen tank strapped to the back of his wheelchair.

"How are you, Mort?"

"Woke up on the right side of the dirt, so I can't complain," he answered, smiling.

Mort used to be a Madison Avenue ad man. He was still mentally sharp and plugged in to current events.

"Sorry to hear about your troubles with the law, Nora," he said softly. "You doing all right?"

I glanced over at Lada, certain that this would start a conversation about the murders, but she was smiling, oblivious. Ann just looked at me with concern. I nodded at Mort.

"Maybe you'll come with us to the film today? Take your mind off things," he said. "They're showing *Hairspray*. John Travolta plays a woman. Wears a fat suit."

I'd gone to see *No Country for Old Men* with Lada and Mort a few weeks back; The Cedars screened movies in the downstairs lounge. The two of them fell asleep about twenty minutes into the film. Holding hands.

"Sorry, Mort. I've got to work after lunch." I gave my arm to Lada. "I have to steal my aunt away for a little bit. Nice to meet you, Ann. See you soon, Mort."

I fully expected Lada to bring up the murders as soon as we were out of earshot, but she didn't. She really seemed to be off in another world.

"I'm so happy to see you," was all she said as we ambled down the hall to the elevator. She was walking slowly but still walking, thank God.

We had a salad bar lunch in the dining room, but Lada didn't bring up the murders there, either. She flitted from topic to topic: "Here's something Ann told me. Did you know Vladimir Putin is a very rich man? Ann says he's worth billions. And still he acts like a baboon thumping his chest!" Seconds later: "Mort's daughter is a social worker. She was so upset about a case. A couple put a lock on their refrigerator.

They made their fourteen-year-old daughter pay for her food using money she earned babysitting." Lada looked distraught. "They're worse than the Stalinists. What's wrong with them?"

I remembered Stokes's story of his in-laws presenting him and Kelly with their grocery bill.

"I don't know, Aunt Lada," I said, patting her arm. "There are some very sick individuals out there."

After finishing lunch, we went back to Lada's apartment, and I shampooed her hair in the sink. She always said, "It comes out so much better when you do it, Nora." But I knew the real reason. She liked being touched. She purred while I massaged conditioner into her scalp. Her silver hair turned soft as corn silk. I set it with curlers made from empty orange juice cans—a recession-proof method as effective and about three hundred times cheaper than a Brazilian Blowout.

While Lada's hair dried, I made her some tea and then returned to the closet in the entrance hall where I'd hung my coat. The large, cellophane-covered cardboard box sat on the shelf above the coatrack. On every visit, I'd think about what to do with it—a carton full of mementos of Hugh. Things I hadn't been able to throw away, but couldn't live with anymore. When I started over in Pequod, I'd left them in Lada's care.

I looked up at the box, reviewing the seemingly endless hurts Hugh inflicted. Helene's pregnancy. A painful and public divorce. Moving to Pequod with Helene and reopening the wound. Now I was a suspect in his murder investigation. What was there to debate? I pulled out the stepladder from the back of the closet.

Lada stared at the cellophane-covered box as I set it down on her kitchen table. There was enough tape on it to wrap a mummy, as if I'd been afraid the detritus of my marriage would claw its way out and hunt me down.

"Nora."

Suddenly present and mentally alert, Lada was looking at me fretfully.

"Tell me about your talk with the police," she said.

"The police . . . yes."

I thought I'd escaped this conversation. Damn. It was probably best not to tell her the whole story. Why stress her? I wasn't under arrest.

"I spoke with them briefly, but I don't think it helped them very much. Where do you keep your scissors, Aunt Lada?"

"In that drawer by the stove."

I walked to the cabinet next to the stove and opened the drawer.

"What's your bra doing here?"

Bunched up between the garlic press and the chicken shears was one of Lada's military-grade brassieres. I lifted the white nylon bra out with two fingers. Lada gaped at the dangling DD cups, and her expression darkened.

"I've been looking for that! Someone put that in there. Someone is playing tricks," she said angrily.

Someone.

She grabbed the bra out of my hand, shoved it in the pocket of her sweater and sat back down in a huff.

"What if you'd put it in the microwave, Aunt Lada? It has metal in it. You could've blown yourself up!"

There was no way around it. I'd have to talk to The Cedars about graduating her to supervised care. It would cost.

Lada muttered words I couldn't make out before she went silent, as if a storm had passed. She stood up, walked to the refrigerator, took out a jar of kosher pickles and picked up where she left off.

"Do the police think you killed them?"

"Of course not."

"Well, that's good."

She opened the jar, stuck her fingers in and eased out a big, fat pickle.

"Do they have a suspect?"

"They're working on it. I'm sure they will."

She snorted and took a big bite. "Don't count on it," she said, chewing. "They never even looked into your father's death."

"But Daddy wasn't murdered," I said gently. "He fell down the stairs in that basement apartment, remember?"

"Eat, bubbala." Lada offered me the jar. "They're delicious. Kosher." I shook my head. She shrugged.

"I think someone maybe pushed him," she said.

"What?"

This level of delusion was new and worrying. No one pushed him. I'll never forget that day. I was working at *New York Spy* when I got the call from my father's landlord, who lived upstairs from him. He told me he had seen my dad come in with groceries. Seconds later, he heard the tumble and shout. He rushed down to help, but death was instant. A broken neck. My chin trembled for a second thinking of it.

"They should have investigated," Lada said.

I wasn't sure how to respond in a way that wouldn't agitate Lada further. Should I challenge her? Ignore her? If she could think logically enough to play gin rummy, she couldn't be *that* far gone. Maybe it made sense to explore her fantasy first, and then appeal to her powers of reason.

"Who would kill him, Aunt Lada? Who do you think would do that?"

"The men he stole from. The mobsters."

"But he paid them back. You know that. That's why he lived in a basement. He was broke. He had nothing."

"What if they killed him anyway? To pay *him* back."

"That didn't happen."

"That's what some people are like, you know. Some people never forgive a betrayal."

A tall, brown metal dumpster sat at the back of the main building near the health clinic service entrance. Filled with God knows what. Ensure cans. AARP magazines. Empty pill bottles. I set the cardboard box on the ground, opened the top and stared inside at our wedding invitation and wedding photos, and the framed pressed daisy from my bouquet. For a second, I saw Hugh at the reception, laughing as friends lifted my chair into the air and the white satin train of my wedding gown covered their heads. I heard my father's sad refrain.

Here's a big tip, kiddo. A tip for living. This world is rough. It's going to keep throwing things at you.

I should have done this a long time ago. I reached into the box and began hurling the wedding mementos over the high brown wall. Then I tossed in the pictures from our summer vacations to Maine and Nova Scotia, winter escapes to Mustique, art jaunts to Europe for Hugh's exhibitions. I crumpled a paper napkin from Harry's Bar in Venice and lobbed it in along with a book of matches from our Valentine's dinner at Les Halles. I was ruthless, scrapping the tinfoil ring Hugh made me that summer in the Pequod barn. If the police saw me doing this, they'd think I was acting out of anger. But that wasn't the case. The past was just too painful to hold on to any longer.

Don't let them break your heart.

I picked up the final item: an eight-and-a-half-by-eleven spiral notebook. On its cover was a photo of Carrie Fisher as Princess Leia wearing her bikini slave outfit. It was the kind of notebook an adolescent boy might buy from a Walgreens drugstore stationery section.

Hugh occasionally used cheap books like this to sketch out ideas when he began a series. He said their tackiness helped him feel free to play around. Some covers featured pop music figures: The Jackson Five, Madonna, Ringo. He also had a Ronald McDonald and an Indiana Jones. All in all, I'd say Hugh filled about ten of them, and he never showed the notebooks to anyone. Except me. "They're a little like diaries," he said. Carrie Fisher contained sketches for a series he called *Loving Nora*.

I wondered if Hugh had shown the books to Helene? Had he made one for the series he painted of her?

The sketchbook I gave you on your twenty-eighth birthday is by far the best.

I remembered the price Picasso's portrait of Dora Maar fetched, and I slipped the notebook into my shoulder bag. I couldn't bring myself to trash it.

From the *Pequod Courier*

Letters to the Editor

Dear Editor,

This paper's push to reduce the Pequod Police Department's budget and earmark those funds for bike paths and solar street lighting is nothing but a politicized press pandering to liberals and jeopardizing public safety. The double homicide committed at Pequod Point this week is proof positive that our citizens need more protection, not less. Unless you want to start seeing vigilante groups patrolling the streets of Pequod, I strongly suggest that the *Courier* change its position.

Sincerely,
Mona Slattery

Pequod Citizens Oversight Committee

Chapter Twelve

"Pow!"

For a second, he looked stunned. Then he jerked violently backward. Struggling to stay upright, he lost the fight and fell at my feet. After a few whimpers, he closed his brown, almond-shaped eyes, went limp and lay still as a stuffed toy. One dead dog.

"Attennn . . . shun!"

The spunky Jack Russell snapped to life and sat up on his haunches. Lifting his left paw to his spotted white muzzle, he gave a snappy salute.

"At ease, Serpico."

Tail in full wag, Serpico jumped up and bounded toward the Barcalounger for a pat from his master before prancing back to me on the couch.

"I'm so impressed with you, Serpico!" I said, scratching behind his perky, triangular ears.

I was also impressed with the robust, sandy-haired young man sitting in front of me, glowing like a proud papa. Eric Warschuk had changed radically since I'd come to interview him six months ago, the day his pup arrived.

"He's pretty great, huh?" he said, grinning.

Back then, the twenty-four-year-old former marine lance corporal was dangerously underweight and couldn't look me in the eye. Afghanistan's goodbye present to him the month before his tour of duty ended was an IED that blew his left leg off below the knee. Since coming home, he'd moved in with his mother, a school bus driver and single mom. He'd been depressed, unemployed and in counseling for PTSD. Melanie Warschuk had learned about the *Canines for Heroes* program and encouraged Eric to adopt one of their rescues—dogs that had been mistreated and needed a loving home. A Jack Russell was an unusual candidate for a vet service dog. Typically, they were larger breeds like German shepherds and Labs, but this one had excelled in his training. He had the heart of a Saint Bernard.

During those first hours with the adorable new pooch, Eric had seemed lethargic. He'd answered me in monosyllables. But he'd transformed since then and become positively chatty. Before aiming his pistol finger at Serpico, triggering the dramatic death scene I'd just witnessed, he'd made me coffee and talked my ear off about the great girl he just asked on a date and about his new dog-training business. He said Serpico was responsible for it all. I wrote down his quote in my black-and-white composition book—I always bring it along for notes when I'm on a story: "There are triggers: a noise, a smell or the way the light looks. They blast me back to that road outside Kandahar. Serpico knows what's going on. He comes over and licks my face. He snaps me out of it, fast. I named him Serpico because he's got my back. The little guy saves my life every day."

I moved from scratching Serpico's ears to rubbing his tummy. Maybe I needed to adopt a Serpico to bring me out of my black moods? We could take care of each other. Instead of searching for my life's meaning, I could create meaning by loving a dog.

"You seem like a nice lady," Eric said.

I looked up at him, perplexed.

"I saw you on the news." He shook his head. "It must be tough for you. Man, the killers are everywhere. You don't have to go to Kabul."

I sensed the interviewee was about to become the interviewer. I stopped rubbing Serpico, stood up and extended a hand.

"Thanks for your time today, Eric. I'll let you know when we're going to run the story."

Serpico rolled onto his back and started singing high notes. He was begging me for another belly scratch. I bent over and gave him a few parting strokes.

"She didn't like dogs," Eric said.

"Who?"

"Helene Walker. She was mean to him." He nodded toward Serpico. I hesitated, and then sat back down.

"You knew her?"

"No."

"I don't understand."

"I still have a tough time sleeping some nights, so I hang out at the Thunder Bar and watch the bowlers. I used to get loaded before I found Serpico. Now I bring him along and nurse a few Cokes. He's like my AA sponsor."

The dog pawed me for more tummy action. I pulled him onto my lap and obliged.

"Anyway, it was late—the place was empty. This was back in early September, around Labor Day, I think. Stokes was closing out the register. I'd just paid my check and was about to go home when Helene Walker showed up. She told Stokes she thought she'd left her favorite scarf there a few days before, when she'd come in for a drink. She asked if he remembered her, if he'd found it. Funny time to look for your scarf, I thought. While Stokes went to check the lost and found, Serpico trotted over and gave her leg a sniff. She kicked him off."

"That's despicable."

"I told her that if she were a man, she'd be eating my fist. She apologized, but I could tell she didn't mean it. She was only saying she was sorry because she didn't want a scene in front of Stokes."

I held Serpico closer and kept stroking his belly to make up for the meanness done to him.

"You know something? After a tour in Afghanistan, you get pretty good at reading when people are hiding things."

"You're saying what?"

"I saw her at the Thunder Bar a couple of times after that. She was always alone and dressed pretty hot. I usually went home before she did. I don't know how long she stayed, if you know what I mean."

"You mean you think Helene . . . and Stokes?"

"I was there last week when she came in again—this time to bowl with your ex for his birthday. They were with another couple. Arty types. The four of them got pretty smashed and were doing stuff like bowling on one leg, bowling backward. Real ass clowns. Some major vibes went down between her and Stokes then, too."

"You're sure it was Hugh Walker?" I shook my head in disbelief. "Hugh Walker would not be having a bowling party on his birthday."

I'd always organized Hugh's birthday dinners at chic restaurants in New York like Odeon or Orso—his favorites. Or catered parties at the loft. We spent weeks fussing over the guest list. But in fact, the timing was right—Hugh's birthday was November tenth. Had Hugh changed that much? Or maybe this is what he'd always preferred and I never knew it? Or him.

"You sound upset. I'm sorry. Maybe I shouldn't be telling you this," Eric said.

"No. No. Go ahead."

"Trust me, it was definitely the Walkers. Serpico and I were sitting at a table in the corner. About a half hour into the party, Helene came up to the bar. She told Stokes they wanted more peanuts. Stokes was filling the bowl, but he kept looking at her while she leaned on the bar and took her index finger and kind of . . . kind of sucked on it. When he gave her the peanuts, she kind of angled herself so her people couldn't see. She leaned across even more and moved his hand to touch her, you know . . . there." Eric pointed to my right breast. "Your ex definitely knew something was up. He kept looking over. She giggled and went back to the bowling party and sat in his lap."

Helene's affair with Stokes could explain why she'd started staying out here during the week in the off-season: more playtimes for her if Hugh was working at his studio in New York. I wondered what she did with Callie on those nights. She must've hired a babysitter.

"Her husband, I mean your ex, kept calling out to Stokes after that: 'Hey, kid! We need some more beer!' 'What about another pizza over here, buddy!' 'The pizza's cold! How about you heat it up?' Whenever Stokes showed up with the goods, Mr. Walker made it a point to grab his wife's ass or make out with her. Humiliation, man. It's the thing men fear most. Really fucks them up. Look at the Afghans."

"Serves him right," I muttered as Serpico rolled out from under my hand, sat up and began to study me with his head tilted to one side. Suddenly he jumped up on my chest and began licking my face.

"Okay, okay!"

"See? Serpico knows. He knows when you're in a bad place."

◆ ◆ ◆

As I walked into the dark evening outside the Warschuks' house and hugged myself in the nippy air, my foot sank into the mushy remains of the smashed, rotting Halloween pumpkin in the driveway.

"Shit."

I wiped off my shoe on the frosty lawn. Helene and Hugh's behavior at the bowling alley seemed just as slimy. The incident Eric Warschuk described was completely at odds with the perfect couple in those press photos, and with the affection they showed when I spied on them. It contradicted Sue Mickelson's TV comments about Hugh and Helene being so in love. Given the story I'd just heard, could it be that the Walkers' marriage was rife with betrayal and contempt? Along with a pinch of sadomasochism?

On the drive home, I reviewed Stokes's behavior on the morning of the murders. He'd hesitated before entering the crime scene, and ultimately avoided it completely by leaving with me. He'd sat right there in the passenger seat of my car, cold-eyed and angry, describing the corpses of his in-laws. What was it he'd said about Helene and Hugh? "I'd want anyone who screwed me over like that to be fucking dead." He must've been enraged at how they used him to spice up their marriage. How they played him in their sick little game. But was he capable of murder? And clever enough to set me up to take the blame in his place? He'd pretended he didn't even know that I'd been married to Hugh. But I felt sure Helene would certainly have told him, if they were seeing each other.

If I hadn't been so wrapped up in these thoughts, the bright, UFO-like glow coming from the vicinity of the Coop would have registered sooner. I might have figured out what was causing it and had more time to prepare. But I was only a few hundred feet from my driveway when I saw that the place was lit up like a movie set with half a dozen blazing spotlights aimed at both the Coop and lawn. It looked like every light inside had been turned on. A cop with a flashlight stood on a ladder checking the gutters. Two cops with rakes combed the grounds. The Coop's front door was wide open.

This game had just changed. My jaw muscles clenched and my insides swirled. I had the impulse to turn the car around, but I knew I had to pull it together and go in there. I reached for the phone in my purse to call Gubbins as I steered into the driveway, searching with one hand while maneuvering around the county police squad cars and vans. A stocky female officer tapped my hood and signaled to stop and roll the window down.

"Leave the keys in the ignition and step out of the vehicle, please."

"What's going on?" I asked, feigning indignation.

"Just put your hands where I can see them and follow my instructions."

"But—"

"Now."

I dropped the phone back into my bag, turned off the engine and opened the car door. "Can I bring my purse?"

She eyed it and nodded.

"Who's in charge here?" I asked, stepping out.

Before she could answer, I saw a cop in my living room through the open front door. He was dropping my MacBook into a heavy-gauge plastic bag.

"Hey! They can't take my computer! My whole life is on there."

Instinctively, I tried to duck the female officer's outstretched arm and run toward the house. But she put a firm hand on my chest.

"Let's go in together calmly, shall we?"

I took a big swallow of air, nodded and straightened up as another officer aimed a spotlight at my car. I stood in its glare, momentarily paralyzed, until my chaperone ushered me along. When we reached the doorway, I hesitated again, disoriented by what I saw. The officer nudged me forward.

"Step inside, please."

I wobbled and held on to the doorframe as I stared.

My living room looked like it was being organized for a moving-day tag sale. The kilim lay rolled up against a wall. The furniture had been pushed to the room's center and the cushions removed from the couch and chairs. Their blue-and-white mattress ticking covers sat in a pile on the rocker. Bookshelves stood empty, hardcovers and paperbacks stacked on the floor. The holiday cards sent by charities I intended to make small donations to had been removed from my desk drawer and laid out on the coffee table along with my bank statements, notepads, old postcards and an assemblage of miscellaneous writing instruments and keys. My father remained upright in his frame on my desktop, surveying the goods.

The cop who'd bagged the computer knelt at the woodstove, sifting through the dead ashes with a poker. What the hell was he looking for in there? I glanced down and spied *Moby Dick* on top of a book pile just as my own personal Ahab came out of the kitchen. He was wearing another one of his tweedy jackets along with blue plastic gloves.

"I'll take the purse over here," Roche said.

The female officer began to lift the shoulder bag off my arm. I started to grab it.

"Hey!"

"You're not going to be trouble now," she warned.

I released the bag, took a breath and gathered my wits. It was best to stay cool and address Roche as a professional doing his job.

"I assume you have a warrant," I said.

"Right here."

Roche pulled some folded papers out of his jacket pocket as the officer delivered the purse. "Permission to search your premises and personal property, including your electronic equipment and car."

"You're wasting time and taxpayer money. You won't find anything, because I didn't kill anyone," I said, trying to sound confident.

"Then you have nothing to worry about," he said, and walked back into the kitchen with the leather bag slung over his arm.

Making my way around the displaced furniture, I followed. I saw him set my purse down on the kitchen table. Then he reached inside, pulled out my cell and began to bag it. My cool demeanor collapsed.

"No, please," I pleaded. "You can't take that. I don't have a landline. I won't have a phone."

"I'm sorry. That's unfortunate."

"I'm entitled to call my lawyer."

"You'll be able to do that very soon."

He lifted out the composition notebook next. Had I written anything incriminating? I couldn't think fast enough.

162

"You shouldn't look in there."

He paused and studied my face. "Really? And why not?"

"Those are story notes for an article I'm writing. They're confidential. If you read them, you'll be violating the journalist shield laws."

"Sounds juicy."

He thumbed through the comp book while I glanced anxiously around the kitchen. The cabinet doors were ajar. Cereal and pasta boxes lined up on the counter next to the mail, which was laid out for inspection. Envelopes had been ripped open, their contents obviously read.

"Enjoy messing with cops?" Roche asked as he closed the comp book.

"What?"

"Vive la Resistance. The speed traps."

I swallowed nervously. "It was a joke."

"Huh."

Seemingly satisfied that there was nothing of interest to him in the notes, Roche set the book down on the kitchen table. He reached into the purse again and found the Princess Leia sketchbook. My pulse rate spiked. How would carrying around Hugh's naked sketches of me look to the police? I had to think of something . . .

"More notes. For an article on women's changing hairstyles," I said.

He seemed intrigued and was about to look further when Sgt. Klish walked in. Klish carried a pair of my black jeans in one of his gloved hands. In the other he held up a faded, wrinkled slip of paper.

"Pay dirt," he said. "I found her jeans in the dryer. There was a receipt in the back pocket from Mao's Take-Out. It went through the wash, but you can still see the date and time. Saturday night. She washed them Saturday night."

I didn't remember washing my jeans. I must have done that when . . . Oh God. My knees began to buckle. I thought I was going to be sick.

"Well, well," Roche said, smiling. "Bag them both and get the jeans to the lab."

He set Princess Leia down on the table. Then he reached into his jacket and offered me his phone.

"You can make that call to your lawyer now if you like."

Chapter Thirteen

It was almost eight o'clock by the time the police left the Coop. Gubbins had agreed to wait at his office. I drove down Crooked Beach Road toward town, pushing the speed limit, anxious to see him.

"In six hundred feet, your destination will be on the right," Madame GPS said. "In six hundred feet, your destination will be on the right."

"That's in the middle of the fucking trees, you idiot," I said.

As I reached the darkest, most deserted stretch, the lights seemed to come out of nowhere. Intense white flashes in my rearview mirror. I squinted. Whoever was driving hadn't realized they still had their high beams on. Annoying. The vehicle continued to gain ground until my Toyota flooded with light. I slumped down to keep the glare from the mirror out of my eyes.

"Come on, buddy. Turn your brights off."

The lights were inescapable and they were blinding. Slowing, I steered toward the shoulder to give the driver room to pass, but another car appeared in the oncoming lane. I tried again, moving from the road toward the shoulder, but the same scenario repeated. Oncoming car. No passing.

"You have reached your destination. You have reached your destination."

The tailgater hovered alarmingly close as we neared the bridge. I gripped the steering wheel, unnerved.

"*What* is your problem?"

Crossing the bridge, the vehicle hung back a bit. I breathed easier. But as I turned onto Pequod Avenue heading into town, it followed. When I reached the *Courier* building and pulled over, I could finally see the beat-up black van speed by. It looked like the driver was male. Was he a cop working an unmarked police tail? Did he need to brush up on his surveillance skills, or was he intentionally trying to intimidate me? Or was the driver simply a jerk? I couldn't tell. The ordinary could appear ominous in my state.

Gubbins buzzed me into his office. His staff had already left. We met in an empty reception room.

"Thanks for staying," I said, still jangled. I was desperate for him to stop the runaway train that my life had become. I didn't care anymore that he had Dr. Spock hair, a shiny suit and an unctuous manner. I really did need a lawyer, and Gubbins was the best choice for now.

"The police took my place apart. I had to get out of there, at least for a while. They went through everything. They took my phone and computer—and my jeans."

Gubbins's brow furrowed.

"Your jeans?"

I swallowed. "Yes. From the wash."

Even if I had been sleepwalking the night of the murders, that didn't necessarily mean I'd killed anyone. Right? Doing laundry wasn't a crime.

"I'm sorry the police were so disruptive. Would you like to stay at The Pequod Inn tonight? I could give them a call."

A pricey tourist draw, the only hotel within town limits was a historic site—a former whaling captain's home. I couldn't afford the $300 they'd charge.

"No, thanks. I'll manage. But look," I began pacing, "they're clearly more interested in me than you thought. What I can't figure out is why they came and took my place apart but didn't arrest me? Not that I want to go to jail, but what's going on?" I stopped in front of Gubbins and clasped my hands on my chin to keep from wobbling like a bobblehead doll. "If this is some kind of mind game, it's working."

"Try to calm down. The judge must've decided that they only had probable cause for a property search at this point. If they'd found the murder weapon in your possession or evidence that placed you at the crime scene, that would justify an arrest warrant."

I knew that. I wasn't thinking straight. I took a deep breath, closed my eyes for a second and tried to slow my racing thoughts.

"Listen, I have another idea about who the murderer could be. I didn't tell Roche. He'd assume I was trying to take the heat off myself."

I was desperate to share my suspicions with Gubbins and have him use his resources to make the case. He might have an investigator on his staff who could check Stokes out. Someone shrewd, like Paul Drake, the PI on *Perry Mason*. I'd come across DVDs of the 1950s TV series at the library. Mason was an imposing criminal lawyer with a baritone voice. Both men wore suits with quarterback shoulder pads. They always uncovered the truth and sent the right party to jail.

"You're shaken up. Let's get you settled first," Gubbins said, leading the way into his inner offices.

We entered an impressive conference room. Gubbins waved me toward one of the six red-leather swivel chairs surrounding a large glass table. His decor was more sophisticated than I expected: modern Italian-looking furniture, George Nelson lamps. I zeroed in on the espresso machine on his granite-topped bar. It had been a very long, draining day, and my head felt like it was stuffed with cotton balls. Mental clarity was imperative if I was going to set out my theory for him.

"You know, I could really use a cup of coffee. Would you mind very much?"

"It would be my pleasure to fix you one," he said.

While Gubbins popped off a pod of Arpeggio, I walked over to the front windows and parted the gray silk drapes. Corwin's Market had closed a few minutes earlier, but the inside lights were still on—I could read the **ORDER YOUR THANKSGIVING TURKEY NOW** sign above the entrance. The manager was doing his usual slapstick routine of collecting shopping carts from the sidewalk and struggling to fit them together while they rolled back toward the curb.

Further down Pequod Avenue, a young woman carried a laundry bag out of the Laundromat. The rest of the stores visible from here were already dark, most of the parking spaces empty. There was no sign of the black van.

"What are you looking for out there?" Gubbins asked.

Once again, my lawyer had shown himself to be astute.

"The van that was tailgating me before," I said, returning to sit at the conference table. "It's gone. For a minute, I thought it might be a cop keeping an eye on me. But I'm pretty sure I was just paranoid. I've been looking through a dark lens lately. It was some guy in a hurry."

Gubbins frowned. "Tell me if he shows up again."

He rubbed a twist of lemon on the rim and set the tiny espresso cup and saucer down on the table.

"Drink this and collect your thoughts while I try Thomas O'Donnell."

"Thomas O'Donnell?"

"He's the county magistrate who issued the warrant. He can tell us what new information sparked the search—they must have something they didn't have two days ago, and we need to know what it is," he said, adding, "I'm close with his sister Mary—the state's lieutenant governor. We went to law school together."

Douglas Gubbins, man of contradictions. A small-town lawyer with a power broker's contacts.

"I missed him at the office, and he hasn't picked up his cell. He doesn't take calls once he's home. But he usually stops at the Massamat Steak and Brew first," Gubbins said. "I want to try him one more time." He checked his watch. "He should still be sober."

Seeing the expensive watch on Gubbins's wrist reminded me of the wealthy collector Hugh and I had known who dressed exclusively in tracksuits. He wore them everywhere—to openings, patron dinners, auctions. He wouldn't attend any event that enforced a strict dress code. "No matter how poorly a man dresses, you can tell how much money he has by what kind of watch and shoes he wears," Hugh had said when the collector showed up to a Christie's auction in his usual attire and purchased nearly $2 million worth of art.

Despite his cheap suit, Gubbins wore a Rolex and Ferragamo loafers. Between flashing that hundred-dollar bill at Eden's, the watch and the shoes, it looked like my country lawyer was highly successful. I just prayed he still knew his way around the county criminal court from his days at the DA's office.

"There's the phone if you need it." He indicated the slim, black cordless on a stand. "I'll be back in a couple of minutes, and then you can tell me *all* about the murderer."

What was that tone I'd just detected? Was Gubbins humoring me? I chalked it up to more paranoia.

The espresso tasted strong and smooth—just what the doctor ordered. I was tempted to phone Grace to tell her about the police search, but she'd be outraged. She'd insist I come to her place and stay the night. She and Mac would want all the details. They'd ask about Gubbins's strategy. I couldn't handle another interrogation. And I was beginning to feel discomfited at my recurring role as the needy friend.

A stack of *Time* magazines lay on the table. The cover on the top issue read "Exodus: The Refugee Crisis." It had a photo of a father carrying his child on the long and dangerous journey to a foreign land that might or might not take them in. Eager for distraction, I perused the story while I finished the coffee, but I couldn't concentrate on the words. I took the cup to the bar to rinse it. As I watched the clear water swirl down the drain, I suddenly felt guilty. Guilty about the waste. About squandering such a precious resource. There were thousands of refugees who had no access to clean drinking water. Or food and shelter, for that matter. They lived in mud and filth. I felt guilty for not helping them, for not having adopted an abused dog, for having two legs while Eric Warschuk had only one. Guilty for everything I did, didn't do, was or wasn't. Where was all this guilt coming from?

You'd think I'd killed someone.

I was jittery, on edge. I should never have had that espresso. When Gubbins opened the door, my heart jumped.

"O'Donnell didn't answer, but I managed to reach Ben. I told him to try his contact at the DA's office to find out what prompted the warrant."

I groaned. "Do we have to involve Ben?"

Gubbins gave me a questioning look. "I can assure you he doesn't mind helping, and we need every resource we have. So . . . what's this theory you've developed? We're done with Jeffrey Volani, I hope."

"We should look into Stokes Diekmann. He was sleeping with Helene."

Clearly interested, Gubbins sat down. I began to share my suspicions about Stokes, reporting on the sexual dynamics between him and Helene, as well as Hugh's response to them at the bowling alley.

"Helene was using Stokes to provoke Hugh, and I'm sure both men knew it. Eric Warschuk saw them all behaving badly at the Thunder Bar. He can confirm the affair and the tension."

Gubbins listened intently from the swivel chair next to mine, his hands in prayer position under his chin, his eyes distorted and magnified behind thick glasses. Big as fly eyes. He was quiet.

"Stokes was also on the ambulance team that was assigned to pick up the Walkers' bodies for the coroner. But he couldn't do the job. He couldn't even make himself go into the house. He abandoned his post. He was very nervous. I think he couldn't face bagging his victims' bodies. Especially in front of the police."

Gubbins was studying me closely.

"How do you know all this? Who told you?"

His speed in analyzing my "testimony" and finding the hiccup was impressive. He could go toe-to-toe with Perry Mason any day. I had to trust my lawyer and tell the truth.

"I was at Pequod Point the morning of the murders. I saw it all. I drove Stokes to work from there."

I didn't give Gubbins a chance to ask *why* I was at the crime scene. I launched into an account of the strange way Stokes had behaved in my car.

"He wanted to talk about dead bodies. His in-laws' dead bodies. They were asphyxiated by a malfunctioning boiler . . ."

"Yes. I read about that in your interview with his wife. Terrible thing. That's how the Diekmanns came into the money to buy Van Winkle Lanes. 'A dream built on tragedy,' I believe you wrote."

"You've got an amazing memory. You're right. Stokes's dream to own a bowling alley was made possible by his wife's inheritance." Oh Jesus. It hit me that Kelly was living with a likely murderer. Would he hurt her? "But listen . . ."

I began spinning the story like a Grimms' fairy tale.

"Since that car ride, I've been thinking . . . Stokes told me he was the first to find the bodies of his in-laws. In their bed. You should have heard the way he spoke about them. He hated them. Suppose he caused that carbon monoxide leak so that he and Kelly could inherit their money? Suppose he was the one who killed them? And just in case there's something he missed, he makes sure he's the first person at the scene. That gives him more control of the situation and an excuse for any of his prints, DNA, etcetera being found in the house, right?"

"Possibly."

"And now we have Hugh and Helene, another couple that Stokes knew. They were also found dead in bed. Coincidence? Or did Stokes kill again? He was Helene's spurned lover. He had two motives: jealousy and humiliation. I'm sure he hated the Walkers. He could have murdered Hugh and Helene. He could be framing me for it. And now Kelly could be in danger."

Gubbins nodded solemnly. "So you went to Pequod Point. Why?"

"Wait. What do you think of my Stokes theory?"

"I'd like to know why you went to Pequod Point."

I felt myself squirming under Gubbins's gaze. "I was curious, I guess."

"Curious."

"Yes."

"Remember, I'm on your team, Ms. Glasser."

I sighed. "Okay. All right." I stood up and walked to the bar, then turned around and faced him reluctantly. "You might not believe this, but I really don't know why I went. I wasn't thinking straight. I was upset when I heard about the murders. I couldn't accept what had happened. I guess I needed to make it real."

Gubbins nodded. "That makes more sense."

"The point is, Stokes was acting guilty about something that morning. He wouldn't go into Hugh and Helene's house. He left the scene. He was talking about seeing dead bodies. He seemed haunted by them. Crazed, in fact."

Gubbins adjusted his glasses. He didn't speak.

"Well? What do you think?" I pressed.

"It's clear you're a writer," Gubbins said, leaning back in his chair. "There might be something to it. But we'll need a better witness to the affair than Eric Warschuk if we're going to interest the DA."

"Pardon me, but Eric Warschuk is a decorated war hero who gave his leg for his country."

"Yes. I also remember reading that a few months ago, in your article about him adopting a dog."

I was astounded. Did he have a photographic memory?

"A very moving piece. But you reported that he'd been under psychiatric treatment for post-traumatic stress disorder. As a witness, he's compromised."

"Dammit, of course." Where was my head? Cross-examination basics. I'd blown my case.

Gubbins rubbed his chin. "There may be someone else who knew about the affair . . . perhaps those people Hugh and Helene went bowling with? The 'artsy' couple?"

"Maybe. But I have no idea who they are."

Gubbins made a note. "I'll look into it. As for Kelly, I wouldn't worry. If Stokes is our man, he'd be playing nice these days so as not to attract suspicion. Now . . . you said the police took your jeans from the wash. Did you launder them the night of the murder?"

"I guess so," I said, exasperated. My jeans weren't what I wanted to focus on.

"Did the police take anything else?"

"A Chinese food receipt they found in the pocket."

"Do you remember the date on it, perchance?"

"From the same night."

Gubbins scowled and made another note.

"That confirms the jeans were laundered close to the time of the murders, which looks suspicious. They're going to test the jeans for evidence that could place you at the crime scene. Soil type, carpet fibers, etc. Washing doesn't fully eliminate all substances. Blood, for instance. Blood is very hard to eradicate completely."

I suddenly saw grisly flesh on blood-soaked sheets. I felt bile rise in my throat.

Gubbins paused, pushed his glasses further up his nose and gave me the stink eye this time. "As your lawyer, and this is important, Nora, I need to know exactly what I'll be dealing with. I can't help you if there are surprises. Are they going to find anything?"

My heart began pounding. What if I was at Pequod Point that night? If I had some kind of soil on my jeans they could trace to that area . . .

"Jesus. What do you think? Of course not. Absolutely not."

The way he stared at me while tapping his pen on the table had me worried. The fake smile that followed increased my suspicion: he didn't believe me. Did he think I might have killed them?

"All right then," he said, opening the brown leather folder in front of him. He pulled out my contract. "Now for the retainer. With this new development, discovering what triggered the search warrant will require more time . . . What if we start with say, fifteen thousand dollars, and see how far it takes us?"

I waited for him to say he was joking.

"Nora?"

"Would you consider letting me pay in installments?"

It was almost 9:45 p.m. I'd come downstairs to use the PC in the *Courier* office, peeking through the door glass first to make sure Ben wasn't working late. On top of everything, his rejection still stung. My eyes watered from the strain of reading in the dark. I'd kept the lights off. I didn't want any of the Piqued who saw me as the murder suspect ogling through the window.

Doing research on the current value of Hugh's drawings felt mercenary, but I needed to be practical. The numbers on the Artworldprices. com database were encouraging; one of the drawings had sold for

$33,000 last month. Granted, the sketches in the *Loving Nora* book were small, but now they were part of the Hugh Walker legend, and the scandal would only increase their worth. I heard that happened with Carl Andre's work. His story was legendary in the art world.

The infamous sculptor had been acquitted of killing his wife back in 1988. He claimed she was opening the oversize window in their apartment when she lost her balance and fell thirty-four floors. Andre was built like a bull. His wife weighed ninety-three pounds. When the police arrived, he had fresh scratches on his nose. *Scratches.* He was found innocent despite the incriminating marks.

Even with a discount for a quick sale, the money from selling Hugh's sketches should take care of my legal bills and Aunt Lada's expenses, plus some. The cash could save us both.

I logged off Artworldprices.com. The caffeine high had petered out, and my energy was flagging. I shut the computer, laid my head down on the desk and closed my eyes. *Just for a moment,* I thought. The smells of pencil shavings and furniture polish invoked kindergarten naps. I must've dropped off.

A faint rattling in the rear office woke me. It sounded like someone jiggling the handle on the building's back door. Or jimmying it, attempting to break in. My first thought: the rock thrower. Was that cowardly bastard back? Or was it a thief after our office computers? Then the black van flashed through my mind.

I heard the creak of the door opening and I bolted, lurching in the dark toward Ben's desk. The bat. Where was his baseball bat? I knelt down and groped. My hand found the smooth wooden knob. I grabbed it and jumped up. Gripping the neck with both hands, heart racing, I lifted the bat high over my shoulder as the lights popped on. Ben stood in the doorway of the back office, still wearing his coat, with his hand on the light switch. As our eyes met, his face flushed. Mine burned. I must be beet red.

"Nora? What the hell . . . ?"

Embarrassed, I lowered the bat.

"I thought . . . I thought you were a robber. Or the rock thrower, breaking in to smash up the office. I didn't hear your motorcycle."

"I got my car back this morning. Sorry. I wasn't expecting to find anyone." He pointed to the Pequod Liquor box by my left foot. "I came for my wine. I bought a case to have around for the holidays and keep forgetting to take it home." He checked his watch. "What are you doing here this time of night?"

"I was checking my e-mail. The police took my computer. And my phone."

"Right." Ben looked at his shoes. "I heard."

Long silence. I wanted to crawl under the desk. Being around Ben felt even more awkward than I feared. Should I say something? Suggest that we forget the kissing incident? Chalk it up to the heightened drama of the day? I leaned the bat against the wall.

"Well, it's late. I suppose I'll be on my way." I squirmed. My nervousness had me sounding so phony.

Ben raised both palms, beseeching.

"Nora. Please. I have to apologize. It won't happen again, believe me. I had no right to do what I did. I crossed the line. It was unethical. It was a Clarence Thomas move—an abuse of power and against everything I stand for. When you didn't respond, I understood what an unfair position I'd put you in. I'm sorry."

How could he think I didn't respond? Was I that rusty? I really went for that kiss, but he thought I was a cold fish.

"Is there any way you can forget what I said in my voice mails?" he went on.

"Voice mails? I didn't get any voice mails from you."

"I left you three messages since yesterday morning."

"No. There were messages from Grace and my aunt. And from Lizzie and Gubbins. The rest were from 'unknown callers.' Probably tabloids. I didn't even listen. I erased them."

Ben looked puzzled for a moment. "Wait. I called you from home . . . I just got a new Internet phone." His whole body seemed to relax. "Your cell wouldn't have recognized the number."

Wait. Ben was the unknown caller? He'd really tried to reach me?

He moved out of the doorway, sat down on the edge of his desk and smiled. "You weren't avoiding me."

I shook my head. "No."

He'd been worried that I hadn't wanted to connect. Concerned he'd offended me. I realized I was smiling, too.

"I was afraid you were going to quit," he said.

He was *really* worried. I'd had it all wrong. I felt sorry I'd misjudged him.

The phone in his pocket rang.

"Hold on."

He took out his BlackBerry, glanced at the number and lifted an index finger.

"It's my guy," he said, putting the phone to his ear. "Wickstein here." He grabbed a pen off his desk. "Okay. Go ahead." He jotted notes on the back of an envelope. "Autopsy confirms both deaths caused by single .22-caliber GSW to the head."

I winced. He stopped writing and listened, his face darkening.

"Say that part again." He wrote some more. "Uh-huh. Huh . . ." He looked at me, expressionless. "Anything else?" He put the pen down and continued listening for another excruciating minute. "Thanks. I owe you." He hung up and frowned.

"What?"

"Three factors triggered the warrant."

"Three factors."

"One, the FBI report came in."

"FBI? When did the FBI get involved in this?"

"The county uses the fed's profiler on multiple murders." He read from his envelope: "Crime scene of a disorganized type. Consistent with a killer who has been rejected or humiliated."

"But that fits him." My heart sped up. "It fits him exactly."

"Who?"

"Stokes Diekmann. He was sleeping with Helene. And she dumped him."

Ben crossed his arms. "Really. I would never have called that one."

"I have it from a reliable source. Kind of."

"That's valuable information. He's worth checking out."

He left the desk and walked toward me, stopping inches away. He looked me square in the eyes.

"The profile also fits you."

I blinked nervously. I knew that too well. But I balked at the idea that Ben might suspect me. He didn't even know about my sleepwalking.

"True, but . . ."

"Number two: the DA has an incriminating document that your ex-husband kept."

"What?" I stepped back, alarmed. "What kind of document?"

"On the advice of his lawyer, Hugh kept a diary during the period you two were divorcing."

"No." I was incredulous. "He did not."

"In case things got out of hand, which they apparently did, once. He made reference to you trying to stab his painting. The same painting I told you was slashed at the crime scene. Somehow you never mentioned that."

"Shit." I looked away.

"And you cut him."

I turned back and faced Ben. "Believe me, that was an accident."

He nodded. "The third factor is a witness who can place you at the crime scene shortly after the murders."

"Let me guess . . ." I swallowed hard, my throat tightening. "Stokes Diekmann."

◆　◆　◆

Ben poured some Beaujolais Nouveau into the two mugs on his desk and offered me one. I took it, gulped half of it down and continued pacing the room like a big cat in a small cage. Wide-awake now, I ran my story by him, including my encounter with Stokes at Pequod Point and my suspicions about the deaths of Stokes's in-laws.

"I think Stokes is a vengeful guy. He must've despised the Walkers. Helene used him. She cock-teased him in front of Hugh. Hugh turned around and humiliated him in front of her and their friends. I think Stokes killed the Walkers and arranged the evidence to frame me, just like you said. Then, to make sure everything is buttoned up, he goes to the police and tells them I was at Pequod Point that morning. I'm really worried about Kelly. How can she be safe with him?"

"Stokes didn't go to the police. They went to him."

I stopped pacing.

"They're interviewing everyone who might have had regular contact with Helene and/or Hugh. That includes your Pilates crew, Kelly and Stokes—he'd have been at the alley on occasion when your class was held, correct?"

"Yes."

"Stokes told the police he found you . . ." Ben checked his notes. "The way he put it was that he found you 'crawling around the crime scene.' Is he lying?"

"No." I looked down and fidgeted with the mug handle.

"Why didn't you tell me you were there? You've done a lot of evading, Nora. Pretending you didn't know the painting had been stabbed. Leaving this little adventure out."

It pained me to ask. "Do you actually think I'm guilty, Ben?"

I wanted him to believe in my innocence, even if I had doubts.

"Of course not. I'd just like to know why you didn't tell me."

Relieved, I turned away and put the mug on my desk, suddenly finding the stains on the wood very compelling. I ran my finger over them. It was scary to feel this vulnerable with him.

"I was embarrassed," I said finally.

I could feel Ben watching me for a few moments before he spoke. He cleared his throat.

"At the beginning, I used to go to the cemetery every day before and after work. In my head, I knew Judy was dead, but I couldn't make it feel real. I had to sit there on the ground next to her gravestone every day, twice a day, so it would sink in. I never told anyone."

I stilled my hand and looked up at him.

"Maybe it was something like that for you," he said. He was looking at me expectantly, his soulful brown eyes asking for confirmation.

"That must've been it," I said.

I didn't mention that I also spied on Hugh and Helene while they were alive, and that if my eyes had been lasers, I might have happily incinerated them.

"Understandable." He nodded. "Don't be hard on yourself." He picked up his BlackBerry and made a note. "I'll reach out to the editor at the *Catskill News* and ask to review the material on Kelly's parents' deaths—to see if there was even a whiff of foul play. And I don't think we should worry about Kelly, in any case. If it's Stokes, he'd be playing it cool right now with the police looking around here so closely."

"That's what Gubbins said. I guess it makes sense." I walked over to his desk tentatively. "Checking out the Catskill story would be really helpful. I appreciate it." Did I really want to pursue this?

"Ben?"

"Yes."

"What did they say?"

"Who?"

"The voice mails."

He stared down into his mug of wine like it was an oracle that would tell him his fate. Then he set it aside and met my gaze. I felt my whole body quake.

"You're sure you want to know?"

I nodded.

"The first one said I couldn't get you out of my head."

I suppressed a slight moan. So, it was the same for both of us. The kiss meant something.

"The second said I was sorry if I shocked you, but I'd been attracted to you since you first walked into the office. Then when I heard that you might be in trouble . . . well, I realized it was more than attraction. I realized how much I cared. 'What the hell are you waiting for, Ben?' I asked myself. 'Let her know how you feel.'" He paused.

Yes, please. Don't stop. Tell me how you feel.

"And the third said I was having a big problem."

My face fell. "Oh."

"I asked for your help," he said.

"With what?"

"Figuring out how to get to know you better. After all this time, it's not the easiest thing for me . . ." He trailed off.

I stepped closer to him. I could feel the heat from our bodies mingling. What was that scent? It was a familiar, happy smell that reminded me of going to the movies. Good & Plenty licorice candy. That was it. Ben smelled like licorice candy. I breathed him in.

"In my experience, when you're trying to solve a problem, it's best not to overthink it," I said.

"Good advice."

"You have to do something to relax your mind and then the answer appears. Or at least part of it does."

"Just like that?"

"No, like this." I leaned in and kissed him lightly on the lips.

Wave after wave broke through me. One final arch of my back and I collapsed in sweet pleasure-pain. Electric shocks were still running up and down my calves from pointing my toes like Anna Pavlova. Ben rolled off me. We were both panting.

"Now I know why the French call it a little death," I said, gazing up at the stars through the skylight over his bed. "We've definitely gone to heaven."

We turned to face each other. Ben ran his hand along the curve from my waist to my hip.

"You are beautiful," he murmured. "Let's spoon. I haven't spooned in years."

As Ben wrapped himself around me, I marveled at what a wreck we'd made of his bedroom in our deliriousness: clothing flung onto furniture and into corners, his nightstand overturned. A clear glass lamp filled with seashells had landed on his sheepskin rug—intact, at least. A watercolor of Pequod's harbor hung askew on the wall where he'd pinned me. We'd gone at each other with such hunger and abandon. I didn't know it was possible to feel this alive again. My body was tingling. Out of the deep freeze into the sun. I smiled; Ben was such a passionate man, all this time disguised as a porcupine.

Even as I was appreciating our connection, I was fighting off demons. *This can't go anywhere. This isn't good. This is the worst possible time to find passion again. I don't know if I've done something terrible or not.* I spotted a windup alarm clock lying on the floor by the glass doors to Ben's balcony. In a few hours, I'd be back to grappling with my status as a murder suspect.

"God, it's almost three o'clock in the morning," I said.

"You have somewhere to be?"

Despite my anxiety, I laughed. "No."

"Nora?"

"Uh-huh."

"Do you do this a lot?"

"You mean do I sleep around?"

"No, I . . . I'm sorry . . . it's none of my business."

"You're my first since the divorce." I groaned. "Why does that feel like I just told you I was a virgin?"

He found my hand and squeezed it. "I'm flattered."

"What about you?"

I already regretted I'd asked. The answer wouldn't feel good either way. I wanted Ben red-blooded and lusty. Thinking of him living like a monk for years would be a turnoff. It was okay for me to grow cobwebs between my legs, not him. A double standard, I knew, but that's how I felt. On the other hand, I'd hate to be merely one of a number of women he'd bedded since his wife died. No win.

"I've had a few encounters," he said. "They didn't feel like this."

"Can you define 'this'?"

My heart sped up, anticipating. He waited a good long time before he spoke.

"There was this giant door inside me and it was closed. We stood in front of it, you and me, and then we opened it together. The whole damn ocean was on the other side. We dove right in."

I felt him grow hard against the small of my back and we made love again. This time very slowly, and we stayed on the bed. We lay quietly afterward, listening to each other breathe. For a few minutes, I felt happier than I'd felt in years. And then I remembered. Watching the tiny, blinking white light of a plane make a trip across the skylight, I envied the night travelers on board. I wished with all my heart that Ben and I could be up there flying far, far away. Thousands of miles from all the trouble I was in.

"Ben, tell me this will blow over. The police will catch the killer and leave me alone."

He didn't answer. I turned to find my new lover fast asleep. *You are beautiful, too, the way the silver sprinkled along your hairline catches the light, the way your chin cleaves perfectly in two around that dimple. How could we have been just inches apart day after day without this happening earlier? Timing truly is everything, isn't it?* I closed my eyes, exhausted. I'd wake up with Ben tomorrow and he'd tell me it would all be okay. Really, how could it not be, eventually?

My hands were stinging and throbbing. The agony jerked me out of a deep sleep. Hot water scalded my fingers, and I yanked them toward me instinctively. Where was I? It was dark. Water splashed and flowed into a hot puddle around my feet. I smelled lemons. A sick, familiar feeling churned in my belly. *Holy shit. Holy fucking shit.*

Still disoriented, I stepped backward, my eyes adjusting to the low light. I saw a sink directly in front of me. Water poured from its faucet, running over the lip of the sink onto the floor. This was a kitchen. Ben's kitchen. My pulse raced as panic took hold.

I stumbled forward and shut off the water quickly. How did I get here? No. This couldn't be happening. After so many years? But the last thing I remembered was falling asleep next to Ben, and now I was naked in his kitchen washing my hands in his sink. More than washing. Scrubbing them raw. This was real. I looked from the lemon dish soap to my hands. What did this mean? the small voice in my head whispered.

Will these hands never be clean?

What?

Here's the smell of blood still.

Lady Macbeth. That was Lady Macbeth's lament.

All the perfumes of Arabia will not sweeten this little hand.

Guilty Lady Macbeth had tried to wash off blood. She and I shared an affliction. Sleepwalking.

Breathe. Breathe, dammit.

Diary entry:

After meeting with my lawyer yesterday, as per his counsel, I am keeping an official record of any aggressive actions on the part of my wife, Nora Glasser. Let me state, also for the record, that I take no pleasure in doing so. My lawyer insisted, after learning that Nora had tried to knife Self-Portrait with Pregnant Helene, and that she also sliced open my hand, accidentally, I believe. ("Mr. Walker, your career is in that hand.") Should there be any more incidents, he advises seeking a restraining order. So far this week, the only event worth noting: Nora picked up some more of her belongings from the loft. She knocked a framed photo of me off the shelf and the glass broke. Another accident, she said.

Chapter Fourteen

At least Ben hadn't woken up. He probably wouldn't think anything of the dish towels drying on the rack in the morning, or the wads of paper towels stuffed in the bin under his kitchen sink. I tried to think what to do next while I let the cool tap water run over my hands to soothe the irritated skin. There was no point in trying to go back to sleep, or even lying down next to Ben while I was vibrating like a tuning fork. And what if I did fall asleep and the same thing happened all over again? Or something even more destructive?

I had visions of a child's hand gripping a steel golf club. The hand lifting my mother's Wüsthof carving knife, its blade glinting in the moonlight. I saw the hand, now larger, wielding razor-sharp scissors and stabbing a sweatshirt. Clutching an X-ACTO knife. All the hands mine. Hands that committed angry, violent acts.

Sickening questions swirled in my head. Was I, the woman who vowed not to let her life be ruined by anger, getting a message from my unconscious that rage had triumphed? Had I been so plagued by my conscience that I'd roamed in my sleep to wash my hands of blood like Lady Macbeth? Was I sleepwalking the night Hugh and Helene were murdered? Did that blood I imagined belong to them?

I'd read the literature on sleepwalking. The morning after I'd cut the heart out of Axel Bartlett's sweatshirt, I'd rushed straight over to the lower level of Bobst Library at NYU. Hunched in a dark booth in the bowels of the enormous library building, I'd scrolled for hours through the *American Journal of Psychiatry*, *Scientific American* and scores of medical publications stored on pre-Google microfilm.

Somnambulists (the name sounded like a circus act: "Now for the flying Somnambulists, ladies and gentlemen!") almost always made their move within the first hour of sleep, before REM and dreaming kicked in. In children, the triggers might be anxiety, sleep deprivation or fatigue. The biggest physical hazards came from falling and bumping into things. Generally, child sleepwalkers grew out of the problem by age eighteen—my age at the time of that last sleepwalk. A small percentage didn't.

Adult sleepwalkers weren't just overtired, nervous pups. Sure, there were harmless, blank-stared strollers who merely wandered from room to room moving furniture, flicking a light switch or raiding the fridge for ice cream. But a good number of adult sleepwalkers had serious medical or mental disorders. They drank heavily or took medication that set off dangerous, sometimes lethal behaviors while they slept.

The legal defense term was "non-insane automatism." Defense lawyers argued that consuming alcohol and/or drugs could produce involuntary actions like "sleep driving," as in getting behind the wheel and accidentally running someone over or slamming a car into a utility pole. "Sexsomniacs" woke up screwing total strangers. And, most terrifying of all, "sleep killers" murdered unconsciously.

Was I one of them? Had I consumed too much vodka last Saturday night and gone "sleep driving" over to Pequod Point? But where would I get a gun?

There were also cases where there was no drinking or medication involved. Killers had been acquitted using a straight up "sleepwalking defense." A sleepwalking father smashed his shrieking baby against the wall: "I was sure it was a wild beast." A sleepwalking fireman beat his wife with a shovel, believing she was an intruder. One major study showed that adult sleepwalkers had difficulty handling aggression in general. Could that be me?

I'd been too horrified to deal with what I'd read back then. I hadn't even told Grace about the disturbing research I'd found. I just prayed the sleepwalking would end. She'd advised watchful waiting after the sweatshirt "heart attack," and counseling if I had another incident. Grace was an unusually light sleeper, and we agreed more nighttime activities would certainly wake her up. There were none. I calmed down, eager to believe this had been a singular event, the affliction's last gasp while I was still in my teens.

But as I shut off the water and dried my tender hands in Ben's kitchen, a high-profile case I'd read about in NYU's library haunted me.

Kenneth Parks drove to his in-laws' house in his sleep. He choked and stabbed them, killing his mother-in-law. Later, he staggered through the doors of a police station, not knowing why he came. His own wrist had been severed, but he couldn't feel the pain. He wasn't awake. Given his history of sleepwalking and the fact that he "adored his in-laws," he was acquitted.

There were sleep experts who theorized that Parks's violent act was the result of a neurological glitch, that when Parks's father-in-law discovered him sleepwalking outside the house and tried to detain him, he'd caused Parks's amygdala—his primitive brain—to kick in. Parks fought him and went on to kill his mother-in-law without (literally) blinking. Or so his lawyer argued.

Did I have that same glitch?

Get a grip, Nora. As Ben would insist: "You're a reporter. Look at the facts."

Okay. Fact: I'd never left my immediate location when I was sleepwalking. Fact: my worst offense had been cutting a hole in a sweatshirt, and tonight all I was guilty of was letting water overflow from a sink. Most important, I'd never had access to a gun, awake or asleep. The facts said "no, not possible."

But it was also a fact that I'd begun sleepwalking again. There were those jeans that I didn't remember washing the night of the murders, and those blazing lights the other morning in the Coop. And what about the scratch, the twig and the leaves? Still, none of that meant I was a murderer.

Remember: no gun, no guilt.

A chill ran through my naked body. I scurried into Ben's living room to look for my coat and spotted a fluffy mohair throw on the back of a leather armchair. I picked it up and wrapped myself in it. The soft wool felt like a warm hug, and for a moment I stopped wanting to crawl out of my skin.

Ben's apartment overlooked the harbor. Moonlight poured through the wall of windows onto two plump white couches in front of the fireplace, a piano and a plush Oriental rug. I crossed the room to the windows. Over the past few days, mariners had hauled out the last of the boats for the season. Light shimmered on the inky water all the way to the horizon under an almost full moon. An achingly romantic view for someone in the mood.

I turned away, my gaze settling on the framed photographs resting on the mantel. A picture of a young, gap-toothed Sam. He looked like his dad. Another of Ben's wife standing behind the wooden wheel of a sailboat, smiling confidently, her hair blowing in the breeze. All I knew of sailing I'd learned during a Channel Island whale-watching trip with Hugh: for seasickness, suck on gingerroot. Had Ben been comparing me to her tonight? Did I even come close to measuring up? I couldn't afford to spend any time worrying about that. I had more important things to figure out, like why this bizarre affliction had returned and how to stop it.

According to everything I'd read, muscle-paralyzing drugs were the standard treatment. A terrible idea. What if there was an emergency in the night? A fire? I'd be toast if I couldn't move. And what about needing to use the bathroom? Not a single article had offered an actual cure, though some sleep-clinic research showed promise for biofeedback techniques. I was afraid to seek help at a sleep clinic. What if Gubbins was right about the police tracking my GPS? If they discovered I went for sleepwalking treatments, they would use it against me, if not as direct evidence, then as a sign of a troubled woman with a guilty conscience.

I moved to the couch and flopped down. My head fell back onto the pillows, and I became aware of a smell almost instantly—subtle but definitely there. Cookies. Chocolate chip cookies. Where was the delicious cookie smell coming from? I sat up again. A large brown pillar candle had been placed in the center of the coffee table. I leaned over, drew it toward me and sniffed.

A chocolate chip cookie candle.

Ben had a chocolate chip cookie candle in his living room.

If I weren't so messed up, I could fall in love with a man like him.

Ben didn't budge when I tiptoed into the bedroom. Or as I gathered my clothes, or even when I accidentally tripped over the alarm clock on the floor and caused it to clang like a tricycle bell for a second or two. I envied Ben's ability to sleep soundly. He lay on his side, arms wrapped around his pillow the same way they'd embraced me. When I finished dressing, I knelt down next to the bed and watched him sleep. All traces of the ornery Ben had disappeared. His expression was sweet, the corners of his mouth turned up slightly, as if he were smiling at some happy thought. I had to fight the urge to kiss him. *He's a good man: a good father, a good friend. Loyal and true. He's lost the love of his life, and he's trying to start over. He's opening his heart to me.* But my heart wanted to run and hide. If Ben knew about the sleepwalking, how would he react?

I'd told Hugh about my distressing sleep history and its genesis: the mobsters showing up at the cinema to strong-arm my father. "That same night, I woke up wielding a golf club. The next night, a knife. I think I wanted to protect us." Ashamed of how vengeful it looked, I didn't share how I'd mutilated Axel's sweatshirt years later.

Hugh was sympathetic and reassuring—even a little intrigued. "Those bastards must've scared the hell out of you, poor kid. This explains something."

"What?"

"You've always given off a kind of dark mystery. I thought it was the Russian in you."

But Hugh had hidden his own darker feelings. That "disturbing" picture he'd painted of the "Nora beast" standing over him while he slept? The one I read about in the review of his *Scenes from a Marriage* show? That was Hugh saying, "This is my ex-wife, the repulsive sleepwalking fiend."

If Ben learned about the sleepwalking, he might also be repulsed. He might even begin to add things up differently. He could have doubts about whether the killer really did arrange a frame-up. He might suspect that I'd murdered Hugh and Helene. How could I expect him to trust me when I was having trouble trusting myself?

Ben's eyelids began to flutter. What was he dreaming? Was I in there with him? Were we opening his door to the ocean, crossing the threshold together and diving deep? I wished I could swim by his side over the coral reefs and discover fish and plants I never knew existed, explore underwater caves and ancient shipwrecks with him. I didn't want our great adventure to end before it started. But I couldn't see having a relationship until I cleared my name of suspicion.

I quietly took a pen from my purse and, fearful that tearing a page out of my comp book would be the thing that would wake him, went back to the kitchen. I returned, righted his nightstand and set my note down on top of it.

A brilliant moon lit my path. The surf slapped against the wooden pilings of the empty docks as I jogged along the edge of the water with my shoulder bag slung across my chest like a bandolier. A halyard pinged against a flagpole. Cold, salty air bit my face, drawing tears from my eyes. Tiny daggers of ice stabbed my lungs. I was headed for the *Courier*. We'd driven to Ben's apartment in his car, and mine was still parked in front of the office. Though blood drummed in my ears and my chest wheezed, I kept moving through the frigid early morning. In a little more than an hour, it would be light, and I'd meet up with Grace at Van Winkle Lanes. I'd tell her everything. She would have some idea of what to do. She always did.

Soon I was making the left on Pequod Avenue and heading toward the golden glow of one of Pequod's solar streetlights. I stopped short when I saw him. He stood a few yards ahead of me under the canopy of the Pequod Bookstore, nibbling on the ornamental cabbage in the window box. A white-tailed buck. Noble, elegant tines sprouted upward on either side of his head. His ears twitched and he lifted his snout. He turned and stared at me, still chewing the cabbage leaves. Daring me to do something about it.

He was fearless, confident. I'd need more of his moxie to deal with what lay ahead.

From the *Pequod Courier*

Letters to the Editor

Dear Editor,

The Point Killer isn't the only one getting away with murder in Pequod. What about that new traffic camera on the signal by the expressway exit? The county sent me a $100 ticket for running the red light there last week. I did not run the light. But they have "photographic evidence." I don't know how they've rigged this one, but I'm not the only resident it's happened to. I demand an investigation.

Nick Lyons

12 Conklin Street

Pequod

Chapter Fifteen

I heard the tires screech before I saw anything.

"What the hell?"

The black van peeled around the bowling alley's back corner as I turned into the Van Winkle Lanes parking lot. I braked hard and sent the thermos of coffee rolling off the passenger seat. The van careened onto Old Route 20 and sped away with its engine roaring and gray-blue smoke trailing out its tailpipe. Shaken, I parked near the darkened Van Winkle Lanes sign. That made the second van sighting in less than ten hours. Clearly, the driver wasn't following me this time. But this guy was dangerous. Reckless. Why was he always in such a rush?

I'd managed to read the faded logo on the van's dented side panel: MASSAMAT DIRT BUSTERS: WE GET YOU CLEAN. It was possible the driver worked as a janitor here. I'd ask Kelly about it when she came in.

I leaned over to retrieve the thermos on the floor under the passenger seat, and as I straightened up, I noticed the tip of Kelly's blue Mini parked at the rear of the building. The dash clock said 7:13 a.m.—way too early for Kelly. She usually arrived five minutes before class to let us in. My breath caught in my chest. Something wasn't right . . . the way that van came racing out of the lot. I turned off the engine and, with a growing sense of foreboding, went to check.

Music seeped out of the rear of the building. Amy Winehouse's smoky, muffled voice. The metal door to the Thunder Bar was unlocked.

I cautiously pulled it open and entered. Inside, the music was set at CIA-torture level, and it blasted my ears. The strong stench of ammonia stung my nostrils. I ran my hand over the wall for a light switch, found one and flicked it on, but nothing happened. The faint glow from the crack at the entrance door's bottom was all I was going to get.

"Kelly?" I yelled.

Pointless. How could anyone hear over the din? I stuck my fingers in my ears and, hugging the wall, made my way down the hall in the dark while the pounding bass line pulsed under my skin.

The only light in the Thunder Bar shone from a single hanging fixture with a stained-glass shade. Behind the bar, a mirrored wall reflected some of the glow into the wood-paneled lounge area. The bowling lanes that filled the rest of the vast, hollow space were hidden in darkness. A quick survey revealed a closed cash register, clean glasses stacked on the counter and liquor bottles displayed in orderly rows on the shelves. Aside from the overly loud music, nothing was amiss. But where was Kelly? I located the stereo in a cabinet next to the minifridge and turned it off. Blessed silence. Then, from the back corner—a faint whimpering.

"Kelly?"

The whimpers turned into soul-wrenching sobs. They were coming from the cluster of wooden café tables at the rear of the Thunder Bar. Shadows obscured the farthest ones. I found another light switch and flipped it. In the back corner, a shapely calf dangled off the red vinyl banquette.

"Kelly!"

I rushed out from behind the bar and ran to her. She lay sprawled on the banquette, wearing purple spandex shorts and a matching purple sweatshirt. The shirt was hiked up, exposing her bulging tummy and its huge belly button, which looked like tortellini. Her pink down jacket was bunched around her head as if someone had tried to smother her with it.

"Are you all right?"

A barely audible voice croaked from under the pink puff.

"He hurt me, Nora." Her body heaved with more sobs. "He hurt me and my baby."

"Oh my God." My hand flew to my mouth. I scanned quickly for blood but didn't see any. "Don't move. I'll call for an ambulance." Panicky, I reached for my cell and remembered I didn't have one. "Where's your phone?"

Kelly slowly pulled herself up to sitting. The jacket fell away from her head to reveal a tangled ponytail sticking out over her ear. Her eyes were bloodshot from crying.

"I'm okay. I don't need an ambulance."

"You do. You're hurt. I need your phone." She might be numb with adrenaline. How to convince her? "Even if you feel okay, we want to check the baby."

"He didn't hurt me physically."

"You're sure?" I ran my eyes over her again for any signs of bruising. She nodded.

"Thank God. But we still have to call the police."

"Why?"

"He tried to attack you!"

"Who?"

She wasn't making sense. Could she have a concussion? "The man in the van." I pointed to her down jacket. "He tried to smother you."

Kelly looked at her jacket, puzzled for a second. Then she shook her head.

"No. No. I was trying to block the light. And that was Al. Al didn't attack me."

"Al?"

"Sinead's husband, Al."

"Al Rudinsky? Tidy Pool Al?"

She nodded.

I was confused. "What was he doing here?"

"He cleans the alley on Fridays."

I sat down on the banquette next to Kelly, trying to process this. Al was the maniac in the van? He's always been such a sweetheart—a shy, mellow man. Since when did he work here? If Al moonlighted as a janitor, that amounted to four jobs between him and Sinead. Money must be even tighter than I thought. Plus, they were still raising teenagers. I couldn't even imagine the strain on them.

"Someone's bowling in my head," Kelly whined and went down weeping again.

"I'll get you some water."

I hurried back to the bar, sprayed water from the soda gun into a beer mug and brought it to her. She sat up, took the mug and handed it back to me after a few sips.

Then she collapsed into me and started crying again. I put my arm around her.

"Stokes was having an affair," she croaked.

"Oh God," I gasped, doing my best to act shocked. "I'm so sorry," I said, which was genuine.

"I came here to sleep last night. I couldn't stay in the house with him another second."

She continued to cry softly while I stroked her greasy hair and shushed her gently. I knew firsthand how betrayed and awful she felt.

"I'm so sorry," I repeated. "So, so sorry."

Kelly finally sat up and rubbed her eyes. I pinched a bunch of paper napkins from the dispenser on the table and handed them to her. She honked into one loudly and then wiped her eyes with another.

"He was sleeping with Helene. Helene Walker."

This was confirmation of Eric Warschuk's story from another source. An unimpeachable one. Gubbins could use this.

"No way," I said in a higher-than-usual pitch. My guilt was kicking in for all this dissembling.

She nodded, and her ponytail fell apart completely. Now her black hair covered her face like a troll doll. I brushed some of it aside for her.

"She's the gift that keeps on giving, isn't she. How did you find out?"

"Stokes told me. He said he wanted me to know before he confessed to the police. They interviewed us yesterday. He didn't say anything about the affair then, and now he's scared they'll uncover it. That not telling them will look, you know, suspicious."

A preemptive move. Smart of Stokes. I wished I could ask her if he was home on the night of the murders. Not the right time. She'd begun weeping again.

"I never thought he'd do this to me. To us."

I handed her another napkin, and she sniffled. I gave her a hug.

"I feel like I've lost my best friend."

I remembered that feeling. Utterly alone and abandoned after I found out about Helene. The unbearable realization that I was replaceable for Hugh. But hearing Kelly speak the words provided a new perspective. Hugh and I were never best friends. Hugh set the terms of our relationship. Terms that allowed him affairs. I could accept them or leave him. Or use a more insidious option: pretend they weren't occurring, which worked until he did something impossible to deny—he made a baby.

"I've been such an idiot," Kelly moaned. "I was actually teaching her how to tone her flabby abs and tighten her saggy butt. Trying to make her sexy while I turned into a blimp."

"Stop it. Your body is gorgeous. You're a beautiful, voluptuous woman."

A few years ago, I was desperate to have a fertile, round-bellied body like hers. But now I understood that if I *had* gotten pregnant, I would have been dealing with Hugh's infidelity, coping with a toxic level of stress at the height of my vulnerability. That's what Kelly was facing. My life would have gone one of two ways: either I would have divorced

Hugh and become a single mom, or stayed and raised a child in a marriage filled with mistrust and resentment. I did not envy Kelly. For the first time, I entertained the idea that I'd gotten off easy with Hugh.

"Believe me, if I'd known what Helene had done to your marriage when she came to Pilates, I never would have let her join the class." Kelly sniffed. "I let the fox into the henhouse. No, that's wrong, I let the . . . no. Anyway, none of this would have happened. Or maybe he'd have cheated with some other woman. I don't know. I feel so confused. I don't know who Stokes is anymore."

I took Kelly's hand. What was the point in telling her that Helene had been with Stokes since September, well before she showed up in class? More important was to soften the impact of the devastating possibility I was about to present her with.

"Sometimes there's a side to people we love that we don't want to see because it's too painful. We can sleepwalk . . ." I squirmed. "We can sleepwalk through a relationship, Kelly. But there's a time to wake up."

Kelly blinked at me and widened her eyes.

"What I'm trying to say is, on the surface Stokes seems one way, but underneath he might be a very destructive person."

She burst into tears and flopped down on the banquette again. "You're right. He's killed everything we had together. I don't think I can ever forgive him."

"No. I mean . . ."

I heard the outside door open.

"Nora?" Grace called.

"In here."

Grace walked into the bar wearing her orange parka and carrying her mat. She looked at me questioningly.

"I thought I was early," she said, heading toward the table but stopping midway. "Oh my God. We're in Oz!" She stood there gawking at my chest as if I'd sprouted a third breast.

"What are you talking about?"

"You're finally wearing a color!"

I looked down at my torso. A few hours earlier, while refilling some of the drawers that the police had emptied, I'd come across the cherry-red hoodie that I'd bought myself as a present last year at Massamat Mall's Valentine's Day sale. Surprisingly, I felt like wearing it.

"What's going on?" Grace asked, concerned. She'd seen Kelly, who was curled up on the banquette rubbing her head.

"I don't feel so good," Kelly muttered.

Grace furrowed her brow. "There's a twenty-four-hour virus going around. Otis had it. Two kids in Leon's kindergarten, too." She turned to me. "We should get her home."

"It isn't a virus," I said.

"Are you sure?"

Kelly rolled over. "What time is it? I have to set up for class."

Grace took one look at her tear-streaked face and moved to sit next to her on the side opposite mine.

"What's got you so upset?"

Was Kelly going to tell her?

"Nothing." Kelly began searching under the table. "Where's my mat?"

Should I tell her?

"Forget that. Tell me what's wrong. And if you're not feeling well, let's get you home. We have to take good care of you and the baby. Right, Nora?"

She shouldn't go home. Stokes might be very angry with Kelly for leaving him. I was afraid for her and the baby, even though he would be taking an enormous risk if he harmed one hair on her head once the police knew about his affair.

"She doesn't want to go home," I countered.

Grace examined me curiously and then turned to Kelly. "Kelly?"

"I'm not going home to a liar and a cheat," Kelly said.

"Stokes was cheating?"

"He was sleeping with Helene," I blurted.

Grace stared at me, stunned for a moment. Then she pounded her fist on the table, making the salt and pepper shakers jump. "Un-fucking-believable. That woman was a man-eater."

"I never want to see him again," Kelly whimpered.

"Of course you don't. I can respect that," Grace said, putting her arm around Kelly's shoulders. "But in these situations, you can't be the one to give ground." She shot me a look. "Let *him* find somewhere else to stay," she said, firmly. "You're pregnant. You can't be living in a bowling alley."

"But I can't see Stokes. I'm not ready."

"You can come to my house," I said. I instantly pictured the wreckage the police left and regretted the offer.

Kelly nodded a little uncertainly.

"Hold on," Grace said. "The Coop can get pretty cold, Nor. She needs creature comforts in her condition. We have a guest room and hey, who better to have watching over you than an EMT? I'll call Mac and tell him you're coming, Kelly. I'll be home after my show later."

"I think Grace is right," I said. "I'll make a sign that says class is canceled. You should go to Grace's and let them baby *you*."

"You guys are great. Thanks," Kelly murmured.

"Think you can drive?" Grace asked her.

"Uh-huh."

"Good. I'll help you get cleaned up," Grace said, taking her hand. "Come on, honey."

While Grace steered Kelly to the restroom, I went behind the bar to scavenge for sign material. In a moment, the outer door squeaked again.

"Who's there?"

No answer.

"I said who's there?"

Still no reply. My shoulders tensed. Was it Stokes? Had he come for Kelly? Instinctively, I reached for a bottle and grabbed it by the neck.

I relaxed my grip when Sinead's husky form appeared in the doorway. Dressed in sweats, she was carrying her usual hanger of work clothes to wear to the bank, along with her exercise mat and a small brown-paper bag. Under her blunt-cut bangs, her eyes had bags, too.

"What is everyone doing here at the crack?" she asked.

"I could ask the same of you," I said, putting the bottle down nonchalantly. "Kelly's sick. I'm making a sign to say class is canceled."

Sinead came over and set her burdens on the bar. I thought of Tidy Pool Al and their four jobs, and I regretted raising my voice to her at the Tea Cozy.

"Sinead, I'm sorry about the other night. The way I spoke to you. I was a first-class bitch."

"Forget it. I handled it arseways. You were in a state. That Detective Roche who interviewed us yesterday? He asked how I thought you were taking it, and that's what I said. 'Even if Hugh Walker was a shite bastard, she shared the same bed with the man for years. She'd have to have ice water in her veins not to be devastated by what happened to him.'"

I rocked slightly, holding on to the bar to keep steady. This meant Roche was asking around about my emotional state, building his case. Would he even look into Stokes as a possibility?

"What else did Detective Roche ask?"

"If I'd noticed anything that might help the police, which I had not. What I thought of Helene. There, I gave him a piece."

I tried to quell my anxiety and concentrate on Sinead.

"I guess things haven't been easy for you, either. I saw Al leaving here this morning in the Dirt Busters van."

Sinead lowered her eyes.

"He didn't want people to know." She looked up and lifted her chin toward the Jameson bottle. "I'll take a wee one."

I picked up a shot glass from the bar, then hesitated and picked up a second one. I poured whiskey into both. We picked up our glasses, clinked them together and took our sips. I saw Sinead's tears welling up.

"Oh, Sinead. Is it that bad?"

She nodded.

"Cleaning pools and digging irrigation ditches was one thing," she said. "But toilets . . . He lost so much business this year that he had to take on this night job, and we're still short. What with the high prices in town and the taxes going up on our house . . ."

"I had no idea."

"Things went from bad to worse after he lost Pequod Point. It was his biggest account. The owner used to be a Tidy Pools client before he sold to the Walkers. Apparently, they replaced him with some bloody fella from Massamat their realtor recommended."

"The Walkers fired Al?"

She nodded. "He hates being a janitor. It's turning him mean. He's mad all the time. He's mad as hell. That's what he's been saying ever since he started this night shift."

I stepped back. He'd been saying what?

"He used to be so good-natured. But now it's: *I'm mad as hell that I'm cleaning other people's piss and shit; I'm mad as hell that your mum's coming for Thanksgiving; I'm mad as hell it costs half a day's pay to fill my gas tank.* He's so knackered he barely eats. He's always running from one job to another."

Sinead knocked back the rest of her whiskey while I gaped at her.

"I wanted to surprise him and bring him breakfast before he left," she said, tapping the brown bag. "I brought his favorite: sausage-and-egg sandwich. But I guess I missed him." She wiped her eyes. "Sorry, I don't mean to be such a whinger. Hey . . ." She pointed at my chest.

"What?" I said, finally jolted out of my amazement.

"Look at you. You're wearing a color."

◆　◆　◆

I had thought of Stokes as a hater, capable of killing Hugh and Helene. Now there was also Al with an ax to grind against the Walkers. No, the idea was ludicrous. Shy, nervous Al Rudinsky, a guy who worried about tracking mud on the floor? He couldn't kill anyone, let alone do it over the loss of an account. Or could he? The only thing I felt certain of as the four of us emerged from the dark Thunder Bar into the bright, brisk morning was that *Mad as Hell* had to be him. He'd used the phrase repeatedly, and he drove like a madman. But why couldn't he come to me directly and say he was offended? Why did he have to express his anger under a nom de plume?

When I thought about it for a second, the answer was obvious. Shame. Humiliation. What Eric Warschuk said was probably true: "It's the thing men fear most."

"Women don't exactly love it, either," I mumbled.

"What did you say?" Grace asked.

Grace, Kelly and Sinead stood by the entrance door in the sun, squinting like moles.

"Nothing."

Kelly shivered in her shorts as she held on to Grace. The skin on her gorgeous calves was covered in goose bumps. Grace bundled her into the Mini and gave her directions and a house key while I tacked the CLASS CANCELED sign to the door. I'd written it on the blank back of a coaster that said, "Due to cutbacks, the light at the end of the tunnel has been turned off."

Grace returned, shaking her head. "What a thing to go through when you're pregnant. I'm surprised she didn't miscarry. I didn't think Stokes was Helene's type."

"You don't know the half of it, Grace. I have a million things to tell you."

Grace dropped her chin to her chest and began picking invisible lint off her parka. "I have stuff to tell you, too. Detective Roche came by last night."

I nodded as my belly turned over. "He was asking about me, right? They searched my house. They commandeered my phone and computer."

Grace jerked her head up. "Shit!"

"Gubbins is working on getting them back. What did Roche ask you?"

"He asked if I thought you were emotionally stable. I said you were a rock. That you'd gone through hell in the past because of Hugh and you'd kept it together. But lately you'd been depressed."

"And you felt you had to share that," I said, recoiling.

Grace was quick to defend herself. "I didn't want him to hear it from someone else and think I was hiding it."

"How did he react?"

"He wanted details. 'How is she behaving differently?' 'Is she spending more time alone? Becoming more secretive?' I told him you were a little colorless, that's all. I also set him straight. 'I've known her for twenty-three years,' I said. 'She's a good person and godmother to my kids. Don't waste your time investigating Nora Glasser. There's a dangerous killer running around out there. Go find him.'"

Loyal as Lassie, like I said.

"Nor, there's another thing. About my program today—"

"Wait. Stokes might show up here soon. Let's talk at the station."

Grace broadcast *Talk of the Townies* live at 10:30 a.m., and her station manager usually stocked the fridge. I couldn't remember when I'd last eaten.

◆ ◆ ◆

As I drove along the commercial stretch between Pequod and Massamat, my mind jumped from worry to worry like a grasshopper dodging a lawn mower. I worried about getting arrested, about Stokes roaming free, about my sleepwalking and what it meant. I even worried about Al working all night scrubbing toilet bowls. The more I thought about it, I knew Al wasn't a killer. I knew it in my bones. My money was on Stokes. Stokes was the one. No matter how mad Al was about my column, his threats were idle. He was a frustrated victim of the changing economy. My heart went out to him.

It was a good thing I didn't have a phone, because I had the urge to call Ben and tell him Tidy Pool Al wrote the letters. I probably shouldn't talk to Ben until he had time to absorb the note I'd left. I hoped he'd understand. My reticence wasn't about him. It was all me.

Grace disappeared through the station's door as I pulled into a visitor parking spot at WPQD. My measly hour of sleep was beginning to take its toll. I climbed out of the car and stomped my feet to shake off the drowsiness before hustling into the warehouse-size brick building— a former party goods store. With their economic challenges, the Piqued hadn't been throwing as many parties. Celebration had gone belly-up.

WPQD was suffering, too—federal grants decimated, ad revenues down. Half the time, some dejected host was chanting the phone number during a fund-raiser and offering hemp tote bags or Bruce Springsteen CDs in return for donations. As I entered, "Uptown Funk" was playing on the air. On the far side of the lobby, Grace's boss, Monty Beers, sang along in his glass studio. He pulled a serious face when he spotted me, gave a big thumbs-up and mouthed, "You go, girl!" before fading the music out and starting the news.

"Good morning. This is Monty Beers with WPQD Weekly News in Review. The town of Pequod is still on edge as the police hunt for Hugh and Helene Walker's killer. Apple-picking season is in its final week. And an economic report released yesterday is forecasting the 2018 economy will be 'okayish.' This and more. Stay tuned." He flipped on a public service announcement and gave me two thumbs-up this time.

What was Monty's big rah-rah for me about? He'd seen me on the news, I supposed. It looked like he believed my statement and was trying to show emotional support—praising me for managing to hold it together given the traumatic events of the week. I was grateful for a little encouragement. I proceeded to the kitchen to snatch two mugs and a peach Yoplait from the minifridge.

Grace's interviewing style is effective. In the way Barbara Walters gets people to cry, Grace gets them to say things they normally wouldn't. She has qualities that make people open up to her: she's a great enthusiast, a flatterer and an empathic listener. Before they know it, guests have let down their guard and spilled a secret or expressed an opinion they regret. Grace could go national, she was so adept at this. But ambition is not Grace's thing. "My porridge is just right in Pequod," she'd said when we'd discussed whether she would pursue an opening at NPR in DC.

I stood outside her small, soundproof studio, watching her through the glass as she prepped for her show. She sat in one of two metal chairs at a long wooden table with her MacBook, pad and pen, two table mikes and two sets of headphones in front of her. The empty chair hosted a pink pillow that said, "Grace is a gift from God" in red stitching. I realized I was reluctant to go in. It was time to tell Grace everything, including the fact that my sleepwalking problem had returned. I dreaded doing it. Telling Grace meant admitting I'd lied to her. Without Grace trusting me, going through all this would be intolerable.

I stepped inside. Her studio was quiet as a confessional—Grace had switched the station speakers off. I set the mugs on the table, along with the thermos of coffee I'd brought. Then I sat on the pillow and dug into my Yoplait.

"Monty just cheered me on like I'm about to run a triathlon," I said, still avoiding the difficult subject. "I appreciated it. I need the boost."

Grace adjusted the mikes and her MacBook unnecessarily. She wouldn't look at me.

"Grace?"

"He thinks you've come in to be interviewed about Hugh."

I stopped eating and set down the spoon.

"I wanted to tell you before at the bowling alley. Monty asked me to do a show on Hugh today. He wants me to interview you as the main event. He said: 'It's called *Talk of the Townies*, and she's what the townies are talking about.'"

"And you said yes?"

Maybe not so loyal.

"I said 'absolutely not' regarding you, but I did set up phoners with the art contingency—Abbas Masout and Davis Kimmerle, the critic. It's hard for me to avoid the topic altogether. I figured you might not mind so much since Hugh is, you know . . . dead. But say the word and I'll pull the plug."

I looked into Grace's clear blue eyes and saw that she meant it. She'd ditch the show if I told her to. I had no right to object to her doing her job; Hugh was a major cultural figure who lived in the area. "I can't participate. But of course, you should go ahead with your other guests. Do what you need to do," I said.

Grace touched my arm. "Thanks, Nor."

I took a deep breath. "Okay, my turn for confessing. And please don't ask questions until I'm done."

It was difficult for Grace not to interrogate me, but she managed to let me speak. It all poured out in a rush. I told her about Ben and Gubbins both subscribing to the theory that I'd been framed. The slashed painting, the posed bodies.

"What the fuck?"

I told her about Hugh's damning divorce diary that documented my attack on the very same painting.

"He was collecting evidence on *you* for the divorce? That's rich."

"You promised not to interrupt."

I gave her my list of possible suspects: an angry drug dealer, a jilted lover of Hugh's and, finally, Stokes. I made the strongest case for him, positing him as a serial killer whose trigger was humiliation. "His in-laws demeaned him. He asphyxiated them and managed to get his hands on their money. Then Helene and Hugh humiliated him, and there was a sexual mortification this time. He took his revenge."

Grace tapped her pen. "I don't know. I can't see Stokes Diekmann having the bandwidth to orchestrate the framing scenario."

"He's a very angry guy. He's scary, believe me. It's good Kelly is staying with you. Now please stop interrupting. There's more."

Then I told her about sleeping with Ben. "Well, not sleeping, except for an hour."

Her eyes widened. "You've finally met someone, and it's Ben fucking Wickstein. Wow. How was it?"

"Wait. I'm not finished."

"Nor, come on."

"It was great. But kind of overwhelming . . ."

"Of course, it's been a while. But that's wonderful. I'm thrilled for you. For both of you."

"Please don't make too much of it. It was probably a one-night thing."

Grace frowned. "What makes you think so?"

I glanced at the clock on Grace's wall. Almost 9:45 a.m. Ben would be at the *Courier*'s weekly staff meeting, where I should be. How could I have walked out on him? I felt lousy about it. Cowardly. Small. But I still cringed when I thought of telling him about my sleepwalking. I took another deep breath.

"Grace. I've been sleepwalking again."

"What?" She stiffened. "I asked you. You told me you weren't."

"I wasn't sure. Then it happened last night at Ben's. And maybe before that, too, I think." I paused. I wasn't going to hedge with her now. "No. I *know* I was sleepwalking before."

Grace stared at me, her expression growing more concerned by the second. What was going through her mind?

"The morning of the murders . . . Nora, you had all that crud in your hair. And the scratch on your face. You said you went for a walk and you fell. Was that a lie? Had you been sleepwalking?"

"I'm pretty sure. I just don't know where I went."

"Holy shit. You must be terrified," she said. I could hear the stress in her voice.

She rolled her chair back slightly and angled her body away. It was subtle, but I knew what it meant. My heart sank. I'd never seen a graver look on Grace's face. I began wringing my hands, anguished.

"You think I did it."

Grace flinched.

"You think I killed Hugh and Helene."

I crumpled into the chair, crushed.

"Stop the crazy talk." Grace stood up and shook her head adamantly.

"I know you. You couldn't do something like that. No way in hell. You are not that person."

"It's just . . . there are so many things that line up," I said. "How can you be sure? Remember Axel? Nora Scissorhands?"

"That was a sweatshirt. These are human beings. It's completely impossible. Never in a million years. You understand? Never." She grabbed both my shoulders and looked me in the eye. "Repeat after me. Never."

It felt like I'd just been yanked back from the precipice.

"Never."

"Good. What does Ben have to say about it?"

I averted my eyes. "I didn't tell him."

"You need to."

"I can't."

"You can."

I looked at Grace again, pleading. "What if it makes him think I killed them?"

"Then he's not the man for you. You've got to tell him."

"No." I stiffened and crossed my arms. As empathic as she was, Grace had no idea what this was like. How exposed and defenseless I felt.

"You're stubborn," she said sternly.

"You're bossy."

She flipped her hair back with her hand and sat back down. We eyed each other, unblinking.

"We'll revisit this," Grace said. "Meanwhile, I think you should find a sleep clinic. You haven't tried that."

"The police are watching. They don't have those clinics out here. Gubbins said if I leave the county, they'd be sure to track me. I can't have them finding out about my sleepwalking. A sleep clinic isn't an option right now."

"Okay. Then we've got to figure out a way to reduce your stress. I bet that's triggering the episodes."

"Finding the killer and getting me off the suspect list would help with the stress, believe me."

"Right."

Grace picked up her pen and began making notes. "As for who committed the murders, we can discount two people right off the bat."

"Who?"

"First, the pissed-off drug dealer. If Hugh and Helene were using drugs, it would've come out in the autopsy report. Ben's source at the DA didn't mention drugs, did he?"

"No," I said, chagrined. Why didn't I think of that?

"And second, like I said, I don't believe Stokes came up with this plan to frame you. He spends half his life bowling. He's kind of a lug."

"You're kind of a snob. Just because Stokes is obsessed with bowling doesn't make him stupid. That's classist. He's playing dumb. He's plenty smart. And diabolical. Helene would have certainly told him I'd been married to Hugh, but he acted like he didn't know. Like *I* was the creep at the crime scene . . ."

Grace narrowed her eyes. "Maybe. And maybe Kelly killed them. What if she knew about the affair, and she's pretending she just found out? Maybe she Googled Helene and read about your history. She realized you'd be the perfect suspect." She gasped. "Oh shit. She's in my house with Mac right now."

"No. No. No. Forget it. It's not Kelly." I was disappointed that Grace wasn't buying the Stokes theory. "She might've whipped them with her ponytail, but shoot them? And why would she kill Hugh? Her grudge was against Helene."

Grace pondered this for a moment and relaxed. "Good point. And she really is a sweet person."

"It's Stokes," I insisted. "Stokes hated both of them."

"Could be . . ." She started doodling. "But what if . . ." She appeared to be sketching a pair of crossed eyes.

"But what if what?" I asked impatiently.

"What if Hugh was messing around again? He might have slept with some nutjob. A pathologically jealous type. 'Bang bang' Hugh and Helene. 'Slash slash' the painting." She scribbled out the eyes. "Then again, maybe it *is* Stokes."

I began massaging my temples, overwhelmed by the possibilities.

Grace continued. "Isn't it odd that Helene was attracted to Stokes? He's so not her type—a bowler from Catskill?"

"There you go again. Classist."

"But Stokes doesn't have all those millions, like Hugh."

Grace doodled a dollar sign. I glanced at it. Looked away and looked back again. My brain started pinging and flashing like a pinball machine. How could I—how could both of us have missed this? I popped out of my chair and tapped the pad repeatedly as I tried to harness my racing thoughts. Grace looked alarmed.

"What?"

"Bob Woodward and Carl Bernstein," I said.

Grace dropped the pen and we both chanted it together: "Follow the money."

My words tumbled out. "Callie is the money. She'll be Hugh's heir. His paintings are worth even more now that he's dead. A fortune, in fact. Fifteen million? More? She's just a child. Someone has to take charge of her, become her legal guardian."

"You're right," Grace agreed.

"That person will have a lot of influence over what happens to her millions during the next few years. And what she does with her money when she's grown. Want to bet it's going to be Uncle Tobias and his wife, Ruth, who petition the court to be Callie's guardians?"

Grace cupped her chin, thinking it over. "I didn't know Tobias was into material things."

"Remember I told you he started that religious foundation? He hit Hugh up for large donations a couple of times, invited us down to fundraisers in Virginia that we never went to. Hugh thought the foundation promoted 'Christian fascism' and never gave him a cent." I sat down again and circled the dollar sign with Grace's pen. "What if Tobias did it for the money?" I pointed to Grace's MacBook. "Can I use this?"

"Please."

"Did you know Tobias was in New York for a 'Save the Family' conference on the weekend of the murders?" I asked, logging on to my e-mail.

"Now, *that* is a suspicious coincidence," Grace said.

"He also knew that Callie was staying with Helene's sister and wouldn't be at home. He told Wolf Blitzer. He was alone and within striking distance of Hugh and Helene. There was no one to keep track of him. He could have rented a car, driven out to Pequod from the city late that night and shot them before driving back to his hotel in the city. No one would have any idea he'd left. And Tobias would know how to set the scene to make it look like I'd done it."

"The police must suspect him. They must be looking into it."

"I think the police are too busy with me."

Grace peered over my shoulder as I reopened Tobias's e-mail.

"He invited you to the funeral?"

"It would be the Christian thing to do, no? He's reinforcing his saintly image."

Grace paused for a moment, then narrowed her eyes. "Tell him I'm grieving and want to come with you," she said.

From the *Pequod Courier*

Obituaries, cont'd from page 11

Nora Glasser, on staff at the *Courier*, was Hugh Walker's first wife and introduced the artist to this area. Both of the deceased moved to Pequod Point earlier this year. Hugh Walker's brother, Tobias Walker of Lynchburg, VA, survives him. Helene Walker's mother, Dinah Westing, and her sister, Margaret Westing, survive her. The Walkers' daughter, Callie, survives both of them.

Chapter Sixteen

I was on a mission. I left WPQD for Reynolds Discount Electronics in Massamat. It was time to shop for a disposable phone, or "burner," in crime-show lingo. I intended to call rental car agencies and try to find out whether Tobias booked a car last Saturday night. If he had, there would be mileage records. With any luck, if the rental car hadn't been cleaned thoroughly, the police might still find traces of Pequod Point's soil on the floor mats or tires. Or carpet fibers on the upholstery. Or even blood. Buying a cheap laptop would also be a good idea for checking e-mails and finishing "Canines for Heroes." I'm no shirker. Despite everything that was going on, I'd fulfill my work obligations.

I thought of work, and a flicker of doubt returned about Ben. Had I done the right thing in pushing him away? In not giving him the opportunity to respond to my situation? I had to shake off this relentless self-questioning and refocus on the plan.

As I drove, I reviewed what Grace and I had discussed. There were two prime suspects now. Stokes had a strong motive, but so did Tobias. He was Cain to Hugh's Abel. He had to be envious of his little brother. Hugh's talent had brought millions, public adulation and a hot blonde. Tobias earned a modest teacher's salary and lived with a frump. If Hugh had donated even one painting to his brother's foundation, it would probably fetch more money than Tobias could hope to raise in his entire lifetime. Behind all the godliness and concern, Tobias must've harbored massive resentment. If Nathan Glasser were alive, he'd lay odds that Tobias had devised a way to kill the Walkers, blame me and enrich himself and his cause.

Grace and I hatched a plan. I'd already e-mailed Tobias from her computer accepting his invitation and requesting that he let Grace pay her respects. Bless Grace, she'd taken it on herself to make it less awkward for everyone at my wedding by giving Tobias and his wife some quality attention, so I doubted he'd refuse her. She'd approach him at the funeral as the caring mother she was and try to suss out his intentions regarding Callie. Grace had also suggested one more possibility.

"We can't dismiss the idea that Hugh had a jealous lover. Along with pedophiles, cheaters have a high level of recidivism. There's a chance that lover could show up at the funeral."

"As a stranger, she'd draw too much attention," I objected. "She would be foolish to risk gloating over her victims in person. And how would she find out about the service, anyway? Tobias isn't advertising it."

"What if she's not a stranger? What if she's one of the people Tobias invited? A friend."

I contemplated this for a moment and someone came to mind.

"Sue Mickelson, the neighbor. She was the first at the scene after the housekeeper. She's very attractive. I wonder . . ."

"I'm just saying we shouldn't rule out that possibility."

We agreed that if we uncovered any useful information, we'd tell Gubbins immediately.

By the time I paid for the phone and computer at Reynolds Electronics and returned to my car, *Talk of the Townies* was almost over. I'd missed the entire Abbas interview. Grace was finishing up with Davis Kimmerle of the *New York Journal*.

"And then there's Walker's brilliant self-portrait with his ex-wife as a distorted, half-bestial figure hovering over him as he sleeps. The portrait evokes both the raw and the sophisticated. It's contemporary yet grounded in classical traditions across many cultures. This is why Hugh Walker will remain profoundly influential. In fact, he has single-handedly paved the way for a revisioning of neo-primitivism."

"That's fascinating, Davis. Your understanding of Walker's vision is very impressive," Grace said. "You really have to write a book."

"Thank you. I admit, I've been thinking about doing just that."

"Oh, you must. Fantastic. Promise me you'll come on the show to talk about it when the book comes out."

"I'm there."

"Again, thank you for speaking with us today and explaining the significance of Walker's paintings so eloquently. Now that he's gone, it's so sad we won't be able to see more of his work and hear your take on it."

"A shame, I know. But you *will* be able to see a number of his previously unexhibited paintings soon. I'd be happy to come back on the show and talk about them."

"Really?"

"Yes. The Abbas Masout Gallery had already planned a comprehensive retrospective for this spring before any of this . . . Oh God, I'm sorry, Grace. I just betrayed a confidence. It's not public knowledge yet. Can you edit that out?"

"I'm afraid this is a live show, Davis."

That's exactly what I meant about Grace eliciting information. It seemed to work with everyone.

It wasn't even noon, but I caught myself drifting over the yellow line more than once on the way home. The car rental calls would have to wait. All I could think about was resting my head on a pillow and closing my eyes. I arrived at the Coop, too tired to address the last remnants of disorder the police had left: a kilim to roll out, books to return to the shelves and a desk to reorganize. With my remaining speck of energy, I gathered materials from the kitchen instead: three frying pans, two large soup pots and two smaller saucepans.

Now that I knew for certain that I was sleepwalking again, I also knew it was a possibility anytime I slept, even in the middle of the afternoon. I wanted reassurance that my wandering was taking place indoors exclusively, the way it always had in the past. The pots and pans would function as a simple alarm system. A noisy barrier that would wake me if I tried to leave. I placed them just inside the front door, and then I hesitated. Did I really want to test myself? If this alarm went off, it would mean I could have gone to Pequod Point the night of the murders.

The answer was yes. I *had* to know.

I retreated to the bedroom and changed into pajamas. Then I crawled into bed, left Grace a message with my new number and phoned Aunt Lada. She wasn't in her room. The call rolled over to Yvonne at the front desk.

"Hi, Yvonne. Do you happen to know where my aunt is?"

"Hiding out."

"What do you mean?"

"Trash-talking magazine people found her. So, you used to be married to dat man got killed with his wife? He sneak out on you and give her a baby?"

"Oh God."

"They been bugging your auntie. Calling her day and night since yesterday. She tell me she turning her phone off."

I sat up. "I'm coming over."

"No need. She okay. Just layin' low. Say she needs a rest."

"I still think I should come."

"I think you just make her feel bad for making you feel bad."

"Okay . . . but listen, I have a new phone number. Can you please make sure she gets it? And ask her to call me?"

"No worries. I'll stop up there before I leave tonight."

I gave Yvonne the number and thanked her.

"Nora?"

"Yes?"

"You take care of yourself."

I hung up, feeling protective of my aunt and angry with the press for invading her privacy. I contemplated driving to The Cedars despite Yvonne's advice, but I was dying to sleep. I must've dropped off right away because when the doorbell rang, I woke with the phone on my chest.

Apparently, I hadn't slept very long—light still streamed in at the corners of the bedroom curtains. My phone said 2:06 p.m. I rolled out of bed, went over to the window and gasped as I spied Ben's car in the driveway. There was no pretending I wasn't home; my car sat right next to his. Besides, my heart wouldn't let me shut him out. Two tiny hands had just grown from the center of it, and they were reaching for him. Ambivalence quickly snatched them back. The problems I'd recognized last night had not gone away. I was still a sleepwalker. The police still suspected me of murder. On some level, I still suspected me of murder. I couldn't see how Ben wouldn't.

The doorbell rang again.

"Just a sec!" I shouted, scrambling for the bathroom.

I checked the mirror. Major bed head, but still kind of sexy. *Take a moment, Nora. Breathe.* I managed to compose myself before strolling into the living room as casually as possible. I pushed a couple of pots away with my foot. How to explain them? Opening the door sent the rest clattering across the floor. I winced. Ben registered the noise and pulled back slightly.

He held a bouquet of red roses. *Totally old school. Sincere. Adorable.* Ben wasn't ambivalent.

"You in the middle of something? Is this a bad time?"

He looked at me questioningly and held my eyes. My stomach fluttered. We stood there for a few seconds, pulsing with electricity. Despite everything, I wished he would kiss me.

"Nora, listen. I want you to know I realize the strain you're under with this goddamn investigation. But we need to talk. Can I come in?"

I stepped aside to let him pass. He closed the door and took in the collection of cookware near his feet, puzzled. I should risk it. I should tell him about the sleepwalking right now. My mind raced through pros and cons and got stuck on "he'll think I'm guilty." If I could just go somewhere and think. I opened my mouth, then closed it, then opened it again.

"I got a great deal on the rent, but the roof leaks," I said, disappointed in myself. It felt crummy to lie to him.

"That's too bad." He glanced around at my living room, nodding his approval. "Your place is nice. Eclectic."

He offered the roses, partially wrapped in clear cellophane and tied with red ribbon.

"These are for you," he said, holding my gaze again.

"Thanks."

As I reached for them nervously, a thorn pricked my index finger. "Ow." I winced.

"Sorry."

I began sucking the blood from the tip.

"Here. Let me," Ben offered, tucking the bouquet under his arm. He coaxed my finger out of my mouth and inspected it. His touch undid me. I felt my knees turn to jelly and I swayed a bit.

"Let's get this under some cold water. Where's a sink?"

A cold shower was what I needed. Ben held up my dripping finger, and I led him to the kitchen. The faint citrusy aroma of his aftershave wafted into my nostrils, mixing with his licorice scent. The combination was an instant aphrodisiac. He leaned across me at the sink to turn on the faucet, and my entire body flushed.

"Just hold it here for a minute," he said, guiding my finger under the cool stream. The water felt soothing on the tiny, throbbing wound. But all at once my jaw clenched as I remembered last night, standing naked at Ben's kitchen sink with pulsating hands.

"You have a vase?" he asked.

I jutted my chin toward the cabinet next to the fridge, afraid my voice would reveal how upset I was.

"In here?"

I nodded. Ben opened the cabinet and found the empty kosher pickle jar that I'd denuded after finishing the pickles Aunt Lada sent home with me a few weeks earlier. He set it on the kitchen counter.

"And where's your garbage?"

Still silent, I indicated a lower cabinet. He frowned at me, perplexed.

"Okay, Harpo."

He gently nudged me aside, pulled out the trash bin and took the fattest Swiss Army knife I'd ever seen from his pocket. The knife I'd discovered riding back from the police station with him. He noticed me looking at it.

"This is my lucky charm. A Father's Day present from Sam. It's called the Champ. There are wire cutters, a metal saw, a magnifying glass . . . The only time I don't carry it is when I fly, which is too bad because they could probably use it to repair a 747."

He opened the scissor attachment and began snipping the rose stems into the garbage. Watching Ben handle the roses—the relaxed, confident way he moved—was calming. I was impressed that he cut the stems on a slant to let them drink more easily. I liked that he carried a lucky charm from his son. I liked everything about him at the moment.

"So, you took off last night, and now you're not speaking to me." He began placing the roses in the vase. "How should I interpret this?"

I shut off the water and cleared my throat. "I guess you didn't see the note I left."

Ben stuck the remaining flowers in the jar. He reached into his other pocket, pulled out a folded square of paper and opened it.

"You mean *Dear Ben. I'm not ready. I'm sorry.*" He balled up the paper and tossed it into the open trash, frustrated. "I can't accept this. You only gave me the lede. What's the rest of the story?"

Tongue-tied again, I avoided his eyes and inspected my puffy, wrinkled finger. It stung like the devil.

"Nora."

Could I trust him? I had a lousy track record picking trustworthy men. I replied with a halfhearted shrug and looked up.

His brown eyes blazed at me as he spoke. "You think it was easy for me to let it happen last night? To open myself up? You think I didn't want to run? I did. But I said, you can't let this one go because you're scared of losing someone again. This one's special."

"Ben, I—"

"It took me hours to work up the guts to come over here to talk. To tell you I reject your 'Dear Ben' note. I'm not going to knock down the castle door again to reach you, Nora. I'm not going to plant the magic kiss that wakes you up. You've got to meet me halfway, for real, or . . ."

I didn't want to hear the rest of that sentence. I didn't want to lose him.

"Shhh," I said, putting my swollen finger to his lips. And then I kissed him until we were swimming in the ocean again.

Our bodies floated on dark swells by the time we finished. We lay there, letting the current slowly draw us to shore as we held hands, utterly spent. Ben finally rolled over and brushed my hair off my face.

"I think you have a right to know that I've been harboring elaborate fantasies about you for at least six months," he said, grinning.

"That's kind of kinky," I teased.

"You think?"

"How did reality measure up?"

"Far superior."

He kissed me. But when our lips parted, I could tell we both felt the mood shift.

The gloom of the murder case had moved in. We couldn't avoid it. Ben sat up and turned on the lamp on the night table.

"So, what have you heard from Gubbins about the case?"

"Nothing yet. But Kelly confirmed that Stokes and Helene were having an affair. She says he's going to tell the police before they discover it."

"He's got motive. That should make Roche take a closer look at him, at least."

"Grace says Stokes isn't clever enough to orchestrate a frame-up."

"If twenty-five years as a journalist have taught me anything, it's that people are like onions. Lots of layers."

That was me, for sure.

"You've already peeled off one of his and discovered adultery. Who knows what else is underneath?" Ben shook his head, worried. "There's nothing on his in-laws' deaths from my contact at the *Catskill News* yet. I wish the police would find the damn murder weapon in this case. A trace on that gun would be a big help."

I was about to tell Ben my new theory about Tobias, and the plan with Grace, but he'd caught sight of his wristwatch and looked stricken.

"Shit. It's almost seven p.m."

"What's going on?"

"Sam's on his way home for Thanksgiving break. I'm picking him up at the airport. He'll be landing at 8:05. It'll take me more than an hour and a half to get there, even without traffic. I lost track of the time."

You'd better get moving then."

He looked uncertain.

"I'm fine. It's fine. Don't worry," I said.

I was actually relieved Ben had to leave and I didn't have to come up with some lame excuse about why he needed to go home before I fell asleep. ("It's not you, Ben. I've never been able to share a bed.")

He hopped out of bed and began dressing, hastily. Then he hesitated.

"Nora, I'm sorry to run out."

"Go. Go. Go," I urged.

"What was the idea you wanted to tell me?" he asked, pulling on his jeans.

"It can wait."

He stuffed his socks in his pocket and slipped into his loafers. "We're driving into Manhattan from the airport so Sam and I can visit with his grandmother for a couple of days. We'll be back Friday afternoon. How about we have dinner Friday night?"

"You don't mean with Sam," I said nervously.

"No, just us. Of course, I'd like you two to meet. But I don't want to rush you."

"Okay. Sure."

He handed me his phone. "And put in your burner number, okay?"

I nodded and entered the number as he buttoned his shirt.

Ben leaned over and kissed me again. Then he took his phone and grabbed his jacket. "If you talk to your landlord about the leaks in your living room, you can mention that the *Courier* is doing an exposé of local slumlords."

"We are?"

"No, but it might speed things up." He winked and then grew serious. "And do me a favor. Double-check that your doors and windows are locked tonight."

I started to nod but stopped. "Hold on. I'm confused. If I'm being framed by someone, I'm not in danger. The killer needs me alive to take the blame."

"That's our theory. And it's probably true. But nothing is a hundred percent until they catch this maniac. So, lock everything, please. And don't open up unless you're sure who it is."

The way Hugh and Helene had been sure?

Before Ben's car even left the driveway, I felt apprehensive about seeing him again. It wasn't clear what we were doing. Had we crossed the Rubicon that afternoon and entered a bona fide relationship? Ben said he didn't want to rush me. And I needed to find the courage to tell him about my freakish nocturnal habits before we got in too deep. The faith to believe he wouldn't question my innocence. But since the debacle with Hugh, courage and faith were not my strong suits.

Dispirited, I put on my robe and went to regroup the pots in front of the door. This was no way to live—building a moat with kitchen equipment every time I went to sleep. There had to be a better solution. I decided to make coffee and at least do some research on sleep clinics. After this murder was solved, when I could get treatment without arousing suspicion, I'd book an appointment.

Entering the kitchen, I noticed Ben's good luck Champ on the rim of the sink. I picked it up. An engraving etched into the red plastic handle read: "World's Best Dad." No wonder he always kept the knife close. He'd be upset to discover its absence. Apparently, he'd already realized it was missing; I heard his car pulling back into the driveway.

It wouldn't do for Ben to be late picking up Sam on my account. Knife in hand, I rushed to the front door, pushing the pots aside again. When I pulled the door open, the hardened faces of Crawley and Roche delivered a virtual punch to my solar plexus. Crawley was in uniform and Roche was dressed in his usual cords and tweed jacket, this time with a navy duffel coat over them.

"We'd like a few words, Ms. Glasser."

I recovered quickly. "Not without my lawyer," I said, clutching Ben's knife inside my fist.

"Actually, this is about your neighbor."

"My neighbor?"

"We have a couple of questions about the property nearby in relationship to the murder case." He peered over my shoulder to the inside of the Coop. "I see you've almost put the place back together. Sorry about the upset." He noticed the pots on the floor and looked puzzled. "Did we do that? We try not to be unnecessarily messy. I'm afraid we don't always succeed."

I hesitated. Would a refusal reek of guilt? How could it hurt to give them five minutes about a neighbor? Especially if it would help them solve the crime. I waved them inside. Crawley stood by the door like a sentry. Roche strode over to my dining table, pulled out a chair, turned it around and sat with his legs spread out cowboy style. He gestured for me to sit next to him, but I caught a glimpse of my father's picture on my desk. His eyes warned me against it.

"I'd rather stand," I said. "How can I help?"

Roche scratched his chin before he spoke.

"I heard they're planning a big show of Hugh Walker's work in New York. I hope that doesn't upset you too much."

You were right, Daddy. I need to be wary.

"I thought you said this was about my neighbor?"

Roche raised a palm. "Just empathizing, Ms. Glasser. The show would stir up a lot for me if I were in your shoes. This *is* about your neighbor. Sergeant Crawley received a call this afternoon regarding a building on the other end of your property. A farmhouse."

I nodded. "You must mean Jack Mance's place. He's my landlord."

"We understand it's a summer home, uninhabited since early September. Is that correct?"

"Yes."

"Seems the meterman came by this morning and found a broken window at the back—near where he takes his reading every month."

"A burglary?"

Roche ignored my question.

"The power company contacted Mance. Mance tried to call you so you could take a look for him, but couldn't reach you."

"That's because you took my ph—" I stopped. The son of a bitch was toying with me.

Roche smiled. "Apparently, he tried you earlier in the week, too. He's been a little worried about you, given everything that's going on. At any rate, he spoke to the good sergeant here and reported the break-in. Sergeant Crawley investigated. Mr. Mance provided a list of valuables to look for. The place had definitely been burglarized, but only a few small items were missing. One in particular prompted Sergeant Crawley to contact me. As a county detective, I don't generally get involved in a local theft, but we believe this item has a direct connection to the case."

"What did they take?"

"A metal lockbox."

◆ ◆ ◆

"Nora? It's Jack Mance. Landlord and bon vivant. David and I have some friends out for the holiday weekend. Don't be a stranger. Come by for a drink this afternoon. Put a face to the name."

Friday afternoon of Memorial Day weekend. The opening of vacation season the spring I moved to Pequod. I'd never met Jack Mance or his partner. A realtor from Town and Country Properties had shown me the Coop and handled all the paperwork. That weekend was the first Mance had visited his house since I'd become his tenant. He sounded very gay and very nice. And funny. It was about time I ventured out and socialized with new people in Pequod. Grace, Mac and the kids made for a limited selection.

"Delighted," I said. "What can I bring?"

"Your charms, and a bottle of olives, if you have them. Corwin's Market was out."

Maybe if he liked me and my olives, which I happened to have, he'd go easy on our next lease negotiation, I mused.

Strains of Sondheim floated on the warm, early summer breeze as I walked across the grassy field between the Coop and the solar-paneled farmhouse. There were cars in the driveway—two Jeeps, a gray Mercedes, an Aston Martin. I heard laughter as I stepped onto the wraparound porch. The front door was open, so I went right in.

A half dozen tanned, attractive men were gathered around a white desk in the corner of the airy living room. I glanced around at the sky-lights, the oversize windows and bleached wood floors. The contempo-rary furniture upholstered in chocolate, pale blue and various creams. A tall, tanned man in jeans and a white linen shirt, who I assumed was Jack Mance, stood at the center of the group regaling them.

"I found it when my sister and I cleared out my father's study last week to get his house ready to put on the market. We had no idea he even owned one."

No one had noticed me yet. They were busy listening to Jack and admiring some object he was showing them.

"I'm registering it in my name and keeping it for sentimental rea-sons, but it's staying out here. I can't have it in the city. I'd be too tempted to use it on Bigfoot, my upstairs neighbor. Or on the Tony Soprano look-alike with the jackhammer tearing up the street in front of my apartment at seven a.m."

The men laughed. Jack lifted a martini to his lips. He finally saw me across the room.

"Ah, this must be Nora Glasser, my tenant. She's a journalist with the local paper. Our resident Joan Didion."

"Thank you. I'm very flattered, but you exaggerate."

"Come in. Come in."

He waved me in with his other hand, the one that held a gun, and I instinctively ducked and shielded my face with the olive jar.

"Jack! Put that fucking thing away," shouted the man I'd pegged as his partner, David.

"Sorry. One martini and I'm Annie Oakley," Jack said sheepishly.

He put down the gun and his martini, opened a gray metal box that sat on the white desk and deposited the weapon in it.

"Ms. Glasser, did you hear me?"

"What? Sorry."

"I've noticed you drift off a lot."

"Yes, well, I haven't been getting enough sleep lately."

Roche gave a fake smile. "That can happen when you've got too much on your mind." He studied me. "I said the lockbox contained a .22-caliber handgun, which happens to be the caliber of the bullets in our investigation."

I experienced a strange sensation in my gut akin to snakes slithering.

"You think the same person who took the box used the gun to commit the murders?"

"That's a possibility we're considering, yes."

"How would they get the gun out?"

"Those boxes aren't difficult to open. Any one of a number of basic tools can do it."

He looked at the Swiss Champ in my hand. We both did. I slipped it into my robe pocket.

"Ms. Glasser, you're trembling."

"Am I? It *is* chilly in here. I need to light the woodstove," I said, and wrapped my arms around myself.

"We wondered if you'd seen or heard anything unusual on the property between say October eighteenth, the last meter reading, and November fourteenth, the night before the murders."

As far as I knew, there hadn't been anyone else on the property besides the mailman and me.

"No."

"Since you're the closest neighbor, I was hoping you might have seen something."

Roche's eyes bored into mine. I blinked first, and he cracked a triumphant smile.

"Well, thanks for your time. Give me a call if you have second thoughts. Even the smallest detail can be helpful."

He rose from the chair and started for the door.

"Detective?"

He stopped.

"If possible, I'd like to have my phone and computer back, please."

He didn't even bother to turn.

"We'd like to hold on to them."

As soon as the police car was out of the driveway, I unpacked my new pink Acer Aspire computer, set it up and did a Google search. There were at least fifteen entries on the subject. Turns out you don't even need a tool to open a lockbox. One video on YouTube showed how to pop it with a paper clip in less than a minute.

Chapter Seventeen

"Yvonne!"

I sprinted down the hall, dodging the empty wheelchairs and gurneys lined up against the wall. A bright-yellow-and-black-striped turban bobbed near the nurses' station like some sort of cartoon bumblebee.

"Whoa. Put on the brakes, girl," Yvonne said, raising her palm traffic-cop style as I closed in on her.

"How is she?" I said between huffs.

"She okay. The doctor's gone, but he says your auntie gonna be fine. No worries."

She wrapped herself around me in a big bear hug, and my nose bumped one of her bracelet-size hoop earrings. After a few pats on the back, she released me. I must've still looked shell-shocked because she grabbed my shoulders and shook.

"She be fine. You hear?"

I nodded. "So, what happened, exactly?"

Yvonne took my arm and headed for the row of plastic chairs across the hall. She plunked herself onto one and patted the seat next to her. I sat down.

"It was eight o'clock when I went up to give her your number like I said I would, I hear her yelling inside. But she don't answer the door. I get security to open up, and we find her in the tub shakin' from cold.

Too weak to stand up. 'Why you don't let out the cold water and fill it with hot?' I ask her. But her mind not thinkin' right. So she freezin' in there. Doctor says she had a ministroke. Lucky she didn't catch pneumonia, too. The doctor be here in the morning."

I leaned back and blew out a long breath. "The stroke. How bad?"

"Not so bad. I say three out of ten, if ten be dead."

I prayed "three out of ten" didn't translate into a permanent disability.

"But she also dehydrated. That's why her mind fuzzy." Yvonne shook her head in disbelief. "She sittin' there in a tub full of water, dehydrated."

"Thank you for staying, Yvonne. Let me pay you something, please." I fumbled for my wallet, but she put her hand on mine.

"You goin' through bad times. Spend it on yourself or your auntie."

She gathered her black patent leather coat and matching purse from the chair on her other side and stood up.

"Show this girl some love, Marie," she instructed the young night nurse who'd been eavesdropping from behind the counter. "She gettin' beat up by the world this week." She turned back to me and tilted her head. "You have somewhere to go for the holiday?"

Thanksgiving. I hadn't given a thought to Thanksgiving. It was coming up the next week. Between Lada's condition and my precarious legal situation, I couldn't imagine making plans for the holiday. I might be spending it in the hospital or in jail.

"I haven't figured that out yet."

"You both welcome at my house," Yvonne offered.

"Thank you. That's very kind. Can I let you know?"

"No worries. Unless you're one of those Tofurky people. I can't help you with that. But we ordered a big bird. We got enough to feed Macy's parade, the New York Knicks and whoever. You just call me."

She squeezed my arm and then sashayed down the hall toward the exit door. I looked after her, touched that she would offer to share her holiday with us. The harsh reality I was facing softened for a moment.

Night nurse Marie gave me a sympathetic look and directions to Lada's room. Finding it was easy—the clinic was small—only ten rooms to a floor. The top of a medical chart labeled "Levervitch" stuck out of the plastic holder outside on the wall. I opened the door a crack, hesitating. The overhead lights had been turned off and the curtains drawn. What shape would she be in?

My stomach rolled as I stepped cautiously into the darkened room, leaving the door half open so I wouldn't have to turn on the lights. Lada had fallen asleep propped up on her pillows. A beeping monitor tracked her vital signs. She looked like Yoda—the bald spots on her scalp showing through unkempt wisps of hair. They'd clipped an oxygen tube under her nose, and she had a bruise blossoming on the pale, thin skin around the IV stuck in her skinny forearm. The bones in her wrist seemed as delicate as bird bones.

I sank into the chair by the wall and put my head in my hands. I began to cry silently. We're such vulnerable creatures, I thought. At least Lada hadn't died or become a vegetable. She was still Lada. But if they sent me to prison, how could I continue to help pay for her care? If she defaulted on payments, they'd transfer her out of The Cedars to some state-run nursing home where she'd get bedbugs and bedsores. I was sick at the thought, and time was running out. The noose was tightening. Gubbins told me so when I called him after Detective Roche's visit.

"I'm afraid this strengthens their case substantially. The most compelling argument for your innocence—not having access to a gun—has just been eliminated," he said.

"But I didn't take the gun," I protested, my voice shaking. "It's all circumstantial. You know there have been more summer home break-ins this season. The burglary was a coincidence."

It had to be a coincidence. It had to. The other option was unthinkable.

"An inopportune one. You have no alibi. And a strong motive."

"It doesn't make sense. Why would I kill them now, after all these years? Answer me that one."

Please give me a reason not to go down that road, Mr. Gubbins. Please.

"The DA will say your wounds reopened when Hugh and Helene moved here."

"They moved here last May. It's November. Why would I wait?" I croaked.

"Helene pushed you over the edge when she joined your Pilates class. Your resentment and hatred got out of control. The DA will also try to prove you found out about your ex-husband's retrospective somehow—the one just announced on the radio today on your friend's show."

I thought of Hugh's letter. He'd told me about the retrospective.

"You were enraged that your story would be in the public eye again," Gubbins said.

"But the murders put my story in the public eye!"

"Good point. We can use that."

"Use it now, before this goes any further," I pleaded.

"I'm sorry, Nora. But I have to advise you to get your affairs in order. We need to prepare for the possibility of an arrest warrant in the next few days."

I instinctively distanced the phone from my ear. "Oh no. No. No. Don't say that. I don't want to hear that."

"Nora. You need to stay focused. Try to breathe."

I brought the phone closer, still panicked, but willing myself to listen.

"If it comes to that, there will be court costs when I file the motion for bail, so I'll need that fifteen thousand dollars as soon as possible."

"Jesus. The bail. How high will it be? It's a murder charge."

"A double-murder charge," he corrected me. "We'll get you bonded for that. I know people . . . There's one other thing I'd like you to be aware of."

"What? What else could there be?"

"A polygraph test. It's up to the judge whether to admit it, but the DA may ask for one."

◆ ◆ ◆

Lada shifted in her bed, startling me. Recounting the conversation with Gubbins had my stomach in knots. I should call Grace. Tell her about Aunt Lada's condition. And my neighbor's missing gun. But what if her certainty about my innocence wavered? I couldn't cope with that right now. I couldn't.

I clung to the facts that were still on my side. A) I'd never traveled beyond my immediate surroundings during previous sleepwalking episodes. *But what about the leaves and twig in my hair? Where had they come from?* B) I'd always woken up in the midst of an episode, so I couldn't have broken into Mance's house to steal a gun. Or committed two murders miles from my bed. *But what about washing my jeans, and those blazing lights in the Coop the other morning? I'd almost certainly been sleepwalking, and I hadn't woken then.*

Terrible thoughts kept creeping in. Thoughts of sleep killers. Kenneth Parks butchering his in-laws. That father slamming his innocent infant into a wall. A killer lived inside me; my vicious fantasies attested to that. But had the unspeakable demon murdered in a whitehot rage while my human side slept? Had it gone on a bloodthirsty rampage?

I reminded myself there were still other suspects. Tobias. Stokes. An unknown lover. But even a trace of self-doubt could cause enough anxiety to skew a lie-detector test. Television crime dramas had taught me that. I had a giant glob of self-doubt living in my belly. It was a horror movie in there.

Whatever happened, I would need a war chest—fast—to pay for legal expenses and what might soon be a small army of caretakers for Lada, not to mention the clinic's bill. I resolved to call Sotheby's, Christie's and Phillips's auction houses tomorrow and offer the sketchbook to whichever one set the highest opening bid. I worried that even an expedited sale would take more time than I probably had.

I pulled myself together and looked around Lada's room for a tissue. There was a box of Kleenex on the heating unit by the window. I rose to fetch one.

"Nora?" Lada wheezed.

I rushed to her side. She still hadn't opened her eyes.

"Welcome back. How do you feel?"

"I'm sorry to be so much trouble," she whispered.

"No apologies." I patted her arm.

"I'm an old car. My parts are rusted. I belong in the scrapyard."

"Don't say that. Take it back," I demanded, my fear turning me shrill.

She opened her eyes. They were vacant. Her voice was flat.

"I can't take care of myself anymore. *Vashna nee to kak dolga tuy prozsheel, a kak horoshow zsheel.*"

"In English, please."

"*How well you live makes a difference. Not how long.* I can't even get out of the bathtub. What kind of life is that?"

She turned away from me, her chin trembling. My heart melted.

"All you need is a little help. They have people here who can help you, Aunt Lada. I'll arrange for someone."

"And pay with what?"

"Let me worry about that." I stroked her cold, bony hand. "Lada?"

"What?"

"I heard a rumor."

She loved rumors. She turned her head back and looked at me. Her green eyes twinkled with life for a moment.

"They're going to show *White Nights* at the cinema club here. Mikhail Baryshnikov and Gregory Hines dancing ballet and tap. Defectors and spies in Moscow and Saint Petersburg."

"Bubbala, don't call it Saint Petersburg. It's Leningrad. It will always be Leningrad to me."

If she was up and around by next week, I'd make them rent the movie. Or rent it myself.

◆ ◆ ◆

Lada fell asleep again, thanks to the nurse's pill. She was snoring peacefully as I left her room to go out to the clinic's courtyard and check my burner—clinic rules demanded that cell phones be turned off inside. Ben had called twice and left a message.

"Hey. I just wanted to hear your voice and tell you that thinking about you makes me happy. Call me."

Ben. Oh God. If only I could listen to that lovely message and feel happy along with him. The situation was so much worse now than before he left for the airport. Even if I came clean about sleepwalking, I couldn't tell him with more than 50, maybe 60 percent confidence that I was innocent of murder. The phone buzzed in my hand. Ben again. My heart stopped. What to do? I couldn't let him worry. I swallowed hard and picked up.

"Hello?"

"Nora. I'm so glad I reached you. I was getting nervous."

"I'm sorry. There was a medical drama with my Aunt Lada, but it's okay now."

"What happened?"

"A ministroke."

"Damn. You must be upset. Is there any way I can help? I can drive back tonight."

"No, no. You're generous to offer. But she's out of the woods. And mostly okay." I started to choke up, realizing how it might have turned out differently. "Ben?"

"I'm here."

I wanted things to be simple. Just for a minute. To pretend we were two normal people beginning a real relationship. To think of him knowing the woman who was so dear to me, and have her know him.

"I'm hoping she won't die anytime soon, because I want you to meet her."

"Of course. And I plan on asking her to fill me in on what you were like as a little girl."

"You'll get an earful."

"There are still so many things I don't know about you. For instance, what's your favorite color?"

I smiled. "Jade green."

"Food?"

"Rice pudding."

"Where do you stand on GMOs and Monsanto?"

I loved that he was trying to cheer me up.

"I . . . well . . ."

"Just kidding."

"How did you get to be such a mensch?" I asked.

"The love of a good woman."

I could still hear the pain losing his wife caused him.

"Of course."

"Sorry. I didn't mean—"

"No, it's all right. Judy was something special. I understand. You were a lucky man."

"I've been lucky twice."

I could hear Ben really meant it. But what do they say luck is? "When opportunity meets readiness." I feared that he was an opportunity I might miss.

"I miss you," Ben said.

"I miss you, too." If I didn't switch gears, I might start crying. "Were you late for Sam?"

"Almost an hour. But he was deep into his new iPhone and didn't mind."

"Please don't worry about me. Enjoy your time with him . . . Oh. I almost forgot. You left your knife here."

"I know. Take care of it for me."

"I will."

"I'll see you for dinner on Friday."

If I wasn't in jail by then.

"Nora?"

"Right. Friday."

"I'm hoping to see you sooner than that. In my dreams. And don't bother dressing."

If only we could meet there. "Night," I said.

It began raining. I returned to Lada's room to check on her one last time before driving home, but it didn't feel right to leave her alone. I decided to take a chance and sleep in the chair by her hospital bed. If I were going to sleepwalk, getting caught by a nurse in a clinic would be a best-case scenario. But when I woke in the morning, there were no signs that I'd gone "gallivanting," a verb Lada often used to describe my post-midnight club crawls in college. Sometimes I'd visit her for breakfast if I stayed out all night dancing with friends. She was always up by 5:00 a.m., delighted to make blinis and hear of my adventures.

It took drinking vats of weak coffee at the nurse's station to reach my functional caffeine level. Then I spent the next few hours holding Lada's hand through another battery of tests. Her doctor came by and gave a cautiously optimistic report but ordered more tests for the afternoon. The gloomy day passed in a medical bubble. It was actually a relief to be focusing on Lada instead of the murders. I managed to leave messages at the auction houses, but I had to stand outside in the rain to do it. The sun broke through after Lada's pal Mort visited. She finally smiled and seemed more like herself. My spirits brightened as well.

By midnight I was headed home, hurrying down the cedar path in the brisk night air toward the parking lot. Above me a cluster of feathery gray clouds surrounded a giant yellow moon. They made it look like the eye of a wolf. I pulled my collar up, wrapped my coat around me more tightly and jogged the rest of the way to the car.

After I crossed the Harbor Bridge, a dark road stretched ahead. Not a single car in sight. No headlights behind, either. Sgt. Crawley's car wasn't parked on the shoulder where he'd waited before, but that didn't mean the police weren't watching. This deserted stretch of Crooked Beach Road offered plenty of secret spots for a stakeout—thick, dark woods on either side. The police could be lurking in there for the night.

As I arrived at the Coop, the clouds moved over the moon. Cloaked in shadow, the long, low building and a small garden shed squatted between two walls of towering hemlock shrubs. The dark forest loomed at the edge of the field behind. I'd forgotten to turn on the outside light when I rushed off to the clinic and had to squint for my house key on the crowded chain. I finally remembered to use the light on my phone.

A strong odor of cigarettes and burned rope greeted me at the doorstep. I stiffened, whipped around and scanned the driveway and bushes with my phone light.

No sign of anyone. Silence. I slowly returned to face the door and sniffed again. I aimed the light beam at my feet and could see two cigarette butts mashed into the sisal mat. I concluded the police must've returned for more questions. But then I remembered I hadn't seen Roche or Crawley smoking. I bent down, picked up one of the butts and held it closer to the phone. I recognized the eagle wing insignia on the paper instantly and went completely still.

American Spirits.

Something rustled the thick hemlocks at the side of the house. I flinched and accidentally dropped the phone. It bounced off the concrete step and landed in the gravel as a bright beam of light shot straight into my eyes.

"Hey, Nora. I've been waiting out here so long, I had to relieve myself back there."

The light kept me blinking, and pretty much blind, but I recognized the voice. "Stokes?"

"You're out late. Been on a date?" he asked. There was a taunt in his tone I didn't like. Stress hormones coursed into my bloodstream.

Stay calm. Just keep talking.

"I was visiting my aunt," I said, discreetly stretching my foot down the step to feel for the phone. "What are you doing here? And where's your car? I didn't see your car."

The light swept away from my face toward the shed.

"I rode my bike."

Spots danced in front of my eyes for a moment, but then I could distinguish the form of a bike leaning against the shed's side.

"These miner lamps are great, but I don't want to wear out the battery," Stokes said. There was a click and everything went black again. "I took the bike so I wouldn't wake Kelly, so she wouldn't hear me leave. Man, I had to beg her to come home. She wanted to stay at Grace's."

Oh shit. Had he done something to her?

"I think you know why she left," he said.

I heard him take a few steps toward me. Bile rose in my throat. My legs pulsed with tension like a runner at the starting line. The only thing I could see was Stokes's dark, hulking form.

"She came back, but she told me I had to sleep on the couch. I couldn't sleep. The fucking voice wouldn't shut up. I kept hearing this goddamn fucking voice inside my head," he said.

I took a step backward. There was nowhere to go—the front door was locked.

"It wouldn't stop. It kept needling me. Wouldn't let me sleep. 'Why did you do it, Stokes? How could you do it? You are a degenerate son of a bitch.'"

Tendons pulsed on either side of my neck. If I could make a break across the field and run like the wind, I could lose him in the forest. But what if he was faster? My hand began working the keys. Everything seemed to be moving in slow motion. It took an eternity to maneuver them between my fingers into a spiked fist.

"You can come to hate the person you once loved. Isn't that true, Nora? You've felt that hate inside, haven't you?"

He took a few more steps. He came close enough that I smelled the smoke on his clothes. The alcohol on his breath. The sharp stink of his sweat. I swallowed hard. My tongue felt heavy as lead.

"Sure," I said.

"You probably couldn't stand the sight of Hugh. What a scumbag that guy was. You must've prayed for bad things to happen to him. You imagined making them happen yourself, didn't you? You wanted to take your revenge. Isn't that right?"

I clenched my barbed fist. *Take one more step, Mister. Meet Gladiator Girl.*

"Isn't it?"

"Yes."

"Shit!"

I heard him slap his jeans, spin around and walk away from me, kicking the dirt as he went.

"So, tell me what the hell I can do to change that, Nora!"

"Huh?"

"Kelly hates me. She wants a divorce. She said she hoped my dick would rot off. And if it didn't rot off, she might cut it off like that woman in Virginia did to her husband. What's her name . . . you know . . . Lorna?"

I was so light-headed with relief, I had to think for a second.

"Lorena Bobbitt?"

"Yeah, her. But I never loved Helene. I've only ever loved Kelly. Help me out here, Nora. Please. You're the only one I can think of to ask. You've been through it. What could Hugh have said or done that would get you to forgive him? Tell me what she wants to hear."

He sounded so sincere and bereft. I sat down on the doorstep and started to laugh.

"What's so funny?"

"Nothing. It's just . . . I'm relieved. You scared me. You know there's a killer on the loose, Stokes."

"Oh fuck. I'm sorry. I'm, like, crazy over this."

"Come inside and we'll talk. It's too cold out here. But do me a favor first? Turn on that headlamp and help me find my phone."

His hair shone with grease. He hadn't shaved for days. Dirt discolored his fingernails. His jeans looked like they could walk away on their own. I poured Stokes a beer and myself some of the Stoli from the freezer while he fidgeted with his headlamp and avoided my eyes. He took out his pack of cigarettes.

"Please, could you not smoke inside?"

"Sorry," he said, palming them. "I started after Kelly got pregnant. I think I was scared of how everything was changing. Kelly wasn't interested in sex anymore. We'd get into bed and all she wanted to talk about was how her boobs hurt and her ankles were sore. But Helene . . . you know she shaved her hooch?"

I recoiled. This wasn't an image I wanted in my brain.

"Gee, no, I didn't."

"We did wild stuff. Triple-X-rated. Things that Kelly would never get near."

Was that it? Had Hugh betrayed me to fuck a sex tiger? Had I bored him in bed? Is that why he cheated with Helene and the others?

"Anyway, it doesn't matter. Helene was just using me, I know that now. I was a dumb-ass. A slave to my dick. All I want is Kelly back. I love her. I can't live without her. And I want to be a family with her and our baby. You've gotta tell me how I can make her love me again."

He was frantic with narcissistic remorse. What could I say to this guy? *So, your wife's sex drive took a dip while she was pregnant. She was physically uncomfortable. She needed some extra love and attention to help get her turned on, or maybe some curated porn? Instead you gave her the shiv. You were feeling sexually neglected, so you broke her heart. Or were you so afraid of becoming a parent that you acted like a selfish child?*

But his question had me wondering if there was anything Hugh could have said to change the way I felt. Could I have forgiven him if he hadn't gotten Helene pregnant? I didn't know. I guess I forgave his road affair without ever confronting him. No. That wasn't forgiveness. That was denial. My silence was complicit. Like Hillary Clinton and countless other women who stayed with their cheating men, I'd made my bed.

"It all comes down to trust," I said, pouring my second shot. "You have to earn her trust again. And that's not going to be easy. It's going to take a very long time."

"You think there's a chance?"

I nodded. Who was I to say there wasn't? Forgiveness comes more easily to some.

"Here's what I think. Take it slow with Kelly. Don't be surprised if she warms up to you and then goes nuts again. Don't answer any 'specific' sexual questions about your affair. She'll ask, but if you answer, it will hurt her in a way she won't be able to recover from. Make sure you tell her repeatedly that you think you were an idiot. And show her that you want to be a good dad. Take those parenting classes with her.

If you really love your wife and want to save this marriage, you just might be able to."

Stokes thanked me so intensely you'd think I'd gotten his finger unstuck from a bowling ball. He even offered to start my woodstove. As I downed my third shot of vodka and watched Stokes build the fire, I was almost certain he didn't kill Hugh and Helene. I didn't know how Tobias put his hands on a gun, but he must have. Yes, Tobias had to be the one who killed them, I thought desperately.

Because currently I was the only other likely alternative.

Chapter Eighteen

I woke up with a start. What time was it? My head felt like a water balloon. I couldn't recall the last time I drank so much vodka. I rolled over and lifted the cell off the night table—the battery was dead. I plugged in the charger and it buzzed almost instantly. Grace. The funeral service. Shit.

"Nora? I'm at the chapel. Where are you?" she whispered.

In bed. But I didn't remember going to bed.

"Did you go . . . you know . . . for a walk last night?"

"I don't know," I admitted, flinging the sheets aside. "I don't think so. Save me a seat. I'm on my way," I said, searching for debris in my hair as I rolled out of bed and hurried to check the rest of the house.

"Listen, Kelly went home last night. I couldn't stop her. But don't worry. She let Mac follow her over and warn Stokes he'd better take good care of her. Even if Stokes is the killer, he won't dare touch her."

The kitchen lights were off. "Stokes came here last night," I said.

"He did?" Grace was incredulous. "What for? Are you all right?"

I stopped short in the living room. The pots weren't in front of the door. They were scattered across the floor. Shit.

"He just wanted to talk. I'm fine. I'll fill you in later," I said. "Tell me what's going on there."

Had I set the pots in place after Stokes left? I was so hammered last night I couldn't remember.

"I made it here early and spoke with Ruth Walker. You were right. They've already asked their lawyer to petition for guardianship. You sure you're okay?"

"Totally. See? I knew it."

I pressed my palm to my heart. This was good news. Tobias was making his moves. He could be the one.

"They're flying home after the burial this afternoon and taking Callie with them," Grace said. "And something else . . . Tobias mentioned his Fund for the American Family. He said he regretted having to go back to Lynchburg right away, but he had a very important meeting with the lawyer for the fund."

"Figuring out how to finance it with Hugh's money, no doubt."

"That's what I was thinking," Grace said. "So hurry up and get over here."

"Any press around?"

"Not yet. I'll save you a seat in the back," she said and clicked off.

Despite the hangover, I rallied and zapped four tablespoons of instant coffee in a mug of water and then gulped it down along with two Advil. I whipped through my closet, pulling out a black pencil skirt, black turtleneck sweater and black boots. The house was colder than usual, which meant it must be freezing outside, so I grabbed my Ushanka—the Soviet Army hat Lada gave me for my birthday about ten years ago—along with my black wool muffler. I dressed, put on eyeliner and lipstick, called Lada to check on her and flew out the door within fifteen minutes. I hoped I wouldn't have to make a late entrance at the church, but the important thing was this: to see Tobias in the flesh. I don't know why, but I had a powerful intuition that if I could look into his eyes, I'd know for certain if he killed his brother.

The day was damp and cold and the sky filled with heavy gray clouds. "Gunmetal gray," I heard myself thinking as I unlocked the car. I had guns on the brain. Mance's stolen handgun in particular. My self-doubt still gnawed. *Wake up and smell the coffee, Nora. Remember Occam's razor. The simplest explanation is that you were sleepwalking and you stole your neighbor's gun. You're a sleep killer.*

I did not. I am not.

The air smelled like snow. Historically, a "coastal effect" kept snow from falling on Pequod until after Christmas, but it looked like flurries might start any minute. I wrapped the scarf around the upturned collar of my trench coat and pulled the Ushanka down over my ears. *Call me Masha*, I thought, catching my reflection in the rearview mirror. Hugh would have wanted to paint the mysterious Russian vixen staring back at me. And have sex with her, too, of course.

Crawley was waiting at the corner in his black-and-white on the shoulder of Crooked Beach Road. He wasn't trying to hide his intentions anymore. He pulled onto the blacktop and followed after I passed.

"Make a U-turn," Lady GPS said. "Make a U-turn."

"Maybe this time you're right," I said.

I stayed well under the speed limit, determined not to let Crawley shake me up. For distraction, I switched the radio on despite knowing it was unlikely I'd pick up much. WPQD offered pure static. The classical station crackled with more high-pitched white noise. But the Christian station came in as clear as holy water: "Why not demand that our elected officials make laws that reflect our Christian values? Abortion is only one of the crimes sanctioned by the godless in Washington," the host scoffed. "Adultery is another. And according to the Bible, it's punishable by death."

I clicked the radio off. Some of these people sounded so extreme—like an American version of the Taliban. Would the Fund for the American Family promote the kind of religious radicalism that led to violence? I suspected Tobias had already hired lawyers to find a loophole that would let him use some of Callie's inheritance. He might need to wait until she turned eighteen to get his hands on the bulk of it. Would he have brainwashed Callie into donating millions to his cause by then?

The turnoff for Charlotte's Cove was coming up. Tobias had picked a quaint Lutheran chapel located in a farming area a few miles south—there was no evangelical church near Pequod. Charlotte's Cove Chapel bordered one of the oldest family farms in the county. Rows of corn stretched from the edge of its yard all the way down to the shore in summer. The congregation had been lured away by larger churches built nearer to town, so the diocese closed the chapel and began renting it out as a hall. I'd attended an Animal Rescue Fund benefit there. The place didn't have a minister; it wasn't part of the church anymore. You'd think Tobias would want a formal Christian service for Hugh—he might be a murderer, but he was a religious one. Were the active churches too big for the modest gathering he envisioned? Were they booked?

The white spire appeared ahead. Crawley slowed down and dropped back. He pulled over next to another squad car parked on the roadside and watched me drive on alone. Mourners' cars lined both sides of the street. Damn! The press had gotten wind of the service—three vans with satellite dishes on their roofs had parked at odd angles in front of the chapel. A gaggle of reporters milled under leafless oaks that bordered a brick path leading to the chapel doors. Entering there would be like walking the gauntlet.

Lizzie was on the street in a black watch cap and navy peacoat. She had her camera slung around her neck, and she'd positioned herself by one of two black hearses. She appeared to be chatting up the driver. Smart girl. She'd get some dramatic shots when they brought the bodies out. But in about ten seconds, she and the rest of the press would spot me.

I spied a tall evergreen hedge jutting out past the chapel and remembered parking in that side lot. There was a second entrance that would offer some protection from the press. I sank lower into my seat, covered the bottom half of my face with my scarf and tugged the Ushanka down over my brow. Out of the corner of my eye, I saw the reporters turn to check out my car as I sped past the hearses and veered around the corner into the lot. Grace's Prius and a couple of other cars were there. I parked and hurried up the steps into the chapel before the cameras could catch up.

Inside, the vestibule smelled of furniture polish and old Bibles. A bulky radiator clanked and hissed against the wall. It masked the words of a female speaker beyond the inner wooden double doors. I checked my watch: probably thirty minutes since the service began. I realized this entrance to the sanctuary was located too close to the pulpit. It would disrupt the speaker and draw a lot of attention if I walked in there. Better to crack open one of the doors and watch unnoticed. Hoping for oiled hinges, I pulled the handle.

Sue Mickelson was sitting on the end of the pew directly opposite, listening attentively to whomever was speaking—I still couldn't hear much over the radiator's hiss. A fur coat rested on Sue's shoulders. Blonde tresses curled down around a string of pearls that ended in the décolletage of her black silk dress. She looked like a sexy Blackglama ad. It wasn't hard to picture Hugh with Sue. But as I watched her wipe a tear from her eye with one hand, I saw her discreetly place the other on the upper thigh of the woman next to her, a reedy woman in a masculine black suit who had short, dark hair and square black glasses. Their body language had me pretty sure Hugh didn't score with Sue.

Adjusting my angle for a better view of the nave, I had to steady myself as my eyes landed on two imposing caskets. Large ebony boxes strewn with white lilies. Hugh was inside one of them, no doubt dressed in a suit he'd never wear and pumped with formaldehyde. I felt instantly, deeply sad for him. I wouldn't feel this grief if I'd killed him. Right?

Behind the caskets, Helene's sister spoke from the pulpit. I recognized her from the newsclip. She looked to be in her thirties. She had multiple piercings in one ear and wore knee-high black boots and a black motorcycle jacket over a black dress that ended midthigh. Her cheeks were stained with runny mascara. A section of her thick mane of auburn hair had fallen over one eye. She kept brushing it away with the back of her hand, revealing a mass of silver bracelets on her wrist.

There was a large projection screen in back of her—only a small portion of it visible from my post. I took a chance I wouldn't be noticed and opened the door an inch more. I could finally hear her speak.

"I guess what I'm trying to tell you is I admired my little sister. You know, she had a rough time growing up."

As she paused to pull a tissue from her jacket pocket and blow her nose, I crouched down to get a better look at the screen behind her. It featured an oversize image of Hugh and Helene toasting toward the camera at a Masout Gallery opening. The image cross-faded into one of Hugh and Helene hugging Callie in a canoe at Pequod Point. There was another of Hugh and Helene in white robes and sunglasses, grinning as they relaxed on chaise lounges by an infinity pool. The slides were a painful reminder of how happily Hugh's life had continued after our demise.

"Our mother isn't here today. Probably because she was too drunk to get on a plane. We haven't seen my father since he left when Helene was ten—that's when my mother started drinking. I was already at college, so my sister practically had to raise herself. Maybe that's why she grew up to be someone who had amazing drive and determination." Her voice cracked. "'Maggot,' she'd say—that was my nickname—she hadn't been able pronounce the 'r' in Margaret when she was little," Margaret said, losing her composure and pausing.

Helene's difficult background came as a surprise. I'd always assumed it was because she was spoiled—used to getting everything she wanted—that she acted without regard to the hurt she caused.

After a moment, Margaret gathered herself. "'Maggot, you need a vision of your life,' my little sister would say. 'You have to see things in your mind first and then make them happen. You have to *manifest*.'"

On the screen, a slide of one of Hugh's paintings—one I hadn't seen before—faded in and stayed there. It was a kitsch homage to *American Gothic* featuring Hugh and Helene in overalls. Helene held a pitchfork in one hand and with the other hand was touching the bulging belly she'd manifested.

"My sister's way of doing things didn't endear her to a lot of people. But I can only see her as that fiercely determined little girl. And when she grew up, she was determined to have a child of her own. The one she brought into this world is incredible."

Margaret broke down completely and collapsed into sobs. Her anguish was heartrending.

"I love Callie. And I loved my sister. I can't do this. I can't bury her."

A bald man in a dark suit swooped in from the side and ushered the distraught Margaret back to the front-row pew. I didn't recognize him at first; his hairlessness threw me off. He wasn't bald; he'd shaved his head. His face was gaunt and the skin under his eyes bruised purple. And he'd lost a shocking amount of weight in the few days since his appearance on the news. Tobias looked like he'd just gotten out of prison. Was his guilt eating him alive? Was his shorn hair a sign of penance or grief? When he finally returned to stand behind the pulpit, he didn't speak. He took his time surveying the crowd. Then he picked up his Bible and waved it over his head.

"You don't have to be a murderer to be a sinner, brothers and sisters. 'As it is written, there is none righteous, no, not one.' Romans 3:10. We are all lowly creatures of appetite. Weak and indulgent lovers of flesh. 'We are all as an unclean thing, and all our righteousnesses are as filthy rags' . . . We are sinners, all of us. Subject to the wily manipulations of the devil."

He placed the Bible back on the pulpit and stroked it before continuing.

"And what is the Devil's nefarious purpose? To close the gates of heaven and seal us in hell." There was a wildness in his eyes. A cruelty that was frightening. "To condemn us to everlasting torment.

"But there is a clear path to return to God's grace. Accept the one who willingly died on the cross so that you might be cleansed. Receive Jesus as your Savior."

He paused and bowed his shaved head.

I suddenly knew why Tobias booked this "defrocked" chapel. He wanted to play minister to another captive audience. To stand up there and feel important and righteous. He raised his head and walked away from the pulpit, placing himself between the two coffins.

"My brother and sister here?" He tapped each of the lids lightly. "They were liars. Coveters. Adulterers. Their thoughts and deeds polluted with greed and carnality."

I could hear the crowd murmuring and rustling in discomfort at this distasteful display. I hoped Callie wasn't hearing this. I scanned the pews in my sight line. I didn't see her. I did find a few other distressed faces.

"They worshipped at the altar of the devil. But still, we must forgive them. They began as children of Jesus."

With a cheap showman's sense of drama, he leaned down and kissed the top of one coffin, then the other, before turning to the crowd again.

"Whether they returned to Him at the end, we cannot know. I pray with all my heart that they did. So they won't suffer the torments of hell. So they can rest in the loving arms of the Lord and enjoy eternity in his glorious Kingdom."

He put his hands together. "Pray with me. Pray for them. And for Callie, their little girl. She is not here with us today—she is far too young to absorb all this loss."

I felt relieved for Callie. Tobias closed his eyes and stayed silent for a few moments. When he opened them, I saw the glint of pride. And power.

"Praise God. All rise."

Clothing rustled again. Pews squeaked. I stuck my head a little further into the chapel for a quick peek at the mourners. It was only three-quarters full. I guessed the majority of Hugh and Helene's friends lived in New York City and would attend the service there.

"'For the wages of sin is death; but the gift of God is eternal life through Jesus Christ our Lord.' Forgiveness begins here. Amen."

A chorus of mumbled "amens" rose to a crescendo and then petered out as a recording of "Precious Lord" began. Tobias gripped a casket handle and waved for the pallbearers to join him up front. I retreated into the vestibule, closing the door. The sizzle of the radiator drowned out the hymn, but it couldn't shut out my own chaotic thoughts. They were slamming into each other like bumper cars. I felt I would explode.

Tobias Walker was a twisted, sanctimonious prick—preaching about sin over their bodies. Using their funeral to gratify his need to aggrandize himself. Would he use their kid? Did he slaughter his own brother and sister-in-law like animals to get control of their money? Had he destroyed my life by setting me up to take the blame?

And Helene. Poor Helene. Her mother was a drunk; her father a runner. She'd been neglected, abandoned and most likely emotionally abused. Despite everything she'd taken from me, I felt sorry for her.

Wait . . . why should I feel sorry for Helene? My childhood was no picnic, either, and I didn't go around getting myself knocked up by another woman's husband. After shattering that woman's life, I didn't show up to plague her when she tried to build a new one. And look at how she burned Kelly. Kelly was about to have a goddamn baby, and it still didn't deter that selfish witch. No. I was glad that Helene and Hugh were dead. I was grateful I'd never have to deal with either of them again. Happy they were off the planet.

God. Oh God. What's wrong with me?

Did Tobias kill Hugh and Helene, or did I?

Wrung out, I just wanted to find Grace and go home. I opened the vestibule door again. A number of the mourners had already filed out of the chapel, following the coffins to the hearses. I slipped into the sanctuary and stood in the shadows against the wall, scouting for Grace.

The white silk rose on her wide-brimmed black hat surfaced from the sea of black by the door. She was about to enter the media circus out front, and I wasn't going to chase her there.

Sue Mickelson and her girlfriend remained in their seats, whispering to each other. They finally rose and brought up the rear of the line behind Hugh's Latina housekeeper and her son. They were the only other people I recognized besides Grace, Tobias and his wife. Where was Abbas? Surely, he'd driven out for this. Who were the rest of these mourners? Granted, it looked as if Tobias meant what he said—"just family and a few local friends." But not that long ago, I would have known everyone. It was as if the life Hugh and I shared for twelve years had never happened. It had been erased.

Sue Mickelson, towering in high heels, was gazing absently across the room over her girlfriend's head when she spotted me. I saw her eyes flicker and her expression change. She leaned down and said something to her partner, who turned to look. So did the housekeeper and her son. The couple in front of them began whispering to each other, glancing furtively in my direction. Word traveled down the line. As more heads turned, my face flushed, and my vision clouded with tears. I was shaking with anger. I wanted to scream: "Did any of you people even know Hugh? He would have hated this funeral. He wasn't religious!"

But I said nothing. I spun around and marched back through the doors and out of the vestibule to wait for Grace in the lot. On the steps I stopped short, still vibrating. Distant voices shouted—probably the press firing off questions around front.

Crawley had moved his squad car directly across the street and was watching me through the opening in the hedges. I wasn't going to let him gawk anymore. Defiant, I charged over to my car, plunged inside and slammed the door.

Staring savagely at the side of the chapel, I cranked up the heat and switched on the radio. Scary pipe-organ music. I turned it off. In the quiet that followed, I heard a familiar voice torturing the English language.

"You are hearing me now?"

There he was. Abbas Masout rounded the corner on the path that led from the front of the chapel along its side to the parking lot. He spoke into the phone while bending and twisting his torso in search of a better connection.

"Hearing me now?"

He wore a black turtleneck under what looked like a black wool painter's jacket topped with a black cashmere scarf. The man was elegant.

"Yes, come to memorial service at gallery tomorrow. Three o'clock. I am seeing you then."

Of course Abbas was going to host the memorial at the gallery. That made sense.

"Sorry, another is calling. I must go. See you tomorrow."

Abbas switched the phone to his other ear and craned his neck.

"Hello, Anina? Anina, did you get my message? I have tried to reach you. Sorry, I am in Pequod now. Yes. A small service. And Hugh's brother wants estimation on his paintings, so I stay this afternoon."

Tobias was already trying to determine what Hugh was worth. Outrageous. But more condemning evidence.

"Yes. Thank you, Anina. I am doing my best. How could I not? But you will come to the memorial tomorrow at the gallery? Good. Then I go to London for some weeks. We will reschedule our meeting after London."

He leaned too far to the right and nearly lost his balance.

"Hello? Anina? Hello? Agh, shit."

Abbas continued cursing his dropped call until he saw me through the windshield.

"Nora!"

I pressed the button and my window rolled down.

"Hi, Abbas."

"My God, Nora."

He came around to the driver's side. Then he leaned in the window to look more closely at my face through the rising steam of our breath. It was good to see him.

I wondered what he thought of that brutal eulogy.

"Dear girl, you came. I didn't see you inside." He shook his head. "The brother. His talk was terrible, no?"

"Awful," I agreed.

"You must come to the city tomorrow. We will do a beautiful thing at the gallery at three."

He began to study me the way I'd seen him evaluate a work of art so many times in the past. Lips pursed. Close-set eyes narrowed and penetrating as he took measure of the painting's effect on him. Analyzing where it fit into the marketplace and how much he could profit from it.

"You are looking stunning today. Like Cossack princess."

"Thank you." I couldn't help smiling a little inside. Even at a funeral, Abbas's chauvinism was irrepressible.

He raised an eyebrow. "I think you must have a new man."

Ben. Our dinner was tonight, and I had so much to tell him. I hoped I'd find the nerve.

"I do."

"I am happy for you, Nora." He sighed. "You know my feeling. Hugh should have never let you go. He should have given you a baby. You were good for him."

So that's how he saw it. I guess he wasn't keen on Helene. But what about whether Hugh was good for me?

"Thanks . . . For the record, *I* was the one who let *him* go."

"Ah, of course. Anyway . . ." He trailed off and looked sad. He rubbed his eye. He was starting to cry. "So much history. I see you and I remember. How much time Hugh and I spent together, how much we enjoyed arguing for sport. How he loved my baba ghanoush." He blinked, fighting back his tears.

"Three, four times a week we were talking. Three, four times a week for all those years. In my mind, I am still speaking with Hugh all the time."

I opened my glove compartment, dug out a recycled, brown-paper napkin and gave it to Abbas. His feelings for Hugh touched me. But I was also a little envious that Abbas could mourn Hugh without ambivalence. Hugh hadn't betrayed him.

Abbas blew his nose. "Now he is gone. And why? Who does this terrible thing?"

"I wish I knew."

I'd had the urge to tell him that the man he was helping today was likely Hugh's killer. But I checked it. I needed to get to those car rental calls and find some real evidence to present to the police. Wait . . . maybe Tobias had said something incriminating to Abbas?

"So, you're going to evaluate Hugh's paintings today? At the studio?"

He tilted his head. "Who told you this?"

"I heard you on the phone just now. Why the rush, if you don't mind my asking?"

Abbas looked defensive. "Tobias asked for my help. He has financial decisions to make for the child. He is flying home this afternoon, right after burial, with his wife and the little one. He asked me to stay and take an estimate on the paintings in Hugh's studio before I leave for London. I'll be gone for almost a month."

His phone buzzed and he checked the caller.

"I need to be answering this. You are coming to the cemetery now?"

"No."

"Then you must come to memorial tomorrow, dear girl. We must talk more." He reached in, grabbed my hand and kissed it, then put the phone to his ear. "Anina? Anina? You can hear me now?" he shouted, turning away.

He crossed the lot doing battle with his phone and finally gave up in frustration, climbing into his dark green BMW. As he backed out of his parking space, my passenger door opened. Grace slipped in beside me. I held up my hand before she could speak.

"I'm pretty sure it's Tobias. It looks like he's already counting the money."

Big, shaggy flakes began falling as soon as we left the chapel. So much for the "coastal effect"; global warming messed with cold-weather patterns, too. A thick dusting already covered the lawn by the time we pulled our cars up to Grace and Mac's house, a mid-nineteenth-century Cape on one of Pequod's prettiest streets. Mac, Otis and Leon were out front wearing dark wool caps and toggle coats, lobbing the season's first snowballs. The scene looked like a Currier & Ives litho—if you cropped out the Pequod Volunteer Ambulance parked by the curb for Mac to jump into at a moment's notice.

We greeted Mac and the boys and went into the house. Behind the traditional exterior, the home's inside was unconventional. Walls lined with dozens of flea-market paintings of flowers—roses, zinnias, sunflowers—all sorts of blooms. Colorful pillows and throws on creamy couches. Eclectic, ethnic furniture set on an assortment of vibrant Turkish rugs.

Grace went into the kitchen to whip up a snack, insisting I rest.

"You look like you need to lie down," she said.

I sprawled on the chaise by the window and stared across at shelves full of books and family photos, lingering on the picture of Grace and Mac at their wedding. I'd glanced at it so many times in passing. But I studied it now. Gallant, snowy-haired Mac stood behind his bride with his strong arms wrapped around her waist. She leaned back into him, her hands covering his, secure at her center. Both of them were beaming and genuinely thrilled.

Snapshots of my own wedding arose in my mind unbidden. Grace's oldest, Leon, toddling down the aisle and flinging rose petals up in the air at whim. Dappled sunlight shining through the windows of our loft onto fluted champagne glasses. The smiling, expectant faces of guests watching the civil-court judge conduct the ceremony.

But had those faces really been smiling? Or was that how I'd chosen to remember them? Because worried expressions began to appear in my mind, on Grace's face, on Mac's and Aunt Lada's. Did they know marrying Hugh would bring me so much unhappiness? Had they suspected his infidelities? Even the groom seemed subdued, in retrospect. Was Hugh in turmoil at the altar? Had he just lacked the nerve to call off the wedding? The trouble with having a partner who lies and cheats is that it can make you question everything.

The snow was still drifting down twenty minutes later. Leon and Otis played outside, winging snow angels. Grace was speaking with her sister on the phone in the kitchen. Mac, in his typical ADD style, had grown bored with the snowball fight. He'd come inside to watch *Deadliest Catch* on TiVo in the den while he worked on his fishing lures and monitored the stock market's afternoon moves all at the same time.

I'd filled Grace in on Lada's ministroke, Stokes's desperate visit and, reluctantly, Detective Roche's "drop-in" about the stolen gun. "Another summer house burglary? Right down the road from you? And they stole a fucking gun. Jesus, why can't you catch a break here?" She never doubted my innocence for a second.

When I told her Gubbins thought I should prepare for arrest in the next few days, she was adamant that I come stay with her and Mac. I argued that I should see Lada again right away, but Grace disagreed. "She's in good hands. You need a little loving care, too."

I lay on the chaise making calls to car rental companies and keeping an eye on the boys through the window. The smell of fresh coffee mixed with the mouthwatering scent of baking brownies. It would have been a typical fall afternoon at Grace and Mac's, except for the snow drifting down outside. And the cop car parked across the street. And the fact that I was tracking down evidence in a double homicide investigation.

I'd spent the last five minutes on hold as Avis played Gershwin's "Rhapsody in Blue." The agent finally picked up. I cleared my throat.

"Hello! I work at Lynchburg Media. My boss rented a car from you last weekend in New York City. Unfortunately, he seems to have misplaced the receipt. I'm trying to get a copy for his expense report. His last name is Walker. First name Tobias. I'd really appreciate your help."

She bought the story. "I'm sure we can locate that for you. It might take a minute," she said. "Rhapsody" resumed while she put me on hold again.

Grace appeared carrying a tray of scrumptious chocolate squares. She set them on a small bamboo table near the chaise along with a stack of paper napkins.

"Take a few. I don't want the kids to eat too many. Did you find anything yet?"

"Nothing at Hertz. I'm on with Avis. If Tobias didn't rent a car there, there are still six more companies."

Grace started back for the kitchen. Suddenly, I felt a crushing weight in my chest. I reached for her hand and held on, barely getting my words out.

"Grace. Sometimes it feels like none of this is real. It can't be. It's too insane."

"I know."

"If I let myself think about Hugh, what happened to him, what he was feeling right before the gun went off. If he watched them kill Helene first or . . ."

"Don't."

Grace squeezed my hand. I took a breath.

"What if they never find out who murdered them? What if I go to jail, or worse? Even if they don't charge me, people will always wonder if I killed them." *I'd* always wonder.

"I feel so helpless," I said.

"You're innocent, Nora." Grace sat on the arm of the chaise, still holding my hand. "We'll do whatever it takes to prove it."

I couldn't summon my own faith, but I held on tightly to hers. "I really needed to hear that. You're my rock, Grace."

"Oh, honey."

Grace released my hand and stroked my head. Mac's voice interrupted us.

"I think I'd better drive to the hardware store and pick up a bag of salt for the driveway," he announced.

I sat up and pulled myself together as he walked in from the den.

"The brownies done already?" He made a beeline for them and grabbed one. "The weather alert just said they're predicting fourteen inches by morning. We're breaking a record. Maybe I'll order takeout at Mao's for dinner while I'm at it?" He bit into his brownie. "Mmm. Outstanding. Do we have enough for me to bring one to Crawley?"

"Why would you do that?" I asked, offended.

"I feel for the guy. He pulled such a crap assignment," he said as he wrapped another brownie in a paper napkin. "He's sidelined here watching you while his buddies at county get to hunt the killer." He walked over to the coatrack and grabbed his coat and cap. "It's only a matter of time before they nab whoever did it, and poor Crawley will have missed all the action."

I was touched. He had faith in me, too.

"What if I pick up a DVD at the library? Or how about Thai food instead of Chinese? Or is Italian better?" he asked, bundling up for the storm.

Grace shrugged, accustomed to Mac's multiple-choice questions.

"Anything you decide is good," she said.

"What makes you so sure they'll catch the killer, Mac?" I asked.

"It helps to think positive." He walked over and gave Grace a peck on the cheek. "Hey, maybe we skip the takeout and cook chili together? I could stop at the market . . . You're staying for dinner, right, Nora?"

No. I was meeting Ben for dinner tonight, and I desperately wanted him in my corner along with Grace and Mac. I was determined to own up to the sleepwalking. I'd tell him about the gun and the arrest warrant. Grace knew it all, and she believed in my innocence. Ben might, too. Grace said he shouldn't be in my life if he didn't.

"Thanks, but I'm having dinner with a friend."

I felt at peace for a moment, until I looked out the window at the heavy, swirling snow. Ben might not be able to make it back.

"Unless the weather makes that impossible," I said.

Mac stopped at the front door. "There you go again. Don't be a neg head. Ben drives a Land Rover. He'll make it."

Frowning, I turned to Grace.

"You told him about Ben?"

She looked sheepish and stuffed a piece of brownie in her mouth. "Pillow talk."

"I think it's great," Mac said. "I'm taking the Jeep. Back in an hour or so. If you think of anything else we need, let me know." He went out, calling over his shoulder, "Remember, Nora. Positive."

I wasn't sure whether my thinking was positive or negative, but I decided to start eating a brownie, suspecting that the rental agent would come back on the line the moment I took a bite. It worked. I swallowed quickly.

"Okay, ma'am. Sorry to keep you waiting. I have—"

"Hello? Yes?"

Grace sat down on the arm of the chaise, eager to hear.

"Hello? Hello? Hello!" I slumped and stared at the phone. "Fuck."

"What happened?"

"I got disconnected."

The front door flew open and the boys tumbled in, bringing a blast of frigid air.

"Mom! Aunt Nora!" Leon shouted. "I made a snow devil! He has horns!"

"Fantastic," I said, trying to rally for the boys.

"Brownies!" Otis screamed.

"No brownies until those wet boots come off and you both get into dry clothes," Grace said.

She helped the boys with their coats and boots and then went off with them to the bedroom. I was about to try the call again when my phone buzzed. I picked up.

"Gubbins here. Bad news, I'm afraid."

A shudder went through me. I sat up straight, steeling myself. "Go ahead."

"Thomas O'Donnell called me as a courtesy. The DA's office is preparing the arrest warrant. They'll take it over to the judge's house in a few hours. You can expect an arrest before sundown and a bail hearing in the morning."

"Oh no. Oh God. No."

"We'll sort this out, Nora. We'll get you out on bail as soon as possible," he assured me. "I think it's better if they pick you up at my office. It will lower the temperature. And I'm sorry to keep pressing, but bring along that check, please, if you would."

I hung up in despair. I knew this was coming. I knew it. And still I wasn't prepared. How could a person prepare for this? What was I going to do? Practical issues first: I had to get money to pay Gubbins, the court, Lada's clinic bill and her Cedars rent, not to mention my own due next week. But I couldn't negotiate with the auction houses about Hugh's sketches from jail. Could I ask Grace and Mac for a loan? They lived on such a tight budget. I knew they would try to raise what they could, but they'd probably have to take out a second mortgage. That would require time I didn't have, and besides, I couldn't bear for them to do it. What about Ben? Should I ask him? Just the thought made me want to shrivel up and disappear.

I was dazed, staring at the plate of brownies with absolutely no appetite as Otis came running back into the living room in his underwear. He was waving a notebook.

"Aunt Nora! Look at the picture I made yesterday. It's a monkey wishing on a rainbow," he said as he grabbed a brownie and plopped the open book in my lap.

I gazed down at the crayon drawing: a hairy brown circle with a smiley face and stick legs standing next to a large, multicolored arc.

"Beautiful, Oatsie," I murmured, ruffling his soft brown curls, realizing I might never see him again.

He smiled, his teeth full of crumbs. What would he think of me if I were convicted of murder? I'd become a scary story in his show-and-tell. "The Point Killer Was My Godmother." No. This was nothing to joke about. He'd be traumatized. His ability to trust might be impaired. That would be an awful legacy to leave him and his brother while I wasted away in a prison cell.

Otis grabbed the last two brownies, holding one in each of his pudgy little hands as Grace walked back in.

"Bunny! Don't eat too many of those."

I closed Otis's book and noticed the image on the cover. A picture of *Sesame Street*'s Big Bird. I gawked at it. My pinball brain began pinging again. What time was it? I checked my phone. 2:16. I had to move quickly. But how could I leave here without Crawley following? I glanced over at Grace. She was cleaning the chocolate off Otis's fingers with a napkin. *Think, Nora. Think. What would Nathan Glasser do?*

"Grace?"

"Hmm?"

"I need a big favor."

She looked up. "Anything."

"I need to borrow you for a few hours. For your own good, don't ask questions."

I walked out right under Crawley's nose, nodding and waving. He rolled down his window and shouted, "Thanks for the brownie!"

He watched Grace clear the snow from her Prius in the same outfit she wore at the chapel. Only Grace was me. I was wearing her coat with the collar turned up. Her long black wool scarf covered the lower half of my face, and my hair was tucked under her black hat with the white silk rose. The wide brim hid the rest of my face in shadow. We'd traded purses, too, after switching out the contents. Grace's large, rectangular, black leather bag hung from my shoulder.

Crawley had already seen Mac leave. The idea was for him to assume Nora Glasser was staying behind to babysit her friends' kids. He didn't suspect anything as I dusted myself off, climbed in the car and threw the snow brush in the back seat. Step one had worked. I hoped Mac wouldn't get too angry with Grace for aiding and abetting.

The car's clock read 2:33 p.m. Somewhere above the blizzard of snow, the sun was still high. It wouldn't set for another two hours. That gave me just enough time to enact my plan. The scarf felt hot and scratchy on my mouth as I backed out of the drive, but I was careful to keep it on until I'd traveled safely out of Crawley's view. The world was in disguise, too. Snow had transformed bushes into pillows and lawns into feather beds. Flakes seemed to drift down in slow motion along the muted back streets as I drove toward the town's center.

Pequod Avenue had a completely different, almost frenzied energy as people converged on the shops to buy storm supplies. Only the Laundromat had closed early. Crossing the bridge, the Prius began to glide on the icy, elevated roadway. The beauty of the blizzard disguised its danger. A hunk of snow flew off the hood and smashed on the windshield, blocking out the road until Grace's wipers swatted it down. I held tight to the steering wheel for the rest of the drive. Despite the weather, I made it home fairly quickly, parked and trekked through virgin snow into the Coop. I marched straight to my bedroom, unconcerned about the trail of white clumps on the rugs and floors.

I changed into jeans, a sweater and warm socks—a skirt wouldn't do for this venture—and then foraged in my closet and found the second hatbox. Inside was another Ushanka, identical to the one I'd left at Grace's. The second hat was a gift from Aunt Lada last year on my birthday—she'd forgotten about the first. I'd stowed the hat away, not wanting to acknowledge it as a sign of her emerging dementia.

Now I replaced Grace's unwieldy hat with the spare Ushanka and pulled my boots back on, but instead of a parka, I slipped back into Grace's long, black coat—it was far warmer than any I owned. I'd need it for what lay ahead. Then I lifted the corner of the mattress, bent and reached further underneath until my fingers found Hugh's sketchbook.

Chapter Nineteen

Wearing the Russian army hat and long, black wool coat, I might have been a character in *Doctor Zhivago* trekking to my dacha in the snowy woods to hide from the Bolsheviks. Such quiet. Silence except for my own breathing, and the faint crinkling of the plastic bag tucked in the waistband of my jeans. I'd stowed Hugh's sketchbook there to keep it dry. Instead of driving into the front entrance of Pequod Point, I'd decided to go by way of the blind in case the county police were still posted on Hugh's road. Tricking them might not be as easy as it was with Crawley.

I was aware that this venture was risky. It wouldn't help my case if I were caught returning to the scene of the crime again. As icy crystals slashed my face, I tugged the Ushanka farther down on my brow. *Golova nyet, shopka nye nooshno. She who has no head needs no hat. Golova nyet, shopka nye nooshno.* Was I a fool? Was this an act of pure recklessness?

Thank God the Dune Club lot had been empty. Snow could bring out hunters. It gave them an advantage by concealing their sounds and smells from prey. Grace and I often saw men in camouflage outfits on our winter walks before the gruesome hunting accident. We'd watch men heading off the trail in pairs, or alone, toting medieval-looking crossbows on their shoulders. But this freak snowstorm must've sent the huntsmen out to shovel their driveways or buy rock salt, like Mac.

The parking lot was deserted. The only trespasser in these woods was yours truly.

I tramped on, wiping the snow from my cheeks and remembering Mac's advice to "think positive." Was it so different from Helene's edict to "manifest?" If Helene could manifest, why couldn't I? I'd manifest the sale of the sketchbook and the arrest of Tobias. I'd manifest a big celebration with a triple feature of Russian movies for Aunt Lada and her friends. *Fiddler on the Roof, Anna Karenina, Reds.* Why not throw in a buffet of blinis, borscht and stuffed cabbage—Lada's favorites? In fact, I'd manifest it every year with The Lada Levervitch Annual Russian Film Festival.

In spite of my grim circumstances, I was trying to be optimistic. I really was. But as I threaded my way deeper into the silent woods, my gut began twisting with anxiety again. It was a certainty: I'd be spending that night in jail, and not a cushy Martha Stewart jail, either. What if I had one of my sleepwalking incidents in prison? I could almost hear my cellmate jeer: "Yo, Guard! There's a fuckin' zombie freak in here!" If she didn't misinterpret my moves and beat me senseless first.

I tried to shift my focus to the immaculate snowy landscape—white earth, white trees and white air. Pristine and beautiful on the surface. But all I could think about was what the white concealed. Mold and rot and insects. A dark and twisted world. A sense of menace increased with every step I took.

As I rounded a curve on the trail, the blind came into view at the bottom of the incline—a gingerbread house trimmed with white frosting. I approached slowly to avoid slipping on the icy trail and finally reached the door. It resisted when I pushed. I shouldered it. Pushed again. Nothing worked until I finally stepped back and kicked, *La Femme Nikita*–style. The smack of my boot cracked like a gunshot in the quiet woods.

Inside, snow blew through the open wall. Drifts covered the floor. The army blanket was still folded neatly on the bench, and I used its scratchy fabric to wipe my face. I assumed I'd be able to assess the situation from the blind, but a thick curtain of falling snow obscured Pequod Point. Only the glow of house lights came through, nothing more. It had been impossible to retrieve Lada's opera glasses from my car with Crawley watching, and I wasn't sure they would have helped. I'd just have to head in the direction of the lights and hope Abbas was alone.

"Protect me, Champ. Bring me luck," I murmured, touching Ben's knife in my pocket before I turned and walked out the blind's door. I had brought it with me to deliver to Ben tonight in case I didn't have time to stop at the Coop after returning Grace's car.

The seagrasses along the edge of the inlet had transformed into giant marshmallow mounds, and they kept me hidden as I followed the shoreline. My skin stung from the cold, but I soldiered on. In a few minutes, I stopped and peered over the snowy humps. The edge of the lawn was right there. Pequod Point was no more than fifteen yards further on, all lit up and sparkling with ice crystals—a Snow Queen's palace in a fairy tale.

Through the glass wall I saw the bright, open-plan living room and kitchen. No one was visible inside. Abbas's dark green BMW, coated in white, was parked in the driveway near the path that led to Hugh's studio. But another snow-covered car sat in front of the garage—a red Ford sedan with a Dollar Rental sticker still detectable on its license plate. Shit. Someone else besides Abbas was there. Who?

His silhouette appeared in the hallway off the living room before Tobias walked into the light. *What?* I thought Tobias was supposed to be on a plane back to Virginia. *The snow. His flight must've been canceled because of the snow.* As I stood freezing and trying to figure out my next move, I chastised myself: Why hadn't I called the cheapest car-rental company first? I should've known Tobias was a Dollar man.

Tobias entered the kitchen area, stopped at the marble-topped island and faced in my direction as he talked on a cell phone. I was still hidden by the wall of grass, but there was no way to reach Hugh's studio without being seen crossing the lawn. My watch said 3:39. Still more than an hour before dark. I wrapped my arms around my chest and stuck my hands in my armpits for warmth. There was no help for my face or my toes. I began to march in place to ward off frostbite.

"Come on, you bastard. Leave. Or at least go into another room," I said aloud.

It seemed like an eternity before Tobias finished his call and changed his position. He began hunting through the kitchen cabinets, but he was still too close to the windows for me to chance a move. He found a bottle of liquor, opened it and took a swig. Then another. What a hypocrite. How smugly he'd preached against his brother's vices just a few hours before. He went to the refrigerator next and rummaged around. Then he removed . . . what was that? A log of salami. No more denying his appetites.

What the hell was he doing now? Trying to bite the plastic shrink-wrap off the salami with his teeth. He couldn't be that drunk yet.

"Can't you be bothered to get a knife, Tobias? It's right there in the island's center drawer."

The chill that went through me didn't come from the frigid air. There were at least a dozen drawers in that kitchen. How had I known which of them held the knives? I must've seen Hugh or Helene take a knife out when I came here to spy. I tried to remember. Yes, that was it. Helene went into the kitchen for wine. She must've . . . No. Had I seen her take a knife from the drawer or not?

Or did I search for a knife after I'd shot the two of them, so I could gouge Hugh's painting and kill them twice?

Abruptly, a whooshing noise sounded in the treetops. Within seconds, it became a roar. A fierce wind swept in and sent snow spiraling upward and then plunging back down. It began to blow in every direction at once, surrounding me in icy chaos. I shielded my eyes and squinted toward the house; I could barely make out Tobias through the white squall, but it looked like his back was finally turned. I prayed I was right. Ready. Set.

Now.

◆　◆　◆

"My God, Nora. What are you doing here, dear girl? You must be frozen!"

Incredulous, Abbas ushered me into the studio. My face burned like an acid peel when my skin hit the warmth. I checked outside as he closed the door. All clear. I'd made it past Tobias undetected.

"I have something to show you, and I don't have much time," I said breathlessly.

"Come in. Come in. Be warm." Abbas gestured across the room to the fire crackling in a large stone hearth between two enormous windows at the rear.

I stamped the snow from my boots, pulled off my soaking wet gloves and tried to get my bearings. Easily twice the size of the studio in New York, this looked more like a gallery. There were polished concrete floors and soaring ceilings with snow-covered skylights. A zebra-skin chaise and an Eames black leather couch furnished the sitting area near the fireplace. Picture windows on either side provided views of the snowy woods and inlet. Hugh's self-portraits were on view everywhere. They hung on the walls, leaned against them and rested on the furniture. It felt like an egomaniac's shrine.

One of the paintings stood out among the others. It sat on an easel in the center of the studio, probably for evaluation by Abbas. A painting of Hugh as a satyr.

He had a smirk on his goatlike face, and a naked erection—exaggerated, by far. Seeing it gave me the willies. I turned away quickly.

"Hugh gave this to me as a birthday gift," I said, opening Grace's coat and removing the plastic bag from my waistband. My hands were still frozen and clumsy. The book slipped out of the bag and fell to the floor. I picked it up gingerly and offered it to Abbas. "I want you to sell it for me. As quickly as you can."

He didn't take it. He merely stared at Carrie Fisher's picture, confused.

"A comic book from *Star Wars*?"

"No. Much more."

I carried the book to Hugh's drawing table. The same custom-made drawing table he'd used in the city. He'd kept his antique Japanese screen, too. It stood at the rear of the studio, blocking off a recessed area—probably hiding his messes. I was almost nostalgic.

"It was a kind of joke for Hugh. Once in a while he'd use these cheap notebooks to sketch out his series, mostly in charcoal and colored crayon or pencil," I explained, placing the book on the table. "I'll bump your commission by ten percent if you can sell it fast. Do you think you can?"

Abbas pursed his lips, studying me for a moment. Then he came to my side and opened the book. He examined the first drawing: my younger self sprawled naked on rumpled sheets, one hand cupping my breast, one arm thrown across my eyes. Hugh lay sleeping facedown on my left. The viewer was meant to linger on my body, soft and voluptuous like one of Pissarro's nudes. The title, *Loving Nora*, was scrawled at the bottom. Abbas leafed through the rest of the nude portraits, fascinated. His expert's eyes were doing that greedy, calculating thing. I blushed as they feasted on me.

"He never showed me this," he said, shaking his head.

"According to my research, the book is worth almost half a million," I said. "Now that he's dead."

Abbas glanced up with what appeared to be a disapproving look.

"Maybe," he murmured, and perused the pages again. He finally set the book down. "Why are you offering me such a good deal?"

"I know you're busy. It's an incentive to make this a priority. I need to sell right now."

"Why? You waited all this time, but now you rush, rush, rush? What is going on?"

I glanced at the door anxiously. He was asking too many questions. I'd have to try to engage his competitive instincts.

"Listen, if you don't want to do this, I'll take it to one of the auction houses."

"Ah, yes, the auction houses," he said, ruefully. "Those temples of art." Abbas crossed his arms and narrowed his eyes. "I think something is wrong. I think you are in trouble."

"My aunt is sick, Abbas. Her care is expensive."

"Ah. I am sorry to hear."

"Do we have a deal or not?"

Abbas paused for a moment, and then tapped the book. "If you can prove you own this."

"What does *that* mean?"

"I need a bill of sale."

"I told you, the book was a gift."

"Was it listed in divorce settlement?"

"No. Hugh gave it to me years before we divorced. For my birthday. It wasn't part of the settlement."

"You have a witness? Someone who saw Hugh give it to you? They will swear to this on paper?"

"A witness? No. He left it under my pillow, you know, in bed. What's the problem?"

Abbas frowned.

"I have seen this many times when an artist divorces. The wives steal. They wait. They try to sell the work years later without getting caught."

"Abbas. You know me." I was stunned. "I can't believe you'd think I'd steal this. I swear it's mine."

"I'm not calling you a thief, dear girl. But you must prove this is not part of Hugh's estate. His lawyers will be watching on a sale of this size."

"Wait. I have a letter. A letter Hugh wrote. He says he gave it to me."

"Let me see it."

"I don't have it on me—"

Out of the corner of my eye, I caught a movement out a window close to the front door. A dark figure hunched against the wind and snow was heading for the studio.

"Shit." I looked around wildly. "Tobias is coming. Please don't tell him I'm here."

"Why not?"

I turned and ran toward the Japanese screen.

"What is going on, Nora? Tell me!"

"Later. Please."

I ducked behind the screen, nearly banging my hip on a utility table strewn with mountains of papers, books, rags and paint tubes. Crouching between a cloth-covered easel and a work sink, I tried to catch my breath as the door opened and the cold wind blew in.

"Mr. Masout," Tobias said, stomping off snow and closing the door. "How are things coming along?"

Silence. Abbas wasn't answering. I held my breath. Oh God. He was going to give me away. Finally, I heard one of the men clear his throat.

"I am almost finished," Abbas said. "Another hour, I think."

I began breathing again. But my nose had started to tickle. It must be all those chemicals: the cans of paint thinner, turpentine and spray varnish reeking on the shelves behind me. I bit my tongue so I wouldn't sneeze.

"I thought I'd be able to stay until you were done, but I've got to go back to the inn. Ruth called. I'm afraid our niece is not doing well. Not well at all."

"That poor child," Abbas said. "My heart breaks."

"She's in a terrible state. She's been crying all afternoon. The loss is overwhelming. I know it must be very emotional for you, too. Looking at these paintings, today of all days. Let me thank you again for staying to help, especially in this weather."

"If it will help Callie, I'm glad to do it."

"It surely will."

I heard footsteps tread further into the room.

"My God. When did Hugh begin painting pornography?"

"What?"

"The beast with the erection."

"That is art, Mr. Walker."

"Really. What is this particular piece of 'art' worth?"

"About one point two."

"Million?"

"Yes."

"And the rest?"

"My estimate is not completed, but including unsold work at the gallery . . . it could be thirty-five million, I think. Maybe more."

I was floored. I knew Hugh's net worth had risen since his death, but that was more than twice what I estimated.

"I'm impressed," Tobias said.

"You should be. Your brother became a very successful artist."

The men went silent. My urge to sneeze was so strong I had to bite my tongue *and* pull my ears. Tobias finally spoke.

"That's thirty-five million minus your commission, correct?"

"Yes, of course."

"Are you a religious man, Mr. Masout?"

"I am not. I've seen too much destroyed in the name of religion."

"What about God? Do you believe in God?"

"He doesn't exist."

"I'm sorry to hear that's your position. I believe God had reasons for allowing my brother and his wife to be killed, Mr. Masout. And now he has called on me to become Callie's guardian and conservator. As such, I will be making financial decisions on her behalf."

"Of course."

"I'll begin with this: if you want to continue representing this 'art,' you might consider donating a portion of your commission to His righteous cause. I have a foundation that does the Lord's work. Perhaps these paintings can redeem their existence. Otherwise, I'm certain there are auction houses that will be eager to negotiate their fees—if you understand my meaning."

There was another long pause before Abbas said, "I understand."

"Good."

Footsteps retreated. A series of electronic beeps sounded before Tobias spoke again.

"I called the security company and changed the alarm code. You'll have to contact me if you need access again in the future. Please press 'Armed' when you leave. And one more thing . . ."

"Yes?"

"Would you be so kind as to move your car? It's blocking the driveway."

More footsteps and the jingle of car keys. The door opened and closed. The men were gone.

So, Tobias believed God wanted Hugh and Helene murdered, and God chose him to raise their daughter. Did God ask him to threaten Abbas, too? To take Hugh's paintings elsewhere if Abbas didn't fork over money to his cause? Tobias had just secured a sizable flow of funds on top of what he might eventually get from Callie. Abbas might be willing to talk to the police about this conversation if I convinced him of my theory. Along with a receipt from Dollar Rental Car and his rush to adopt Callie, there might be enough evidence—circumstantial, but so was mine—to stop Tobias from getting on a plane. Maybe even enough to keep me out of jail until the police could investigate further.

I should tell Gubbins what was going on. I whipped out my burner phone, but the battery was dead again after all those rental car calls.

There must be a phone in the studio somewhere. I grabbed on to the easel to steady myself as I rose from my squatting position, accidentally pulling off the drop cloth. When I saw the image on the canvas underneath, I paused.

Abbas sat in an old wooden banker's chair facing the viewer. He wore a suit and his signature turtleneck. The painting style superficially suggested a portrait by Lucian Freud, but unlike Freud, this artist painted violence. On the right side of Abbas's chest, a ragged hole had been torn in his jacket, revealing gored and bloodied flesh. The painting wasn't finished—the faceless outline of a man stood behind him. I knew that man had to be Hugh. Hugh only painted self-portraits.

I was perplexed: Hugh would often use sex in his work, but, like Freud, never carnage. Had he been angry with Abbas? Maybe Abbas had critiqued the new direction Hugh was taking with that grotesque satyr? Or was he unhappy with the retrospective Abbas organized? I couldn't imagine what inspired this vicious image. I scanned the utility table for a phone amid the disarray as I began rifling through the mess. No phone. Maybe something in the heaps of papers would explain what was going on with that sadistic painting.

I found shipping invoices, a book on Marc Chagall, and then I noticed the garish green turtles—Teenage Mutant Ninja Turtles half-hidden under a Christie's auction catalog. I pushed the catalog aside, and the turtles grinned manically from the cover of a cheap spiral notebook. I opened the book. Hugh had written a title on page one:
Leaving Abbas.

One fanciful image followed another, all drawn in graphite pencil and crayon. Hugh's head emerging from the shell of a giant turtle; Hugh holding up a skull, like the gravedigger in *Hamlet*; Hugh riding a horse into the sunset in a cartoonish Western landscape. Halfway through the book, I found the completed study for the unfinished painting I'd unmasked on the easel: Hugh standing behind Abbas and squeezing his dealer's bloody heart in his hand as if he'd just torn it out of his chest.

Shocked, I stopped turning the pages. *Leaving Abbas.* That meant Hugh had planned to leave the dealer who'd nurtured and supported him for years. The man who'd helped to build his stellar career. Hugh's departure would signal that Abbas was on the decline. Other artists would smell failure and they'd defect, too. That's how it worked in the art business. Abbas would lose a fortune. Clearly, no one else knew about this, or drums would be beating all through the art world.

Hugh must've understood this act of betrayal would bring a bitter end to their friendship. The painting on the easel proved it: he was ripping out the man's heart. But Abbas had still spoken so lovingly of Hugh. He'd given no indication he was aware of Hugh's intention to leave. Hugh must have died before he dropped the bomb.

I flipped to the last page. The final drawing showed a familiar image. Hugh stood at an easel. He was in the process of painting Abbas, who was curled in a ball on the floor. It was a variation on the painting Hugh had done of me after I discovered Helene was pregnant. He'd given this one a similar title:

Self-Portrait with Abbas, Knowing.

Wait. *Did* Abbas know Hugh was about to dump him? If he *had* known, he would have also recognized that Hugh's death would be a boon to him. Abbas Masout, Hugh's beloved dealer, would be the keeper of the Hugh Walker legend and make more money off Hugh's paintings than ever before. The hard truth was sinking in, and it was chilling down to my soul.

Money. Follow the money.

The door creaked open. "Nora?"

I whirled around in a panic. My arm hit the screen, and it went down with a crash. I stood there paralyzed as Abbas stared at me from the doorway.

"Was it you?" I asked, astounded.

"Was what me?"

Abbas shut the door and started toward me.

"You are upset, dear girl. What is it?"

I came to my senses, reached in my pocket and took out the Champ, fumbling to open it.

"Don't come any closer," I warned, shaking and pointing the knife unsteadily. "Stop right there."

Abbas halted at the edge of the fallen screen. His face was wet. Melting snow dripped off his silver hair onto his black cashmere scarf. I watched his eyes move to the easel and take in the image of himself with a hole in his chest. His right eye began to twitch.

"You killed them, didn't you? In cold blood," I rasped, the fear stealing my voice. "You murdered Hugh and Helene."

Abbas frowned. "And why would I kill them, Nora? Why would I kill my good friend and his wife? A man I adored and represented for years. He was like my own child. There's no reason in the world."

"Because Hugh was going to leave you. You knew he was leaving. And that meant you'd be ruined."

Abbas flapped his hand dismissively. "Who told you this nonsense?"

"You drove out here and shot them in bed. You posed them and stabbed the painting. You're trying to blame me for it. All the evidence is in the book," I said, glancing at the utility table.

No! Why did you tell him about the book?

"What book?"

He followed where my gaze had led him. He saw the ninjas.

"That book?" He took another step forward.

"I said stop!"

I jabbed the air with the knife and tried to look menacing. What to do? I had at least thirty years on Abbas. Could I grab the book, do an end run around him and make it out the door? Almost before I finished the thought, his hand went into his coat pocket and emerged with a small, silver gun. He aimed it at my chest.

"Drop the knife and move over there," he said, waving me away from the table toward the shelves.

I thought my heart would pop; it was beating so hard. Obeying, I backed up. I heard the beautiful Japanese screen crack as Abbas walked across it to get at the ninja book.

"You are a real problem, Nora," he said, keeping the silver muzzle pointed and steady as he perused the pages of the sketchbook.

I looked around frantically, my heartbeat thrashing in my ears. *I can't die here*, I thought. *Not here on the floor of Hugh's studio, lorded over by his goat erection.* Incredibly, that's the first thing that came into my mind. Next—advice from some random crime-show psychologist. *Best chance to stay alive. Make eye contact. Show empathy. He has to see a human being.*

"What happened, Abbas? What went wrong between you two?"

Abbas looked up. I made contact with orbs hard as marble.

"Damien Hirst."

"What does Damien Hirst have to do with it?" I asked, confused.

The artist Damien Hirst had rocked the art world decades ago by placing a rotting cow's head in a large container made of glass and steel. Along with the head came maggots that turned into flies, which fried in a nearby fly zapper. Later on, he displayed a bisected shark under glass. His bold and edgy work shocked, and it made him about as rich and famous as an artist could get.

Abbas gestured with his free hand at the display of paintings in the studio.

"We planned a big show for Hugh at the gallery next spring. A show to run six months and change each month—old work, new work, work-in-progress. A big idea. No one has done this before for a gallery retrospective. We would announce to the press at the Art Basel market in December."

Abbas stepped away from the utility table. Closer to me. I leaned back instinctively.

"But last Saturday morning, Hugh brings Callie to her aunt in the city for the weekend. I think he does this because he is fighting with Helene—they need time alone out here. He comes to the gallery after. 'Abbas, I've been thinking,' he says. 'Remember how Damien Hirst let Sotheby's auction his work in '08? He didn't use his dealer.' He tells me Sotheby's gave Hirst a show much bigger than the one I offer. That they brought in collectors from all over the world, and Hirst sold over two hundred million. 'He broke Picasso's sales record. It worked for Hirst—the free-agent thing.' Hugh says he wants to do what Hirst did. 'I'm thinking I'd like to go solo, Abbas.' Those were his words. 'I'm thinking I'd like to go solo.'"

Abbas stepped back, still aiming his gun at me. My heart thundered while he examined the book again in silence. Then he suddenly snapped his fingers. I flinched.

"Just like this," he said. "I am one of Hirst's dead flies."

I blinked, absorbing this. "After all you'd done for him, he dropped you," I said. "What a bastard he was."

Abbas didn't seem to have heard me; he'd reached the final drawing. I flinched again as he let out a loud, guttural sound and swept the book to the floor.

"This is how he would paint me?" he snarled. "Like a weak, submissive animal at his feet? And he calls it *Abbas Knowing*?"

He spat on the book. The hairs on the back of my neck lifted.

"Abbas knows this: when no one wanted Hugh Walker, I gave him a show at my gallery. When he didn't have money, I paid his rent. When he was lonely, I took him into my home to sit with friends at my table. I believed in him. I made his career. And he dismisses me like I am a boy who does yard work." Abbas paused and began rubbing his right temple again.

I tried to stay focused on connecting with him, but my head was swimming.

"He betrayed you. I know how that feels."

"You don't know betrayal." He let out a quick, disgusted snort.

"When a man acts like a man, when he wants to taste other flavors, a woman calls it betrayal."

This tack wasn't working with him. I had to stay cool and think. Think what to do. But it was impossible with Abbas glowering at me.

"During the war in Beirut, men had to betray to stay alive. Betrayal meant food. It meant water. It meant wood and oil for heat in the winter. The difference between being able to buy medicine on the black market and dying of dysentery." He kept kneading the flesh over his eye. "You became an artist of betrayal. You betrayed the ones who trusted you, and they never suspected. Your friends. Your neighbors. Your dog."

His dog?

"Did you ever taste dog?"

Cringing, I shook my head. All these years and I'd never imagined he was capable of such things. I had to get away from him. How?

"After I arrived in this country, I worked hard to forget the ways of war. I became human again. I behaved with honor and loyalty. But if it means survival, I use the old methods."

Grimacing, he mashed the heel of his palm into his brow as I scanned the room. No other exit. Had he developed a brain tumor? Was that how he got so crazy? Or maybe he was about to have a stroke or an aneurysm? My only hope was to stall, then use the element of surprise and run.

"Did you talk to Hugh? Did you at least try to convince him to stay?"

Abbas snorted. "I am not a beggar. I only asked him for time. Until I worked out my strategy for damage control. Not to go to Sotheby's, not to talk to anyone until I spoke with my publicist. 'You owe me this at least,' I told him. 'Let me keep the respect I deserve.'"

"But you had another plan, didn't you?"

Abbas's eyes had begun to water. They narrowed into slits and his face contorted. His mouth opened wide. He looked like one of Francis Bacon's screaming popes as he started a bout of uncontrollable sneezing.

"Hachooo! Hachoo! Hachooo! Hachoo!"

Now! This is your chance. Do it! Charge him and run.

The fit ended abruptly. It was too late. Abbas grabbed a rag off the utility table.

"Yes, I had a plan."

He sniffed the rag and his eyes grew small again. He was probably reacting to the chemical fumes. The rag must reek of them. Hugh's dirty rags were releasing toxic chemicals, and Abbas was overly sensitive to them. He sneezed violently and threw the rag down. My pulse raced.

Toxic chemicals from the cans on the shelf.

"You weren't going to talk to the publicist, were you?" I said. Slowly, carefully, I angled my body so I could move my right arm behind me unnoticed while Abbas wiped his eyes. "You were buying time."

Buy time.

"You drove out here that Saturday night," I continued, blindly exploring the shelf with my trembling hand.

Don't knock anything over.

"You came here to the house unannounced and told Hugh you were very upset, you needed to talk, right? You knew he'd let you in. Very smart, Abbas."

"I gave him one more chance. Only one. No pleading."

"And when he answered?"

Abbas sniffed and used the gun in his hand to jab at an imaginary Hugh. "I made him go back to bed."

"Did you make them pose before you . . ." I shuddered. "And then you slashed the painting to make certain the police would think about me. Oh God."

"I thought they would arrest you sooner," he said, scowling. His eyes were beginning to swell. "What will I do with you now?"

All his phony concern. I'd been nothing but a "thing" for him to use in his scheme.

I saw him glaze over and focus inward for a few seconds. I could almost hear him calculating. Then he began rubbing his eyes again with his coat sleeve. I took a small step to my left and continued frantically searching until my fingers found a tall, round can. Bless Hugh's messy work habits: the cap was off. Abbas finally brought his arm down and looked at me again. Red light.

"Walk over there, back toward the door. Away from the art," he ordered.

If I obeyed, I'd lose my only chance to get out alive. I stayed put, terrified.

"What are you going to do? You can't get away with another murder," I said.

"No?"

Think. Think.

I challenged him, desperate. "How will you explain killing me?"

He paused again, the plan still forming in his mind.

"We spoke in the parking lot at the funeral. You knew I would be coming here. You followed, uninvited, and offered to sell me a notebook you stole from Hugh." He nodded toward the Princess Leia sketchbook on the worktable at the center of the studio.

"I refused. I said I would report you." He shook his head and clucked his tongue. "You got very, very angry, Nora. You went mad, dear girl. You admitted you killed Hugh and Helene and shouted that you'd kill me, too. Then you pulled out a knife and attacked me." He brandished the gun. "I had to defend myself."

Think. Think. Think!

"Now move," he ordered, waving the gun.

"But you used that gun to shoot Hugh and Helene," I said, firming up my grip on the can. "They'll match the bullets."

Abbas smiled.

"*That* gun is at the bottom of the Hudson. *This* one is legal, and it's not a .22."

He stooped to pick up the ninja book.

"I must thank you for finding this," he said. "Now I can burn it."

I seemed to stop breathing. Blood thundered in my ears. Everything was slowing down except my racing thoughts: if I tried to run, he would shoot me; if I didn't run, he would shoot me. I had nothing to lose. *Make your move.*

I bent over, dropped into linebacker stance and rammed my head into Abbas's belly, knocking the wind out of him. The gun fired above me with a deafening crack as a sharp, burned smell hit my nostrils. I raised my hand high and pressed the nozzle on the can of Blair's spray varnish, aiming at his eyes. Abbas howled. I pressed again. He screamed and fired a second time, shattering glass somewhere in the studio before the gun clattered to the floor. Abbas dropped the book next and tore at his eyes, shrieking.

"I will kill you, you fucking bitch!"

I sprayed one more time.

"Fuck!" he screamed. "Fuck!"

Tossing the can and snatching the ninjas off the floor, I scrambled to my feet and ran like the wind.

◆ ◆ ◆

Bursting out of the studio into the cold twilight, I blasted through the driving snow, shin-deep in snowdrifts. My coat flew open. Freezing air bit my face and lungs as my arms and legs kept pumping. I looked over my shoulder and saw Abbas's dark shape emerging from the studio.

The ninja book dripped with melting snow. I shoved it inside the waistband of my jeans to protect it and realized, shit . . . Princess Leia was still on Hugh's worktable. There was nothing I could do about that. It was too late to backtrack.

I struggled to close the buttons on Grace's coat as I labored on, breathing heavily. The sky was darkening and I had to find the hunting trail while I could still see where I was going. Stay low. *Keep moving. Stick close to the snowbound seagrass so Abbas can't see you.* The ground near the inlet had turned slushy and was slowing me down. My pants were soaked up to my knees, my toes ice. Was I close to the blind? I looked around pointlessly—the flying snow obscured everything. I could barely make out what was right in front of me. Had I already passed it? Suddenly my foot met with something hard and my big toe exploded in pain.

"Fuck!"

I went flying. I landed on my right shoulder at the edge of the inlet. The icy water began seeping through Grace's coat almost instantly. Rolling onto my back to save the ninja book, I felt a pain in my foot so sharp I knew I'd be hobbled and unable to run. But I couldn't stay there; I had to keep going. I managed to turn over onto my hands and knees and try to stand. A loud pop sounded as the bullet whizzed by my head and sent me diving face-first into the icy mud. Another pop.

And another. I curled into a fetal position and clasped my hands over my ears.

"I know you're in there," Abbas yelled.

I couldn't stay where I was. I rolled back onto my belly and crawled commando-style behind a large clump of snowbound grass. Through a small gap in the reeds, I could see him lurching through the snow a few yards away. There were no more moves to make except into the water behind me. I might not be able to walk, but I could swim. I could shed the coat, swim underwater, and pray that I didn't freeze to death before Abbas ran out of bullets.

The Polar Bear Club jumps in every winter. They survive. You can do it, kiddo.

Daddy? Is that you?

I began to inch backward on my elbows through the mud, but I hesitated. The ninja book. The ninja book would be ruined. Even if I survived the freezing water and bullets, without those sketches, I couldn't prove Abbas's motive to kill. Instead, he could tell a story that would get me convicted. Especially since he still had the other sketchbook. He'd claim I stole it from Hugh and tried to sell it to him.

Kiddo, the water has got better odds than a bullet. You gotta bet the odds. Go.

I started inching backward again, grunting with the effort. But my hesitation had cost me.

"Give me the book," Abbas commanded.

I raised my head. Abbas stood over me. His right eye had closed, and it was the size of a golf ball, the skin burned red from chemicals. His mouth twisted into an ugly grimace. He was aiming the gun at the center of my forehead. Black spots swam in front of my eyes as I started gasping for air.

"Take it out slowly and hand it to me," he commanded.

I managed to get hold of the book inside my coat and pull it out shakily, but I kept it close to my breast. Teenage Mutant Ninja Turtles were the only thing between oblivion and me.

"I swear I won't tell anyone you killed Hugh and Helene. Let me go," I begged breathlessly.

"Sorry, dear girl. It will be quick. You will not suffer."

It happened so fast. He was reaching for the book when I heard a whistling sound, followed quickly by a thud. The gun plopped into the mud. Abbas let out a deep grunt. Amazed, I stared at the steel arrow sticking out of his right shoulder. Bright red blood oozed from the wound through his wool coat. He staggered sideways, lowing like a cow giving birth, and then fell over. He writhed on the ground, clutching his arm, his horrid, bulbous eye aimed at me.

I finally let out a scream.

A man in khaki camouflage came running through the curtain of white holding a crossbow in one hand. I saw the alarm on his face as he rushed over and bent down at my side. His breath steamed warm mist at my cheek.

"Lady, are you all right?"

I couldn't speak, only gasp and nod. With eyes wide, I stared at Abbas as he whimpered and bled all over the snow.

"I had to do it," the hunter said in a panicky voice. "I heard what he said. He was going to kill you."

He pulled off his belt, hurried over to Abbas and began tying a tourniquet around the bleeding arm. As I watched him work, I came back to myself. I could feel the throbbing pain in my foot again, the burning sting of icy water on my legs and arms. I also felt an enormous surge of gratitude toward this stranger. If he hadn't acted so quickly, I'd be dead. Or if I'd survived the gunshot to my head, I'd possess the mental capacity of a parsnip.

"What's your name?" I rasped.

He glanced over.

"Jake."

He'd finished with the tourniquet and was packing snow on the wound.

My throat was thick. "I'm Nora," I said, trying to get up. I saw the gun lying in front of me, steaming in the muck. Overwhelmed, I collapsed again. "Thank you, Jake," I said. "Thank you for saving my life."

Abbas moaned as Jake finished tending to him and returned to my side.

"You're freezing." He helped me sit up and peel off Grace's coat, which was sodden and heavy with brackish water. My lower legs and feet were soaked. He stripped off his camouflage jacket. "Here, put this on," he urged. Shaking, I managed to slip into the dry jacket and stick the ninja notebook back in my waistband. Jake removed a phone from his pants pocket.

"I'll call 911 and stay with him until the ambulance gets here. You need to get warm. Think you can make it to the duck blind over there?"

"Where?"

I peered in the direction he indicated. I was completely snow-blind.

"Hold on," he said. "This will help."

Jake unzipped a compartment at the back of the hunting jacket and removed an emergency flare. He struck a match, lit the fuse and planted it in the ground. A fountain of orange sparks spouted into the air. I could finally make out the dark, rectangular shape of the duck blind less than a dozen yards away, barely visible in the waning light. Limping through peach-colored snow, shivering and growing numb with cold, I was suddenly overwhelmingly tired.

Wailing sirens, men's shouts and crackling radios clashed in the distance. I opened my eyes, completely dazed and confused. Why was I lying in the corner of the duck blind, curled in a ball, trembling all over, and hugging myself for warmth? How did I get there? What was going on? Hypothermia was muddling my brain. It felt like I was underwater. Ice-cold water. My body was sinking, incredibly heavy, while at the same time my thoughts were slowly rising to the surface. I remembered waiting in the snowy woods outside Pequod Point, watching Tobias in the kitchen . . .

Suddenly Mac burst through the door with an EMT bag. He dropped it and roared.

"Nora!"

Al followed in his red Pequod Ambulance jacket and Little League cap, carrying a small oxygen canister. On the verge of swooning, I tried in vain to sit up.

"Don't move," Mac ordered, bending down and taking my wrist. "Rudinsky, get the thermal blanket. Stat!"

"I'm on it," said Al.

Mac's white hair flashed red and blue hypnotically, in sync with the pulsating lights coming through the open wall of the blind. He let go of my wrist, wrapped a blood pressure cuff around my arm and pumped. In a trance, I watched Al float a large, silver rectangle of foil onto my body and tuck me in. Then he stood up and glanced toward the ruckus outside.

"I think the cops are about to head over here, Mac."

I was still struggling to emerge from my stupor.

"Cops?" I repeated, bewildered.

Mac released the pressure ball. It hissed and he frowned.

"She's disoriented. Her pulse and BP are low. We need to get her warmed up," he said, and began rubbing my legs briskly under the blanket through my jeans. They felt like wooden logs. He mumbled and shook his head as he worked. "What the hell did you get yourself into, Nora? What happened out there?"

I closed my eyes and attempted to make sense of the scrambled images.

"There were turtles. Hugh was a goat."

Mac stopped massaging and clipped an oxygen line under my nostrils. A sweet stream of air flowed in.

"We need some preheated saline in here, Al. Is the PQ Fire Team still outside?"

Al nodded. "I'll get them to warm up a drip. Looks like they're just about to load the victim into their rig."

I opened my eyes as the oxygen cleared out the brain fog.

"Oh my God," I gasped as Al went out the door. "They're taking Abbas. You can't let him get away." I tried to get off the floor again, but Mac put a firm hand on my shoulder and pushed me back down.

"The police have to arrest him!" I cried.

"Okay, okay, Nora. Calm down. I knew I recognized that guy. Abbas, the art dealer, right? He was at your wedding."

"Yes! He's the one who killed Hugh and Helene!"

"Hold on. An hour ago, Grace said you were sure Hugh's brother killed them."

"We were wrong. It's Abbas. Don't let him go. He'll leave the country!" I attempted to sit up once more, but Mac wouldn't have it. "I need to go out there and stop him—"

"No, Nora. We'll have the police look into it. We need to get you to the ER. That's the priority now. What the hell was Grace thinking, letting you evade a police officer and come here by yourself?"

"Don't be mad at Grace, please."

His face softened and he touched my shoulder. "I'm not mad. I'm relieved you're not worse off."

The door opened and Detective Roche swaggered in, brushing the snow off his broad cop shoulders and stamping his boots.

"I'd like a minute with Ms. Glasser."

Mac scowled and stood up.

"She could be hypothermic, Detective."

Roche waved him off. "This won't take long."

Reluctantly, Mac stepped aside.

"Did you arrest Abbas Masout?" I asked, anxious.

Roche sat on the blind's wooden bench, looking down at me. He cleaned snow off his brown corduroy pants and then blew on his hands.

"No."

"You have to! He killed Hugh and Helene."

"And you have the right to remain silent. Anything you say may be held against you in a court of law."

"No!" I cried. "You've got it all wrong."

"What?" Mac cried out. "That's crazy—"

Roche shot him a hard look.

"You're making a mistake, Detective. Arrest Abbas," I pleaded. "He killed them."

"You have a right to an attorney. If you cannot afford an attorney, one will be provided for you."

"He tried to kill me."

"Mr. Masout says otherwise. He says you came to the studio to sell him valuable artwork you stole from your ex. When he refused to buy it, you attacked him with a knife. You told him you'd killed the Walkers and would kill him, too."

"That's a total lie."

"He fired his gun in self-defense and you ran. He chased you. Found you injured from a fall. Before he could call us, the hunter misread the situation and shot him in the arm."

"No, he's lying. I swear. Ask the hunter. Ask Jake."

"We're about to get his statement." Roche paused. "You know, you're pretty good at deception yourself. Nice trick there with Sergeant Crawley."

I put my hand under the blanket. Before I could reach the ninja book, Roche had already whipped out his gun.

"Don't move."

"Fuck," Mac said.

"I'm just taking out a notebook."

"Do it *very* slowly."

I removed the battered book gradually and passed it to Roche.

"Abbas wanted to get his hands on this. That's why he tried to kill me. His motive is in here."

He took it and puzzled over the cover.

"There are sketches in there showing that Abbas knew Hugh was leaving the gallery and taking away millions of dollars' worth of business," I said. "Abbas would have been ruined by it. I can explain more if you need me to."

"You and Mr. Masout will have a lot of explaining to do," Roche said, standing up. "After you're stabilized, I'm bringing both of you in."

"No!" Mac cried out, unable to control himself.

"Abbas Masout killed them," I insisted, frustrated.

"We'll see."

At least Roche is taking Abbas into custody, I thought fearfully.

"Mac, please call Douglas Gubbins. Tell him I'm under arrest."

The klieg lights reflected off the snow, bathing the area in brilliant white as Mac and Al carried me out of the blind. The police were working the crime scene, tromping through the snowdrifts wearing plastic gloves and Tyvek paper shoes, measuring angles and trajectories, distances and shoe sizes. They'd collect DNA and blood samples. The powder they sprinkled on Jake's arrow and on Abbas's gun would capture fingerprints. Their labs would confirm that the gun had been fired numerous times near the inlet—evidence (I hoped) that Abbas had attempted to kill me because of what I knew.

The police were after the same "five w's and an h" a reporter would seek: "Who? What? When? Where? Why? How?" They were using all the science at their disposal to compile the facts and help the district attorney build an airtight case. But "why?" was a question their methods couldn't address. I was counting on the ninja notebook providing an answer to that one.

◆ ◆ ◆

Mac radioed ahead to the hospital while he drove. His voice carried through to the back of the ambulance: "Coming in heavy. Forty-one-year-old Caucasian female. Possible hypothermia." He gave them my stats as we traveled along the dark roads, snow crunching under the tires, a police car following behind. I had a warm saline drip in my left arm. My right wrist was cuffed to the gurney's side bar. The tight metal bracelet pinched the skin, and I wriggled in frustration, rattling my chains against the railing.

Al looked up briefly at the sound, but avoided my eyes. He'd perched his bulky body on the end of the bench by the ambulance doors and was filling out a form on his clipboard in silence. He went back to writing, obviously nervous about being alone with me. I decided to break the ice.

"Isn't Stokes on your team anymore?"

"He's at the hospital."

"He's sick?"

"Their baby was in distress."

"Oh no," I groaned.

"It's okay. The baby is out of danger. Mother and child are fine."

We drove over a nasty pothole and Al looked up again. This time our eyes met. I knew that look from a man. Guilt. He lowered his gaze swiftly and went on with his paperwork.

"I'm sorry, Al. I didn't mean for anyone to get hurt."

"You don't have to apologize," he said, still writing. "You didn't put the arrow in the guy. And you didn't kill the Walkers. I'd bet money on it."

"Thanks. But I was talking about you, and my Tips column."

Al's hand stopped moving.

"I get why you're mad as hell. You felt I was making fun of you. Believe me, I wasn't. I'm really sorry it hurt you."

Al pulled his cap down and stayed focused on the form.

"Al?"

After a few seconds, he sighed.

"I've never worked so hard in my life, and I'm barely making it," he said, sadly. "The expenses get higher and higher. And with two more kids coming up on college . . . The bills are piling up. I'm always rushing from one lousy job to another to make my nut. I never have any time. I hardly see Sinead and my girls. I just get so frustrated. And angry. Really angry."

He shook his head and clammed up.

"I didn't mean any disrespect. You're a solid guy, and I admire you."

"Yeah?"

"The way you care about your family, and the community. I mean, besides working so hard, you're still volunteering. Coaching kids. Saving lives. Please, can you forgive me?"

He was quiet. Then he removed his cap and studied its crown. He finally ran a hand over his buzz cut, put the cap back on and raised his head.

"This is all going to be over soon, and you'll be back to work at the paper," he said. "I want you to do something for me then."

It was heartening to hear that Al was confident of a positive outcome.

"What would that be?"

"If you're going to keep doing the column, write funnier stuff."

I smiled, relieved. "I'll try my best."

Mac's voice crackled though Al's hand radio. "I've got Ben Wickstein on the phone. He said to let Nora know he's on his way to the hospital. Check if there's anything she wants me to tell him?"

I shook my head no.

I was glad Ben was back. I had a lot to say to him. But I'd say it in person.

"She's good, Mac," Al said into his radio. He clicked it off and gazed at me curiously. "So, you and Ben? You're an item?"

Chapter Twenty

Seventeen miles from Pequod Point, we reached Massamat Hospital—it had the closest ER. We backed into the emergency bay. Sounds of a commotion carried over from the street as soon as Al opened the ambulance doors. He glanced at me.

"Reporters," he said.

Waiting for a break in the case, the press corps would have been scanning police and ambulance radios 24-7. They must've tapped into the 911 call. At least they were far enough away that I didn't have to pull the sheet over my head. I cringed at the thought that Lizzie might be out there covering my arrest for the *Courier*.

Al and Mac unloaded my gurney and pushed me up the ramp into the ER. A county police officer accompanied us.

"We can stay with her, right?" Mac asked him.

The officer nodded. "Long as I'm there."

We rolled into a small examination room and he took up a guard post outside. A male nurse arrived, said "hello" to the three of us and proceeded to place an electronic thermometer in my mouth. While he waited for a reading, Mac started for the door.

"Hold tight, Nora. I'll see if I can find Ben and get him cleared to come in."

The nurse finished and left the room. There was only Al standing by. He shuffled over to the gurney and took off his cap.

"I'm sorry about the letters to the editor, Nora. I was letting off steam, that's all."

"I know, Al. We're good. Stop working and go home. There's nothing more you can do here now. Thanks for everything. And say hey to Sinead for me."

Al nodded. "I will. And good luck."

He walked out. While I lay there alone waiting for a doctor, I started thinking about Al's anger. My anger. Anger's importance. Anger told you when someone crossed your line. "Don't tread on me," anger said. You had to pass through anger, and the hurt underneath it, before you could get to forgiveness. Otherwise, it seemed to me, you skipped a step. But there was also plenty of danger there. How long could you hold on to that dark fire before it scorched all that was good in your life? And what was the best way to let anger out?

I was turning this over in my mind, thinking of the murderous rage Abbas had unleashed on Hugh and Helene, when a massive sense of relief washed over me.

I hadn't killed anyone.

"Ms. Glasser?"

A tall, fiftyish Indian man in surgical scrubs entered and closed the door behind him. He had a black, bushy unibrow above kind, almond-shaped brown eyes. He checked the name on my bracelet.

"You are indeed Ms. Glasser, and I am Dr. Patel," he said, smiling. "How are you feeling?"

"Exhausted," I said, smiling back at him weakly.

He lifted my free wrist and took my pulse. Then he pulled down my lower eyelids one by one and shined a bright penlight in each of them. Next, he pressed a stethoscope to my chest and listened. After a few moments, his dark brow furrowed. He left my side and walked over to a cabinet.

"You are mildly hypothermic, but you also seem to have a slight arrhythmia."

"What's that?"

"An irregular heartbeat. I'd like to give you an EKG and check a few other things," he said, returning with a tray of needles and vials. "Just to be prudent."

"Is an arrhythmia a big deal?"

He tied a rubber tube on my arm.

"It's probably just the excitement." He patted my hand. "I'll give you some Valium to relax you after your blood sample is taken and the EKG is done. We don't want it interfering with the results."

Despite Dr. Patel's reassurance, I fretted all through the EKG.

"Definitely an arrhythmia," he said, checking the readout when the test was done. "We'll see what the other tests show in a day or two. It's entirely possible that a good, long rest could take care of this." He rubbed my arm with an alcohol pad, and while he injected the Valium, he looked at my cuffed wrist sympathetically. "You've been through a lot. You'll be staying here tonight. I'll tell the detective your health won't permit a move yet. You need sleep."

"Thank you."

I was grateful for the kindness and, unless Roche decided to believe my story, a respite from the county jail.

◆ ◆ ◆

The Valium had taken effect by the time Ben walked in. I was floating on my back in the Caribbean.

"Hi," said Ben.

"Hi."

He smiled and bent over to kiss me. His lips felt like little soft pillows.

"How are you feeling?"

"High."

"Hi."

"No, high."

"Yes, hi."

I gave up and kissed him again. I could feel the drug dissolving my inhibitions like paint stripper.

"You are incredibly wonderful, Ben Wickstein. You are a good man. And I mean that as the highest compliment. Goodness does nothing to diminish your sex appeal."

Ben looked amused.

"Maybe you want to pull the curtain and climb in here?" I suggested.

He laughed. "I think they're keeping a pretty close eye on us," he said, nodding at the door. "The officer actually frisked me before I came in."

"As if you might try to pull off a jailbreak?"

The gravity of the situation dragged me down, despite the buoying effect of the drug. Ben's expression turned serious, too.

"Mac brought me up to speed. You were incredibly brave," he said, taking my cuffed hand in his and squeezing it. "I don't know what I would have done if anything had happened to you."

"What do you think will happen now?"

Ben furrowed his brow and sat down on the edge of the gurney. "Depends what they make of the hunter's statement. It could come down to Masout's word against yours."

I was indignant. "What about all those shots he fired at me? And his motive for killing Hugh? I gave Hugh's sketches of Abbas to the police. They're proof."

"Remember, they think you had a motive to kill, too. And you attacked Abbas with that spray varnish. I think it could be time for the New York City criminal lawyer I told you about."

"I think you're right."

I sighed heavily. It was now or never. When else would I have the aid of a tranquilizer to ease the way? I swallowed hard.

"Ben. I have to tell you something. I haven't been honest. I've been holding back information."

Ben looked at me, curious.

"Okay. I'm just going to say it really fast. Get it out there."

"I'm listening."

"I walk in my sleep."

"You what?"

"It used to do it when I was a kid, but I grew out of it. Then that first night in your apartment? I woke up standing in your kitchen naked, washing my hands. I was sleepwalking. That's why I left. I was pretty freaked out."

"You walk in your sleep. Really?" His eyes widened.

"I think I might have walked in my sleep the night of the murders, too. And I probably left the house. I found leaves and a twig in my hair in the morning. You saw the scratch on my cheek."

He openly stared at me.

"You sleepwalk. And don't know where you've gone or what you've done?"

"If I don't wake up in the middle of an episode, yes."

"You can drive in your sleep?"

"I'm not sure. I've read about people who have."

Ben became completely still. Silent and unreadable.

"I was worried that you'd think I went to Pequod Point and . . . and that you'd suspect me."

He looked dazed.

"Ben?"

He finally blinked.

"You're insane," he said quietly.

My heart stopped.

He shook his head. "You really think I'd believe you murdered the Walkers because you walk in your sleep? I've been sitting one desk away from you for more than two years now. I've seen you," he began ticking off fingers, "depressed, disappointed, sad, confused and, yes, angry—to name a few of your darker moods. I know what you're capable of. Not murder. Not you. I know your heart, Nora."

And that heart was singing. It meant so much to hear Ben say he had confidence in my essential goodness. Especially after he'd witnessed my less attractive attitudes.

"I only have one question," he said.

"What?"

"Will you ever trust me?"

I looked down, uneasy. "I want to. I really do."

"But?"

"But I'm afraid. I didn't see that seismic betrayal coming with Hugh. I feel like I should have. Like there's something wrong with me."

"Nora. It's not your fault."

I looked up. "No?"

Ben reached out and touched my cheek. "You're supposed to trust the person you're in a relationship with. That's the whole point."

Of course it was. So simple. So true.

"Loving someone is a risk," he said. "A leap of faith you have to take if you go all-in."

I knew he was right, but could I let myself jump? I wanted so much to be brave. Ben wiped a tear off my cheek.

"You okay?"

I nodded a little uncertainly.

"Okay. Now we have to put everything into getting these charges dropped. I can call the criminal lawyer in the city—his name is Marhofer—and put him in touch with Gubbins to bring him up to speed. I think Gubbins will cooperate."

I noticed a traffic ticket sticking out of Ben's coat pocket.

"Looks like you had your own run-in with the police today," I said, trying to lighten things up.

He nodded and pulled the ticket out.

"I hit the Old Route 20 speed trap." He shrugged and smiled. "I was in a rush to see you. I should've known Pequod's finest would be out with their radar guns, even in a snowstorm."

I couldn't stop staring at the ticket. A storm had started brewing in my brain, complete with thunderbolt. Ben sensed something was up.

"What's going on, Nora?"

"I have an idea. It's a long shot, but it's something."

"What?"

"Traffic signal 2234. Late last Saturday night. Or early Sunday morning."

Ben sat there for a moment and blinked, taking in my words. Then he stood up quickly, excited.

"That might work. I'll tell Roche. And Gubbins. Cross your fingers. Maybe we'll get lucky."

He kissed me and rushed out.

"Traffic signal 2234" was Ben's story in the works at the *Courier* about the signal at the expressway exit. Almost everyone who drove out to Pequod from the city took that route, unless for some reason they wanted to drive an extra half hour and backtrack on a long detour.

Just before the county highway supervisor was removed from office on charges of embezzlement and corruption this summer, he'd had his department install a camera at the intersection to record "no right on red" violations. But there were complaints. It looked as if the pressure reader under the pavement had been placed in the wrong location. If a vehicle that was about to turn went over the stop line by even a few feet, the camera would take a photo. A few weeks later, a ticket for an illegal turn arrived in the driver's mailbox. Was it the highway department's ineptitude? Or was it intentional, to generate more tickets and fill the county's coffers? Ben was looking into it.

If there had there been a red light when Abbas exited the expressway on his way to kill Hugh and Helene, *and* if he had driven his BMW over the stop line, we'd have photographic proof that he was in the area during the time of the murders. That is, if Detective Roche would agree to check it out. Those were a lot of ifs. But, as Ben said, maybe we'd get lucky.

And I especially liked that he'd said "we."

◆ ◆ ◆

Orderlies moved me to a small room upstairs where another officer guarded the door. When they left and I heard the lock click, claustrophobia set in. I looked around in a panic. The bare room had a tiny window and no TV. No phone. This was a hospital room for prisoners. I'd done nothing to deserve it, but they were treating me like a criminal when Abbas was the guilty one. Were they holding him up here, too?

Almost instantly, I felt nauseous at the thought of Abbas staying anywhere near. I saw him towering over me in the blowing snow, pointing the gun at my head, the barrel like a long, black tunnel. I began to sweat and shake. I heard his cold, hollow voice. "It will be quick. You will not suffer." I had the urge to run. I scrambled out of bed, yanking pointlessly at the handcuff as it cut into my wrist. I slid to the floor, chained and in pain, stuck in a nightmare of Abbas's making. I started to cry. Was that psychopath perfecting his story? Would he send me to a place much worse than this? It was still a terrifyingly real possibility.

A female nurse arrived this time and gave me a stronger sedative to help me sleep. Even if I hadn't been handcuffed, I had about as much of a chance of sleepwalking as a bowl of Jell-O. I didn't know if anyone checked on me during the night, because I was practically comatose. The next morning, the male nurse was back with oatmeal and orange juice. And Sanka.

"No coffee?"

"Not on your list," he said.

"Oh." I frowned, imagining a withdrawal headache to add to my troubles. "When are visiting hours?"

307

He looked at me sympathetically. "I'm not sure. You're in a . . . a special unit. I can ask, though."

I shrank back into the bed. "I see. Well, could you please tell the officer outside I'd like to make a call to my lawyer right away? I'm entitled to that, at least." I wanted to learn whether Gubbins had any news from Ben on the traffic signal. Or if he'd heard from the criminal lawyer.

"Sure."

I ate, skipped the Sanka and lay there waiting. And waiting. No phone. No visit from Dr. Patel with word on the lab tests. No headache from caffeine deprivation, either. Thankfully, the drugs must've short-circuited that. I pressed the nurse call button. Why hadn't anyone delivered a phone yet? Surely, they'd have to allow contact with my lawyer. My anxiety level was beginning to climb again. Could I get more Valium?

Finally, the door opened. Gubbins and Detective Roche walked into the room together. Roche looked rough, like he hadn't slept or shaved. He was still wearing yesterday's clothes. Gubbins was in another shiny suit, freshly showered and smiling. A good sign. I sat up, eager to hear the news.

"Good morning, Ms. Glasser," Gubbins said.

"What's happening?"

Detective Roche positioned himself at the foot of my bed and cleared his throat.

"We are in possession of a photograph of Abbas Masout's car, taken at 12:28 a.m. last Sunday, November fifteenth, 15.3 miles from Pequod Point. We ran preliminary tests and found a trace of blood on the driver's seat upholstery. Probably off clothing Masout disposed of. We don't know whose blood it is yet, but I'm willing to speculate. We also recovered shell casings indicating Mr. Masout's gun discharged multiple shots at the site where we found him yesterday, in addition to the shots fired inside. Foot and handprints corroborate your story. You were in a prone position when he fired and no threat to him."

"So, you're charging Abbas?"

Roche nodded. "For the murders of Hugh and Helene Walker. And the attempted murder of you."

"You mean I'm not a suspect anymore."

"You're cleared of all charges, Nora," Gubbins said. "It's all over."

I moaned and fell back against the pillows, absorbing the news. Deliverance. I wanted to leap out of bed and hug him.

"Except for your testimony in court," Roche added. "Good detective work, Ms. Glasser. You helped put the puzzle together." He came to my side and unlocked the cuffs.

"Free as a bird," he said.

I rubbed my sore wrist and looked at him reproachfully. He pulled his shoulders back and straightened his posture.

"I was doing my job. I'm never sorry about that. But I do regret how it came down on you."

"Could you do me a favor, then?"

He eyed me warily. "What's that?"

"There's another sketchbook. The one Abbas told you I'd stolen. It's mine. It's at Hugh's studio. There's a picture of Carrie Fisher on the cover. I'm assuming the studio is off-limits. Could you arrange to get it back to me? It's quite valuable."

He raised an eyebrow. "You mean the notebook on 'Women's Changing Hairstyles' you had in your purse?"

"Uh-huh. And there's also a red Swiss Army knife, engraved to the 'World's Best Dad.'"

"Sorry. Everything in that studio has been logged in as evidence for the DA. It stays with the police."

"For how long?"

"I can't really say."

"Please. Can you at least release the notebook? I need to sell it. I have a cash-flow situation."

Gubbins piped up behind him. "I'd like to have a word with you about that, Detective Roche."

The door opened again and Dr. Patel walked in.

"Gentlemen, would you please step outside?"

It couldn't be soon enough for Roche. He took my cell phone from his pocket and set it next to me on the bed. "That's it, then. I've left your computer with Mr. Gubbins here."

Gubbins placed his attaché on the nightstand, opened it and removed my laptop.

"I'll let Ben know about the dropped charges. And don't worry about anything else. We'll speak later," he said, closing his case and following Roche out the door.

When we were alone, Dr. Patel approached the bed and looked at the skin on my wrist where the handcuffs had chafed.

"I'll give you some cream for that. I'm happy to see your troubles with the law are over. How are you feeling today?"

"Pretty damn good. Have my test results come back?"

"They have. Do you drink a lot of coffee, Ms. Glasser?"

"Every chance I get. Why?"

"You'll need to stop drinking coffee immediately. No dark chocolate, either. Caffeine is your problem. Caffeine leaches calcium and magnesium. The tests show that your calcium is low, but more seriously, you have quite a severe magnesium deficiency."

"I do? Is that dangerous?"

"It's probably responsible for the exhaustion and arrhythmia. It can cause a host of other difficulties over time. Confusion. Violent muscle spasms. With severe magnesium deficiencies, we've even seen brain seizures. And parasomnias."

"Parasomnias."

"Yes. Like night terrors, for instance. Or sleepwalking."

That gave me a jolt.

"Sleepwalking? You're sure of that?"

"Have you . . . ?"

"Yes," I said excitedly. "I've been walking in my sleep recently. A couple of times. It was a problem when I was a kid. But the doctor said I'd grow out of it after puberty. I thought I had."

"You probably did. But if you have a predisposition, it can become a 'weak spot.' It's likely been triggered by this deficiency. I want to observe you for another day or so, but my thinking is, if we replace your magnesium and cut out coffee, your arrhythmia *and* the sleepwalking will cease."

I fervently hoped the problem boiled down to coffee and magnesium.

"You think I can be cured?"

"I'm very optimistic, but of course, we'll have to wait and see."

"Today is Sunday, right?"

"Yes. It's Sunday," Dr. Patel said.

A week since the bodies were discovered—a life-changing week, to say the least. Having ascertained that my heart held a steady rhythm, Dr. Patel ordered my release. After two nights under strict observation, the night nurse reported that I had not done any sleepwalking. It seemed Dr. Patel's prognosis was correct. His only prescription besides magnesium pills and a ban on caffeine was "pleasure and leisure."

"Don't jump right into anything. Take it easy for a couple of days. Stay home. Read books. Watch movies. Drink wine, in moderation. Enjoy the company of your loved ones."

That would be Aunt Lada, Grace and Mac and the boys and, maybe, Ben. When he picked me up at the hospital, I asked if he could stay at the Coop for the rest of the day.

"Unless because Sam is home you'd rather . . ."

"Sam is busy hanging out with his other friends who are home on break. It would be my pleasure."

The temperature had remained cold since the storm, which meant the snow hadn't melted. The sun shone on a beautiful, shimmering wonderland as we turned onto Crooked Beach Lane and approached my driveway. A few dogged city reporters waited there. They were eager to get a statement from the woman who had faced down her ex-husband's murderer. Ben shooed them away. "Unless you want to stay and help me shovel this snow," he said. "Seriously, Ms. Glasser will call you if she decides it's in her interests to speak to the press."

Then he accompanied me inside and insisted I go right to bed while he brewed his favorite tea for us. "I was hoping you'd invite me to stay. I brought supplies," he said, pulling two tea bags out of his coat pocket.

I fell asleep before the water boiled. When I woke, Ben was in bed next to me, reading my April Krim book on artists' muses.

"You've been asleep a long time."

"How long?"

"Eleven hours."

"Wow. Catching up, I guess."

He tapped the book. "Interesting women. Most of them talented in their own right. Passionate. Generous. But some of these male artists . . . It's disappointing to read how they treated the women who loved them. Let's just say these sons of bitches are best known through their work."

I closed my eyes and mused on Ben's observation. Was Hugh "best known through his work?" If I could go back in time and leave that art gallery before he introduced himself, would I? Did I regret our entire relationship? No. But I let the admiration I had for his talent and success overshadow his hurtful behaviors. I got hooked on being his muse and betrayed myself. I had to forgive me before I could forgive Hugh. It was time to do both.

I opened my eyes and looked over at Ben.

"Hungry?" he asked.

"You are pretty terrific," I said.

He smiled, kissed me, went off to the kitchen and returned with a bowl of mushroom soup from a pot that Grace delivered. I thanked him, drank the soup and dropped off to sleep again.

For the next two days, I happily heeded Dr. Patel's advice and stayed home. I kept tabs on Aunt Lada, who was lucid and recovering well. The first time I called, she wanted to talk about Abbas.

"I remember him from your wedding. He was such a charmer, that one. *But na yazeekey myed. A na seardsea lyod.*"

A tongue of honey. A heart of ice.

"I don't want to . . . I can't talk about him, Aunt Lada. I'm just glad it's over."

Since I'd panicked in the hospital, I'd used Ben's method and put up another curtain to keep that monster out of sight. I never wanted to think about Abbas or my terrifying night at Pequod Point again.

I spent much of the time reading a delicious mystery novel and watching Harry Potter movies with Grace and the boys. They'd brought DVDs from the library. I told Ben it wasn't too rushed to invite Sam for lunch and was pleased to discover his son was a delightful kid with an interest in history and politics. We had a lively discussion about the rise of fake news. The days ended making love with Ben. And at night there was still no sign that I'd done anything but sleep peacefully.

On the morning of day three, I took a magical walk across the snowy farm field into the glittering, frosted woods. I followed a half-frozen stream, water gurgling beneath the ice floe, and circled back to the top of the road where Crawley had parked to keep tabs on me when I was a person of interest. No police car. Just a snowbank. The hunt really was over.

Only the money worries remained. I still had to pay for Gubbins's services, my own and Lada's rents and the clinic bills. I called Gubbins, hoping he'd be amenable to negotiating a payment plan until the police returned the Princess Leia sketchbook.

"Good news. I've convinced the DA to accept slides of the sketchbook to use as evidence at the trial," Gubbins said, clearly pleased with his win. "I warned them that the book was an important source of my client's financial stability. 'Your withholding it directly affects the physical well-being of Ms. Glasser and her aunt, a senior citizen,' I said. They agreed to return the original to you by next week, as long as you can prove ownership."

"Thank you. That's fantastic. I have a letter from Hugh saying *Loving Nora* was a gift. Does that help?"

Gubbins paused, and I worried that the letter wouldn't do. Finally, he said, "I know a handwriting expert. If he verifies your letter, that should be completely acceptable."

My brilliant lawyer.

"But they insist on holding the knife until the trial is over."

"I'll let Ben know. It belongs to him. Thanks again."

"One more thing. I took the liberty of calling Sotheby's and asking an appraiser the approximate value of a sketchbook by Hugh Walker. He wouldn't give an estimate without seeing it first, but he was extremely eager to have a look. When I told him that the police were holding it for a few days in a criminal investigation, he indicated that would increase its value substantially."

Just like that, "snap," my money troubles were over. *Like one of Damien Hirst's flies*, I heard Abbas hiss. I shivered and shook off the memory.

"Nora?"

"Wonderful," I told Gubbins. "Just wonderful."

I drove to the *Courier* office in the afternoon on Wednesday, unlocked the door and turned on the lights. We were basically closed through the holiday. Ben had put the Thanksgiving issue to bed the night before, except for the weekend calendar. I'd come in to finish it. Afterward, I planned on joining him and Sam at the Pequod Food Pantry, handing out fresh turkeys to some of the town's less fortunate residents to take home and cook.

I breathed in the comforting aroma of old wood. Worn pine floors. Creaky oak doors and window frames. Scratched and coffee-stained maple desks and armchairs. This was a newsroom of a bygone era, and I loved it. My eye was drawn to the framed picture of Judy and Sam on Ben's desk. Instead of worrying about living up to Judy, I appreciated Ben's devotion to her. For a second, I felt a twinge of concern. What would it be like to work here with Ben now that we were involved? I hoped we'd be able to navigate without too much tension.

A stack of the *Courier*'s special issue, published after Abbas's arrest, sat on my desk. The headline emblazed across the front page read:

HUNTER'S ARROW TAKES DOWN POINT KILLER
Courier Reporter Confronts Murderer

I moved the stack of papers onto the filing cabinet. "Chapter closed," I resolved. "Forever." I'd already called Jake, the hunter, earlier and thanked him again. "If you'd hesitated, I wouldn't be here today," I said. He was humble about it. "I'm just glad I turned up in the right place at the right time, ma'am."

I sat down to work on the calendar. Glancing through the window, I noticed Lizzie on the other side of the street wearing her army jacket and a boiled wool hat from Afghanistan. She was speaking to a woman bundled up in black in front of Eden's Coffee Shop. The two of them turned and began to cross directly toward the *Courier* building. I stood up when I recognized the woman with Lizzie was Helene's sister.

They reached the building entrance on the left and I couldn't see them from the window anymore. The outer door creaked. Then the *Courier* office door opened and Lizzie scurried in from the cold.

"Hey, Nora! You're back! Great. I didn't think anyone would be in today."

"Wasn't that Margaret Westing who just walked across the street with you?"

"The very one." Lizzie set her camera bag on her desk and plunked down in her chair. "I went to Eden's for breakfast and saw this woman I recognized from the funeral having coffee at the counter. I sat next to her and introduced myself. She was here to pick up some of her sister's belongings. Get this: she's applying for guardianship of Callie Walker."

"Really?"

"Uh-huh."

From what I'd heard at the funeral, I didn't think Margaret wanted Callie for the money. I had the impression Margaret really cared for her niece.

"That's great. She'd be a whole lot better than Ruth and Tobias. Only, it's going to be a tough win for a single woman coming up against a family for guardianship. But if she pulls it off, it could save that kid's life."

On my darkest days, I'd been saved by the love of an aunt.

"Right," Lizzie said, getting up and walking over to the Mr. Coffee machine. "Here's the thing: Tobias Walker is in deep trouble with the IRS. He's about to be charged with fraud. His 'nonprofit educational' Fund for the American Family gave oodles of money illegally to political candidates with religious agendas. So, the court might not look too kindly on him as a responsible, ethical parenting option."

"Margaret told you that?"

"Crawley did. He said the cops had been looking into Tobias since the beginning of the murder investigation." She picked up the coffee carafe, carried it to the water cooler and began filling it. "I bring

Crawley doughnuts when he's parked at those speed traps, so he gives me some pretty good tips."

I could learn a few things from this girl.

"You know, you're an excellent reporter, Lizzie. In case I haven't mentioned it."

"Thanks." She beamed. "You want coffee?"

"Nope. I'm off caffeine," I said.

The Coop was filled with the mouthwatering smells of the feast that Grace and I prepared together: turkey and gravy with chestnut stuffing, cranberry sauce, sweet potato casserole and green beans with pearl onions. It was also full of the people I treasured. Ben. Grace, Mac and the kids. Aunt Lada. She'd gotten the okay from her doctor to celebrate with us as long as she took it easy. Ben and I picked her up in his Rover, along with her wheelchair. "She won't need it for long," her cardiologist said. "She's recovering beautifully."

There were also guests I looked forward to knowing better. Like young Sam. Also, my neighbors, Jack Mance and his boyfriend, David. They wanted to check on their house, so I invited them. The police had located Jack's stolen gun the day before. It turned up in a botched gang robbery at the Massamat Pizzeria. "Now there's a story for the *Courier*," Jack said.

We were about to sit down to our meal when I remembered that in the bustle and prep of the holiday, I'd forgotten to take my pill. I excused myself and sneaked off to the bathroom. "Take one pill every morning, just before breakfast," Dr. Patel had instructed.

I reached into the medicine cabinet and removed the high-dose magnesium supplements Dr. Patel prescribed, filled a glass with water and then examined myself in the mirror. I looked rested for the first time in months. My skin was in great shape, the scratch under my eye barely visible. I placed the bottle back in the cabinet, turned toward the tub and popped the horse-size pill in my mouth. As I drank the water, I watched the light play on the snow-covered field through the window and listened to the voices rising and falling in my living room. The laughter.

The afternoon sun was reflecting strongly off something outside directly under the window, flashing sparks of light on the glass. I leaned over the tub awkwardly to see exactly what it was. Near the Coop's foundation, half buried in snow, my hand hoe lay next to a pile of dead rose branches and a burlap bag emptied of daffodil bulbs. The hoe's silver tip was glinting in the sunlight.

I touched my cheek. The scratch. That was where I'd gotten the scratch. I must've ripped out the dead, thorny branches and planted the bulbs during one of my sleepwalking episodes. A twig and leaves had stuck to my hair and clothing. I'd knelt right there by the light of the moon and dug holes with my hoe. I smiled to myself. There would be blooms in the spring after all.

Maybe this was a sign. Should I ask Jack Mance if he was willing to sell the Coop? I could make a bid with the sketchbook money. Despite the Coop's flaws, I was fond of it, and I'd already put down roots. It looked like there'd be a windfall—enough to pay for a renovation.

As I straightened up, I saw him standing in the field midway between the Coop and the forest. The wind was blowing sprays of snow from the ground into swirls of powder around him. His noble head was lifted, nose to the sky. Long whiskers graced his muzzle. His rack was high and wide, his chest massive and his waist almost as big, giving him the shape of a small cow. He was the oldest buck I'd ever seen.

"How have you lasted through such cold, harsh winters and with so little food?" I wanted to ask him. "How have you escaped the hunters? Avoided getting hit by a car? How have you survived this long? Dealt with your losses and traumas? Do you have any tips for living? You must have tips."

He turned his head toward me, tilted it and shook his antlers as if to say, "Lady, I'm a deer," as the rest of them approached.

They came out of the forest one by one, walking slowly in a line. All shapes and sizes. Fawns, does, yearlings and younger bucks. They stopped and gathered around him for a moment, protecting each other from the wind, steam rising off their warm bodies. Then they began to move back toward the forest, forming their line again with the old buck at the head. They walked into the woods with their white tails flashing in the last of the light.

"Nora, come on! We're hungry!" Ben called out from the living room.

They were all out there. Waiting. And they weren't going to start without me.

From the *Pequod Courier*

Tips for Living

by Nora Glasser

Aunt Lada's Advice

Do the best you can. Give it your all.

And if things don't come out well the first time, try again.

As the Russians like to say: "The first pancake is always a blob."

And, furthermore, "She who takes no risks, never gets to drink champagne."

ACKNOWLEDGMENTS

I am grateful to all the readers, advisers and encouragers who helped bring *Tips* into the world, starting with my elementary school librarian, Mrs. Walker. She sat me down with magical books and a safe space to read. Lucy Childs, my supersmart and determined agent, never stopped pushing to make *Tips* a better book. Melanie Fleishman provided wise editorial input and unceasing support. Susan Scarf Merrell read the first draft and left the "go, go, go, go, go!" voice mail that spurred me on. Bettina Volz and Libby McGuire cheered, too. Mary Corey prompted the addition of a crucial ingredient. Susan Dalsimer gave invaluable notes and confidence. Florence Falk gave me faith. For decades.

Special thanks to the aces at Lake Union, starting with the wonderful Liz Pearsons, who fell for *Tips*. She has been a constant ally and advocate. Tiffany Yates Martin: working with you was my grad school. Also thanks to the great communicator Gabrielle Dumpit, and to Kimberly Glyder for her inspired design.

A shout-out to the late, great Nora Ephron, who told me I should write books. To Cis Wilson, Steve Molton, Pamela Galvin, Annette Chandler, Will Chandler and Vicki Polon for their friendship throughout. To Marcelle Tosi and the team at Miracle Management for their support and enthusiasm. To Geoffrey Nimmer for the "cedar" talk. To Dr. Karen Langone for enabling me to walk out ideas. To my beloved dog, Hitchcock, who comes along on the walks when he's not sitting patiently in my office waiting for me to return to reality and give him treats. And to my clients, who continue to show me what courage it takes to heal and go on to thrive.

But most of all I want to thank my wonderful partner, Nick Gazzolo, who inspires, supports, applauds, advises and brings coffees and laughter at just the right moments. Nick makes everything better. Always.

ABOUT THE AUTHOR

Photo © 2016 Nicholas Gazzolo

Renée Shafransky is a writer and psychotherapist. Her articles and essays have appeared in various publications including the *Village Voice*, *Condé Nast Traveler*, and the *Southampton Review*. She has written screenplays for major motion picture studios and teleplays for HBO and PBS, working with renowned directors such as Harold Ramis. Previously married to actor and writer Spalding Gray, Ms. Shafransky produced the acclaimed film of his monologue, *Swimming to Cambodia*, directed by Jonathan Demme. She currently practices as a psychotherapist in New York City and Sag Harbor, where she makes her home with her partner, Nick, and her dog, Hitchcock. *Tips for Living* is her first novel.